CRITICAL ACCLAIM FOR PETER MURPHY

'Racy legal thrillers lift the lid on sex and racial prejudice
at the bar' – *Guardian*

'Murphy paints a trenchant picture of establishment cover-up,
and cannily subverts the clichés of the legal genre in his all-too-
topical narrative' – *Financial Times*

'Peter Murphy's novel is an excellent read from start to finish and
highly recommended' – *Historical Novel Review*

'An intelligent amalgam of spy story and legal drama' – *Times*

'A gripping, enjoyable and informative read'
– *Promoting Crime Fiction*

'The ability of an author to create living characters is always
dependent on his knowledge of what they would do and say in
any given circumstances – a talent that Peter Murphy possesses
in abundance' – *Crime Review UK*

'Murphy's clever legal thriller revels in the chicanery of the
English law courts of the period' – *Independent*

'The forensic process is examined in a light-touch, good-
humoured style, which will evoke a constant stream of smiles,
and chuckles from non-lawyers and lawyers alike' – **Lord Judge,
*former Lord Chief Justice of England and Wales***

'A gripping page-turner. A compelling and disturbing tale of
English law courts, lawyers, and their clients, told with the
authenticity that only an insider like Murphy can deliver. The
best read I've come across in a long time' – **David Ambrose**

'If anyone's looking for the next big court
further. Murphy is your ma

T0323174

ALSO BY PETER MURPHY

The American Novels
Removal
Test of Resolve
A Statue for Jacob

The Ben Schroeder Series
A Higher Duty
A Matter for the Jury
And Is there Honey still for Tea?
The Heirs of Owain Glyndwr
Calling Down the Storm
One Law for the Rest of Us
To Become An Outlaw

The Walden Series
Walden of Bermondsey
Judge Walden: Back in Session
Judge Walden: Call the Next Case

A Week On Mount Olympus

PETER MURPHY

NO EXIT PRESS

First published in 2023 by No Exit Press,
an imprint of Bedford Square Publishers Ltd,
London, UK

noexit.co.uk
@noexitpress

ISBN
978-0-85730-570-1 (Paperback)
978-0-85730-571-8 (eBook)

2 4 6 8 10 9 7 5 3 1

Typeset in 11.5 on 14.5pt Minion Pro
by Avocet Typeset, Bideford, Devon, EX39 2BP
Printed and bound by CPI Group (UK) Ltd, Croydon CR0 4YY

CONTENTS

PART ONE

A WEEK ON MOUNT OLYMPUS

A WEEK ON MOUNT OLYMPUS

A few weeks ago

I was flattered, of course. Well, who wouldn't be, in my position? When you're labouring away on a daily basis at the coalface, as a circuit judge in the Crown Court, the prospect of consorting with the gods on Mount Olympus for a week or two is bound to be seductive, and your instinct is to shout 'yes' as loudly as you can before they can change their minds. That was exactly my reaction when Mr Justice Gulivant called me one day just before lunch, and suggested that I might like to sit with him in the Criminal Division of the Court of Appeal for a week. A minute or two later, after the call had ended, I felt the chill hand of reality on my brow, as I reflected on what would actually be involved in sitting in the Court of Appeal. But by then, the trap had been sprung: the temptation was irresistible: I'd already said 'yes'.

The idea of a mere circuit judge sitting in the Court of Appeal would have been unthinkable until relatively recently. Traditionally, the Lord Chief Justice presided with two High Court judges, and lesser mortals never darkened the Court's door. But, given that the function of the Criminal Division is to hear appeals from the Crown Court, it does make a certain amount of sense to have one judge who actually sits in the Crown Court and has some idea of what goes on there. High Court judges tend to come mainly from the refined world of commercial law, and although they are expected to try cases of serious crime from day one, many of them have never been involved in a criminal case before, and have absolutely no idea what they are doing. Some, though by no means all of them, will admit as much over dinner in their Inn of Court after a glass or two, but it doesn't seem to deter them. Oddly, the Establishment seems to regard this madness as a loveable eccentricity, a quirk of English life that sets us apart from bureaucratic foreigners who insist on submitting to the tyranny of experts. In England, the gods love an amateur and will smooth his path regardless of the potential collateral damage. Stephen Gulivant himself is a case in point. A former planning Silk, Stephen came to sit with us at Bermondsey for several days not long after he was appointed, and I had to hold his hand through a simple offensive weapon case, which took two days longer than it should have, and came perilously close to bouncing back to us from the Court of Appeal. I don't know whether Stephen has tried a criminal case since then, but now he's hearing appeals from those who do.

But before I go any further, I ought to introduce myself. I'm Charles Walden, Charlie to my family and closest associates. I've been a circuit judge for twelve years or thereabouts, and I'm currently the RJ – Resident Judge – at Bermondsey Crown Court in South London. According to the job description, an RJ is a judge who takes on the overall administrative responsibility for the work of all the judges at a court, in addition to his or her own work. In fact, the RJ's main role is to be the person to blame whenever something goes wrong. When I say 'something goes wrong', I mean that the Grey Smoothies think we could be doing whatever it is more efficiently than we do.

The 'Grey Smoothies' is the name we have adopted at Bermondsey to refer to the civil servants who oversee the working of the courts. The Grey Smoothies' main goal seems to be to make the RJ's job ever more difficult, if not actually impossible. In the name of their mantras of 'value for money for the taxpayer' and 'business case' – without which phrases most of them find it difficult to compose a sentence – they launch assault after assault on the already sparse resources of the court, which as RJ, I do my best to repel. Among the rearguard actions I've fought with the Grey Smoothies over the years are: their refusal to spend money on a secure dock to prevent defendants from absconding and assaulting court staff during a case; their attempt to close down our cafeteria, the only safe place for jurors and witnesses to have lunch during a trial; and even a campaign to close Bermondsey Crown Court altogether for economic reasons. With a certain degree of good fortune, I've held them off so far, but RJs elsewhere have been less fortunate, and I can't shake the feeling that it's only a matter of time before resistance becomes futile.

Being an RJ carries with it no extra pay, no administrative support, and no protected time, and it's a legitimate question why anyone ever agrees to do it. Some circuit judges take it on as a career move, hoping that it will lead to an assignment to the Old Bailey, or even promotion to the High Court bench. But in my case, I confess, it's a simple matter of lifestyle. You see, my good lady wife, the Reverend Mrs Walden, is priest-in-charge of the parish of St Aethelburgh and All Angels in the Diocese of Southwark. Being priest-in-charge is just like being an RJ, really, but with different robes. Her living carries with it the privilege of residing in a huge Victorian vicarage, which has many fine architectural features; a large weed sanctuary, euphemistically referred to as a garden, at the rear; and no modern amenities whatsoever. It is hot in summer and freezing in winter, and generally looks as though it hasn't been decorated since the First Boer War. And with both our daughters having long since flown the nest to make their way in the world as single career women, it is a fair bit bigger than we need. But it is close to work for us both, and I enjoy my short stroll to court in the morning.

Along the way I stop at a coffee and sandwich bar run by two ladies called Elsie and Jeanie. The bar is secreted in an archway under the railway bridge, not far from London Bridge station, and it gets crowded if they have more than two customers at a time. But they do a wonderful latte, and a nice ham and cheese on a bap – a temptation if, as is often the case, I'm not relishing the thought of the dish of the day in the judicial mess. The only downside is that I have to listen to their various woes while the process of latte-making is going on. Elsie has a couple of grandchildren who get themselves into occasional scrapes with the law, about which I have to be non-committal because I suspect it's only a matter of time before we see one of them at Bermondsey. Jeanie has a husband who seems to spend most of his time, and most of his benefits, at the pub and the betting shop. So, one way or another, they are rarely short of things to grumble about, and they usually take full advantage. Next door to Elsie and Jeanie is George, the newsagent and tobacconist, from whom I collect my daily copy of *The Times*, and who is always ready with my newspaper, a cheerful greeting, and a penetrating insight into the shortcomings of the Labour Party.

But, to return to my story: after Gulivant's call, I go into lunch in the judicial mess, and, with a growing sense of trepidation, wonder whether I should share the news with my colleagues. Bermondsey is a small court, and there are only three other judges in addition to myself.

There's Judge Rory Dunblane, mid-fifties, tall with sandy hair, a proud Scotsman, and devoted rugby enthusiast, who still plays a good game of squash and enjoys his nights out with 'the boys' (whoever they may be). No one calls him Rory. He has been known to all as 'Legless' for as long as I have known him, and that is quite a while now. The nickname dates back to an incident during his younger days while he was at the Bar, something to do with the fountains in Trafalgar Square after a chambers dinner. No one, including Legless himself, seems to remember the details of the incident, but the name has stuck. Legless is what you would call a robust judge, who likes to get through his workload without any nonsense.

Then there's Judge Marjorie Jenkins, slim, medium height, dark hair and blue eyes. In her late forties, she has already been on the bench for eight years. When she was appointed, Marjorie was an up-and-coming Silk doing commercial work, representing City banks and financial institutions, and everyone was surprised that she took what, in her world, would be seen as a menial job. Marjorie is what they used to call a super-mum, a perpetual motion machine who balances a high-powered career with her family and various voluntary works. Her husband Nigel speaks six languages fluently and does something very important for an international bank. They spend holidays in Provence, where they have a house, or in Lausanne or Rome or Cape Town, as the muse leads them. Their two children, Simon and Samantha, are away at boarding school. It seems to be generally assumed that becoming a circuit judge is a kind of career break for Marjorie, and that she will resume her upwardly mobile path once the children are older. She does tend to disappear without much warning if anything goes wrong at school. But she is a great asset, particularly for fraud cases, in which she effortlessly assimilates tons of material which would take the rest of us weeks even to read, let alone digest.

Finally, there's Judge Hubert Drake. Hubert is what you might call 'old school'. He would have made a first-rate colonial magistrate in India in the days of the Raj, his approach to sentencing certainly being reminiscent of that era. Many is the time when we have had to talk him down over lunch in the judicial mess, to restrain him from passing a sentence the Court of Appeal would strike down instantly with howls of indignation. But he has a seemingly inexhaustible fund of intriguing stories about the old days, which he is always ready to share with us, and which always seem to illustrate some point we've been discussing perfectly. We suspect that many of them have the additional merit of being true. Hubert has been widowed for some years. He has a nice flat in Chelsea, and divides his time more or less equally between the flat and the Garrick Club, of which he is a devoted member. Altogether, despite – or perhaps because of – the eccentricities, we regard him as a treasure, as do the many who know him, far afield from Bermondsey. I know it's a cliché, but they don't make them like Hubert any more.

But Hubert is also a bit of a problem. No one seems sure exactly how old he is, and he shows no inclination to enlighten us. Apparently, some official record has him down as sixty-eight, but I would bet good money that the train left that station some time ago. Our main worry is that he is determined never to retire, and he says they can't make him. When he reaches the age of seventy-two, they can in fact make him, and I have nightmares about the scenes we will have when that happens. In Hubert's good old days, there was no retiring age for judges, but that changed when Parliament finally realised that there were judges clinging on when they were, shall we say, rather past their sell-by dates. That's not true of Hubert. The Bar grumble about him quite a bit, but that's because they see him as being extremely right-wing and reactionary – which he accepts, and regards as an accolade.

So far, nobody has suggested that he is losing the plot, which is reassuring in one sense, but doesn't offer a solution to the approaching retirement dilemma. At some point, I will have to make a serious effort to find out how old Hubert is, and I'm not looking forward to it.

Over my ham and cheese bap from Jeanie and Elsie's, I finally decide to tell my fellow-judges about Stephen Gulivant's call. To my surprise, instead of incredulity, their reaction is positively enthusiastic.

'Marvellous, Charlie,' Marjorie enthuses, 'well done. You'll be brilliant – just what they need up there to keep them on the straight and narrow.'

'Couldn't agree more,' Legless adds. 'They need more like you.'

'You can talk a bit of common sense into them,' Hubert agrees, looking up from his oriental chicken with noodles, the guise in which the dish of the day presents itself. Hubert is known for his fortitude in tackling the dish of the day on a regular basis, whatever it may be - something the rest of us prefer not to commit to these days, given the vagaries of the kitchen in a time of high turnover among institutional chefs. 'Good for you, Charlie.'

'I'm not at all sure I should have agreed to do it,' I confess. 'I'm thinking of calling Stephen Gulivant back and saying I have a trial I can't get out of.'

'Why on earth would you do that?' Marjorie asks.

'Marjorie, you know what goes on in the Court of Appeal. We're used to having juries to do most of the hard work for us, and we don't have to write judgments. But up there, you have to give several judgments a day – extempore, as soon as counsel have finished their arguments. No time to think about it. "His Honour Judge Walden will deliver the judgment of the Court," Stephen will announce, and there I'll be, on stage, exposed, for all to see. What if I make a compete fool of myself? I'll never live it down.'

'Why should you make a fool of yourself?' Legless asks. 'Charlie, you've forgotten more criminal law than Stephen Gulivant will ever know. Your judgments will be the highlight of the day.'

'Absolutely,' Marjorie chimes in. 'And they don't just spring it on you, Charlie. Stephen will assign cases to each judge in advance each day, and you'll have a conference before court sits, so you'll know which files you have to concentrate on before you start, and which counsel you really need to listen to and ask questions of. It's no different from what we do here every day of the week, like deciding whether or not to admit evidence.'

'I don't think you can get away with, "I think the evidence should come in" or "stay out", with that lot,' I protest. 'I think they expect a bit more substance in the Court of Appeal, a touch of law. I think they expect you to explain why.'

'Marjorie's right, Charlie,' Legless insists. 'Most of the cases they get up there are about evidence anyway. There won't be anything you don't know inside out.'

'It's not that difficult, Charlie,' Hubert says. 'It's not so much what you say as how you say it.'

'How so?' I ask.

'The secret is to sound confident,' Hubert replies, 'even if you're talking complete nonsense. That's the important thing.'

Marjorie smiles. 'There's a bit more to it than that, Hubert.'

'No, not at all. I got it from one of the true masters,' Hubert replies. 'I had dinner with Sandy Froggett at Lincoln's Inn one evening – years ago now – and I asked him how he did it. Of course, he sat in the Court of Appeal for years – in the Civil Division in his case, but I don't suppose it's any different in the Criminal Division. Sandy told me that the way he did it was: he would decide which way he wanted to go, and then, if he wasn't sure he understood the law, instead of buggering about with it, he would just say that the rule was "self-evident" or "axiomatic" or "well established". As long as you said something like that, no one would question it, and you moved on to the next case.'

'That may have worked for Sandy Froggett back in the dark ages, Hubert,' I say, gloomily. 'I don't think you can get away with it today.'

'You won't need to get away with anything, Charlie,' Marjorie replies comfortingly. 'You'll be the best criminal lawyer on the panel. You'll do just fine. Once you've got one or two cases under your belt, you'll wonder why you ever worried yourself about it.'

'And in addition to everything else,' I whine, 'I don't have the right outfit. I can't wear the robes we wear here, can I? You have to have the Silk's black gown and all the rest of it. God only knows how much that will set me back.'

'You don't need to buy all that stuff,' Legless suggests. 'You can borrow it from somebody.'

'Even better,' Marjorie says, 'try the circuit judges' website. There are retired judges advertising second-hand robes for sale all the time. You can pick them up for a song. Just make sure you buy them from a judge about the same size as you.'

I look at her, surprised. 'Why would retired judges sell off their robes?' I ask.

'Why not?' Hubert asks. 'Better than having them cluttering the place up at home. I'd try selling them to a theatre company or a film studio. They're always on the lookout for costumes, aren't they?'

Marjorie shrugs. 'If that doesn't work, ask Stephen Gulivant. He'll find you something. It doesn't have to cost a fortune.'

'Well, that's something, I suppose,' I concede.

* * *

Monday Morning

As Marjorie promised, I am not to be thrown in the deep end without any warning. I have been assigned small, but functional temporary chambers, so that I have a quiet corner in which to flick through the case files before the morning conference. Two of the files have a red sticky on them, which doesn't register as significant at the time, but, as I will learn shortly, is actually rather important. The conference begins at nine o'clock in Stephen Gulivant's chambers, with Stephen, myself, and the third member of the court, Mr Justice Julius Hendry, whom I haven't met before, but who seems perfectly pleasant and introduces himself cheerfully as a recent appointment from the marine insurance Bar.

'I know sweet Fanny Adams about crime, Charles,' he confides. 'I've only done this once before myself. So I'm very glad you're here.'

'Charles taught me all I know about crime,' Stephen Gulivant adds, 'when I sat at Bermondsey for a few days. I was supposed to do a nightmare of a case about whether the defendant could claim sovereignty over an island – well, more like a lump of rock, really – off the south coast. He was claiming that we couldn't try him because he was a foreign head of state. But it turned out I had a conflict of interest, and I had to hand it over to Charles, and take over his – what was it, Charles?'

'Offensive weapon.'

'Offensive weapon, that was it. They say there's no real law in crime, but my word, there was lots of law in that one, terribly complicated stuff. But Charles walked me through it, and we got there in the end, didn't we?'

'We did,' I agree.

'Well, let's make a start then,' Stephen suggests. 'We have ten cases in the list today. Charles, since it's your first day, we'll go easy on you. I've got two cases for you to deliver the judgment, and they both seem pretty straightforward. The first one is Ledbetter, an appeal against a sentence passed by a recorder at Birmingham.'

My Ledbetter file has a red sticky attached to it – my first indication that this isn't a coincidence. I make a note to study the files bearing red stickies rather more carefully in future.

'I'm no expert,' Stephen comments, 'but it does look a bit on the high side.'

I open my copy of the file to remind myself. He is absolutely right. The sentence passed by the recorder – a part-time judge of the Crown Court – was not so much high as stratospheric. Chummy, who was gainfully employed, and of good character except for a couple of previous for shoplifting and possessing cannabis, hit the victim over the head with a chair during an altercation in a pub, apparently caused by a dispute over someone's girlfriend. The victim sustained a couple of nasty cuts to the head, and one or two bruises when he fell down, but they didn't keep him in hospital overnight and he made a full recovery within a few days. The charge was assault occasioning actual bodily harm. The defendant pleaded guilty at the first available opportunity.

The recorder, after pontificating in his sentencing remarks for some time about how the country was going to the dogs, and about how there was too much mindless violence, and other such amateur stuff, weighed Chummy off for four and a half years. It was a sentence out of line with the sentencing guidelines – of which the recorder seemed to be only dimly aware – as well as one lacking in any sense of proportion. He also ignored the one-third reduction the defendant was entitled to for his early plea of guilty. I quickly calculate that, taking into account the absence of any previous for violence, and the one third discount, I would probably have given him six months, and on balance, I would have suspended the sentence for two years, ordering him to do a hefty chunk of unpaid work for the benefit of the community, and pay the victim some compensation. I suggest to Stephen that we should allow the appeal and substitute that sentence for the one imposed by the recorder. Both he and Julius Hendry agree immediately, without any debate.

My second red sticky file, a case called Winters, is slightly more challenging. It's an appeal against conviction. Chummy, who is forty-five, was convicted at Norwich of a sexual assault on his seventeen-year-old stepdaughter. The prosecution asked the highly experienced trial judge to allow them to tell the jury about a previous conviction he had for an offence against another girl, one that sounded somewhat similar but was some twenty years old. Another complication was that the earlier conviction had been by way of a plea of guilty in the Magistrates' Court, so there was no detailed record of the proceedings. The only indication of its history was a note on the court file, probably made by the clerk of court, which was a bit vague about the details, including the age of the victim. Besides, that kind of evidence would only be relevant to the current case if it tended to prove that the defendant had engaged in very similar behaviour in the not-too-distant past, a conclusion which, at first glance, seems less than compelling.

'The previous matter is a bit on the old side, isn't it?' Stephen observes. 'And the judge wasn't given much in the way of evidence about it. I must say, Charles, I'm not at all sure she should have let it in.'

He's hit the nail on the head, and initially I'm disposed to agree with him. But I know the judge who tried this case, and she's a first-rate lawyer. Not only that, but when I put myself in the judge's shoes, and ask myself what I would do, I know exactly what was going through her mind. You just know that Chummy has been trying to portray himself to the jury as the perfect stepfather, not at all the kind of bloke who would interfere with young girls, and without the previous conviction, it's an image the prosecution might have some trouble debunking. Any judge would love to show the jury the other side of the coin. I'm acutely aware that in her position, I would have been itching to let the evidence in. I might well have given myself a good talking to and done my best to resist the temptation, but I'm by no means sure I would have succeeded.

I glance at the extract from the judge's summing-up to the jury, in which she deals with the previous conviction. As I would have expected, it's impeccable. She makes it clear that it was all some time ago, the details are rather sparse, and she warns the jury in the clearest terms not to give it too much weight. She explains, equally clearly, what its relevance is, and isn't. I couldn't have improved on her directions at all. All the same, the evidence was there when perhaps it shouldn't have been, and the jury couldn't have ignored it.

I'm almost ready to agree with Stephen that we should think about allowing the appeal, when it occurs to me that not only was the summing-up impeccable, but also, the evidence against Chummy, leaving aside the previous conviction, was more than enough for any jury to convict. And I can't shake off my sympathy with the judge.

'On the other hand,' I venture tentatively, 'the evidence as a whole was quite strong, wasn't it? If we felt that the conviction was safe overall, we could uphold the conviction. I don't know about you, but I would say the judge's summing-up was right on point. She went out of her way to warn the jury to be cautious in looking at the evidence. I honestly couldn't improve on it.'

'If your experience leads you in that direction,' Julius says, graciously, 'I wouldn't dissent.'

Stephen shrugs. 'He obviously did it, didn't he?' he comments. 'But is that something we should take into account?'

'No,' I reply. 'But the real question is whether the conviction is safe. If the judge hadn't been so clear in her directions, I would probably take a different view. But she got it absolutely right, and with the rest of the evidence, there was a solid basis for the jury's verdict. I will understand if you disagree, but that's the way I'd go.'

'If you're comfortable giving that judgment, Charles,' Stephen says, 'I don't mind climbing on board.'

And so it comes to pass. I ask prosecuting counsel a number of questions designed to illustrate just how strong the case against Mr Winters was, and by the time I come to deliver the judgment, I feel I'm starting to get the hang of this appellate stuff. And then, for the rest of the day, I'm listening politely to cases in which one of my colleagues will give the judgment, joining in now and then with the odd question. I must say, my first day on Mount Olympus hasn't been nearly as daunting as I'd expected.

* * *

Tuesday Morning

On Tuesday, there's no longer any hesitation, or sense of 'going easy' on me. Stephen immediately assigns me all four of the appeals against sentence we have in our list. Fortunately, there's nothing too difficult about them. All four sentences are on the high side, but they are either in line with, or not too far away from, what you'd expect under the guidelines. They are sentences the judges concerned were fully entitled to pass, and we quickly agree to dismiss the appeal in each case.

Stephen also assigns me one appeal against conviction, which is not quite so straightforward. Chummy was convicted of several counts of fraud at Newcastle, the gist of the offences being that he duped some elderly and other vulnerable victims out of thousands of pounds of savings and pensions, by luring them into a bogus investment scheme, which had no substance at all. To bolster his credibility with his victims, he falsely pretended to be a man of the cloth, and sometimes wore a dog collar when making his sales pitch. He told them that a large proportion of any profits he made would go to charity.

Chummy gave evidence in his defence. Having taken the oath on the New Testament, which is quite usual, he then refused to return the book to the usher, and insisted on holding it tightly to his chest for the whole of the one and a half court days for which his evidence lasted – which is not at all usual. The prosecution suggested to the judge that, in so doing, he was trying to mislead the jury into thinking that he was a man of good character, and argued that they should be permitted to tell the jury about his three previous convictions for theft. The judge agreed. He was duly convicted, and the judge duly weighed him off for a richly deserved four years.

As counsel point out to me in the course of argument, this is not a novel point. There is already a certain amount of precedent – previous decisions of the Court – the gist of which seems to be that it would be a bit over the top to let in previous convictions just because a defendant wants to hold the New Testament while giving evidence. Defence counsel argues that given the highly prejudicial effect of telling the jury about convictions for theft in a case where Chummy is charged with fraud, the appellant was not given a fair trial and the Court has no alternative but to allow the appeal. But the prosecution counters, equally cogently, that the defendant's behaviour was such an obvious attempt to give the jury a false impression of his character that the judge was right to allow them to hear the full story. Although I started the hearing with an open mind, as the argument proceeds, I find myself agreeing more and more with the prosecution. But I'm also acutely aware that I haven't spent enough time on Mount Olympus yet to be comfortable about suggesting that the Court might have got it wrong on earlier occasions. On the other hand, if my two colleagues feel the same way, it might just be possible. I ask Stephen if we can rise to consider our decision in chambers.

'So, you think the current authorities are wrong do you, Charles?' Stephen asks, once we are safely in chambers with the door closed. 'You think we ought to depart from them?'

'No reason why we shouldn't,' Julius observes, 'is there, technically speaking?'

'No,' Stephen agrees, 'well, not if we have a good reason. But we would need a good reason.'

They are both looking at me expectantly.

'I think this case is different, factually, from the earlier cases,' I say. 'For one thing, he's charged with thoroughly dishonest conduct – serious, repeated instances of fraud – during which he wore a dog collar, cloaking himself in the trappings of religion.' As I'm saying this, I can't help thinking of the Reverend Mrs Walden, and what she would have to say about it, which would not be at all favourable to the appellant, and would very likely be couched in distinctly non-liturgical language. 'And when he holds the book while giving evidence, he reinforces that impression. Essentially, he's trying to con the jury in exactly the same way he conned his victims. I think it would have been wrong for the judge not to let the prosecution put the record straight.'

'That makes sense to me,' Julius says. 'He's obviously a nasty piece of work. Look at all that money he took from those poor people – in some cases, their entire savings.'

Stephen is nodding. 'If we can distinguish the earlier cases factually, I'm happy to dismiss,' he says.

So, there I am, back in court, ready to rewrite the law as if I were one of the Olympian gods. The only problem is that I now have to give a reasoned judgment based on the law. I experience a few moments of panic as I begin the chronological recitation of the facts, but suddenly, as I'm staring at my notes, getting ready to move on to the law, from somewhere, an image of Hubert comes into my mind. I pause for effect.

'It is well established,' I say, 'that where a defendant seeks to mislead the jury by making a false claim of good character, it is proper for the prosecution to rebut that suggestion by adducing evidence of the defendant's actual character. In fact, one might say that it is axiomatic.' Glancing to my right, I see my two colleagues on the bench nodding. 'Whatever may have been the position in the earlier cases to which counsel referred us, we are satisfied that in this case, given the appellant's reliance on religious imagery to perpetrate his frauds, the learned judge was entirely correct in allowing the jury to hear about his true character. Accordingly, this appeal fails.'

Chummy hasn't had the gall to appeal against his sentence, so there is no more to be said, and I'm off the hook for the rest of the day. Wednesday and Thursday prove to be straight-forward, and by now I'm carrying my full weight in terms of giving the judgments. I'm actually starting to think that perhaps I have found my true vocation. I could get used to this appellate way of life.

But then comes Friday.

* * *

Friday morning

There's only one case in our list today, and it is sporting a red sticky. I open the file and start to read. It stops me in my tracks. 'Appeal against Conviction and Sentence,' the heading announces, 'The Queen v Leo Bradley, Len Bradley and Lance Bradley, on appeal from the Crown Court at Bermondsey, His Honour Judge Hubert Drake and a jury.'

I know all about this case. Stella consulted me about it because it seemed to have a few distinctly tricky issues involving identification, on which basis we decided that it should go to Legless, who is very solid in tricky identification cases. But when the day arrived, Legless was immersed in a trial that had already overrun by several days, Marjorie and I had fixtures we couldn't hand off, and so with some misgivings, she had to assign Bradley to Hubert. I have a terrible premonition of what I'm going to find as I explore the file, and as I begin to read, I watch the premonition take solid form and rise up to confront me.

The brothers Bradley are members of a large family which migrated to south London from Hong Kong in the 1950s, to became one of Bermondsey's celebrated 'disorganised crime families', also known to the Bar as '*le Cinque Famiglie di Bermondsey*'. I represented members of one of the *Cinque Famiglie*, the Fogles, myself when I was at the Bar. I never acted for anyone from the Bradley family, but I heard a lot about them from the Fogles. The Fogles detested the Bradleys, not only because they were rivals, but because of the Bradleys' fondness for gratuitous violence, which was a feature of almost every crime they committed. To their eternal credit, the Fogles had no truck with violence, and were not above quietly grassing a Bradley up from time to time, when they thought the violence had gone too far.

The case Hubert tried was one of robbery, and featured a

familiar Bradley *modus operandi*. The three brothers were alleged to have carried out the robbery at a small, family-owned 24-hour supermarket, late at night, armed with baseball bats and one firearm. They got away with about £400 and a quantity of cigarettes, leaving the father and son, who were manning the shop at the time, bruised and battered, though mercifully, nothing worse. There had been several customers in the shop at the time, and between them, they gave the police fairly detailed descriptions of the three robbers. But needless to say, the Bradley brothers were the beneficiaries of an alibi provided by numerous family members, who maintained that, at the relevant time, they were at a family party in honour of a great-uncle's ninetieth birthday. Nonetheless, each of them was identified in a formal procedure at the police station by at least one witness as having been one of the robbers, so the prosecution was certainly viable.

As I delve deeper into the file, I begin to find my worst fears confirmed. Fairly early in the trial, Hubert has lost track of which brother was which, and which brother was alleged to have done various things – such as threatening those present with the firearm, assaulting the father and son, emptying the till, and stuffing cartons of cigarettes into bags. Even worse, when it comes time to sum up, he is far too cavalier about the very real issues of identification. Visual identification is a notoriously dangerous kind of evidence. Even honest and conscientious witnesses can be mistaken about an identification, while at the same time, because they are honest, they are often very credible witnesses. It's a natural breeding ground for miscarriages of justice, and the history of the law is replete with them. The Court of Appeal has said over and over again that, in his summing-up, the judge must warn the jury fully about the dangers of identification evidence, and even withdraw the case from the jury if the evidence seems too tenuous.

Hubert decided not to withdraw the case, and reading through the file, I find myself agreeing with him. But his summing-up is another matter. He doesn't come close to warning the jury in strong enough terms, and he is obviously still confused about who is alleged to have done what. Even worse, there are two sentences in which, while he doesn't actually say so in so many words, he seems to imply that they all – meaning, presumably, people of Chinese ethnic origin – look the same, which is not the kind of warning the Court of Appeal had in mind. The three brothers were convicted, they all have form for similar offences, and Hubert weighed them off for seven years each. I can't argue with the sentences. But they are probably academic. The convictions on which they depend seem to be fatally compromised by the problems with the summing-up.

The outcome of the appeal seems inevitable. But that's not my only concern. This was a serious case. Hubert lost control over it at an early stage, and never recovered. The record suggests that counsel did their best to intervene and put him straight, apparently without success, because Hubert was adamant that he understood the facts and didn't need their help. That in itself is worrying, because we all need counsel's help sometimes, and the only sensible reaction when they offer it is to engage with them. Hubert knows that perfectly well. What was he thinking? Suddenly, the case feels ominous, bringing to mind his earlier episode of confusion and the vexed question of his retirement. I've always been determined that, if Hubert does ever reach the point where he can't go on, he should have the option of deciding to retire with dignity. The alternative, of course, is that the Grey Smoothies decide for him, regardless of considerations of dignity. Now, in fairness, they would only do that as a last resort. Even the Grey Smoothies would normally allow a judge to bow out gracefully, rather than being removed. But there's a problem with that in Hubert's case. Hubert has always made it abundantly clear that he has no intention of bowing out under any circumstances, and I'm by no means sure that he would take the hint – which means that Yours Truly would have to embark on a diplomatic campaign to persuade him to change his mind. It's not going to help that campaign if I have to give the judgment in this case myself.

I decide to raise my concern with Stephen Gulivant as soon as we begin our morning conference. I don't allude directly to the question of retirement, of course. I don't want to plant the idea in his mind if it hasn't occurred to him. I do my best to couch it in terms of the potential embarrassment involved in my giving a judgment so critical of one of my colleagues in a small court such as Bermondsey; how bad for morale it will be; and how it will affect my relationship with my colleagues as RJ. It cuts no ice at all.

'Oh, it's something we all have to do, Charles. As you know, I'm a presiding judge on the South Eastern Circuit, so I know every judge on the circuit quite well. But I've still had to allow appeals from cases they've tried from time to time. It's nothing personal. It's part of the job – might as well get used to it. If you come back to sit with us again, you're bound to allow appeals from judges you know from time to time.'

I try my best to couch the judgment in moderate terms, but just reciting the factual background to the appeal tells its own story vividly enough, without any need for embellishment. Defence counsel pulled no punches during the hearing of the appeal, and the prosecutor's muted response amounted to a tacit acknowledgement that there was only one possible outcome. I have no alternative but to tell like it is, as they say.

'In the judgment of this court, the learned judge failed to give the jury the clear warning this court has said, time and time again, is necessary when dealing with evidence of visual identification. The summing-up must make clear that such evidence is potentially dangerous, and must explain clearly what the dangers are. The jury must be told to exercise the utmost caution in evaluating evidence of that kind. Not only did the learned judge's summing-up fail to make those matters clear, but in effect, it invited the jury to give considerable weight to the identifications of the appellants made by the witnesses, while mentioning the evidence of alibi only in passing, and in a way which the jury may have found suggestive that the judge was sceptical about it. It must at best have confused the jury, and at worst, misled them.

'In addition, it is clear that the learned judge himself became confused during the trial about the evidence dealing with the roles said to have been played in the robbery by the three appellants. This is reflected in the way in which he reminded the jury of the prosecution's allegations against the appellants during the summing-up, which, as counsel have pointed out in the course of argument, was inaccurate in a number of important respects. We make no criticism of the learned judge for experiencing some confusion about the evidence. All of us who sit in criminal trials have that experience from time to time, especially in a case of some complexity. But in that situation, the proper course is for the judge to confer with counsel in the absence of the jury at some convenient moment during the trial, and to ask counsel for their help in clarifying the matters he is finding difficult. It has been our experience that counsel are always ready to assist the judge in that way. In this case, not only did the learned judge not seek the assistance of counsel on his own initiative, but he gave every indication of being reluctant to hear from them *when they asked to address him in the absence of the jury, before the closing speeches and the summing-up. In the course of argument, counsel on both sides of the case told us candidly that they were concerned that the learned judge's command of the evidence was not adequate to allow him to sum the case up to the jury properly. Unfortunately, the summing-up shows that counsel's concerns were amply justified.*

'In the circumstances, we cannot say that the convictions in this case were safe. In the case of each of the appellants, the appeal against conviction is allowed, and the conviction quashed.'

Three armed robbers are going to walk free because the trial judge made a hopeless mess of the case, and the worst of it is that I can't be sure it won't happen again.

We have finished our list just before noon. Stephen insists on taking Julius and myself to lunch at Lincoln's Inn to celebrate the end of the week, and in my case, the end of my sojourn on Mount Olympus. I'm not feeling in much of a mood for a celebratory lunch, but I don't want to be a wet blanket, so I go along and join in the conversation as best I can.

* * *

Friday afternoon

After lunch, I return to Bermondsey, to see Stella and find out what awaits me next week. I haven't heard anything from the court during my week away – which is a good sign. Marjorie always fills in for me as RJ when I'm away from court. She is a safe pair of hands, and she would let me know if anything untoward was going on; and even if she didn't, Stella would. So, silence doesn't concern me. But I still have some pangs of conscience about having once left her in charge in a week during which threatening demonstrations were going on outside the court on a daily basis. There was no way we could have anticipated the demonstrations in question, and Marjorie dealt with it all admirably; but there's this cloak of responsibility you wear as an RJ, and it's one you can never quite take off. Fortunately, nothing bad seems to have happened this week.

'Hello, Judge,' Stella says cheerfully as I knock and enter her office. 'Welcome back. How was the Court of Appeal?'

Stella is our list officer, the only person at any Crown Court without whom the court would, literally, fall apart. She has the almost impossible task of planning the work of four judges over a prolonged period of time, without the advantage of a crystal ball to tell her which cases will fold, which will go the distance, which will overrun, and so on – not to mention that all the players, counsel, solicitors, the CPS, and even we judges, who should know better, are always ready to offer their unsolicited advice, to which Stella listens patiently before explaining why something can't be done. As a result, Stella always has an air of doom about her, as if she is anticipating disaster around every corner. I've got used to that – and in fact, I've concluded that it's simply a realistic state of mind for any list officer. It's an almost impossible job, and Stella is absolutely bloody brilliant at it.

'It was interesting,' I reply.

'I'm sure it must have been. Well, nothing much to report here. It's been quiet.' She picks up two files from the pile on her desk. 'Judge Drake finished his trial, and I've got an ABH for him to start on Monday.'

'How many defendants?' I ask.

She looks up at me curiously. 'Just the one. Why?'

'Oh, nothing.'

'Judge Jenkins and Judge Dunblane are both part-heard, juries likely to go out on Monday or Tuesday, and I'm listing two sexual assault cases for them when they become free, which have been hanging around for too long and really need to be tried.'

She selects two more files.

'I have a GBH for you next week, Judge.' She opens the file. 'Name of Remert. It's a weird case. A 55-year-old wife deliberately boils a kettle of water and pours it all over her husband's head.'

'Ouch,' I say, grimacing.

'Yes. The photographs are horrible. But the odd thing is, no one seems to know why she did it. She's of previous good character – actually, she was a probation officer in her younger days – and there was no prior warning at all.'

'And she's not pleading?'

'No. It's a trial.'

'What's her defence?'

'She's blaming her cat,' Stella replies, enigmatically.

'Of course she is.'

'And then, the following week, we've got O'Finn – another strange one. It's been moved to us from Ipswich because local feeling is running too high for her to have a fair trial there.'

'She can't get a fair trial in Ipswich? What is the world coming to? What's the charge?'

'Affray and ABH. It's all to do with a dispute about whether a statue should be taken down in a nearby village. Apparently, things got out of hand when the local council decided to leave the statue where it was. The defendant's the leader of the group trying to take it down. Ipswich thinks we might get an influx of locals for the trial, and we may have to keep the two sides apart, so I've assigned it to you, and I thought I'd better give you advance notice. I've warned security, of course.'

'All because of a statue?'

'So it would seem, Judge.'

'All right.' I pause. 'Stella, do you remember that case of the three Bradley brothers we wanted to give to Judge Dunblane, but had to give to Judge Drake?'

She nods. 'The robbery at the corner store? Yes. They were convicted.'

'Not any more,' I say.

She looks at me, and then holds her head in her hands.

'It was in your list, was it?'

'It was worse than that, Stella. Stephen Gulivant made me give the judgment.'

'Oh, dear. How bad is it?'

'Very bad… Look, I know we've talked about this before… but…'

She nods. 'I do keep my eyes and ears open, Judge. Counsel and court staff talk to me, and I always listen. But apart from that one incident – you remember, he thought he'd seen his wife in court – apart from that there's been nothing of concern. I mean, there's always the usual whining, you know, his sentences are too high and he takes the prosecution's side too much. But that's just par for the course with Judge Drake, and for all the grumbles, he's hardly ever been appealed – not successfully, anyway.'

'Well, he has now,' I say.

'Yes.' She thinks for some time. 'Will you speak to him? I suppose there's no way to avoid it now, Judge, is there?'

'No,' I reply. 'I'm going to have to talk to him. Hopefully he will have something to reassure me.'

'Yes… Judge, do you think it might help to talk to the Grey Smoothies or the presiders first?'

I shake my head vigorously. 'No. I want to keep this in-house, if possible. I'm not sure it will be: Stephen Gulivant is one of our presiders, as you know. But we have to try.'

'You might try our regular counsel, ask if they've noticed

anything unusual,' Stella suggests. 'They might tell you things they wouldn't tell me.'

I smile. 'I'm not sure about that, Stella. It might be the other way around. And we'd have to trust them not to…'

'They're a discreet bunch, Judge.'

'Yes, they are.'

We sit silently for some time.

'If there's anything really wrong,' Stella resumes eventually, 'someone will have noticed. They don't miss much.'

I nod. 'What I'm dreading is the thought of having to suggest to Judge Drake that the time may have come for him to retire.'

Stella sighs. 'Yes. He's so…'

'Stubborn…?'

'Dedicated. He loves the work so much, Judge. I'm not sure he'll ever retire unless they make him.'

'Well, if the worst comes to the worst, we may have to persuade him otherwise.'

'May I make a suggestion about that, Judge?'

'Of course.'

'You might consider enlisting Judge Jenkins's help. I know she and Judge Drake get on well, and she's…'

I laugh. 'You don't have to say it. She's more of a diplomat than I am.'

Stella's face has turned slightly red, but she can't suppress a shy smile.

'I was going to point out that she didn't give the judgment in the Bradley case,' she adds.

'Good point,' I concede.

We are silent again for some time.

'So, Judge, apart from Judge Drake's case, how did you like the Court of Appeal?'

'Apart from that, Mrs Lincoln, how was the theatre?'

We laugh.

'Would you do it again?'

'Yes,' I reply. 'I think I would. I'm not sure I'd want to do it all the time, but now and then a week on Mount Olympus with the gods can be quite uplifting.'

* * *

Friday Evening

My spirits have revived by tea-time, because the evening promises to be very agreeable. Marjorie and her husband, Nigel, have invited the Reverend Mrs Walden and myself to dinner, to celebrate the conclusion of my week on Mount Olympus. We don't see a lot of Nigel. He spends a good deal of his time in Geneva, where his bank is based, but he is on one of his periodic visits to London, and we shall have the pleasure of his company this evening. The only slightly odd thing about the invitation is that the venue is to be the Delights of the Raj. Marjorie and Nigel are generally to be found in far more upmarket establishments. But as the Reverend Mrs Walden points out when I mention it to her, it is probably an act of kindness. The Delights is one of our two favourite local haunts when we need to unwind after a hard day, or can't be bothered to cook, the other being its Italian counterpart, La Bella Napoli. Marjorie is well aware of our fondness for both, and it was thoughtful of her to indulge us.

The owner and head chef of the Delights is Rajiv, who can always be relied on to serve up a splendid repast. There are few things better calculated to restore morale at the end of a long day than a selection of delicious samosas, a powerful Chicken Madras with a side of Saag Aloo, and a Cobra or two to wash it all down: the only comparable remedy being the Insalata Caesar and sea bass at La Bella Napoli. There's another, fortuitous factor, too. Our usual table is set in an alcove presided over by a small statue of the Hindu elephant god, Ganesh. Odd as it may sound for one in her line of work, the Reverend Mrs Walden is a huge fan of Ganesh. The elephant god is associated with wisdom and benevolence, and she willingly concedes that we could do with some influence like his in Christianity. She would gladly adopt Ganesh and take him into the Church of England's pantheon if she could, although I suspect that her bishop, who cheerfully tolerates most of her theological eccentricities, might see that as a step too far. On the other hand, of course, her enthusiasm is music to Rajiv's ears, as a result of which we always benefit from his personal attention.

We are settling in with a selection of samosas and onion bajis, and Cobras all round, served personally by Rajiv, when the Reverend Mrs Walden happens to ask Nigel about his flat in Geneva, which, to her surprise, and Marjorie's amusement, prompts him to take her on a comprehensive virtual tour of the place, using his phone.

'All you have to do is ask him,' she says, confidentially, 'and he'll go on about it for hours. To be perfectly honest, Charlie, between the two of us, I've never thought there was anything very special about the place. Still, each to his own, I suppose. Perhaps that's the real reason he spends so much time in Geneva – nothing to do with the bank, just that he loves the flat so much he can't bear to leave it.'

We laugh together. She continues in confidential mode.

'Charlie, Legless heard a rumour that you gave judgment quashing a conviction in a case of Hubert's: is that right?'

I nod. 'That's not the half of it. We reversed him because he got totally confused in a four-handed visual identification case, and refused to let counsel help him recover – as a result of which he made a complete dog's dinner of the summing-up. I kept it as low key as I could, but I had to explain why we were allowing the appeal, and I'm afraid it won't make pleasant reading for him.'

'Oh, dear,' she replies. 'Is it something we have to worry about – you know, longer term?'

'I don't know, Marjorie. The real question is whether the presiders and the Grey Smoothies think it's something to worry about. Stephen Gulivant was presiding on my panel, as you know, so it's possible I might hear something from him next week.'

'Who was the third member of the panel?'

'Mr Justice Julius Hendry, late of the marine insurance Bar.'

She shakes her head. 'The name rings a vague bell. I don't know anything about him.'

'Neither do I, except for the fact that, in his own immortal words, he knows sweet Fanny Adams about criminal law. At least he didn't get in the way, I'll say that for him.'

Seeing the Reverend Mrs Walden's eyes about to glaze over, Marjorie reaches over to touch Nigel's arm and bring the virtual tour to an end.

'I think Clara's seen all she needs to see of the flat, darling, don't you?'

Before Nigel can protest, Rajiv and his merry band of waiters appear, as if from nowhere, bearing dishes of Chicken Madras, two different vegetable curries, Saag Aloo, bowls overflowing with perfectly boiled white rice, and assorted heaps of breads, chapatis, and naans, plain and garlic – not to mention another round of Cobras. The Geneva flat is quickly forgotten. The conversation dies down while we do justice to this wonderful feast, and I really do begin to feel the cares of the week receding. As we sit back contentedly with the remains of the Cobras, there is a silence for some time, before Marjorie and Nigel exchange meaningful looks, and Marjorie suddenly sits forward in her chair.

'Actually, Charlie, in addition to congratulating you on your first week in the Criminal Division – the first of many, I'm sure – there is something else I want to tell you. It's supposed to be confidential for a few more days, but you're my RJ and you should know, and I can't see any harm in telling you and Clara...'

'Our lips are sealed,' I reply.

'They've offered me an appointment to the High Court,' she says, 'and obviously, I've accepted. Queen's Bench Division.'

The Reverend and I exchange smiles.

'I am delighted, Marjorie,' I say, and I mean it. 'Not that it was ever in doubt. It was always a question of when, not whether.'

'I thought they were getting close, after all the sitting I've been doing as a deputy, but they called me on Tuesday, and asked me to come in for a final interview.'

'Well, we will be sorry to lose you, that goes without saying, but I couldn't be happier for you.'

'That's marvellous, Marjorie,' the Reverend adds, 'very well done. And doesn't that mean you will soon be *Dame* Marjorie Jenkins?'

She smiles. 'Yes. I haven't had much time to digest it all yet. I suppose I'll have to work out what to wear for the occasion.'

'I'm sure they will let you know,' the Reverend replies reassuringly.

'When do you take up your appointment?' I ask. 'I'm sure that will be Stella's first question.'

'I'm sure it will. They haven't given me a firm date yet, but probably about two months. So, Stella will have plenty of time to lobby for my replacement.'

'It's all so bloody unfair,' Nigel whines, with a grin. 'If they were giving me a K, Marjorie would be entitled to call herself *Lady* Jenkins. But when she becomes a Dame, I get nothing at all. I'm still plain *Mr* Jenkins. It's a clear case of gender discrimination.'

'Nigel,' Marjorie replies, 'if you ever want to call yourself Lady Jenkins, I promise you, you'll get no objections from me.'

PART TWO

THE CURIOUS INCIDENT OF
THE CAT JUST AFTER LUNCH

THE CURIOUS INCIDENT OF
THE CAT JUST AFTER LUNCH

Monday morning

On Sunday mornings, in deference to the Reverend Mrs Walden, I'm usually to be found in a pew at the church of St Aethelburgh and All Angels in the Diocese of Southwark. I enjoy the services generally, but for me, the highlight is always the Reverend's sermon. Part of this is attributable to the fact that I often watch it take shape during the week. The Reverend Mrs Walden works hard on her sermons. Her research is very impressive. As Sunday approaches, her desk starts to groan under the weight of open books; and in addition to the usual online sources for more pedestrian matters, she will sometimes take herself off to King's College library to track down some obscure point of church history. Sometimes, I do more than just watch it take shape. Over dinner, she will often bounce ideas off me, and sometimes she even asks for my candid opinion about some point of view she's thinking of putting forward that may prove to be a tad controversial. Once in a while, she will read a whole section to me, and invite comments. So, by the time Sunday comes, I feel that I've had some modest influence on the sermon, and I look forward to hearing the final version, to see how it has evolved during the week.

She varies the theme of the sermon from week to week, of course, but inevitably, over the course of time, there are some subjects that tend to recur, simply because they are such staples, for example, forgiveness, the family, the pressures on young people and in the workplace – and, of course, marriage. In my opinion, the Reverend Mrs Walden is very good on marriage, and indeed, on relationships generally. She is wonderful at counselling engaged couples. It has to be said that this is a view not necessarily shared by all her colleagues, or indeed by every member of her congregation. Some of them tend to bridle at her easy acceptance of gay and trans relationships, and her positively encouraging couples to acquire some experience of living together before tying the knot in church; and there is certainly some resistance to her interesting take on the relationship between Jesus and Mary Magdalene, which doesn't correspond exactly with standard church doctrine. But she is so obviously genuine in her views that she tends to get away with it where some other vicars might not. It helps that she and her bishop get on famously. He is always very supportive of her, even in some of her other less orthodox endeavours, such as campaigning for the legalisation of cannabis for both medicinal and recreational use. So I always look forward to her sermons on marriage. There is a certain nervousness involved, it's true, because she not infrequently illustrates what she has to say by referring the congregation to aspects of our own marriage. She's very discreet about it, of course, but it is an odd experience to sit in my pew and hear my marriage being analysed in front of an audience, and wonder how many of the people around me are staring at me.

I've noted, too, that the Reverend Mrs Walden's sermons occasionally seem to refer, directly or indirectly, to a case I've tried, or am about to try. It's not unusual for her to ask me, in the evenings while we are partaking of our pre-prandial sherry, about whatever case I have going on, and I've noted that the case sometimes provides some inspiration for a point to be made from the pulpit on Sunday. Yesterday's sermon dealt admirably with the importance of understanding, treating each other as equals, and respecting each other in marriage; and I would be very surprised if it didn't owe something to a conversation we had over dinner on Saturday evening about the case I'm starting this morning. I wonder, too, whether history might have been different if those involved in the case could have listened to her sermon before it was too late.

'Members of the jury,' Aubrey Brooks begins, 'I appear to prosecute in this case. My learned friend Miss Cathy Writtle represents the defendant, Marie Remert, the lady in the dock.'

Aubrey Brooks has a pleasant, understated manner, and cuts a dapper figure, which sometimes leads an unwary opponent, or witness, to lower their guard, to their cost. Despite his laid-back manner, Aubrey is quite capable of landing a knock-out blow, seemingly from nowhere, which makes him a very effective prosecutor. He also sits as a recorder, and the understanding of the judicial role he has derived from that experience has given him an additional string to his bow. Defending is Cathy Writtle, who is certainly not understated, and who tends to rely on direct, relentless aggression where Aubrey would employ humour or innuendo. But she can be just as effective when it comes to finding the knock-out blow, and it's going to be interesting to see how the contrast plays out in this case.

'Members of the jury, if you all have your copies of the indictment, would you please look at it with me for a moment? You will see that Marie Remert is charged with causing grievous bodily harm to her husband, Bert Remert, with intent to cause him grievous bodily harm. Members of the jury, at the end of the trial, His Honour will sum the case up and explain the law to you. That's His Honour's province, and you must take the law from him, not from me. But I think I can safely tell you this much now: that "grievous bodily harm" is just an old legal term, which means simply any really serious bodily injury. The Crown say that by the end of the trial, you will be left in no doubt that Marie Remert caused her husband to suffer really serious bodily injury, and that she fully intended to cause him really serious bodily injury.

'Members of the jury, you will hear that in the early afternoon of 6 March this year, a Friday, Bert Remert was sitting at his laptop computer, doing some work. Mr Remert is the husband of the defendant, Marie Remert, and at the time, they lived together in a semi-detached house in Wheatley Road, in Isleworth. They had finished lunch not long before, and having cleared the dishes away, Mr Remert had set his computer up on the dining table. The defendant, Marie Remert, had been in the kitchen, washing up after lunch. As she told the police when interviewed, having finished the washing up, she filled the kettle with water, put it on to boil, and waited. It was her usual practice to make coffee for herself and her husband after lunch. But on this occasion, members of the jury, instead of making coffee, she took the kettle, walked the short distance into the dining room, where her husband was sitting with his back to her, approached him, and deliberately poured the entire contents of the kettle – somewhere in the region of two and a half pints of boiling water – over his unprotected head.'

There are audible gasps in the jury box, and Aubrey pauses for effect, to allow the images they are forming in their minds to sink in. In due course, he will provide them with some of the actual images of the damage, which, if anything, will be worse than whatever they are imagining now.

'Members of the jury, Mr Remert suffered extensive third degree burns to his head, shoulders and back. He was in hospital for more than a month and eventually underwent a number of skin grafts. You will hear the full medical report read to you later in the trial. Suffice it to say that he sustained very painful and serious injuries, the effects of which, the doctors say, will remain with him for the rest of his life.

'You may already be asking yourselves: why did Mrs Remert do this to her husband? Members of the jury, I am by no means sure that the prosecution will be able to explain it to you. Mr and Mrs Remert had been married for more than twenty years. There is no record of the police ever being called out to the Remert residence, no evidence of any previous acts of violence taking place between them. Moreover, Mrs Remert is a woman of previous good character – indeed of excellent character. At the time of her arrest, she was working for an insurance company in their claims department, but in earlier life, she had served for a number of years as a probation officer, whose job it was to help men and women who had been convicted of crimes. Mrs Remert herself called 999 to bring an ambulance and the police to the house. She was arrested, and later interviewed in the presence of her solicitor by the officer in the case, DS Watson. You will hear the interview read to you.

'At the outset, Mrs Remert submitted a prepared written statement, which you may find to be quite extraordinary. In this statement, Mrs Remert denies that she deliberately poured the boiling water over her husband's head. She says that she was approaching him to ask a question about his coffee, when suddenly, her cat, whose name is Ginger, leapt up off the floor on to the dining table and swiped Mrs Remert's right hand, causing her to lose control of the kettle, and causing its contents to spill over Mr Remert's head accidentally. She makes some suggestion that Ginger had done something similar on at least one occasion in the past. Members of the jury, the prosecution will call expert evidence about the pattern of the burns on Mr Remert's head, the effect of which will be to show that the distribution of the boiling water appears to be in direct, almost straight lines, consistent with a deliberate act of pouring rather than an accidental spillage. Suffice it to say that the prosecution does not propose to charge Ginger with any offence arising from this incident.'

The jury and I chuckle, and even Cathy can't resist a smile.

'But then, members of the jury, in answering DS Watson's questions, Mrs Remert takes a rather different tack. She makes a long litany of complaints about her husband behaving in a dominating and overbearing manner towards her throughout their married life. She does not suggest that he was physically violent, but she says that he tried to control her life in intimate detail, for example, by regulating her use of her computer, restricting her movements outside the house, denying her access to her friends, and cross-examining her about the amount of money she spent. Although she stops short of saying so in so many words, the suggestion appears to be that, after silently enduring so much abuse over so many years, she finally cracked, and impulsively took her revenge.

'Be that as it may, members of the jury, the Crown say that this was a deliberate act on Mrs Remert's part, which caused her husband really serious bodily injury, and which she intended to cause her husband really serious bodily injury. That's what we have to prove to you, but it's all we have to prove to you. Why she did what she did may well remain, at least to some extent, a mystery. It is our burden to prove what Mrs Remert did, but not necessarily why she did it. It is a burden of proof we fully expect to meet. If, after considering all the evidence, you are sure that Mrs Remert acted intentionally, with intent to cause really serious bodily harm to her husband, then the Crown has met its burden of proof, and it will be your duty to return what we say is the only possible verdict in this case – a verdict of guilty.'

Aubrey turns towards me. 'With your Honour's leave, I will call Bert Remert.'

Bert Remert's head is covered by what looks like a cap of a very soft material, and we can see that there are still one or two bandages underneath the cap. No doubt the same is true of his shirt. He walks like a man in pain, and I know from the medical report that he will have taken a good dose of his pain medication this morning, just to get himself to court today. But he walks unaided to the witness box, and takes the oath on the book Dawn, our usher, hands him.

'Mr Remert,' Aubrey asks, 'are you the husband of Marie Remert, the lady in the dock?'

'I'm getting a divorce,' Bert replies.

'Yes,' Aubrey says, 'I understand. But as of today, are you still married?'

'Yes, but only because it takes so long to get anything done in this country.'

'And you were husband and wife on 6 March of this year?'

'Yes.'

'For how long have you been married?'

'I gave her more than twenty-three years of my life.'

'For how much of that time did you live together at the house in Wheatley Road?'

'All of it. I bought that house not long before I met Marie. She moved in when we got married. But it's my house.'

I see Cathy smile briefly. She's probably thinking what I'm thinking – that is, if by 'my house' Bert means that his wife has no interest in it whatsoever after twenty-three years of marriage, a family court may well disabuse him of that idea before too long, even given the circumstances of this case.

'Mr Remert, I know this is bound to be painful for you,' Aubrey says, 'but I want to take you back to the early afternoon of Friday 6 March of this year. Please tell the jury what you were doing at that time.'

Bert takes a deep breath. 'We had lunch at one o'clock – as we did every day. Marie cleared the lunch things away to the kitchen, and washed them up – as she always did – and I was expecting her to bring my coffee – as she always did. I was writing a report for work.'

'What was your work at that time?'

He hesitates, biting his lip. 'I was the section manager for the claims department of an insurance company.'

'Have you been able to work at all since the incident?'

'No. I've been off work ever since. The company kept me on the books for a few months, but they had to let me go eventually.'

'By any chance,' Aubrey asks, 'is that the same insurance company your wife works for?'

'Yes. I got her the job in the first place, just after we got married. I didn't want her being a probation officer, so I got her this job, where she reported to me. She was making a lot more money than she was with the probation service, but I never got a word of thanks for it.'

I see Cathy furiously scribbling notes.

'You were writing a report,' Aubrey reminds him.

'Yes. I wanted to get it finished that afternoon. So, I set my laptop up on the dining room table – as I always did when I was working – and I was busy writing.'

'Were you aware of your wife entering the living room at any stage?'

'No. She must have come in very quietly. I never saw her.'

'What happened, Mr Remert?'

There is a long silence, during which he is looking down at the floor.

'Are you all right, Mr Remert?' I ask. 'Would you like a break?'

He shakes his head. 'No. I'd like to continue.'

'All right. Take your time.'

'I don't really remember much about it. One minute I was typing away on my computer, and the next minute, my whole head was burning up. It felt like it was about to explode. The pain was unbelievable. I remember screaming and falling out of my chair, but I don't remember much after that until I woke up in hospital, and even then, I was in so much pain, they had to put me under straightaway. So, I have no real memory of what happened.'

Aubrey thinks for some time, looking down at his notes.

'Mr Remert, the jury will have the medical report read to them in due course, so I don't see any need to ask you about the details of your stay in hospital now. Just tell the jury, if you would, how you feel today, all these months after the event.'

'I'm still in a lot of pain. I take painkillers all the time. I still have to go to hospital to have my bandages changed every two days. And my doctors say I will have some degree of pain, and the scarring, for the rest of my life. All thanks to my dear wife.'

'Did your doctors also tell you that the shock from contact with such a large quantity of boiling water could have had very serious effects, and might even have been fatal in some circumstances?'

'Yes, they did. It was one of the reasons they put me in an induced coma.'

'Mr Remert, do you know of any reason why your wife should have attacked you in the way she did?'

'No. I mean: I married her; I looked after her; I got her the job she has today; I gave her everything she could have wanted. And this is the thanks I get. I don't know whether anyone else can explain it, but I certainly can't.' He turns towards the dock. 'Why don't you explain it to them, you ungrateful bitch?' he shouts.

In the dock, his wife remains impassive, staring straight ahead.

'That will do, Mr Remert,' I say. 'Mr Brooks, do you have much more?'

'That's all I have, your Honour,' Aubrey replies. I have a shrewd suspicion that he might have had a few more questions planned, but his experience is telling him to cut this witness loose as soon as he's got the basics of the story in front of the jury. Let Cathy have a go at him. Come back in re-examination only if necessary.

This trial is starting to feel like a good old-fashioned 1950s defended divorce case, in which the spouses set out to tear each other apart trying to prove adultery, cruelty, or desertion in order to 'win' their divorce proceedings. Defended divorce cases were mercilessly adversarial, and the general rule was 'to the victor, the spoils' – the spoils consisting of the lion's share of the family assets and custody of the children. The scorched-earth approach to divorce had fallen out of favour by the time I came to the Bar, thank God, but I heard all about trials of that kind from my pupil-master, Basil, and they sounded really awful. I really don't want to preside over one now in what's supposed to be a criminal case. I'm not the only one feeling the developing atmosphere. The jury are shifting a bit uneasily in their seats. I need to calm things down a bit.

'In that case, let's take a short break, members of the jury,' I suggest. 'Let's say twenty minutes. You'll have time for a quick coffee.' They look at me gratefully.

'Do you have a cat, Mr Remert?' Cathy begins when we resume.

'A what?'

'A cat – small, furry animal with…'

'Miss Writtle…' I say.

It's a gentle warning shot across the bows. I don't want to make her task any more difficult than it already is. But I also don't want her taking this trial too far down the defended divorce road, and my sense is, neither do the jury.

'Sorry, your Honour. I asked you whether you have a cat, Mr Remert, a tomcat called Ginger, to be precise?'

'Ginger is my cat. Yes.'

'*Your* cat, meaning yours as opposed to your wife's?'

'I was the one who found him and took him in.'

'Did Marie help to look after Ginger? Did she feed him, change his litter box, play with him and his toy mouse, and so on?'

'Sometimes.' It is said grudgingly.

'But he's *your* cat?'

'Yes.'

'Was Ginger in the living room just before the incident began?'

'Yes. He always used to sleep on the sofa while we were having lunch.'

'Did you see Ginger anywhere else just before the incident began, apart from on the sofa?'

'Not that I recall: no.'

'All right.' Cathy does pauses well. She turns over a couple of pages in her notebook, just for punctuation, to allow the jury to digest what they've heard. 'Mr Remert, about three weeks before the incident, do you remember Ginger knocking over a cup of tea in your bedroom, while you were in bed?'

'Yes,' Bert replies.

Cathy raises her eyebrows. I have a feeling that this wasn't the answer she was expecting. A quick smile suggests that the witness might just have opened a door for her.

'Was this when Marie brought you a cup of tea before you got up?'

'She always brought a cup of tea to my bedroom for me in the morning, at 6.45.'

'*Your* bedroom,' Cathy interposes. 'Do I take it from that that you didn't share a bedroom?'

'That's correct. I always liked to have my own bedroom.'

'And what happened on that occasion?'

'She brought the tea into the room. I noticed that Ginger was with her. She put the tea down on the mat on my bedside table, as always, kissed me and wished me a good morning, as always, and turned to leave. At that moment, Ginger leapt off the floor on to the bedside table and crashed into my tea cup. The tea spilled on the bed and the carpet, and Marie had to clean it up.'

'*Marie* had to clean it up?' Cathy asks, 'even though Ginger is your cat?'

Bert doesn't reply. Cathy doesn't bother asking me to order him to answer. She's making her point perfectly well without him.

'Isn't it the case, Mr Remert, that Ginger didn't crash into the cup, but swiped at it with his paw? Isn't that what happened?'

Bert closes his eyes, and seems be trying to relive the scene.

'I didn't really see what happened,' he concedes eventually. 'I was only half-awake. I saw Ginger leap up on to the table, but it was all a bit of a blur. I don't know exactly how he hit the cup. But he did hit it, and knock it over.'

'Thank you, Mr Remert,' Cathy says. So, Ginger has form. Time to turn over a page or two of notes again. She doesn't want the jury to forget this feline criminal record, and I'm sure she's surprised how little effort it took to get the evidence of it.

'Now, Mr Remert,' Cathy continues, unhurriedly, 'at the time you got married, Marie was a probation officer, wasn't she – a job she'd held for a number of years?'

'Yes.'

'But you told the jury that you got her a job at the insurance company, reporting to you, is that right?'

'Yes.'

'Did Marie ask you to get her that job?'

'No. But we discussed it. She couldn't continue being a probation officer.'

'Why not?' Cathy asks.

'She was dealing with criminals the whole time,' Bert replies.

'That's what probation officers do,' Cathy points out.

'Yes, but it would only take one of them to find out her home address, wouldn't it? We could have been burgled, murdered in our beds – anything might have happened. The insurance company was a good job, and it paid more money. It was obviously the right thing to do.'

'Is it what Marie wanted?'

'We were married. We both had to think differently than when we were single.'

'Did Marie tell you that she enjoyed her work as a probation officer?'

'Yes. I believe she did.'

I'm trying not to stare at Cathy, but I'm trying to work out where she's going with this line of questioning. It's already

becoming clear to me, and I suspect, to the jury, that Bert
Remert isn't going to come out of this looking like the ideal
husband. He's obviously a boorish, narrow-minded man,
who would like to control his wife's life to suit his own
predilections to the extent he can. It's already becoming
apparent that Marie Remert must have suffered years of
misery under her husband's thumb. But unfortunately for
her, 'He asked for it' isn't a defence in English law. The remedy
in English law is to consult a solicitor and start divorce
proceedings, not to pour two and a half pints of boiling water
over your husband's head. Cathy has laid a foundation for
blaming the whole thing on Ginger. But she'd love to have a
second string to her bow, in case the jury isn't impressed by
her *Felis ex Machina* theory, and gaining the jury's sympathy
would be a good start. So, she has to give Bert a hard time,
but if she overdoes it, she may play into Aubrey's hands – he
will be arguing that, the more controlling and domineering
Bert was, the more a calculated act of revenge on his wife's
part makes sense.

'Did you allow her a limited time to use her computer in
the evenings?'

'I only made sure she didn't overdo it, so that she wasn't too
tired for work in the mornings. Her job was one that called
for concentration.'

'Did you prevent her from seeing some of the friends she
had from before your marriage?'

'No. I advised her that one or two of the women she knew
were unsuitable, but I didn't prevent her from seeing them.'

'In what way, "unsuitable?"'

'Their main interest seemed to be going out drinking, even
on work nights.'

'Did you require her to write down the names of the friends
she was going out with on any particular evening?'

'And their phone numbers. It was just to make sure I knew she was safe.'

'Was there a particular kind of biscuit – a kind of digestive biscuit, I'm instructed – that you bought for yourself, and that were off limits to Marie?'

'Yes.'

'Did you at one point go to the lengths of sticking a note on the packet, which read, "BR only" – the BR referring to yourself, Bert Remert – telling your wife, in effect, to keep her hands off them?'

'I don't see what the problem is with that. She was free to buy her own, if she liked them.'

Cathy pauses again, and I see her decide that she's scored enough points, and it's time to stop. But knowing Cathy, I feel sure she won't be able to resist a parting shot of some kind.

'Mr Remert, are you familiar with the initials OCD? Do you know what they stand for?'

Cathy is back in her seat before Aubrey can complete his outraged objection, or I can tell her to behave herself.

Next, we have the medical report. It's all agreed, so it can be read to the jury without a witness being called, and they will have copies of it, including the images of Bert's injuries that are probably worse than the jury had imagined when Aubrey opened the case to them. Their reaction seems to confirm that, and one or two dark looks are directed towards the dock. The report's precise medical terminology does nothing to dispel the overwhelming horror of what it describes: the unimaginable pain caused by the scalding water, the induced coma, the confinement in hospital for weeks on end, the constant changing of dressings, and ultimately, the skin grafts. Its dismal prognosis of pain continuing throughout the patient's life somehow has the air of inevitability about it. By the time Aubrey has finished his reading, the jurors are looking a bit white around the gills. Fortunately, the prosecution's expert will not be available until two o'clock, so we can't make any more progress this morning, and to the general relief, we break early.

And so to lunch, an oasis of calm in a desert of chaos.

Marjorie and Legless shower me with endless questions about my experiences in the Court of Appeal. They want to know every detail, and in normal circumstances I would be only too glad to oblige them. If it hadn't been for their encouragement, I might well have found some excuse for ducking out of my stint on Mount Olympus and missed the whole thing. But they had insisted that all would be well and, amazingly, the week went almost exactly as they had predicted. Far from being cast as the clueless comedic character, in danger of making a fool of myself at every turn, I had quickly become a figure of authority. I had undertaken the role of counsellor, explaining the facts of life in the Crown Court to two commercial judges who were the first to admit that their knowledge of criminal law was almost non-existent. Where I'd expected barely suppressed grins and patronising comments from counsel, I found that I was actually treated with respect; and it may have been my imagination, but I even came to feel that there was a hint of relief at the Bar when Stephen Gulivant announced that I would be giving the judgment of the Court. I could have talked about it all for hours.

But Hubert's spectre is hovering menacingly over the judicial mess. He hasn't spoken a single word while Marjorie and Legless are bombarding me with their questions. He's sitting at the opposite end of the table, apparently oblivious to the discussion, and absorbed in his copy of *The Times*, while toying with his hot and sour eggplant and mushrooms with rice, today's dish of the day. Only when Marjorie and Legless appear to run out of questions for a moment does he suddenly seem to become aware that conversation has been going on around him.

'So, Charlie,' he asks, 'how many dangerous criminals did you manage to put back on the streets during your week in the Court of Appeal?'

Marjorie and Legless pick up the atmosphere immediately. I'm not sure how much they know about the Bradley case and my judgment. Inevitably, there will have been some gossip among the court staff this morning, quite possibly started by Hubert himself; and so it's not at all unlikely that Legless heard all about it from his usher before going into court. Marjorie, of course, heard it from me, but knowing Marjorie, I wouldn't be surprised if she has also read my judgment over the weekend. If so, she's being typically discreet about it.

'The object of the exercise isn't to put criminals back on the street,' I reply.

'You could have fooled me.'

'The object of the exercise is to decide whether convictions are safe, and in some cases, the answer is "no." In some of those cases, unfortunately, criminals do end up back on the street, but we don't set out to do that.'

Hubert snorts. 'Note the "we,"' he says, apparently addressing Marjorie and Legless. 'You're one of the team up there at the Royal Courts of Justice now, are you, Charlie?'

'Not as far as I know,' I reply as calmly as I can. 'I have no idea whether they will invite me back or not.'

'Of course they will,' Hubert says. 'You're just the kind of chap they want.'

I must admit, I'm getting a bit irritated. Ever since I took over as RJ, I've done my best to shield Hubert from the consequences of his own folly. I have done my best to accommodate the Raj-era approach to sentencing, to ignore the more reactionary attitudes to defendants and counsel; and I've connived at his staying on the bench for as long as he can before retiring. I have deliberately refrained from inquiring into his true age, and I have discouraged the Grey Smoothies from inquiring into it. Partly, that's been in the interests of a quiet life – every RJ's secret, unattainable dream. But of course, there's more to it than that.

We all treasure Hubert as one of the last of the dying breed of genuine judicial eccentrics. They don't make them like Hubert any more – I doubt whether he would be appointed if he applied today; and in this age of awareness and continuing education, which is about approved attitudes as much as it's about judicial skills, I doubt we will see his like again. Many would say that's just as well, and I understand their point of view. Eccentrics can be very difficult on the bench, and judicial history is replete with stories of judges who took the affectation too far. But I have a feeling that we are losing the colour in our courts, that we're trading it in for a monotonous black and white, and that's something I, and other judges of my generation quietly regret, even if we can't say so openly. The last thing we want is to lose Hubert. But all things come to an end, and I'm rather miffed that he's taking it out on me.

'I understand you're upset about us quashing the conviction in the Bradley case, Hubert,' I say. 'But you left us with no alternative.'

'They were as guilty as sin,' Hubert insists.

'Perhaps they were. But the case against them depended on evidence of identification, and you didn't give the jury any real warning about how dangerous that kind of evidence can be.'

'The witnesses picked them out in the identification procedures.'

'It doesn't matter. You still have to give the warning. You don't need me to tell you that, Hubert. You've been doing this long enough.'

'The evidence was perfectly clear,' Hubert insists, 'to everybody except their Lordships of the Court of Appeal.' He stands, snatches up his copy of *The Times*, and leaves the mess abruptly.

There is a silence for some time.

'The summing-up was a bit off base, then, was it?' Legless asks, eventually.

I nod. 'It was worse than that. It was obvious that he'd never sorted out in his own mind which of the brothers was which, and who did what. He was totally confused, and I'm sure the jury were too. There was nothing we could do. We couldn't allow the conviction to stand.'

'Don't worry about it, Charlie,' Legless advises. 'Hubert's been around long enough to know you had no choice. He's a resilient fellow. He just needs a bit of time to get over it, that's all. A few drinks and a good dinner at the Garrick tonight should do the trick.'

'Would that it were that simple, Legless,' I reply.

* * *

Monday afternoon

'Professor Elgin, describe for the jury your area of study, please,' Aubrey says.

Professor Martin Elgin, an academic at Nottingham University, and the prosecution's expert witness, is short and wears thick black spectacles. He has chosen a brown three-piece suit and bright green tie for the occasion.

'I specialise in the physics of liquids, which means that I'm interested in everything about liquids, from their molecular composition to their behaviour in motion and reaction to stress.'

'Is your work important in an industrial context?'

'Very much so.'

'But are you also able to assist the court by describing the movement or behaviour of a liquid in cases such as this?'

'Yes, I am.'

'Professor, were you asked by the prosecution to read the case papers?'

'Yes.'

'And based on your reading of the papers, what did the prosecution ask you to evaluate?'

'I gathered from the papers that there might be a dispute about whether Mrs Remert poured the water over her husband's head in a deliberate manner, or whether the water was released involuntarily as a result of a cat pawing at the kettle while Mrs Remert was holding it.'

'How did you go about trying to answer that question?'

'By looking at the pattern of the burns on the husband's head and body. The burn pattern reflects the course taken by the water, and that in turn provides us with evidence about how the water was released from the kettle on to his head and body.'

'For that purpose, did you study the photographs of Mr Remert's injuries, which we have in the medical report?'

'Yes, I did.'

'And are you now in a position to share with us the conclusions you drew from your study of the photographs?'

'Yes.'

'If your Honour would bear with me,' Aubrey says, 'it may be helpful to have a larger image. I have a projector in court, and if the usher would assist by setting up the easel and the screen...?'

Dawn has done this before, and she has the screen assembled in a matter of moments. Dawn is small of stature, but she is a veritable bundle of energy, who positively bustles around the courtroom. She always wears something bright under her usher's robe, and is unfailingly cheerful. She is also the court's designated first aid officer, and renowned for her knowledge of home medicinal remedies – some, I suspect, rather more reliable than others. The only time Dawn looks in any way downcast is when we have a verdict of not guilty, which she takes almost as a personal affront. 'Oh, Judge,' she will lament in chambers, 'after all that work.' I've tried to explain that sometimes juries don't feel sure that a defendant is guilty, and so have to acquit, but it never seems to satisfy her. But she's wonderful in court, very efficient and always in control. Jurors and witnesses love her.

'Members of the jury, you have the photographs too, of course, if you would like to compare them with the larger images you will be seeing on the screen,' Aubrey says.

The jurors turn up their photographs slowly and with a noticeable lack of enthusiasm, as do I.

Aubrey points the projector at the screen and pushes a button. A reasonably clear image of the first photograph appears, adding to our discomfort.

'Taking photograph one as an example, professor, what do you notice?'

'The most obvious thing,' Professor Elgin replies, entering lecture mode, 'is that the burns to the head are in a straight line. When I say that, I don't mean a straight line as you would see it on a flat surface. The top of the head isn't a flat surface, of course. But the burns follow a straight path, allowing for the shape of the head, given the assumed angle of the impact of the water.'

'How do you work out the angle of impact?' Aubrey asks.

'We note the fact that Mr Remert was seated at his computer, and that his head would very likely be tilted forward slightly, to allow him to see the screen clearly. Mrs Remert was standing behind him, and behind the sofa, so perhaps one or two feet away. You can see that the edges of the burns aren't right at the back of the head. They start three inches in, or thereabouts. From that, applying a bit of basic trigonometry, we come up with an angle of about 30 degrees, give or take. It's an approximation, obviously – we don't have arithmetically precise evidence about it. If I may have the next slide, please…?'

The jury and I grin, as does Cathy. Aubrey obediently presses the button again.

'Is this the one? I think this is our photograph four,' he says.

'Yes. This shows several burns to the shoulders and back,' Professor Elgin points out. 'And once again, allowing for the slightly greater height and a steeper angle of impact, we see the same pattern of straight lines. There's some deviation at the edges because of some splashing caused by the greater angle of impact. But the basic pattern is clear enough.'

'Professor, based on your observations, your calculations, and your long experience of studying the movement of liquids, what conclusions, if any, do you draw about the question the prosecution put to you?'

'The presence of straight lines indicates that the impact occurred under controlled circumstances,' Professor Elgin replies. 'It is likely that Mrs Remert was in control of the kettle, held it still at the angle of impact, and that she retained control of the kettle throughout. I would further conclude, therefore, that she poured the contents of the kettle on to her husband's head deliberately.'

'What is your opinion about the suggestion that action by

the cat might have caused Mrs Remert to lose control over the kettle, so that the contents spilled accidentally?'

'I would regard that as extremely improbable. If that had happened, you would expect to see much more uneven lines, probably having no real pattern at all, and a high degree of splashing. It would appear chaotic. That is not consistent with the evidence provided by the photographs, or by the physics of the event, given the relative positions of Mr Remert and Mrs Remert, the likely angles of impact, and so on.'

'Thank you, professor,' Aubrey says, 'wait there, please. My learned friend may have some questions.'

'Professor,' Cathy begins, 'I want to make sure I understand this. The prosecution gave you two choices, and only two choices, didn't they? It was either a deliberate act, while Mrs Remert was in full control of the kettle, or an accident caused by the cat taking her control of the kettle away completely: isn't that right?'

'Yes.'

'You weren't asked to consider any alternative scenarios?'

'I'm not sure what alternatives they could have asked me to consider,' Professor Elgin replies.

The answer is given almost dismissively, as if the question had come from a wayward student. I can't resist a smile. It's not the wisest of attitudes for an expert witness to adopt. Even if he hasn't seen an alternative yet, Cathy is probably about to suggest one to him.

'You weren't there, of course, professor, were you? You didn't see how the incident occurred.'

'That's true. But I had access to the evidence.'

'And that allows you to say that there are two alternatives and two only?'

'As far as I can see, yes.'

'As far as you can see. Well, let me ask you this, professor.

Assume with me that Mrs Remert is standing behind Mr Remert, as you observed before, but that the cat jumps up and paws at her hand. Assume further that, as a result of that, water begins to pour from the kettle. Mrs Remert is holding the kettle firmly enough, but she can't prevent some water from leaving the kettle. With me, so far?'

'I'm following you.'

'So, water would have cascaded down on Mr Remert's head while she was in the process of regaining full control, but she would not have lost control entirely – she didn't drop the kettle. Would that not account just as well for the patterns you have described to the jury? May we have the first slide back, please…?'

Aubrey complies with something of a grimace.

'In my opinion, the straight lines are too well defined for that,' the professor replies.

'The lines depend partly on the angle of impact, don't they?'

'Yes. That's true.'

'And the angle of impact would be the same, wouldn't it, as long as Mrs Remert was holding the kettle? The fact that the cat might have caused the spillage of water, rather than Mrs Remert, wouldn't affect that, would it? There would be some irregularity, of course, some degree of splashing as she tried to regain control. But we see some of that in the photographs, don't we?'

The professor does not reply immediately. He is staring at the photograph. Cathy doesn't try to rush him.

'I doubt that a cat would have enough force in its paw to start the water flowing,' he replies in due course. It doesn't sound altogether convincing.

'Have you ever seen Ginger?' Cathy asks. 'That's the cat's name, by the way, Ginger. Have you ever seen him, or a photograph of him?'

'No,' the witness admits.

'Well, let's put that right, shall we?' Cathy says, with a mischievous grin.

She turns around to nod to her instructing solicitor, who stands, makes his way to the entrance to the courtroom and steps outside.

'If your Honour would allow me a moment…' Cathy says.

Mere seconds later, the solicitor returns with an animal carrying case, which, to judge by his demeanour, is rather heavy. He deposits it on the floor, and stands poised for further action. I notice that he is donning a pair of heavy-duty gloves.

'Perhaps you would like to see for yourself, professor,' Cathy says. The solicitor opens the carrying case, and there is some loud, discontented miaowing, followed by a flurry of flailing limbs, with impressive claws deployed.

Aubrey is on his feet. 'Oh, really, your Honour,' he protests, 'this is completely improper. My learned friend is engaging in theatrics.'

'I'm doing nothing of the kind,' Cathy insists. 'My learned friend's expert witness has given the jury his opinion about the ability of a cat to throw a kettle off balance with his paw, without having had the advantage of seeing the cat in question, even in photographic form. I'm just offering him the chance to see the cat now.'

'Is there any dispute about identity?' I ask.

'I have no reason to doubt that the cat my learned friend has produced is Ginger,' Aubrey concedes, rather stiffly. Glancing towards the dock, I see Marie Remert nodding.

'In that case,' I say, 'I agree with Miss Writtle. There's no reason why we shouldn't all see Ginger. But let's try not to let him loose to go on the rampage, shall we?'

'I'll do my best, your Honour,' the solicitor volunteers. He sounds less than confident that he will succeed.

As swiftly as he can, he carries the still-protesting Ginger to the jury box, and stands in front of it, so that the jurors can all get a good look. A woman in the front row makes an effort to stroke Ginger, which he doesn't seem to appreciate; she quickly withdraws her hand. He then moves on to the witness, where Professor Elgin examines him from a safe distance, but wisely makes no effort to touch.

The solicitor gestures an offer to bring Ginger up to the bench for my benefit. But I note that the limbs with the claws are still flailing, and I sense that his patience with being shown off to everybody is wearing thin.

'That's all right,' I say. 'I can see him perfectly well from here.' I can't resist it. 'Are you asking for Ginger to be made an exhibit?' I ask Cathy.

'No, your Honour,' she replies with a grin. 'I'd hate to inflict that on the court, or the jury. But he can always be brought back if he's needed.'

Mercifully, the solicitor succeeds in returning Ginger to the carrier without incident, and he leaves court.

'Now, professor,' Cathy continues, 'he's a good-size cat, isn't he?'

'He is,' the witness concedes.

'And obviously, quite energetic?'

'It would appear so.'

'And if Mrs Remert wasn't holding the kettle as tightly as she might have, a good swipe of the paw from a cat as big as Ginger could have the effect of forcing it forward, couldn't it, resulting in some spillage?'

'It's not likely,' he insists.

'Can you rule it out?'

Another hesitation. 'No. I can't rule it out completely. But I consider it to be highly unlikely.'

Cathy resumes her seat contentedly. She's as good as anyone at the Bar at that kind of smash-and-grab cross-examination, which is over almost before the witness knows it's begun, and generally results in the witness making one or two concessions. She'll take 'highly unlikely' all day long. She started with what seemed like a totally outlandish tale, and she's elevated it to a possible theory, one the prosecution's expert can't altogether exclude – and that's without even considering that Ginger has form for the same kind of offence. Aubrey asks a few questions in re-examination in an attempt to shore up his witness, but he's not getting anywhere, and he wisely abandons the effort before that becomes too obvious.

Aubrey is almost ready to close the prosecution's case. We deal with a few formalities, such as giving the jury a number of agreed facts in writing, after which he calls the officer in the case, DS Watson, to deal with Marie's arrest and her police interview. As Aubrey suggested when he opened the case, the interview is a bit odd. She begins by presenting DS Watson with a prepared statement, no doubt written by her solicitor, which advances the Ginger theory, but doesn't really explain why she was walking around the house holding a kettle full of boiling water. But then, when she is questioned by the officer, she mirrors Cathy's ambivalence in cross-examination – we hear very little about Ginger, but we are treated to a whole litany of complaints about her husband's controlling and domineering behaviour, the many restrictions he placed on her life, and above all his insistence that she abandon the career she loved in favour of working under him at the insurance company. She sounds very much like a woman ready to take revenge of some kind or other on this man who has destroyed her life. By the time Aubrey and DS Watson have read their way through the interview, it is almost four o'clock. There's no question of asking Cathy to open her case today. Once Aubrey has closed his case we adjourn for the day.

* * *

Monday evening

'I think you may be taking the wrong approach, Charlie,' the Reverend Mrs Walden says.

We have just adjourned to the sofa with a glass of the Lidl's Founder's Reserve Chianti we were drinking to accompany her excellent vegetarian lasagne. During dinner, I've been telling her all about my exchange with Hubert at lunch, my fear that the time for his retirement may be at hand, and my proposed strategy for gaining further evidence while hopefully keeping the whole affair in-house. She doesn't seem unduly impressed.

'How so?' I ask, very slightly miffed.

'Well, you keep talking about gathering more evidence, and then somehow telling Hubert that you think he may be losing the plot.'

'I have no choice, Clara,' I insist. 'He may get confused in other trials, and end up in the Court of Appeal again. It may only be a matter of time – and that's not something I can just ignore and allow to happen. Apart from anything else, he could cause a serious injustice one of these days. I'm the RJ. It's my duty to protect the court.'

'I understand that,' she replies. 'But you don't need to tell Hubert he's starting to lose the plot. If you do that, he's going to fight you tooth and nail, and his retirement really will turn into a major battle.'

'But…'

'Charlie, if it's true that Hubert is losing the plot, he knows already. He doesn't need you to tell him. What you should do is wait for *him* to tell *you*. That way, the retirement won't be the terrible fight you're expecting. It's something he will suggest himself.'

I consider this for some time.

'I can't see him ever admitting it,' I reply. 'You should have heard him at lunch today. According to Hubert, we got it all wrong, and put three dangerous criminals back on the street – he did nothing wrong at all.'

She touches my hand. 'Well, of course, Charlie. His pride has taken a huge knock, hasn't it? He's made a terrible mess of a case, and his own RJ has delivered the judgment in the Court of Appeal. And today, he has to sit there and have lunch with you and the others. His emotions must be very raw. He's bound to come across as rather angry and defensive. He'll get over it and start to face up to the truth eventually, but it's not going to happen overnight – it's going to take time.'

'I didn't say anything to him about his case today,' I protest. 'Marjorie and Legless were asking me about my week, and I was telling them about it. But I didn't even mention Hubert's case. Hubert didn't say a word until he suddenly made his outburst.'

'Charlie, you've been reversed a couple of times yourself,' she reminds me. 'You know how it feels. Whenever it happens to you, you go on and on for days about how the Court of Appeal are all idiots, and how they know nothing about criminal law.'

'I do not,' I object, though with no real conviction.

'Yes, you do. And you've only been reversed for some technical legal reason. No one's suggested that you're losing the plot. In Hubert's case, it's not just a matter of the Court of Appeal disagreeing with him about the law. You were saying that he may no longer be up to the job. Put yourself in his shoes. Try to imagine what he must be feeling.'

I walk back to the dining table to retrieve the bottle of Chianti, and pour us what remains of it.

'Do you remember when his wife died?' she asks.

'Yes. He came to see you once or twice, didn't he? You must

have given him good advice. He told me how helpful he found it.'

'He came to talk to me three times, just after the funeral. But I didn't give him any real advice, Charlie. That's my point. All I did was listen to him. He knew what he needed. Talking to me just let him say it out loud. Not straightaway, of course.' She smiles. 'We had to get past the usual bluster – Hubert being Hubert – but once we got that out of the way, he was very honest with me, and with himself. I think he can do the same over this. It may take some time, but he will get there.'

I nod. 'The only problem with that, Clara, is that I'm not sure how much time we have.'

'What do you mean?'

'All presiding judges keep their eye on what's going on in the Court of Appeal. They like to see who's being appealed, and why, and part of that is to give themselves advance warning of problems like Hubert's. Stephen Gulivant is bound to be thinking about following up. And the Grey Smoothies will be on the case before too long. That's partly Hubert's own fault. He's always irritated them by avoiding the question of his age. They suspect he's already past his sell-by date, and they may well be right. Part of that's my fault too. I've been shielding him from the Grey Smoothies.'

'Only because you all love him so much at Bermondsey.'

'But I can't shield him any more – and I shouldn't, not now, when he might do some real harm. It's probably out of our hands. They may force him to retire, whether he's ready to admit that it's time, or not.'

'Well, there's nothing you can do about that, Charlie,' she replies after some thought, 'and at least, if the High Court judges or the Grey Smoothies do it, he can't blame you. But I think he'll get there, one way or the other, if they don't put too much pressure on him. It's just a matter of his finding a dignified way out – and your job is to go along with that when the time comes.'

* * *

Tuesday morning
'It's a bit extreme, though, isn't it, sir?' Elsie says, finishing up my ham and cheese bap. 'I mean, all right, he asked for it, the way he treated her, but still… you know… to boil the kettle, wait for it to boil, and then…'

Inevitably, the case of Marie Remert has become an item of interest overnight, and has enjoyed extensive coverage in the *Standard*, and on the television news, and so it was equally inevitable that it should become a topic of debate at Jeanie and Elsie's coffee and sandwich bar. Jeanie and Elsie enjoy a good scandal or a juicy crime, and they're always ready to interrogate me about it, especially when, as is occasionally the case, it's going on in my courtroom.

'I'm not sure I could do something like that,' Elsie concludes, 'however pissed off I was with him.'

'I've been tempted,' Jeanie replies, attaching the lid to my latte and taking my money, 'and I don't mind who knows it.'

Elsie looks up. 'What, to pour boiling water all over your old man?'

'Yeah, and I might have done, too, if I'd been closer to the kettle. Last year, this was.'

'What did he do to make you want to do that?' Elsie asks.

'He comes in round about tea-time, doesn't he, and tells me he's lost our rent money on some horse that came in last at Chepstow or wherever,' Jeanie replies. 'Bold as brass. No apology, nothing. Just, "I've lost the rent money on a horse", like it was no big deal, just one of them things that happens.'

Elsie nods. 'Not even an apology?' she protests. 'I can see why that would rub you up the wrong way. Can't you, sir?'

'Oh, indeed,' I agree, taking possession of my latte and bap in the hope of making good my escape.

'And that wasn't all,' Jeanie adds. 'Having told me he'd lost the rent money, he then wants to borrow my housekeeping allowance, so he can do down the pub and have a couple of pints with his mates.'

'You are joking,' Elsie says, horrified.

'That's terrible,' I agree again.

'And, as I say, if I'd been anywhere near the kettle, and it had boiled, he might have ended up wearing the whole lot.' She paused. 'But it's like you say, Elsie, to put the kettle on to boil, and stand there watching it, and then carry it to wherever he was and pour it all over him, well, that is a bit pre... pre-something...what's that word you use in court, sir?'

'Premeditated?' I suggest.

'Yes, sir, premeditated, that's the one. I mean, you'd have to think about it for a long time, wouldn't you?'

'I reckon he must have done some very bad things to her,' Elsie says. 'Well, you'd know, sir, wouldn't you? You're hearing all about it. What do you think? Do you think she might get off?'

'It's too early to say,' I reply. 'The trial still has some way to go yet.'

'I hope she does,' Jeanie says. 'Serve him bloody well right.'

'My Auntie Grace found a way to get her own back on my Uncle Tommy,' I hear Elsie say, as I'm on my way out.

'Oh, yes?' Jeanie replies. 'What did she do, then?'

'Uncle Tommy was brewing some of his home-made beer, wasn't he?' Elsie explains. 'He had those, what do you call them, home brewing vats. He used to keep them down in the basement, all lined up against the wall. So, one day, my Auntie

Grace goes down to the basement, takes the lids off of the vats one by one, and doses them up with Ajax, doesn't she?'

If Elsie reveals what misdemeanour on Uncle Tommy's part merited such condign punishment, I'm too far away to hear. Next door, George is holding out my copy of *The Times*.

'It's coming to something, guv, innit?' he says. 'You're not safe anywhere these days, are you? I mean, I could be sitting there, in my own home, reading my paper with a nice glass of something after I get home from work, and the next thing I know, my old lady's confusing me with the teapot.'

'George, I'm sure you wouldn't do anything to make her even think about something like that,' I offer hopefully.

'Well, I don't keep my favourite biscuits locked away from her, do I? And I'm not going to send her out to work at her age. But you never know, guv, do you? What if she imagines I've done something to her? How long does it take for a kettle to boil?'

'I'm sure you have nothing to worry about,' I say as soothingly as I can.

'That's probably what her husband thought, guv, innit?' he replies.

Cathy announces that she will call Marie Remert to give evidence. She is wearing an almost drab-looking brown jumper and grey slacks, and hardly any trace of makeup. There is an air of sadness about her, and it seems to take something out of her physically just to make the short walk from the dock to the witness box. When she takes the oath, she is almost inaudible, and I have to ask her to speak up, which I do as kindly as I can.

'Mrs Remert, tell the court your full name,' Cathy begins.

'Marie Remert.'

'And, as the jury have heard, are you married to Bert

Remert, and until your arrest in connection with this matter, did you live with him at *his* house in Isleworth?'

'Yes.'

'I emphasise the word "his" because we've heard that it was in fact his house, as far as the legal title went, but also because I also want to ask you this. I don't want to drag it out too much, and the jury have already heard what you told the police when you were interviewed, but it's important for the jury to understand: can you tell the jury in general terms how your husband behaved towards you during your marriage?'

Marie nods. 'The word "his" sums it up, really. I had to be his. Everything I had was his. It was like, once the ink was dry on our marriage certificate, I ceased to exist except as his wife. Everything had to be the way he wanted it. I had to bring him his tea at the time he wanted, cook his meals at the time he wanted…'

'I'd like you to give the jury one or two other examples of that, Mrs Remert. Let's start with a very important one: your job. When you got married, what work were you doing?'

'I was employed by the London probation service as a probation officer.'

'What were your duties in that role?'

'When requested by the court, I would prepare a pre-sentence report. I would interview the defendant, talk to him and his family, try to identify any problems such as drug or alcohol use, look at his work record, any previous convictions, and generally try to make helpful recommendations to the court about sentence. I would usually be at court for the sentencing, in case the judge had any questions.'

'And if the court imposed a non-custodial sentence, would you have some role in that?'

'Frequently, yes. We would supervise the defendant to some extent, make sure he was complying with the terms of the sentence, advise the court if we saw any problems developing, and so on. If the defendant was given an order for drug or alcohol treatment, the court would often ask for continuing reports.' She looks up at me. 'I think what we did was useful to the courts. I hope so.'

'Very much so,' I reply.

'And how did you feel about your work as a probation officer?'

'I felt very good about it. I felt I was making a contribution, doing something useful, and once in a while we would actually see some positive results – not always, it's true, a lot of the time, you'd give them a chance, but they would just re-offend – but sometimes they would turn it around.'

'Could you give the jury an example of a positive result?'

'I remember one case, where the judge accepted my recommendation to give the defendant a suspended sentence. He'd been convicted of several non-residential burglaries, and he'd done it before. He was going the wrong way in his life. But there was something about him. I felt there was still time for him to turn the corner, so I asked the judge to give him one last chance. Fortunately, the judge went with my recommendation. One of the conditions of his sentence was unpaid work in the community, and they sent him out to do some gardening for elderly people. This was a lad from the inner city, who wouldn't have known a tulip from a rhubarb plant before that. But when he started doing it, he fell in love with gardening. When he completed his sentence, he started his own business as a gardener, and never looked back. I still hear from him from time to time.'

There are tears in her eyes, which she wipes away. I understand completely. There are many times as a judge when you feel it's all a complete waste of time – you give someone a chance, only to see them waste it and come back before you for something else a few months later. But once in a while, a sentence works. I remember one case, where I ordered a defendant who had committed a street robbery to fund his habit to undergo drug treatment, without much conviction that it would do any good. But he came through it, he did not re-offend, and he now mentors young men in similar situations. So I know how Marie Remert feels, and I sympathise with her.

'Did your husband know what you did for a living before you married?'

'Yes, of course.'

'Did he ever raise any objection then to your working as a probation officer?'

'No, never.'

'Did anything change after you were married?'

'Yes. When we'd been married two or three months, he suddenly started asking me whether I wouldn't prefer working at the insurance company where he worked. He told me that I could earn more money there.'

'How did you respond to that?'

'I told him that it wasn't about the money, that I did my job because I loved it, and I tried to explain to him why. But then, he started saying that he was worried about me mixing with criminals, as he put it. He kept saying, "What if they try to hurt us?" or "What if they find out where we live, and break into my house?" He kept inventing these scenarios. I told him, I'd been doing the job for years, and nothing like that had ever happened – my clients were usually grateful for what I tried to do for them, and they didn't blame me for what happened to them. But he wouldn't have it. He just went on and on about it, day after day, and in the end, I gave in.'

'How do you feel about that decision today?'

'I'm heartbroken. I don't know why I gave in so easily. I suppose I thought, I hadn't been married long, I just had to get used to it, and everything would be all right. But it wasn't. It was the biggest mistake of my life.'

'Did your relationship with your friends change after your marriage?'

'Yes. I'd always had lots of friends, and they were very important to me. I used to go out for a drink or dinner, or to see a film with them, you know, one or two nights a week. I introduced Bert to quite a few of my friends before we got married, and it seemed to be all right, he seemed to get on with them. But once we were married, it was like he became jealous of them.'

'What do you mean by that?'

'Well, he didn't really have any friends, and he seemed to resent it that I did. He wouldn't come out with me. He would stay at home and sulk, and if I went out, before I left, I had to tell him where I was going, who with, what time I'd be home, and I had to give him their phone numbers. He would often call them to check up on me during the evening, which didn't go down well, as you can imagine. Eventually, it all became too much of a hassle, and I gradually stopped going out – I didn't really go out or see anybody any more. I became very isolated.'

'How did all that make you feel?'

'I was very sad – actually, I was depressed, I'm sure. I still am.'

'Did you ever talk to your doctor, to seek medical treatment for depression?'

'No. That was another mistake. I should have, but I didn't.'

'The jury have already heard that your married life was very regimented. Can you expand on that?'

'Bert had to control everything. He had to have his own bedroom. As I say, I had to bring him his morning tea at a certain time. We had to have dinner at a certain time. It just went on and on.'

'Mrs Remert, why didn't you divorce him?' Cathy asks.

'I should have. If I hadn't been so depressed, if I'd still had friends to talk to, perhaps I could have put it in perspective, seen things as they really were, and I'm sure I would have done something. But – it's difficult to explain – when you're isolated, you start to feel that there's no way out, you have no energy, and eventually, you just give up.'

'Mrs Remert, what happened on the day your husband was scalded?'

She looks down for some time. Cathy doesn't rush her.

'We'd had lunch as usual,' she replies eventually, 'and for some reason I was feeling, I don't know quite how to put it, but… panicky, almost desperate. I'd tried to talk to him, but he kept fobbing me off, saying he was busy, he had some report to write. And it all welled up in me. I always made coffee for us after lunch, so I'd boiled the kettle. And before I knew it, I'd grabbed the kettle, and I was standing there, behind him, when he was working on his computer. I suddenly realised what I was doing, and I thought, well, this is silly, I'll ask him a question about his coffee, how much sugar he wanted – which was ridiculous because I knew that already, obviously – but I couldn't think of any other way out. You have to understand, I don't know what had come over me, but I wasn't thinking clearly.' She pauses. 'And then, it happened.'

'Tell the jury what you mean by that,' Cathy says encouragingly. 'Take your time.'

'I'm just standing there, right behind him, holding the kettle in my left hand, quite high up, when suddenly, out of nowhere, Ginger leaps up, and takes a swipe at it. He's a very strong cat – well, you saw him in court – and he almost knocked the kettle out of my hand. Somehow, I managed to hang on to it, not to drop it, but I was thrown off balance, and

I couldn't stop a lot of the water from pouring out, and it went all over Bert.'

'Mrs Remert, did you deliberately pour scalding water over your husband?'

'No. I did not.'

'Mrs Remert, had anything similar ever happened with Ginger before?'

'Yes. Two or three weeks before that, I was taking Bert his morning cup of tea, as usual, at seven o'clock…'

'This was in his bedroom?'

'Yes. I'd just lifted the cup from the tray I was carrying, and put it down on his bedside table, when Ginger did exactly the same thing – he leapt up without any warning and took a swipe at the cup. He knocked it over, and the tea spilled on the carpet and on to the bed. I don't think Bert got any on him, but it made quite a mess.'

'How did your husband react to that?'

'He told me to clean it up, and bring him more tea.'

Cathy glances in the direction of the jury.

'Thank you, Mrs Remert. Wait there, please.'

Of all the skills advocates need in court, cross-examination is the most difficult to acquire and hone. To do it at all well requires several years of experience, and although most barristers, and some solicitors, end up doing it well enough, there are only a very few who turn it into the art form it can be at its best. Aubrey is a decent enough cross-examiner, but until today, I would never have put him in the same league as Marshall Hall, FE Smith, or Norman Birkett. Today, however, he does something quite remarkable. One of the most difficult lessons to learn is the value of brevity. All good advocates know this in theory, but they also tend to like the sound of their own voices, and the main fault with most cross-examinations is that they start well, but then go on too long, allowing the effect of the good work done to dissipate. Aubrey is certainly no exception to this rule. But today…

'Mrs Remert, why were you standing behind your husband's chair holding a kettle full of scalding water in your hands?'

She seems to think for some time. 'Obviously, because I was going to pour it all over him,' she replies.

'Thank you,' Aubrey says, resuming his seat.

There is a very long silence in court. I have a sense that this cross-examination will live long in the annals of Bermondsey Crown Court. Like everyone else, Cathy is visibly taken aback and doesn't quite know how to react. In due course, her mind starts working again, and she realises that she needs to do something to try to rehabilitate her witness. Cathy's instincts, as ever, are good – and she opts to emulate Aubrey's brevity.

'Mrs Remert, you say that you were going to pour the water all over your husband, but did you change your mind at any stage?'

'Yes, as I said before, it occurred to me that it was just silly.'

'Did you actually pour water over your husband deliberately?'

'No,' Marie replies. 'Ginger swiped the kettle before I got the chance.'

'Thank you,' Cathy says. 'Nothing further.'

Next, Cathy calls Marie Remert's former supervisor at the London Probation Service, as a character witness. She does an admirable job, painting Marie as reliable, honest, caring with the clients, easy to work with, and generally the last person you would expect to be pouring scalding water over somebody's head. Gratuitously, she adds that Marie's marriage was, in her opinion, the ruin of her. This is, strictly speaking, outside the witness's remit, but in the circumstances, Aubrey isn't going to be churlish enough to object. Cathy couldn't have asked for more. But the chemistry – as the Reverend Mrs Walden would put it – of the trial has shifted, and everyone in court knows it. This happens sometimes, in much the same way as a brilliant try can turn a rugby match, or missing the black off its spot can turn a frame of snooker. It happens in an instant, and in the case of a trial, it's usually the result of cross-examination.

Somewhat dispiritedly, Cathy closes her case, and we are ready for closing speeches, followed by my summing-up. But not until this afternoon.

And so to lunch, an oasis of calm in a desert of chaos.

I don't go into lunch immediately, however. This is partly because I'm rather dreading another encounter with Hubert. Despite the Reverend Mrs Walden's sage advice, we still have to find some acceptable topic of lunchtime conversation until Hubert is ready to admit that it's time to retire, and I have no confidence that he's going to reach that point any time soon. But there's another reason too.

The change in the chemistry of the trial raises the spectre of the sentence I may have to pass on Marie Remert if Ginger doesn't come to her rescue. There is, of course, no real excuse for what she did, but it's impossible not to feel some sympathy for her. I unearth my copy of the sentencing guidelines, and remind myself of the applicable guideline. This was a premeditated offence, and one that caused very serious injury, some of which will be permanent. The guideline indicates a range of between ten and sixteen years, with a starting point of ten years. Judges have some leeway to depart from the guidelines, and taking into account the undeniable provocation she suffered during many years of marriage, and her excellent character, I can certainly come down to some extent. But if I come down too far, it's likely that the Attorney General will take my sentence to the Court of Appeal on the ground that it is unduly lenient. In the end, I'm probably going to have to impose a sentence I don't want to impose, and I'm not seeing a way out. I sit brooding over this for some time.

When I do finally go into lunch, mercifully, I am spared the worst of my fears. Legless shares a difficult point of law he has to decide in the case he's trying, and we all contribute to the debate about which way he should go. I'm pleased to note that Hubert joins in, apparently quite cheerfully, in between bites of his ham omelette and chips, the dish of the day, with his usual robust suggestions. He doesn't mention the Court of Appeal once.

* * *

Tuesday afternoon
Aubrey's closing speech is short and to the point. Well, in his position, why shouldn't it be? It's not often you get an admission of intent during cross-examination. All right, it's not a complete admission of guilt, but it takes the prosecution most of the way. Marie Remert may well have thought that what she was about to do was silly, but the fact is that scalding water ended up on Bert Remert's head, and unless Ginger is the real culprit, it's hard to see how the case can end well for her. There's no need for Aubrey to overdo it. Wisely, he reminds the jury of the evidence as quickly as he can, comments very fairly on the burden and standard of proof, and sits down, leaving the field to Cathy.

I don't envy her. She begins with a prolonged attack on Bert Remert's shortcomings as a husband, emphasising his depriving his wife of the career she loved. There's no harm in making sure that the jury have some sympathy for Marie, as I'm pretty sure they already do, but obviously, it can only go so far. However much he may have deserved some retribution, it's difficult to justify Marie's intention to take her revenge, and sadly, even her professional history goes against her – surely, a probation officer, of all people, should have known that pouring scalding water all over him couldn't be the right solution. So, inevitably, Cathy shifts seamlessly to Ginger. She now has the advantage that the jury have seen Ginger in the flesh, and I'm sure, like me, they are quite prepared to assume that he might be given to leaping up and swiping things. And, as Cathy is careful to remind them, he has previous for spilling tea by doing exactly that – as Bert Remert himself has conceded. Even so, it's a stretch, and a remarkable coincidence, that Ginger was prescient enough to leap up just in time to save Marie from the consequences of her own folly, leaving her a helpless spectator as scalding water cascaded accidentally down on to Bert's head. And that's before you consider Professor Elgin's evidence – over which, understandably enough, she skates rather quickly. Cathy does her best, of course, but I can't help wondering whether she is regretting not having asked for a psychological, or even a psychiatric report. I'm not sure it would help in this situation, but perhaps there may be some room for a variant on the 'battered wife syndrome'. I'm going to order a report if it comes to sentence, but, of course, it won't influence the outcome of the trial.

It's going to be too late for me to get the jury out this afternoon, but I can get through most of my summing-up before the close of play, and ensure that they can retire early tomorrow morning. I take them through the antiquated language of section 18 of the Offences against the Person Act 1861, and confirm that the definitions of the offence Aubrey gave them when he opened the case were correct. I reassure the jury that it's only natural for them to feel some sympathy for Marie Remert, but I also explain to them that it is not a defence to a charge of causing grievous bodily harm that you are taking revenge on someone, however richly that someone may have deserved it. There is an alternative verdict open to the jury. They could convict her of causing grievous bodily harm, but without the intent to cause really serious bodily harm, under section 20 of the Act. Unfortunately, in the light of her admission in cross-examination, although I can offer the jury this alternative, I can't do so with any real conviction. It's a shame. The difference in the maximum sentence is five years rather than life imprisonment, but the verdict doesn't seem realistic in this case.

I remind the jury briefly of the prosecution's evidence, but by then, it's after four o'clock, and I will conclude the summing-up tomorrow morning. I extend Mrs Remert's bail for what may be the last time, and we adjourn for the day.

* * *

Wednesday morning

This morning, Stella comes to see me before I sit. I've been expecting her. With a jury about to go out, she will have something new for me, and she has come to brief me about whatever it is, and give me the file. There are always a few cases on standby during the week, in case one of the judges finishes a trial and needs something to do. But unusually, today, she has brought Bob with her. Bob is our court manager, responsible for the fabric and the everyday practicalities of keeping the court running, everything from emergencies such as water leaks and broken toilets to longer term projects, such as redecoration. He played a very important role in one of our greatest triumphs, namely: persuading the Grey Smoothies to allow the court to keep the Bermondsey Cannon, a perfectly preserved eighteenth-century naval cannon, which was discovered during routine operations to deal with some flooding in the car park. The Grey Smoothies would have handed it over to some museum, probably one that already had a collection of naval cannons, but Bob and I found a way to keep it, to have it housed in a suitable casing, and exhibited in the court foyer, where it remains to this day.

'Jury out this morning?' Stella asks.

'Should have them out by eleven at the latest,' I confirm.

Stella pauses, pretending to read some note she's made for herself.

'I'm not giving you a new trial to start, Judge,' Stella says, 'because you've got that case of O'Finn starting next week. That's got to start on time. We can't have you running over.'

The name rings a distant bell.

'O'Finn? Isn't that the case Ipswich unloaded on us, claiming they can't have a fair trial there, or some such nonsense? There was a brawl in Suffolk somewhere, over some statue.'

'That's the one, Judge,' Stella replies. 'But it sounds more like a civil war than a brawl. I'm getting regular daily phone calls warning me what to expect. Apparently, there are two factions, one determined to remove the statue, the other equally determined that it should stay where it is, and both are planning on attending court to make their views clear.'

'How is it our job to decide what happens to some statue in Suffolk?' I ask, not unreasonably, in my opinion.

'It isn't, Judge,' Stella replies. 'But it seems the locals think that's what the case is about.'

'Have we alerted security?' I ask.

'Oh, yes, Judge,' Bob replies, 'and I've warned the police that we may be in for some demonstrations. We've dealt with this kind of thing before, obviously, but I don't want us to be caught with our pants down.'

'No, quite,' I say.

'Security are happy as long as they know the police are available with some back-up, if needed. But we will limit public access to your court, as usual, and keep the two sides apart, and see what happens. It may all come to nothing. It's a long way to come, from Suffolk, just to protest about a statue. I doubt it will last more than a day.'

'Better to be prepared, though,' Stella says.

'We will,' Bob says, with the air of a man used to managing such crises.

'Also, Judge,' Stella says, 'the High Sheriff of Suffolk wants to come and sit with you for a day, in view of the importance of the case to his county, he says. I told him you'll be too busy on Monday, getting the case started, so he's planning on being with us on Tuesday.'

'What?' I protest. 'Are you saying I have to have him up on the bench with me?'

'And we'll give him lunch in the judicial mess.' She sees my doubtful look. 'It is one of the High Sheriff's historic roles, Judge, acting as a protector of the courts.'

'But surely, they must have some courts in Suffolk he could protect. Why does he have to protect ours? Isn't he outside his jurisdiction?'

She nods. 'There is a protocol, Judge, that you don't appear outside your county in your official capacity without the permission of the local authorities. Apparently, the High Sheriff approached the Lord Mayor, who said he'd be welcome to pay us a visit.'

'How very kind of him,' I say.

'It may not be such a bad thing, Judge,' Bob suggests. 'It may just help to calm things down a bit to have a local presence.'

'Or it may make it worse,' I grumble.

Bob and Stella exchange glances.

'There is one other thing, too, Judge,' Bob says hesitantly. 'I don't think it's anything for you to worry about, but it will come up during the trial. I know you will read about it in the file, but we thought we should just flag it up.'

'Go on,' I reply.

'Well, the defendant's name is Deirdre O'Finn,' Stella explains. 'She's the headmistress of a local girls' school, and she was leading the charge to get rid of the statue. But she wasn't born Deirdre – she was born Desmond O'Finn.'

'I see,' I say.

'Her solicitors have already been in contact, demanding that she be treated as a woman for all purposes, including being allowed to use the women's facilities at court.'

'She's presumably on bail?'

'Yes, Judge.'

'Well, it shouldn't be a problem, should it?' I ask Bob. 'It can't be the first time we've had someone at court who's – what's the term – transitioned?'

'I'm sure that's true, Judge,' Bob replies. 'But if so, it's gone smoothly, without our knowledge and without any input from us. This time, we'll have to be seen to manage it. I'm sure it won't be a problem, logistically speaking.'

'But the pro-statue faction did try to use it against her once the civil war started,' Stella adds, 'and there's no guarantee they won't try to stir it up again at court.'

'Make sure security and the police know about it,' I direct, 'just in case.'

'Yes, Judge,' they reply in unison.

'Anyway,' Stella says handing me a file, 'this is all I've got for you for the rest of the day. Masterson – it's a plea to arson, being reckless as to whether life was endangered.'

I look up. 'Is this the man who burned his own house down?'

'Yes, Judge.'

'Is there a psychiatric report?'

'Yes, Judge. It says that there's no evidence of any psychiatric illness, or psychological abnormality.'

'Then obviously, whoever wrote it didn't dig deep enough,' I reply.

I didn't mean to sound totally cynical in my reply to Stella. In my experience, arson is a very strange offence, almost always committed by very strange people. At Bermondsey we tend to order a psychiatric or psychological report as a matter of routine when such cases arrive at court, and they always seem to be relevant. If you're burning down your own house, as it's alleged Chummy, Terence Masterson, did in this case, one would think that there has to be something going on behind the scenes. I'm sure counsel will explain it all to me. Aubrey has been asked to prosecute, since he's in my court anyway, and Chummy is represented by Emily Phipson, who will be well prepared, and will have a good feel for what is going on. If she's allowed to, that is. When my court clerk, Carol, comes in to chambers to tell me that court is ready, she whispers that Chummy wants to dispense with Emily's services and represent himself. That would be ill-advised on his part, but it's something he is entitled to do if he insists. I can't stop him.

As anticipated, the jury in the Marie Remert case retire just before eleven, with my final direction, to the effect that at this stage, their verdict must be a unanimous one, ringing in their ears. For some reason, watching them as Dawn takes her oath to keep them in some private and convenient place, and so on, I can't shake off a feeling that unanimity may be an issue. We shall see. I can't worry about that now. I have Terence Masterson to deal with.

When I take my seat on the bench, no one mentions Chummy wanting to represent himself.

*

'May it please the court,' Aubrey begins, 'I appear to prosecute in this case. My learned friend Miss Phipson appears for the defendant, Terence Masterson. Your Honour, Mr Masterson pleaded guilty, at the plea and case management hearing before Judge Dunblane, to one count of arson, being reckless as to whether life was endangered. Judge Dunblane granted him bail pending sentence, and ordered a pre-sentence report and a psychiatric report, which I think your Honour has?'

'I have read them,' I confirm.

'I'm obliged, your Honour. Briefly, Mr Masterson has lived for more than twenty years in a terraced house he owns in Methley Street, in Kennington, no great distance from the Oval cricket ground. It appears that he had finally paid off the mortgage on the property last year, so that he owns the property free and clear. But on the occasion in question, at about eleven o'clock in the morning, he drenched his living room with white spirit, an accelerant, and set fire to it. Your Honour will have seen, from the report of the prosecution's arson investigator, that the fire would have spread fairly quickly. Mr Masterson himself called the fire brigade almost immediately after the fire had started, and as they arrived on the scene quickly, he was rescued without suffering any injury. Fortunately, his call was also in time to prevent the fire from spreading to the other houses in the terrace. The house next to Mr Masterson's suffered some minor external damage to the walls and the roof, but the fire did not penetrate inside the building. Your Honour, that was just as well. The occupier, Mrs Rachel Candy, was inside the adjoining house at the time, with her two children, aged three and six months, and the report makes clear that they might well have been placed in serious danger, had the fire spread any further.

'Your Honour, the police were called to the scene, and once it was established that he had not been injured, the officers asked Mr Masterson what had happened. He immediately admitted to having started the blaze. He was arrested, and later interviewed at the police station under caution, in the presence of his solicitor. Your Honour has the interview in the file. Mr Masterson gave the police a full account of the matter, which, on any view, is quite remarkable. He told DS Stewart, the officer in the case, that when he purchased his house in Methley Street, more than twenty years earlier, it was a very pleasant residential neighbourhood. But over the years, Mr Masterson claimed, the area had gradually gone downhill, with criminal elements and yobs, as he put it, moving in and taking over the streets. He described for the officer drunken brawls and drug dealing going on in the street outside his house, and more recently, incidents involving knife crime. On several occasions, windows in his house were broken, and on one occasion, his front door was spray-painted with graffiti. Mr Masterson said that he had complained repeatedly to the police and to the council over the years, but it was his perception that nothing was done about it.'

'That's not a perception, mate,' Masterson protests from the dock. 'That's how it was. They never lifted a finger to help me. I might as well have been talking to myself.'

'Don't interrupt, please, Mr Masterson,' I say. 'You'll get your chance to give the court your point of view in due course.' I have no idea how right I am in saying that.

'Mr Masterson concluded,' Aubrey continues, 'by telling DS Stewart that he became at first depressed, and then desperate. On several occasions, he considered suicide. He reported these feelings to the council, but they simply advised him to consult his doctor, and took no further action. It seemed to Mr Masterson that he had no way of drawing the attention of anyone in authority to what was going on in the street around his house, and the situation was getting worse by the day. Eventually, in his desperation, the idea occurred to him that if he set his house on fire, someone would have to listen to him.'

Aubrey pauses. 'And in a sense, one supposes, he may have been right. Fortunately, having set the house alight using the accelerant, Mr Masterson realised almost at once that what he had done had been a mistake. He told DS Stewart that, once he realised that he was putting people in danger, including himself, he called the fire brigade. That action on his part did prevent the fire from spreading, but it was not enough to save Mr Masterson's house, which was not only gutted internally, with the loss of his furniture and possessions, but also suffered serious structural damage, the full extent of which is still being assessed. Clearly, there is no question of Mr Masterson living in the house again in the short term. He has been staying with friends while on bail. Mr Masterson did have an insurance policy, which covered him in the event of fire, but of course, in the circumstances, there is no question of any payment to him in respect of his loss – although I understand that the insurance company has agreed to pay for any necessary repairs to Mrs Candy's property.

'Dealing with the sentencing guideline, Your Honour, this is a case of recklessness rather than intention, and so falls within category B as to culpability. As to harm, it would seem to be a case of damage of significant value, and so falls within category 2, although, of course, the case does have the slightly odd feature that all the damage was suffered by the defendant himself – he is the only victim of the offence. Your Honour, making those assumptions, the guideline indicates a starting point of four years, with a range of two to six years. I will call the officer, DS Stewart.'

DS Stewart confirms that Terence Masterson is a man of previous good character, a locksmith by trade, with his own business. Intriguingly, under questioning by Emily, DS Stewart displays considerable sympathy for a man who has committed a very serious offence. He agrees that the area around Methley Street has deteriorated a good deal over the years, and tells me that Masterson has not exaggerated at all in describing it as a hotbed of crime, spiralling out of control. He also confirms that Masterson made many complaints to the police over the years about acts of violence, drug dealing, and vandalism, including damage to his own house; and that with one or two exceptions, although local drug dealers were arrested, his complaints produced little in terms of results. Many of the offences, he adds, especially those involving knife crime, are clearly linked to gang activity. While, of course, he doesn't in any way condone what the defendant did, DS Stewart assures me that he fully understands why he felt desperate enough to do it. In his own way, DS Stewart is asking me to take a lenient view, which is, to say the least, highly unusual coming from the officer in the case. Both he and Masterson have someone's attention now – mine.

'I'm in a rather difficult position,' Emily says, rising to her feet. 'I am, of course, prepared to address your Honour in mitigation, but just before your Honour came into court, Mr Masterson indicated that he wished to speak for himself. He is content for me to remain in court, and deal with any legal issues that may arise, but he feels that, at least for once in his life, he wants to be heard himself.'

I nod. 'Let me try,' I suggest.

'Thank you, your Honour,' Emily replies, resuming her seat.

I think for a moment. 'Officer,' I say, 'please bring Mr Masterson out of the dock. He can sit alongside Miss Phipson.'

The officer is looking doubtful, and is about to object that it's against procedure. It is, technically, but no harm is going to come of it.

'He's been on bail,' I add. 'He's not going anywhere. You can sit by his side, if you like. I need to hear what Mr Masterson has to say to me, and I can't hear him clearly while he's in the dock.'

Reluctantly, the officer complies, so now I have Emily, Masterson and the officer huddled together, looking rather like sardines, in counsel's row.

'Mr Masterson,' I say, 'stand up, please. Look, I understand why you want to speak to me yourself, and I'm going to allow you to do so.'

'Thank you, sir.'

'But in return, I have a request of you. You heard what Mr Brooks said to me about the kind of sentence I should have in mind, didn't you?'

'Yes, sir. It's no more than I've been expecting.'

'Well, nothing has been decided yet, Mr Masterson. That's why we're having this hearing. But if I'm going to pass the right sentence, I need your help.'

'Sir?'

'It would be very helpful to me to hear from Miss Phipson. She's a very experienced barrister, and she will have some legal points to draw to my attention that may suggest a more lenient sentence than the guideline suggests. You might not be able to make those points yourself, but Miss Phipson can make them for you very well. So, I will make a deal with you: if you will allow Miss Phipson to address me first, I will then listen to whatever you have to tell me, for as long as you wish. What do you say?'

Masterson considers for some time. 'Fair enough, sir,' he says, sitting back down.

So, I listen to Emily for some ten minutes, and then to Masterson for the best part of an hour. The two presentations couldn't be less alike. Emily is focused and precise, and comes straight to the point, which is that, remarkably for an offence of arson, the defendant has harmed no one but himself; and that his quick action in calling the fire brigade as soon as he realised his mistake prevented injury and further damage. She argues that this would justify me in departing downwards considerably from the tariff suggested by the guideline. Without asking specifically for a suspended sentence – which would be a rarity in any case like this – she points out the utter pointlessness of sending this man to prison, a sentence which would serve only to complete the ruin of his life he has begun himself. Instead, he needs to rebuild his life, Emily insists, and he can: he has his business to run, and the close friends he's been staying with while on bail have offered him a home for as long he needs it.

Masterson, on the other hand, is neither focused nor precise. He treats the court to a rambling account of the decline of the neighbourhood over many years, the goings-on in the street outside his front door, and his many fruitless attempts to get the council to take an interest in his plight. He says not a word in mitigation of the pending sentence. But he adds one poignant detail that Aubrey didn't mention in his opening, presumably because he didn't know about it. Among the many possessions he lost to the fire was £1,000 in cash, which he kept under his mattress for a rainy day. In his despair, he'd forgotten about it.

'Thank you, sir,' he says in conclusion. 'You can pass whatever sentence you like, now. I feel someone's listened to me at last.'

But I've made my mind up long before he ends his address to me. He's not going anywhere near prison today. I sentence him to imprisonment for twelve months, suspended for two years, during the whole of which period he is to remain under the supervision of the probation service, and accept whatever treatment, medical or psychological, they may recommend.

* * *

Wednesday afternoon

Lunch is almost normal today. Hubert seems to be in a good mood, and regales us with an account of his current trial, a Saturday evening sexual assault at the Blue Lagoon night club, a reliable purveyor of work to Bermondsey Crown Court, said to have been committed after both parties had been partaking of some illicit substances in the ladies. Having done the plea and case management hearing some time ago, I remember this case. It features a near-total absence of credible witnesses, and seems destined for a verdict of not guilty. But Hubert's description of the morning's proceedings is detailed and rational, and would suggest to anyone listening that he is completely on top of the case. That is encouraging, as far as it goes, but unfortunately, it doesn't go all that far.

Stella hasn't given me anything else in court this afternoon, which allows me some time to put on my RJ hat and deal with a stack of written applications. We get quite a few written applications for various things in the course of the average week, matters that don't require a formal court hearing, and it's up to me to sift through them and say yes or no. The applications are mainly for variation of the conditions of bail, due to alleged changes of circumstances. It's surprising how often a defendant's circumstances suddenly change once bail has been granted. Some defendants seem to think that the court wasn't being serious about the conditions, and will change them on demand if they are cramping their style too much. But conditions are imposed for a reason, and we don't allow changes lightly. Besides, if we didn't take a reasonably firm line, we would be inundated with applications to vary conditions in almost every case. We get enough as it is.

There is one slightly unusual application today. Four members of the darts team at a pub in Kennington have been nicked and are awaiting trial on a charge of supplying class A drugs. It's not a case of commercial supply in the usual sense. Their idea was to keep themselves and their mates supplied, and turn a small profit on the side. When I granted bail, I imposed a curfew, requiring the defendants to be at home at night by ten-thirty at the latest, and to remain at home until six o'clock the following morning. I'm now told that the curfew is interfering with their ability to represent their pub at the darts board, especially for away matches, and I am asked to vary the curfew to begin at eleven-thirty, which would allow this very talented team – the Chelsea of pub darts, as their solicitor describes them – to continue their relentless climb towards the top of the league. Initially, I'm not unduly impressed, but before I can decide, my phone rings, and I'm distracted.

'Charles, sorry to disturb,' a familiar voice says. 'Jeremy Bagnall here. Could we come to see you tomorrow, to mention a matter? How would lunchtime be?'

Sir Jeremy Bagnall is a high-ranking member of the Grey Smoothie High Command, and is said to have the ear of both his minister and the Lord Chief Justice. Jeremy was knighted some years ago now, for services to the Courts, a citation which defies satire. His use of 'we' indicates that he will be accompanied by our cluster manager, Meredith, who in accordance with strict Grey Smoothie practice, will take notes of every word spoken. Meredith's title indicates that she is responsible for more than one location of the Crown

Court – any quantity greater than one being referred to in Grey Smoothie-speak as a cluster.

'Of course, Jeremy,' I reply. 'I'll tell everyone to expect you. Can you tell me what it's about?'

'It is a bit sensitive,' he replies. 'I'd prefer not go into it over the phone.'

He doesn't have to. We have ongoing points of discussion with the Grey Smoothies on a variety of subjects, but there's nothing pending at present urgent enough to lead to lunch at twenty-four hours' notice, which in Grey Smoothie terms is tantamount to a minor crisis. No, if it's 'sensitive', there's only one thing this can be about. Jeremy has either been reading judgments of the Court of Appeal or having a chat with Stephen Gulivant.

When I turn back to the darts team, it suddenly occurs to me that, compared to the activities alleged in the indictment, playing darts with a view to winning the league constitutes quite a benign use of their time, and they can't really get into any trouble they wouldn't get into anyway in an additional hour or so. It probably can't be anything worse than an extra pint or two. I grant the application.

Just after three, Carol knocks on the door to tell me that we have a note from the jury. It is neatly folded, written in a clear hand, and signed by the foreman, whom I think I identify as a youngish man sitting in the front row of the jury box. The note reads as follows.

> Judge, we have a request. We would like to have the cat, Ginger, brought back to court, so that we can see him leap and swipe at something. Could this please be arranged?

I never deal with a note from the jury without consulting counsel first. It's important that we all understand what the question is, and in most cases, some brief discussion of the law is involved. Not so in this case – both the note and the answer it's going to get are quite clear – but since we're not in court, I ask Carol to invite Aubrey and Cathy into chambers and rustle up a quick cup of tea for us all before we send Dawn to fetch the jury.

I show counsel the note and we have a good laugh about it.

'I don't know what experience you have of cats, Judge,' Cathy says.

'We had one or two, years ago, when our daughters were growing up,' I reply, 'but I certainly can't claim to be an expert.'

'Aubrey and I have both been around them a fair bit,' she continues, 'and we agree that you can't make a cat perform tricks to order. It's not like having a dog. With a dog, you can teach it to recognise a command, and it will respond whenever you give the command – as long as you keep handing out the treats. But you can issue commands to a cat until you're blue in the face, and it will just lie there and stare at you. Ginger will only leap and swipe when he feels like it.'

'Which will probably be half an hour after the court has risen for the day,' Aubrey adds.

'That's what I remember from my cat days, too,' I agree. 'In addition to which, having seen Ginger when your instructing solicitor was taking his life in his hands just to hold him, I'm not going to unleash him in my courtroom. Lives might be lost – or he might just make a dash for freedom. I'm not sure we'd catch him if he did.'

I ask Carol to send Dawn to bring the jury to court. She leaves. Aubrey and Cathy stand to return to court too. But a fleeting image of Jeremy Bagnall wanders uninvited through my mind, and I call them back.

'Before you go, can I ask you both something?'

They both sit back down. One of the good things about a small Crown Court centre such as Bermondsey is that you tend to have a small Bar. You see the same members of the Bar in case after case, and the feeling of being in a close-knit community encourages a trust between them, and between Bench and Bar. In most courts, I could never have the conversation I'm about to have with Cathy and Aubrey.

'I'd be grateful if you would treat this as confidential,' I begin.

'Is it about Judge Drake?' Cathy asks.

I look at her in astonishment.

'We read your judgment in the Court of Appeal, Judge,' she explains. 'It made the rounds. All the Bermondsey regulars have seen it. We were wondering when you would ask.'

There is a silence for some time.

'I think we all feel that something's not quite right,' Aubrey says. 'In the cases I've had in front of Judge Drake recently, he seems to be easily confused.'

'Confused about what?' I ask.

'About which case he's dealing with, what the defendant's charged with, and sometimes about the law. I've had to correct him several times about directions he's given to the jury, which just weren't right – and they were all basic things, standard of proof, and so on. He's always accepted what I've said, and altered his direction, but still…'

'I've had the same experience as Aubrey,' Cathy adds. 'I wouldn't say it's a serious problem as yet. It's been easy enough to correct him, and he always thanks you when you do, and makes a bit of a joke of it with the jury, about how terrible it is getting old and so on. But you sense that he's not happy with himself – he knows there's something wrong – and the case you had in the Court of Appeal…'

'…was a serious matter,' I reply. 'Yes. I know.'

'Judge, you should really talk to Piers Drayford and Emily Phipson,' Cathy suggests. Aubrey is nodding. 'They had a case where a number of things happened that shouldn't have. It went badly wrong, and in the end, they had to ask Judge Drake to discharge the jury.'

'Thank you,' I said. 'I will.'

We return to court. I explain to the jury why we can't have Ginger the cat running unrestrained around the courtroom on the off-chance that he may be inclined to favour us with a demonstration of leaping and swiping. I tell them that they must concentrate on the evidence they have, and not speculate about evidence that hasn't been given, and probably couldn't be given. They don't seem too put out. They retire again. I return to chambers, but I'm finding it difficult to concentrate on the paperwork. I call Stella, to find out when we are expecting Piers Drayford and Emily Phipson at court, and she tells me that Piers is prosecuting Emily in two sentencing hearings in Marjorie's court on Friday morning. Just after four-thirty I bring the jury back again. They're not giving any indication of having reached, or being close to reaching a verdict, so I release them for the day, instructing them to stop deliberations until tomorrow, and reminding them not to discuss the case with anyone outside their number.

* * *

Thursday morning

This morning, Stella has given me what is politely termed 'the list', that is to say, everything the court has to deal with today that isn't a trial – any applications that must be argued in court, plea and case management hearings, and sentences following pleas of guilty. I'm not complaining – you're always liable to get 'the list' if you get your jury out before Friday, because it means that Stella can make sure the other judges can get on with their trials, without keeping their juries waiting while they deal with such matters. But it's not the most enthralling way to spend a morning in court.

At about eleven-thirty, I am allowed a brief respite. The jury have sent another note.

'Judge, if we can't have the cat, could we please have the kettle, and try filling it with water?'

I rise to allow Dawn time to bring the jury down to court, and ask Carol to show the note to Aubrey and Cathy. When I return to court, I confer with them before we bring the jury back in.

'Miss Writtle,' I point out, 'the kettle wasn't made an exhibit during the trial. I suppose one could argue that the jury shouldn't receive any further evidence once they've retired to consider their verdict.'

'One could, your Honour,' Cathy replies. 'But it's a very reasonable request, and I would argue that it's not so much new evidence as providing the jury with a way of testing the evidence they already have. I certainly don't object to their having the kettle. I assume my learned friend or the officer in the case can produce it?'

Cathy is wearing a contented grin. She has every right to feel pleased. Apparently, at least one member of this jury is treating Ginger as a serious suspect. Aubrey isn't going to be the one to object to the jury having their fun with the kettle. He turns to DS Watson, and they whisper briefly.

'Your Honour, we have the kettle,' he confirms. 'DS Watson will arrange for someone to bring it to court. We should have it here before lunch.'

The jury brighten up considerably on hearing this welcome news. They were looking a bit discouraged when Dawn brought them in. I ask them whether I can help them in any other way. This is a device on my part, designed to enable me to make some kind of assessment of what's going on with them, if I can. One of the things on my mind is the timing of the majority verdict direction.

The ideal outcome of any trial is a unanimous verdict. But you develop a feeling for these things, and I've always suspected that we might not get one in this case. The majority verdict direction informs the jury that, while it is desirable for them to be unanimous, the court may accept a majority verdict as long as not less than ten jurors agree to it. Technically, a judge can give that direction at any time after two hours and ten minutes have elapsed since the jury first retired to consider their verdict. The ten minutes was someone's idea of a reasonable allowance of time for the jury to make their way to and from court: the basic rule was intended to be that they should have deliberated for at least two hours before receiving the direction. In practice, no judge would ever give it after such a short time unless, perhaps, the jury send up a distress flare indicating that they are hopelessly deadlocked, and that there's no real chance of their reaching any kind of verdict. You can't discharge the jury until after you've given the direction, but you might decide that you don't want to keep them sitting around if it won't serve any useful purpose. But even in that case, I usually wouldn't let them off that lightly, after just two hours and ten minutes. Sometimes, playing the 'hopelessly deadlocked' card is no more than an attempt to get out of the work involved in reaching a verdict – which may explain why it is particularly prevalent on Fridays. Once in a while, a 'hopelessly deadlocked' jury succeed in returning a verdict if you give them some time.

In this case, I decide, I'm not going to give them the direction today. They haven't sent up a distress flare. On the contrary, they seem to be making some progress. They will have the kettle to play with this afternoon. We will see how it goes tomorrow.

And so to lunch, although today, I have no illusions that it will be anything like an oasis of calm.

'He's seventy,' Jeremy Bagnall says. 'It took Meredith and Jack a day of trawling through the records of more than one government department to establish it, but there's no doubt about it.'

'He turned seventy about a month ago,' Meredith adds, poised with pen in hand.

'So, he has to retire in about two years,' I suggest hopefully.

'In normal circumstances,' Jeremy replies, 'that would be the case. But in the light of your judgment in the Court of Appeal…'

I've been expecting this, of course. But when Jeremy actually articulates it, I'm not sure how to respond.

'I was concerned about that case, of course,' I admit eventually. 'But we all have our bad days. I think what led Hubert astray was his irritation at the brothers Bradley deliberately trying to confuse the jury about who was who and who did what. They did the same with the witnesses when the police were trying to identify them. We see a lot of this family at Bermondsey, and they're notorious for trying every trick in the book.'

'That may well be the case,' Jeremy replies. 'But that's why we have judges, isn't it, to keep the trial on track, and make sure everyone understands what the case is about?'

It's hard to argue with that.

'My concern, Charles,' Jeremy continues, 'is that the confusion you had to deal with in the Court of Appeal may not be an isolated case. What about the cases that don't reach the Court of Appeal?'

'I'm looking into that now,' I reply. 'I've asked the list officer to let me know of any problems that may have arisen, and I'm talking to counsel who have appeared in front of Hubert recently. I've spoken to two already, and I will be seeing two more tomorrow morning. If I come across anything that causes further concern, I will speak to Hubert and get his reaction to it.'

'Actually, Charles,' Jeremy says, 'we were thinking that you might prefer Stephen Gulivant to have a word. I know how awkward it is when it's someone you've worked with for a number of years and become friends with.'

I look up. This isn't like Jeremy at all. In my experience of Jeremy, issues as personal as someone's feelings don't usually feature in his calculations. I even catch Meredith eyeing him curiously between making her notes. It suddenly strikes me that I may have misjudged him. Is there somewhere a part of Jeremy that rather likes our cantankerous, reactionary throwback to the Raj-era judiciary? Perhaps he genuinely does want to make it easier for us all. In any case, he may be throwing me a lifeline. If Jeremy talked to Hubert himself, Hubert would dig in – we'd have to drag him kicking and screaming from his chair on his seventy-second birthday, by which time the Court of Appeal might have enough work to keep them busy for months. If I try to talk to him, it might not be much better, given our recent history. Jeremy may be right – a High Court judge with no personal history with Hubert may be just what's needed.

'I think that might not be a bad idea, Jeremy,' I agree.

'Mr Justice Gulivant was sitting with you in the Court of Appeal,' Meredith points out, 'so we thought it would be natural enough for him to speak to Judge Drake.'

'I agree,' I reply.

'Good,' Jeremy says. 'Well, it's settled, then. Once you've finished your inquiries in, shall we say, a week or so, why don't you send me a short report – strictly confidential, of course – and I will have a chat with Stephen and set up a meeting.'

'By all means,' I reply.

'And meanwhile, perhaps the list officer could steer – how should I put it – steer some of the less difficult cases in Hubert's direction?'

'She's already doing that,' I reply. It's true. I have already whispered in Stella's ear. 'But it's surprising how often simple cases turn out to be less simple that you expect.'

'Even so,' Jeremy says. 'Let's narrow the odds in our favour, to the extent we can. And Charles, I'm sure you understand: Hubert has to go within a reasonable time. He can retire with full honours, of course, but we can't let him loose for another two years.'

'Doesn't that rather depend on whether he is able to continue?' I ask. 'It's entirely possible that the case I had was an aberration.'

Jeremy shakes his head. 'We can't take the risk, Charles. Not when the confusion is so obvious. We'll wait and see what else you dig up, of course, but I don't want you to be under any illusions. Barring something quite remarkable, we will be thinking in terms of months rather than years.'

They gather up their things and make as if to leave, but at the door, Jeremy turns back.

'Oh, I meant to ask you, Charles: how did you like your week in the Court of Appeal?'

I smile. 'To tell you the truth, Jeremy, I was rather apprehensive beforehand, but once I got used to it, I must say I enjoyed it.'

He returns my smile. 'I'm glad to hear that. Stephen was

impressed. He tells me you did very well. He'd like to have you back.'

'I'd be very happy to do it again,' I say.

'Good. Well, we'll have to see what we can do about that.'

Towards four o'clock, there's another note from the jury.

'Judge, we have a question. If Ginger did leap and swipe the kettle while it was in Mrs Remert's hands, and she lost control of the kettle, would she be guilty anyway because she admitted she intended to pour the boiling water over Mr Remert?'

I explain to the jury that I am about to release them for the day, so I will confer with counsel now and answer their question tomorrow morning, when everybody's fresh. There's nothing very much to confer with Aubrey and Cathy about – the answer to the question is clear enough – but it's certainly going to be more productive to give them a direction first thing in the morning rather than at the end of a long day. Before leaving for home, I ask Dawn whether they have received the kettle.

'Oh yes, Judge,' she replies. 'They filled it up with water several times. I wasn't in there with them, of course, so I couldn't see what they were doing; but after the first time, I had to take them some big towels from the kitchen. Even with the towels, the floor in the jury room is still a bit damp, but I'm sure it will dry out overnight.'

'Please try your best not to let them flood the place,' I ask. 'I'm not sure how we'd explain that to the Grey Smoothies.'

''I'm sure it will be fine, Judge,' she replies. 'Whatever they were doing, they seemed to be enjoying themselves. I was sitting outside, and I could hear them laughing nineteen to the dozen. That young man in the red sweater in the back row was playing the part of the cat.'

'How on earth do you know that?' I ask.

'When I went in with the towels, he was soaking wet – his hair, his clothes, everything. He was trying to make do with one of these small towels from the loo, and the others were having a right old laugh. He was drenched to the skin, poor lad. I think he was all right once I gave them the big towels, and he could dry himself off properly.'

'He could have been playing Mr Remert,' I suggest.

'No. I asked,' Dawn replies. 'They told me he'd been cast as Ginger, because he's a good leaper and swiper.'

* * *

Thursday evening

As the Reverend Mrs Walden prepares our evening repast, her signature fettucini primavera, I pour both of us a glass of Sainsbury's Founder's Reserve Italian red table wine, and break the news that the plan of inducing Hubert to tell us when he's ready to retire may have been overtaken by events.

'The Grey Smoothies are in haste,' I explain. 'They're worried about Hubert making a mess of other cases, and they want him gone. They've given me a week to finish my inquiry, after which they want a report. Once they've got that, they're going to bring in Stephen Gulivant, to talk him into beating a dignified retreat. It's out of my hands.'

She pauses in her methodical destruction of the vegetables, puts down the knife, and sips her wine.

'That may not be a bad idea, Charlie,' she observes. 'It would take some of the pressure off you, and maybe off Hubert as well.'

'Well, yes. But what if he tells Stephen exactly where he

can stuff it? You know Hubert. He's determined to stick it out until the last day he's eligible to sit.'

She nods as she resumes her work with the knife. 'You can't protect him from himself, Charlie,' she points out. 'He has to see which way the wind is blowing, and his options may be limited – unless you can persuade them that there's no need to do anything right now. How is your inquiry going? Is it really that bad?'

'There are some worrying signs,' I reply, 'and I have a feeling that I'm going to find some more tomorrow.'

'You may have to talk to him after all, then,' she suggests. 'You can't let Stephen Gulivant descend on him with no warning at all. It wouldn't be fair.'

'But if I tip him off,' I reply, 'he may just batten down the hatches before Stephen can get to him.'

She walks into the living room and sifts through a pile of papers she's allowed to accumulate on the floor on her side of the sofa, until she finds what she wants, a thin, home-made brochure she produced on her computer.

'Give Hubert this,' she suggests. 'Better still, leave it on his desk, or get someone else to deliver it.'

I flick through it. 'This is about your growing older group, preparing for old age before you actually have to do it.'

'Yes. Hubert saw an earlier edition of this when we were talking after his wife died. He seemed to find it interesting. I wouldn't expect him to come to any of the meetings, but perhaps it will remind him that I'm still here.'

Over dinner, to lighten the mood, I recount the saga of Ginger the cat, and we share a good laugh at the thought of the jury trying to reconstruct his leaping and swiping in the jury room.

'So, that's really her defence?' she asks. '"It wasn't me, guv; it was the cat wot done it?"'

'Either that, or he had it coming. I'm not quite sure which one she's going with yet. What would you think if you were on the jury?'

'What, about the cat?'

'Yes.'

She thinks for some time. 'You know, I might just buy it,' she says with a smile.

'Really?'

'You said the jury saw the cat, and he looked strong enough to take a bit of a swipe at something.'

'Well, yes, but…'

'You remember the cats we had when the girls were young, don't you, Charlie? They were quite capable of jumping on you at the most inconvenient moments, like when you were holding a cup of hot coffee. Let's put it this way: I wouldn't dismiss it out of hand.'

* * *

Friday morning

'Let me deal with the note you sent yesterday afternoon, members of the jury,' I begin. 'First, I must make it clear that Mrs Remert isn't on trial for what she intended. It's not an offence to imagine doing something, or to intend to do something unlawful. It's only an offence if you carry out your intention. In other words, as I said when I summed the case up to you, the prosecution have to prove, so that you're sure, that Mrs Remert deliberately poured scalding water over her husband, intending to cause him some really serious bodily harm. If Ginger the cat leapt up and swiped the kettle, in such a way as to cause Mrs Remert to lose control of it, so that the water went all over Mr Remert without any deliberate action on her part, then she is not guilty of any offence, regardless of what she may have intended. On the other hand, if she remained in control of the kettle, despite Ginger leaping up and swiping it, to such an extent that she was able to pour some quantity of scalding water over her husband, even if some of the water went astray, then she would be guilty.

'And, members of the jury, while I'm on that subject, a note of caution: please bear in mind that you can't reconstruct what happened – you can't recreate the conditions in the Remerts' living room in your jury room. I know you have the kettle with you, but we simply don't know enough about the sequence of events. Any re-enactment you do is bound to be an approximation, and it would be easy for you to mislead yourselves by drawing the wrong conclusions. So, I'm not saying you shouldn't make use of the kettle to help you to evaluate the evidence, but you must focus on the evidence you've been given, rather than trying to speculate about what may have happened.'

To balance the books, I also remind them of Dr Elgin's evidence, and warn them that it would be wrong to substitute speculation based on their own experiments with the kettle for his expert opinion. Then, it's time for the direction that may make all the difference.

'Now, before you retire again, members of the jury, I'm going to give you a further legal direction. When I summed up, I told you that, unless and until I directed you otherwise, you had to return a unanimous verdict, in other words, a verdict on which all twelve of you are agreed. I now direct you that the time has come when the court may accept a majority verdict, provided that the majority is an acceptable one. The rule is that the verdict must be one on which at least ten of you are agreed, in other words, it must be by a majority of eleven to one, or ten to two. Nothing less than that will do. It's obviously desirable that verdicts should be unanimous, so

I'm going to direct you to do your best to reach a unanimous verdict. But, if you are unable to do so, the court will now accept a verdict on which at least ten of you are agreed.

'Please retire again to consider your verdict.'

I send the jury out at ten-thirty, and turn to the plea and case management hearings Stella has assigned to me. But something tells me that we're not going to have to wait for long now that I've given the majority direction; and sure enough, just before twelve, there's a note from the jury proclaiming that they have reached a verdict. Dawn is dispatched to bring them down to court, Marie Remert resumes her seat in the dock, Aubrey and Cathy take their places in counsel's row. To a man or woman – jury, counsel, and Marie Remert – everyone is giving the impression of being glad this depressing case is over, regardless of the result. I feel the same way, except I'm only too aware that it's not over – at least, not if she's convicted, which still seems to me to be the overwhelmingly likely result.

Once the jury are in place, Carol stands and invites Marie Remert, and the foreman of the jury, to stand. She turns to me, and assures me, and everyone in court, that more than two hours and ten minutes have elapsed since the jury first retired to consider their verdict.

She turns back towards the jury. 'Mr Foreman, please answer my first question either "yes" or "no." Has the jury reached a verdict on which at least ten of you are agreed?'

The foreman, none other than the young thespian cast in the starring role of Ginger the cat in the jury-room follies, looks briefly to either side, and behind him, as if to make sure that he's got it right.

'Yes, we have.'

'On the sole count of this indictment, charging the defendant, Marie Remert, with causing grievous bodily harm to Bert Remert, with intent to cause him grievous bodily harm, do you find the defendant guilty or not guilty?'

'Not guilty,' the actor replies.

For some moments, there is a stunned silence in court.

'You find the defendant, Marie Remert, not guilty?' Carol inquires, in a tone of voice that suggests she's wondering whether she heard him correctly. 'Is that the verdict of you all, or by a majority?'

'By a majority,' the foreman replies.

As the verdict is one of not guilty, we don't ask about what the split was; but, to judge from the demeanour of the two oldest male jurors, who are sitting with arms tightly folded across their chests and looking considerably displeased, I would hazard a guess that it was ten to two. Very sportingly, Aubrey is giving Cathy a smile, and surreptitious thumbs-up. When I order that she be discharged from the dock, Marie Remert registers nothing at all. I hear her thank the officer for opening the door, but her face is just as impassive as it has been throughout the trial. She's giving nothing away and there doesn't seem to be anyone in court to meet her. I rise and retire to chambers, to give her time to thank Cathy too – and those thanks will be richly deserved. I'm not sure how many barristers besides Cathy could have got the Ginger defence up and running.

Having returned the jury to their assembly room, Dawn brings me a quick cup of coffee.

'Oh, Judge,' she says sadly, 'I can't believe it, can you? After all that work…'

Carol knocks and puts her head around the door.

'Sorry to disturb, Judge, but Mr Drayford and Miss Phipson are here. You wanted to see them. They're in Judge Jenkins's court today, but she's just risen for lunch.'

'Oh, yes, thank you, Carol,' I reply. 'Show them in. Dawn,

could you rustle up another couple of coffees for us? It will take your mind off Remert.'

'Coning right up, Judge,' Dawn replies. Deep down, Dawn is a cheerful soul, who can never hold a grudge for very long. She's already brightening up.

Piers and Emily are looking wary. I'm sure they know exactly why I want to see them, and understandably, they're not looking forward to it. They're both Bermondsey regulars, and in a small court centre, it makes your life easier if you get along well with all the judges. But they're both responsible, and professional enough to know that that's not always possible. They know I can't guarantee to keep anything they tell me today confidential, or conceal where the information came from. I settle them into chairs. Dawn brings the coffee and leaves, closing the door behind her.

'Thank you for coming,' I say. 'I'm sure you know why I've asked to see you. I take it that, like everyone else, you've seen my judgment in the Court of Appeal?'

'Yes, Judge,' Piers said. 'Cathy Writtle tipped us off to expect to hear from you. She said you'd already spoken to Aubrey and her.' He looks at Emily. 'We would have asked to see you, anyway. We feel badly about it, but in the circumstances…'

'We have no choice, really,' Emily confirms.

I nod. 'Well, why don't you tell me what the circumstances are?'

Piers takes a deep breath. 'I was prosecuting Emily in a case called Williams, a GBH – your usual Saturday night at the George and Dragon thing, lose your temper, smash a beer glass and lash out, nasty injury, you know the kind of thing…'

'All too well,' I reply.

'Chummy's saying it wasn't him – he wasn't the one who swung the broken glass in the direction of the victim – wrongful identification, quick-moving incident, crowded bar, most of the witnesses three sheets to the wind, and he has a run at it. But Chummy has form for ABH about five years ago. It was in completely different circumstances. In that case, he ran self-defence, and as far as the officer in our case was concerned, it was a defence that had some merit.'

'He was defending his girlfriend against a couple of yobs who were trying to grope her at a football match,' Emily adds. 'But unfortunately for him, the jury didn't buy it. The injury wasn't serious, and the judge gave him a community order.'

'I didn't ask Judge Drake to let the previous ABH in,' Piers continues. 'The circumstances, and the defence, were completely different. Even if it was admissible, I didn't think it would be fair.'

'Quite right, Piers,' I say, 'well done.'

'Typical Piers,' Emily says, with a smile, 'not like some I could name.'

'Judge Drake didn't say anything when I told him that was what I was going to do,' Piers says, 'and I had the impression he agreed with me. But then…'

'Go on,' I say encouragingly.

Emily takes over. 'He seemed confused about whether my client was on trial for the GBH or the previous ABH,' she says. 'He mentioned the ABH a couple of times. The first time, it was just a passing reference, and I don't think it registered with the jury, so I didn't say anything. But then, it happened again, when Piers had the officer in the case in the box, and Judge Drake asked him some direct questions about it, you know, what football match was it, what exactly happened to the girlfriend, and so on. So, I had to ask him to send the jury out.'

'We both suggested that he should discharge the jury,' Piers says, 'but he didn't want to. Emily had made her point in case it came to an appeal, so we moved on. But then, when it came to the summing-up…'

Emily jumps in again. 'He started summing up as if he were trying the previous ABH. He defined ABH, and explained that Chummy wouldn't be guilty if he used reasonable force in defence of another. It was some time before he would even let Piers interrupt him. Eventually, he did: he sent the jury out, and this time, Piers persuaded him that he had no choice.'

'I said that if he didn't discharge the jury, I would offer no evidence and put a stop to the case that way,' Piers says.

'He got confused between the offence Chummy was charged with and the previous conviction?' I ask, with some astonishment. 'He was summing up the previous conviction to the jury?'

'Yes, Judge,' Piers replies.

'When they weren't even supposed to be hearing about the previous?'

'Yes. In fairness, at this point, Judge Drake did seem to realise that something had gone wrong, and he did agree to discharge the jury.'

I shake my head sadly for some time.

'Did you tell anyone what had happened?'

'No, Judge,' Emily replies. 'We decided to tell you, once you got back from the Court of Appeal. I'm sorry for the delay – it's been a hectic week.' She pauses. 'But unfortunately, you can't keep something like this quiet. The court staff chat among themselves, and I'm sure it spread like wildfire. Everyone has probably heard some version of the story.'

Yes, I think: and that includes Hubert, Marjorie and Legless, none of whom has said a word to me. After they've gone, I glance at my watch. It's a bit late to go into lunch now, and in any case, I think I prefer to eat Jeanie's ham and cheese bap on my own in chambers. Somehow, once again, I don't think lunch in the mess would be much of an oasis today.

PART THREE

SOME MUTE INGLORIOUS MILTON

SOME MUTE INGLORIOUS MILTON

Monday morning

I've known Roderick Lofthouse for a long time. I suspect we must be the same kind of age – certainly, we started out at the Bar at more or less the same time. He's been a Bermondsey regular for many years, since long before I arrived, and is generally acknowledged as the doyen of the Bermondsey Bar, an accolade he exploits by wearing a rather-too-light single-breasted jacket, which is a bit too small for him, and is held in place precariously by a single button at the waist. He knows, of course, that none of the judges is going to take issue with him about it. It's one of the privileges of being the doyen, and he is highly regarded for more important reasons. Apart from anything else, Roderick is scrupulously fair, particularly when prosecuting, which all judges appreciate. Sadly, from what I hear from my fellow RJs at other courts, such old-school values are not universally shared by prosecutors today. And although his attention to detail is not what it was, he has an instinctive feel for the strengths and weaknesses of a case, which makes him a formidable opponent. His invariably polite and self-deprecating manner sometimes lures opponents who don't know him into a false sense of security, which they tend to realise only when it's too late.

But one thing I've never really associated with Roderick before is a poetic streak. Like most advocates, he's quite capable of reeling off the odd burst of Shakespeare when the case seems to warrant it, but it's rare for any advocate to venture much further than that into the literary jungle. Today, however, as he rises to make his opening speech to the jury in the case of Deirdre O'Finn, Roderick seems to be under the influence of an altogether different muse. I don't feel in the least poetic about this case. As I may have mentioned before, I'm not exactly ecstatic about having this case at Bermondsey to begin with. We've been threatened with an invasion by hordes of angry villagers from darkest Suffolk, not to mention an inspection by the High Sheriff of that county, trespassing far outside his jurisdiction. The case's natural home is Ipswich, and I can't see any good reason why it isn't being tried in Ipswich. Too much local feeling, they say, impossible to hold a fair trial. It all seems a bit unlikely, but our presiding judge, Stephen Gulivant, has bought the story, so we don't have any real choice in the matter.

At least we have Roderick. If anyone can impose order on a trial that could get out of hand, it's Roderick. I'm less sanguine about defence counsel. I have every reason to be grateful to Kenneth Warnock. When the Bermondsey cannon, a perfectly preserved eighteenth-century naval cannon, was unearthed during an excavation at the court, I immediately saw the possibility of keeping it and proudly putting it on display in the foyer. The Grey Smoothies had other ideas, which involved making some money out of it as 'treasure trove' and which they shamelessly advanced by trying to sell us a version of the law some twenty years out of date. I had Kenneth in front of me at the time, and it happens that he is well informed about the law of treasure. He quickly demolished the Grey Smoothies' arguments, as a result of which, the cannon stayed, and graces the foyer to this day.

Kenneth is not the easiest of advocates to deal with. He is given to putting forward outlandish legal theories that probably wouldn't even occur to most lawyers, as evidenced in the infamous Foggin Island case, in which he advanced the defence of sovereign immunity on behalf of a defendant charged with fraud, who claimed to be the king of a lump of rock in the English Channel. As he was a king, Kenneth argued, the English courts had no jurisdiction over him. Yet, even that bizarre suggestion worked out well for the court. It turned out that the lump of rock in question had been ceded to France by England as part of the Treaty of Calais in 1360, a fact which both countries had somehow overlooked ever since then – and which, of course, instantly demolished the defendant's claim of sovereign immunity. But the French government were so grateful for my pointing this out that they declared Bermondsey Crown Court to be a historic beacon of international law, which was enough to prevent the Grey Smoothies from closing the court down, which they had planned and fully intended to do, to allow them to sell the land on which the court stands at a profit. So, I am genuinely grateful to Kenneth on two counts – but I'm also slightly nervous to see what he's going to come up with in this case.

'Members of the jury,' Roderick begins, after introducing himself and Kenneth, 'the events you are going to hear about in this case took place a long way away from this court, and indeed, from London. They took place in the bucolic surroundings of Little Brewing, a village in a rather remote corner of Suffolk. Little Brewing, members of the jury, is exactly the kind of place that might have inspired the poet Thomas Gray when he wrote his famous *Elegy Written in a Country Churchyard*, and it's appropriate that, in the context of the case you're about to try, I should mention it. No doubt you're all familiar with the *Elegy* – indeed, like me, you were probably made to learn it by heart and recite it when you were in school.

> *The curfew tolls the knell of parting day,*
> *The lowing herd wind slowly o'er the lea,*
> *The ploughman homeward plods his weary way,*
> *And leaves the world to darkness and to me.*

The jury, a typical Bermondsey mix of ages and ethnic backgrounds, are looking at Roderick in such a way as to suggest that the experience of having to learn and recite Gray's *Elegy* isn't springing instantly back to mind. But, if Roderick notices this, as I'm sure he does, he's not going to allow it to deter him.

'In the quiet setting of that country churchyard, members of the jury, Gray found himself imagining the people who had lived in the village in days gone by – and he was writing in 1750 – what their lives must have been like, but also what their lives might have been like. There must have been those who had great talents and who, in another place and time, would have been able to share those talents and be recognised for them. In particular, Gray mentioned –

> *Some village-Hampden, that with dauntless breast*
> *The little tyrant of his fields withstood;*
> *Some mute inglorious Milton here may rest,*
> *Some Cromwell guiltless of his country's blood.*

'Members of the jury, three of those four characters feature in the case you're about to hear. Little Brewing's "little tyrant of his fields" is the woman sitting in the dock, Deirdre O'Finn. The man she tried to reduce to the state of being "mute inglorious" was a local poet by the name of John Bonhomme,

who lived in the eighteenth century, during the very period
when Gray was writing the *Elegy*. Little Brewing's "village-
Hampden, that with dauntless breast withstood" Deirdre
O'Finn is a man called Monty Beveridge, a member of the
Little Brewing Village Council, whom I shall be calling as a
witness before you.

'Members of the jury, at the centre of this case is a statue
of the poet John Bonhomme which stands on a plinth in the
village square, and has occupied that prominent position in
the life of the village since the year 1802, when the citizens
of Little Brewing raised a public subscription to pay for a
monument to their most famous forebear. But you will hear
that, earlier this year, a controversy erupted around it. As you
may know, members of the jury, there has been a tendency
in recent times for some people to demand the removal of
monuments to those they disapprove of, and that is what
happened in this case. Sadly, the question could not be
resolved amicably. Eventually, it led to serious public disorder
and violence, in the course of which at least one person was
injured, and of which this defendant Deirdre O'Finn was the
ringleader.

'You will hear that Miss O'Finn was the leader and
orchestrator of the campaign to remove the Bonhomme
statue. Miss O'Finn is the headmistress of a residential school
for girls situated not far from the village, and she encouraged
some of her more senior pupils to do some research into the
life of John Bonhomme. They discovered that Mr Bonhomme
was born in France in 1721, but settled in England in 1762,
marrying a local woman and making his home in Little
Brewing, where he lived until his death in 1783. But between
1745 and 1762, he had spent a number of years living in the
British West Indies, on the islands of St Kitts and Bermuda,
and Miss O'Finn's students found evidence that, during that

time, he had been involved in the slave trade. They also found some of his writings, in which he argued that women and girls should not receive an education, because it would serve only to distract them from their domestic duties towards their husbands and families. Miss O'Finn found all of these things distasteful – as did many of her pupils – and she began a campaign, in the columns of the local newspaper, the *Star*, to have Bonhomme's statue taken down and destroyed.

'Members of the jury, whatever view you may take of that, you must bear in mind that Miss O'Finn was perfectly entitled to argue for the removal of the statue, and she continued to do so quite properly for some time. One step she took was to invite the village council, which is responsible for such local issues, to debate and vote on the matter. But it won't surprise you, I'm sure, to learn that while a number of people agreed with Miss O'Finn, there was also considerable resistance to what she was suggesting. The opposition was led by Councillor Monty Beveridge, and it had considerable support within the village. The villagers are, in general, very proud of their association with Bonhomme, and of the statue, and they were not prepared to allow it to be taken down, based on what many saw as an exercise in political correctness, the pointless delving into events that had occurred thousands of miles away in the mid-eighteenth century.

'Members of the jury, on the evening of 3 March, the village council duly debated Miss O'Finn's request in the course of a session attended by a large number of members of the public. Miss O'Finn and Councillor Beveridge both spoke at some length, as did the vicar of Little Brewing, the Reverend Mr Phineas Pratt, a supporter of the statue, who will also give evidence to you. Not surprisingly, the meeting was tense at times, with a good deal of shouting and name-calling going on. But at the end of the session, when a vote was finally taken, the proposal to take down the statue was defeated by a substantial majority. Members of the jury, up to that point, you may think, the question was dealt with in an entirely appropriate and democratic way. But after the vote, that quickly changed.

'Miss O'Finn, you will hear, was determined to rid the village of the statue regardless of the outcome of the vote. She let it be known that, if the council would not take it down, she would. This, of course, was a departure from the lawful and appropriate way of doing things, and it caused a good deal of local concern. You will hear that Councillor Beveridge formed what became known as the John Bonhomme Defence League, which met in the Cat and Fiddle public house and enjoyed wide support, and which soon began a round-the-clock vigil in the square, in an effort to ensure that Miss O'Finn and her supporters had no opportunity to interfere with the statue. But on the evening of 15 March, the Ides of March – a rather appropriate coincidence, you may think – the inevitable happened.

'In the early evening, Deirdre O'Finn, with some supporters and a few of her pupils, numbering about twenty people in all, approached the square, some carrying hammers, and some carrying lacrosse sticks taken from Miss O'Finn's school. At that time, Councillor Beveridge was present, keeping the vigil, with five other members of the Bonhomme Defence League. You will hear that Miss O'Finn demanded that Councillor Beveridge and his colleagues should withdraw, and allow them to take the statue down without resistance. Councillor Beveridge refused to comply with that demand, and started to make calls on his mobile phone. Within a minute or two, members of the jury, four other members of the Defence League, who had been drinking in the Cat and Fiddle, joined Councillor Beveridge, bringing with them an assortment of brooms, bar stools, sticks and other items taken from the pub. The stage was set for things to get seriously out of hand, members of the jury, and get out of hand they did.

'You will hear from PC Barnett, the only police officer based in Little Brewing, who was present, in uniform, throughout the ensuing brawl. PC Barnett will tell you that he saw Miss O'Finn start the brawl by leading her followers in a charge towards the statue, while screaming at the top of her voice, encouraging those with her to tear it down. Councillor Beveridge and the other members of the Defence League took action to defend themselves, and the statue, against the onslaught. PC Barnett will tell you that he made a vain effort to stop the fighting, but he was unable to do so on his own, because he was hopelessly outnumbered, and those involved simply ignored him. He put out a call for back-up from two neighbouring police stations, which arrived in due course in the form of six additional uniformed officers, but they were too late to prevent the injury and considerable damage that was done. Pending their arrival, PC Barnett stood in plain view near the statue, and made sure he observed what was going on. As a result of that, members of the jury, he was able to see what Miss O'Finn did throughout the brawl.

'You will hear, in particular, that as a result of one blow struck by Miss O'Finn with her lacrosse stick, Councillor Beveridge sustained cuts to his forehead and the top of his head, which required a total of ten stitches. Miss O'Finn also did considerable damage to Mr Bonhomme's left arm with the aid of a hammer. Now, of course, members of the jury, many other blows were struck, both to persons present and to the statue. All the members of the Defence League suffered some cuts and bruises, as did a number of Miss O'Finn's supporters. As far as the statue is concerned, Mr Bonhomme, I'm afraid to say, sustained very serious injuries, mainly to his head and arms, although he remained in position on his plinth. We have before and after photographs, which show the extent of the damage, and with the usher's assistance… My learned friend has been good enough to indicate that there is no objection, your Honour. May they be Exhibits 1 and 2?'

'No objection, your Honour,' Kenneth confirms.

Dawn, today resplendent in a bright pink dress under her black usher's gown, collects the photographs from Roderick, and provides the jury and myself with copies. I see the jury wince slightly. Mr Bonhomme has not come out of it well. Most of both his arms are gone, and his head is severely dented in several places, with the loss of part of his nose. He may still be in possession of his berth on the plinth, but it's going to take some work to restore him to his former glory.

'Members of the jury,' Roderick continues, 'only when the additional officers arrived was order fully restored. By then, many of those who had taken part had left the scene, and it was not possible to identify everyone who had committed an offence. In the end, on the advice of the Crown Prosecution Service, the police decided to deal with the vast majority of those involved – a total of more than thirty people – by way of caution, and to prosecute only Miss O'Finn. They made that decision for the simple reason that she was the instigator of the violence. Without Deirdre O'Finn, the prosecution say, the evening would have passed peacefully, without the multiple assaults and acts of criminal damage which occurred at her instigation.'

I must say, I thought the way Roderick put this was fairly innocuous, but the reaction in the dock and the O'Finn section of the public gallery is very different. We've had a security officer stationed in court, and I have been keeping a wary eye on the public gallery all morning, and so far, it's all been quiet. That's about to change.

'You're only doing this because she's trans,' a female voice from the O'Finn section shouts. 'You wouldn't be persecuting her if she was cis. The police are institutionally transphobic!'

'No platform for slave traders!' a male voice adds, to general approval from his section.

'I'm the victim here!' Deirdre O'Finn shouts from the dock. 'I've been singled out because I stood up against slavery.'

Needless to say, the Defence League section of the gallery is not going to let this pass without some response.

'You're not a victim, you're a fucking pervert!' one woman shouts, pointing a finger towards the dock. She is wearing a t-shirt bearing the legend, *Woman, noun: adult female human being*. 'You shouldn't be allowed anywhere near a girls' school!'

There is then a chorus of '*John Bonhomme stays, John Bonhomme stays, Ee Aye Addio, John Bonhomme stays*' accompanied by some suggestions directed to Miss O'Finn that she might prefer to return to her native Ireland. By now, Dawn has quietly taken the jury to their room, the security officer has positioned himself between the two feuding sections, and we have the two uniformed police officers we've had waiting in the wings, summoned by Carol using her panic button. The noise gradually subsides. I wait for it to die down completely.

'I don't know what goes on in courts in Suffolk,' I say, 'but here in Bermondsey we like our trials to take place in calm conditions, so that justice can be properly done. We don't tolerate interruptions to the proceedings, especially in the form of this kind of outburst, directed to counsel, the bench, or others in court. I want it clearly understood that if there is any further occurrence of this kind, I will close the public gallery, and have you all removed from court. You are also liable to be charged with contempt of court, which means that you may be fined or imprisoned, and leave here with a criminal record.' I turn to the dock. 'As for you, Miss O'Finn, if you interrupt again, I will have you taken down to the cells, and I will revoke your bail.'

I look at each offending section of the courtroom in turn. 'Have I made myself clear?'

There are some reluctant nods. I decide it's not enough – I need to do a little more to ensure that I'm being taken seriously. I can't have the jury being exposed to this kind of behaviour throughout the trial. I can identify the woman who started it all off, and the woman from the Defence League section who responded by calling Deirdre O'Finn a pervert. I decide to make an example of them. It's not entirely fair – they weren't by any means the only ones involved – but I want to stamp this out now, before it goes any further, and I need to make a gesture, *pour encourager les autres*. These two will just have to take one for the team. I order them both to leave court, and not come back. They comply without protest when Dawn ushers them out of court.

'Mr Lofthouse,' I say. 'Let's take a short break. I will rise for fifteen minutes, when hopefully, we shall be able to continue with your opening without further interruption.'

'Much obliged, your Honour,' Roderick says.

I sense that he could do with a cup of coffee, as could I; and the jury will undoubtedly need a few minutes to relax under Dawn's watchful eye.

'Let's make sure the jury know they have some time,' I say to Carol.

When the time comes to resume, I am pleased to see that a few of our Suffolk visitors, from both sides of the divide, have left court, presumably as an act of solidarity with those I excluded. Good, I think, let's hope the rest follow suit. They aren't showing any signs of doing so at the moment, but on the positive side, they are looking a bit more subdued. When Dawn brings the jury back, I am relieved to see that they don't seem any the worse for the experience. In fact, one or two of them are glancing in the direction of the dock and the public gallery in such a way as to suggest that they find the whole thing amusing. But, just in case, I explain to them that I have expelled two of those responsible for the uproar, and that anyone who behaves like that in future will also be expelled, and may be held in contempt. As I say this, I realise I'm offering a hostage to fortune. It will be a miracle if we get through this case without further interruptions, including some from the dock, and I can't expel Deirdre O'Finn. But I do have other remedies, and we will just have to cross that bridge when we come to it. At least for now, no members of the jury are asking for police protection, and it seems that we can carry on with the case.

'Members of the jury,' Roderick continues, 'if you would look with me, please, at your copies of the indictment, you will see that Miss O'Finn faces three charges. His Honour will explain the law to you in detail when he sums the case up, so for now, I just want to explain in outline what the charges relate to. In count 1, Miss O'Finn is charged with affray. An affray, members of the jury, occurs when someone threatens or uses unlawful violence towards others, and behaves in such a way as to cause a person of reasonable firmness to fear for his or her personal safety. We say that, once you have heard the evidence, you will be left in no doubt that Miss O'Finn behaved in exactly that way. In count 2, she is charged with assault occasioning actual bodily harm in relation to her attack on Councillor Beveridge with the lacrosse stick. And finally, in count 3, she is charged with criminal damage in relation to the damage she did to the statue of John Bonhomme, using the lacrosse stick and a hammer.

'Members of the jury, the prosecution bring this case, and if you are to convict, the prosecution must prove the case so that you are sure of the defendant's guilt. Nothing less than that will suffice, and you must consider each of the three counts separately. The defendant doesn't have to prove her innocence. In fact, she doesn't have to prove anything to you at all. But we say that the evidence in this case is clear, and that, when all is said and done, you will have no doubt whatsoever that Deirdre O'Finn is guilty on each of these three counts.

'With your Honour's leave, the prosecution calls Phineas Pratt.'

As the Reverend Phineas Pratt enters court and walks towards the witness box, Deirdre O'Finn shoots him a look of pure poison, and there is a brief outbreak of muttering among her supporters, but I'm able to quell it with a stern look. He takes the oath in a strident tone, as if beginning one of his sermons in the pulpit of his country church.

'Mr Pratt,' Roderick begins, 'please give the jury your full name.'

'Phineas George Pratt.'

'By profession, are you a clergyman of the Church of England?'

'I am.'

'And for how long have you been in holy orders?'

'For slightly more than thirty years.'

'Do you hold the living of vicar of Little Brewing in Suffolk?'

'That is correct.'

'For how long have you been in charge of that parish?'

'For almost twenty years.'

Roderick pauses briefly. 'Mr Pratt, I understand that you were present when the disorder occurred on 15 March of this year, and I will come to that in due course. But first, I want to ask you this: in addition to being the vicar, are you also something of a local historian?'

'I am indeed. I am a Suffolk man, born and bred, and I grew up in the Little Brewing area. I've always taken a keen interest in the history of the village, and in addition to studying all the local sources, I am the author of a monograph on the subject, which was printed, and can be found in most of the libraries in the area.'

'I would like to ask you about John Bonhomme, the man represented by the statue on the village square.' Some further muttering, again suppressed with a stern look. 'Have you made him an object of study, and if so, what can you tell us about him?'

'He bought and sold black people,' a voice from the non-Bonhomme section mutters, loudly enough to be heard throughout the courtroom.

'Out,' I say, 'and don't come back during this trial.'

The speaker stands immediately and leaves court, which is just as well, because I really couldn't have identified him, and the last thing I want is to waste further time conducting an inquest into this. Pratt seems annoyed by the interruption.

'John Bonhomme,' he replies, a little testily, 'is by far the most important figure in the history of the village. He was a poet of considerable renown, which is all the more remarkable, given that English was not his first language.'

'Can you sketch his life for us briefly?' Roderick asks.

'Certainly. Bonhomme was French by birth. He was born in the Languedoc, in a small village between Nîmes and Avignon, in 1721. His given name was Jean, but when he moved to England, he adopted the anglicised version, John. We don't know much about his early life, but evidently he had some desire to explore, to see the world, because in 1745 he appears in the British West Indies.' Pratt stares at the dock and the public gallery in turn, as if daring them to interrupt. He's just as good at the stern stare as I am, and no one mutters anything. 'He lived on St Kitts, and later Bermuda, for a number of years, until 1762.'

'And in 1762…?' Roderick asks.

It's a noticeably abrupt move forward in time. I'm sure Roderick doesn't want his witness to get started on how John Bonhomme made his living during his seventeen years in the British West Indies. The witness is going to be confronted with that subject eventually, but Roderick would prefer him to get angry at Kenneth Warnock instead of himself when the time comes. Besides, he needs Pratt to remain calm while he takes him through the rest of his evidence.

'In 1762, Bonhomme made his way to England, because of a young Suffolk woman called Daisy Hitch, whom he had met in Bermuda while she was travelling with her father. They had fallen in love, and he wanted to marry her, which he did the following year. The couple settled in Little Brewing. Their house is still there for all to see, in what is now the High Street.'

'When did he start writing his poetry?' Roderick asks.

'When he was still in Bermuda, probably in the mid-1750s. His earliest known work seems to have been inspired by the beauty of the islands, and it may have been in part an effort to improve his English. This part of the *corpus* feels highly original in style, perhaps because he's writing in a foreign language, and hasn't quite come to terms with it yet. Then, when he meets Daisy Hitch in 1760, 1761, he reels off a number of poems about her – rather conventional stuff, to be honest, how beautiful she is, how much he wants to be with her, nothing very original – certainly not to be compared with his writing about the islands.'

Roderick smiles. 'Nothing to rival the Sonnets, then?'

The witness ventures a thin smile in return. 'No, he's no threat to the Bard. But then, once he's in England and has

Daisy as his wife, he really starts to branch out, and between 1764 and 1780 we have a very fine body of work dealing with all kinds of subjects, some rather sentimental pieces looking back on his time in the West Indies, but on the whole far more mature, some romantic, some philosophical, but still with the sometimes curious use of his second language, which marks him out from other writers of the same period.'

'And was his work eventually published in this country?'

'It was. Of course, living as he was in an out-of-the-way location like Little Brewing, it took longer than it might have otherwise for him to become known. His fame did spread, but slowly. Not only that, but Bonhomme himself was not what you would call a self-publicist. He was reluctant to have his work published at first. He thought it wasn't good enough. They say that Daisy was responsible for talking him into it. Eventually, a Mr Tasker, printer of Stowmarket, read his work and agreed to publish it. After that, he became far more widely known. But that wasn't until the late 1770s, not too long before his death.'

'I see,' Roderick says. 'Your Honour, Mr Pratt has been kind enough to bring with him several more modern reprints of Mr Bonhomme's work in case we need them. I don't propose to offer them all into evidence myself, but they are available if my learned friend wishes to do so.'

'No, thank you,' Kenneth says, a touch dismissively.

'I do, however, propose to adduce one of them, a compendium of what Mr Pratt tells me is generally regarded as Bonhomme's most important work, which will give the jury a flavour of it, if they are interested to learn more about him. I would also like the jury to have a catalogue of his work, which Mr Pratt also brought with him, because it contains a good summary of the time-frame. May these please be exhibits 3 and 4?'

'If my learned friend thinks that Bonhomme's timeless verse may appeal to the jury,' Kenneth replies, with a glance in their direction, 'who am I to stand in the way?'

The jury have a bit of a giggle.

'Mr Pratt,' Roderick continues, once the exhibits have been delivered into Carol's safe custody, 'after Mr Bonhomme's death in 1783, did there come a time when the inhabitants of Little Brewing decided to take steps to commemorate him?'

'Yes. In 1802, the inhabitants took up a public subscription for a statue in John Bonhomme's honour, to be placed in the centre of the Little Brewing village square. The work was executed by a Mr Harmsworth of Bury St Edmunds, and was put in place in November 1802, where I'm happy to say, it remains to this day, notwithstanding the efforts of someone I could name to destroy it.'

'It's gone, mate,' a male voice insists. 'You can't protect him forever. We'll bring the bastard down next time, you mark my words. The slave trader is gone.'

So is another member of the public, for the duration of the trial.

'Now, Mr Pratt,' Roderick says, changing tack, 'did there come a time when it was brought to your attention that there was a movement to take the statue down?'

'Yes. Late last year, the *Star* – our local newspaper – reported that some of the girls at the school…'

'"The school" being St Cecilia's Academy for the Daughters of Gentlefolk, which I believe is a prestigious girl's boarding school, not far from Little Brewing. Is that right?'

'Yes. The *Star* reported that the new "headmistress" as they were calling him had asked the sixth form to inquire into John Bonhomme's history, and they'd come up with what they claimed to be information linking him to the slave trade. They said Mr O'Finn wanted to "cancel" John Bonhomme, as I believe the phrase is, and take the statue down. He was asking the village council to vote on it.'

'Don't talk about me like that!' Deirdre O'Finn screams from the dock. 'Call yourself a vicar? You're just a transphobic bigot, that's what you are! They should do you for hate speech!'

I thought I might have misheard when Pratt said 'him' the first time, but the second time, combined with 'Mr' O'Finn, was both clear and unmistakeable. There is a veritable explosion from the public gallery. General pandemonium breaks out, with people on all sides shouting, and ironically, I'm starting to worry that we may soon have another affray on our hands. No wonder they didn't want this case in Ipswich. I ask for the jury to retire, and for the public gallery to be cleared – both of which, due to the swift reaction of Dawn, the security guard, and our two officers, are already underway without my having to ask.

I rise for fifteen minutes to allow things to calm down again. When I return to court, the public gallery is empty and Deirdre O'Finn is seething quietly in the dock. The vicar of Little Brewing, on the other hand, is looking smug, as if he is rather pleased with himself. It's irritating. I've seen that look of superiority on ecclesiastical faces before, when I've been with the Reverend Mrs Walden at gatherings of vicars, and I've never warmed to it. But my more urgent concern is that I have to regain control of my courtroom – and, the carrots having apparently failed, it's time to switch to the stick. I have the jury brought down to court. In most cases, when I have to give a witness a dressing down, I would do it in the absence of the jury. But I want them to hear this one.

'Mr Pratt,' I say, 'I'm assuming that a stint in the cells for contempt of court would do nothing to endear you to your bishop. If you want to avoid spending time in the cells, I strongly advise that you refer to Miss O'Finn in the appropriate way from now on.'

He looks outraged. 'I did refer to... O'Finn... in the proper way. The doctrine of the Church of England is quite clear. God created men and women, male and female, and that's all there is to say on that subject of gender. O'Finn was born a man and given the name of Desmond, and that's the end of it. I don't expect you to understand.'

'As a matter of fact, Mr Pratt,' I reply, 'it so happens that I do have some insight into the doctrines of the Church of England.' Roderick gives me a supportive smile. I have no doubt that he has tried to reason with Pratt himself, without success. 'However, I have no intention of debating Church doctrine with you. This is a court of law, not a general synod. And in this court of law, Miss O'Finn is entitled to be addressed in the feminine form. I order you to do so. I expect you to obey my order. If you fail to do so, I shall hold you in contempt of court and have you taken down to the cells. It's up to you.'

I turn towards the dock. 'Miss O'Finn, in the circumstances, I will not have you removed from court for your last outburst. But it stops now. No more. Understood?'

'Yes, your Honour,' she replies quietly.

I nod to Roderick. 'Then, let's resume, Mr Lofthouse, shall we?'

Carol stands and whispers to me. 'Judge, should I open the public gallery back up?'

I shake my head. 'No,' I whisper back. 'It can stay shut until tomorrow. We'll have the High Sheriff of Suffolk to protect us then, won't we?'

'Thank you, your Honour,' Roderick says. 'Mr Pratt, have you brought with you to court two articles from the *Star* in November of last year, in which Miss O'Finn goes into some detail about her demand that the village "cancel" or "no-platform" John Bonhomme – or his statue, anyway – by taking the statue down, and either destroying it or removing it to some other location, where it would be viewed only together with some explanation of what it represented?'

'Yes.'

'Your Honour, I won't take the time to read them now, but may they be Exhibits 5 and 6, so that the jury can read them at their leisure?'

'No objection, your Honour,' Kenneth says. 'It will make a nice change for them, after wading through all that poetry.' The jury have another snigger.

'Mr Pratt, were you present in the Little Brewing village hall on the evening of 3 March of this year when the village council voted on Miss O'Finn's request to remove the statue of John Bonhomme?'

'Yes, I was.'

'What was the result of the vote?'

'The Council rejected the request by a vote of eight to one.'

'And were you present in the village square at about seven o'clock on the evening of 15 March?'

'I was. I'd been doing some work in the church, and I noticed from a distance that there was quite a gathering of people in the square, so I went to see what all the excitement was about.'

'What did you see when you arrived?'

'I saw that Monty Beveridge – Councillor Beveridge – was in position, guarding the statue, together with one or two other members of the John Bonhomme Defence League. They were standing guard round the clock by then because there'd been so many threats – including the ones she made in those interviews in the *Star*. I also saw that M… Miss… O'Finn was present together with several pupils from her school and a number of other people I didn't know – I don't think they were from the village.'

'What, if anything, did you notice about Miss O'Finn and her group?'

'Some of them were carrying those sticks for playing lacrosse, or whatever you call it, and several had hammers in their hands – Miss O'Finn had both.'

'What did you think was happening?'

'It was obvious what was happening. She'd been talking about tearing the statue down ever since the Council voted against her, and now she'd brought a group of thugs to help her do it. Monty was calling over to the Cat and Fiddle to get other members of the Defence League to come and help, which they did, eventually.'

'What did you do?'

He hesitates. 'I'm a member of the League too,' he admits. 'I joined Monty and the others, to do my bit defending the statue.'

'Mr Pratt, I'm not going to ask you about everything that happened after that. I will ask PC Barnett in due course. But briefly, please tell the jury what you saw from your vantage point. How did the trouble start?'

'Miss O'Finn started screaming to the mob she had with her that it was time to do something, and they charged the statue. We tried to stop them, but we were outnumbered. PC Barnett was there, but there was nothing he could do on his own. He called for other officers to attend, but they had to come from outside the village, so it took some time. After that, I couldn't give you much detail about what was going on – I was too busy defending myself against the mob. We managed to stop them taking the statue down, but they did a lot of damage to it with the hammers.'

'May the witness please see Exhibits 1 and 2?'

Dawn retrieves the before-and-after photographs of John Bonhomme from Carol and takes them to the witness box. Mr Pratt inspects them.

'Yes. That's what those vandals did. And she had her pupils with her, in their school uniforms, hitting people with their sticks. No wonder our schools are going to the dogs, with teachers setting that kind of example to children.'

'Yes,' Roderick says quickly, no doubt in the hope of cutting off any further outburst from the dock. 'Did you see anything happen between Miss O'Finn and Councillor Beveridge?'

'Yes. I saw Miss O'Finn in a heated argument with Monty, in the course of which she struck him on the head with her lacrosse stick. It was really dreadful. There was blood everywhere. Monty was in a terrible state. He had to go to the hospital later for stitches. It was shocking – another fine example to her pupils.'

'Did Miss O'Finn hit Councillor Beveridge once, or more than once?'

'Just the once that I saw, but that was more than enough.'

'How did the altercation end?'

'Eventually, a few more police officers arrived and they assisted PC Barnett in calming things down. Quite a few of the mob ran away when they saw the officers, but they took the details of as many as they could – including those of us defending the statue. It took some time, but eventually, the square cleared. There was no one left except for myself and Bill Yates, who volunteered to stay on duty to look after what remained of the statue, since we hadn't been injured. I think we were the only two fit for duty.'

'Mr Yates also being a member of the Defence League?'

'Yes.'

Roderick consults his notes to see whether he's covered everything he absolutely needs. There is a lot of detail he could ask him for, but I'm sure he doesn't want to spend a moment more examining the Reverend Mr Pratt than he has to.

'That's all I have, Mr Pratt,' he concludes. 'I'm sure there will be further questions for you. Wait there, please.'

'Two o'clock, Mr Warnock,' I say decisively. I've had enough for this morning, as, I sense, have the jury. I'm ready for lunch, which hopefully will today be an oasis of calm in a desert of chaos.

By the time I take my seat in the judicial mess, Marjorie and Legless are already in place, attacking the lunches they've brought with them – a bacon sandwich in Legless's case, and some kind of oriental concoction involving bean sprouts, in Marjorie's. I have my ham and cheese bap from Jeanie and Elsie's. But there's no sign of Hubert, who is the only one of us brave enough to face the dish of the day, which today, according to the menu, is spaghetti Bolognese with garlic bread.

'So, how is the great Suffolk cancelling case going?' Legless asks with an irritating grin on his face. I'm quite sure he knows the answer to that question without my telling him. News of any sensational goings on in any of the courts spreads quickly at Bermondsey via the court staff's bush telegraph, which will have been working overtime this morning.

'Don't ask,' I reply. 'If I had my way, I'd send the whole bloody lot of them packing back to Ipswich. The RJ up there is going to get a piece of my mind when it's over and done with, I'll tell you that for nothing.'

'That doesn't sound so good, Charlie,' Marjorie observes. 'What on earth has been going on?'

'Well,' I reply, 'in no particular order, I've had to close the public gallery – after having first expelled several individuals for interrupting the proceedings; I've threatened that I'll have the defendant taken down to the cells and revoke her bail if I hear any more outbursts from her; and I've threatened a witness – a clergyman of the Established Church, no less – with being jailed for contempt if he doesn't behave himself.'

Marjorie smiles. 'My goodness, it sounds as though you've had quite a morning. Do tell: how did the clergyman of the Established Church misbehave?'

'He called my trans defendant "Mr" and used the pronoun "he", which, of course, set her off – not that it takes very much to set her off, but still… And when I told him to knock it off, he started lecturing me on the doctrine of the Church of England about God creating human beings as either male and female, while at the same time commenting that he didn't expect me to understand.'

'Oh, dear,' Marjorie says.

'I understand where he's coming from, Charlie,' Legless says. 'If you're a minister, you can't just write off everything you believe overnight and conform to the new woke wisdom about choosing from an infinite number of genders, can you?'

'I'm not asking him to write off his beliefs, Legless,' I reply, 'it's just a matter of formal correctness in court. Roderick would have made that clear to him before we started. He just wanted to make his point – and wind the defendant up, of course.'

'What does Clara think about all that kind of thing?' Marjorie asks.

'She's not judgmental about it. She may not agree with everything the trans lobby says, but she's quite happy to use whatever pronouns people prefer. She's much more concerned with the important aspects of it all, such as protecting children until they're old enough to understand what's going on.'

'Well, I hope you have a calmer afternoon,' Marjorie says.

'I fully intend to, Marjorie,' I say. 'The public gallery will remain closed until tomorrow, when we will have the High

Sheriff of Suffolk to protect us. He will be with us for lunch, by the way, so I'd appreciate a full house; and speaking of full houses, where's Hubert? It's not like him to miss his spaghetti Bolognese.'

'He said he had some phone calls to make,' Marjorie replies.

'Phone calls? Sounds rather mysterious.'

'I'm sure he'll be with us tomorrow,' Marjorie replies.

* * *

Monday afternoon

'Mr Pratt,' Kenneth Warnock begins, 'you know, of course, don't you, that Deirdre O'Finn is the headmistress of St Cecilia's Academy for the Daughters of Gentlefolk – I'll refer to it as "St Cecilia's" for short?'

'I'm aware of that unfortunate situation.'

'And when she gave her first interview to the *Star*, Exhibit 5, in which she began her campaign to take the statue down, she explained, did she not, that the information she had about John Bonhomme was the result of a research project she had assigned to her sixth form?'

'I believe so, yes.'

'Well, we have it here. Usher, please… Perhaps you'd like to look at it again? His Honour and the jury have copies.'

Dawn takes Exhibit 5 over to the witness box, where Pratt accepts it ungraciously.

'I don't need to look at it again. I regret to say that I remember it perfectly well.'

'As you wish, Mr Pratt. She said this, didn't she: that she wanted the young women in the sixth form to question authority and established wisdom, and she chose Bonhomme as a subject of study simply because he was such a local icon?'

'Something to that effect, yes. But what did she know about John Bonhomme? She'd only been in the Little Brewing area for five minutes.'

'Well, that's rather the point, isn't it, Mr Pratt? She didn't know, and she wanted to find out.'

No reply.

'What the sixth form discovered,' Kenneth continues, 'is that during the years he spent in the West Indies, Bonhomme had worked for a slave trader. That was how he made his living: isn't that right?'

'What they came up with was a lot of rumour and innuendo. I don't recall them finding any real evidence to that effect.'

'Really?' Kenneth asks. 'Perhaps you should look at the interview again, Mr Pratt. If you look at the third page, you will see references to Bonhomme being employed by a man called Simple, a rich merchant who lived and worked on St Kitts, and was known to be engaged in the slave trade.'

'Simple was also engaged in exporting local produce from St Kitts. There's no evidence of what work Bonhomme did for him.'

'Yet, the sixth form's research also shows that Bonhomme was a wealthy man in his own right by the time he settled in England. He and Simple didn't become wealthy by trading in local produce, did they?'

'I don't know, and neither does the sixth form.'

'But…'

'And in any case,' Pratt continues, before Kenneth can formulate his next question, 'that's how things were in the eighteenth century: there was a slave trade. It was wrong, obviously, but that's how things were back then. That doesn't mean John Bonhomme wasn't a great poet, and it doesn't give her the right to storm into Little Brewing without so much as a by-your-leave and demand that we take down his statue after more than 200 years. She needs to show the village some respect.'

Kenneth allows some time to pass, to let this sink into the jury's minds.

'I take it, then, Mr Pratt,' he asks in due course, 'that you're perfectly content that the statue of a slave trader should be the centrepiece of the village in which you're the vicar: is that right?'

'As I've already said, there's no real evidence that he was a slave trader.'

'And in any case, it was all a long time ago?'

'Yes: it was.'

'Mr Pratt, on the Sunday following the publication of Exhibit 5, did you preach a sermon at the morning service in your church, in the course of which you referred to the Church's teaching that there are only two genders, male and female?'

You can almost see Pratt grinding his teeth. 'Yes, I did.'

'In the course of that sermon, did you also say that there is no such thing as transitioning, and that anyone who claims to identify, or attempts to transition to another gender, is a sinner and unacceptable in the eyes of God?'

Pratt does not respond immediately.

'Oh, come on, Mr Pratt,' Kenneth goes on, 'there's no secret about it, is there? The jury heard the way you referred to Miss O'Finn as a man this morning.'

'Yes, I did.'

'And his Honour had to threaten you with being held in contempt of court, didn't he, before you grudgingly used the feminine form to refer to her?'

Roderick is on his feet. 'My learned friend knows better than that,' he complains. 'It's not proper for him to attack the witness for trying to express his religious beliefs, even if the way in which he did so may have been misguided.'

'I'm not attacking him because of his religious beliefs,' Kenneth replies immediately. 'What Mr Pratt said is evidence of his bias and prejudice against the defendant, which is relevant to the credibility of his evidence, and I'm entitled to ask him about it.'

'I'm inclined to agree, Mr Lofthouse,' I say.

'As your Honour pleases,' Roderick says.

'I referred to O'Finn using the male form,' Pratt replies, 'because that is what he is in the eyes of God. However, his Honour having advised me as to the practice thought desirable for use in court, I have been complying with his directions.'

'Last chance, Mr Pratt,' I say, staring at him. 'No more.'

'Going back to your sermon, Mr Pratt,' Kenneth resumes, 'did you also tell your congregation that Miss O'Finn was a danger to all the girls at St Cecilia's, and that she should never have been appointed headmistress of the school?'

'Yes, I did.'

'And isn't that what this is about, as far as you are concerned? It's not just about John Bonhomme, is it? You resent a trans woman coming into your community and asking the children under her care to think for themselves?'

'I have a duty to preach the doctrine of my Church from my pulpit,' Pratt replies, 'and that's what I did.'

Kenneth nods and changes tack. I'm a bit puzzled about where he's going with all this. I'm sure he's having fun taking Pratt on about his religious stance on gender. But even if Pratt is prejudiced against Deirdre O'Finn, that doesn't really address the clear evidence of a violent attack on the statue and its defenders, led by Deirdre, which Roderick has put before the jury. Kenneth can't assert sovereign immunity in this case. At some point during the cross-examination, we should be picking up at least some clue about what defence he is going to raise. We haven't heard it yet. Kenneth's written defence statement doesn't help much. Apart from a suggestion of self-defence in relation to the alleged assault on Councillor Beveridge, it's all rather vague. It asserts that Miss O'Finn was acting in accordance with her legal rights, but doesn't really elaborate about what legal rights are in question. Perhaps he's hoping for a sympathy verdict.

'Mr Pratt, Miss O'Finn wasn't the only person who tried to take the statue down on the evening of 15 March, was she?' he continues. 'She had a number of people with her, didn't she?'

'Yes, she did – outsiders, mostly, like herself.'

'You told the jury that you saw Miss O'Finn hit Monty Beveridge on the head with her lacrosse stick?'

'Yes.'

'Did you by any chance hear what was said between them immediately before that?'

'No. There was too much noise – people shouting and carrying on, everyone shouting at once. It was pandemonium.'

'But did it appear to you that they were arguing?'

'Of course they were arguing. Miss O'Finn was inciting the mob to destroy the statue and use violence against the Defence League, and Monty was shouting at her to call the mob off and leave them alone.'

'Was Monty Beveridge armed with anything?'

'Armed?'

'Yes, armed: was he carrying anything he could use as a weapon?'

'Only for self-defence.'

'Well, what was he carrying for self-defence?'

'A cricket bat,' Pratt replies. He pauses. 'He's a member of the village team, you see – he goes in first wicket down.'

'Did you see Mr Beveridge try to score a few runs off Miss O'Finn with his cricket bat?'

'What?'

'Did you see him practising his cover drive while she was standing right in front of him?'

'No. I did not.'

'Thank you, Mr Pratt,' Kenneth says, resuming his seat.

'Your Honour,' Roderick says, 'I call PC Barnett.'

PC Barnett, in uniform, strides confidently into the witness box. 'I swear by almighty God that the evidence I shall give shall be the truth, the whole truth, and nothing but the truth. Ernest Barnett, police constable, Suffolk Constabulary, attached to Little Brewing police station, your Honour.'

'Officer,' Roderick begins, 'did you make any notes to which you would like to refer?'

'I did, sir.'

'No objection,' Kenneth says at once.

'Much obliged,' Roderick says, and he means it. If Kenneth insisted, certain conditions would have to be satisfied before the officer is allowed to refresh his memory using his notes. His evidence in this case is bound to be quite complicated, and I'm certainly not inclined to make PC Barnett give evidence without his notes in such a detailed case. But still, Kenneth could have made Roderick jump through all the hoops. Of course, he has his own reason for being cooperative – it opens the door for him to inspect the officer's notebook later, if there's anything odd about the evidence.

'You may refer to your notebook as you wish, officer,' Roderick says.

'Thank you, sir.'

PC Barnett positions his notebook on the ledge in front of him, pulls himself up to his full height and joins his hands behind his back.

'Officer, how many police officers are stationed at Little Brewing police station?'

'I am the only officer stationed at Little Brewing on a full-time basis, sir. If more are needed, I have to ask for them to be brought in on an occasional basis – if I'm on leave, or there's some special event going on, such as the summer festival. It doesn't happen very often. It's usually pretty quiet in Little Brewing.'

No one in court can resist an ironic smile at this, Roderick and myself included.

'Officer, when did you first become aware that Miss O'Finn wished to have the statue of John Bonhomme in the village square taken down?'

PC Barnett turns over a page of his notebook.

'It was when I read her interviews in the *Star*.'

At a gesture from Roderick, Dawn takes Exhibits 5 and 6 over to the witness box. PC Barnett examines them briefly.

'Yes, sir. These were the articles I read.'

'Now, initially, Miss O'Finn was calling for the village council to vote for the statue to be removed, wasn't she? But, as the jury have heard, the Council voted against her.'

'That's correct, sir, yes.'

'And after the vote, Miss O'Finn announced that she would take the statue down herself, notwithstanding the vote; did you become aware of that?'

'Yes, sir.'

'Which led to a certain tension in the village: would that be fair to say?'

'It did indeed, sir. Most people in the village are very attached to Mr Bonhomme's statue. Well, it's been there for a long time, and it's what the village is known for. We are all very proud of it. So as soon as Miss O'Finn made her intentions known, there were meetings in the Cat and Fiddle, which resulted in Councillor Beveridge and others setting up what they called the John Bonhomme Defence League, to protect the statue. The League arranged to provide the statue with what they called round-the-clock protection.'

'Was that an indication of a fear that there might be trouble?'

'It was indeed, sir.'

'Did you take any steps to try to defuse the situation?'

'I did, sir. I made several visits to the Cat and Fiddle, and urged the Defence League not to overreact, to wait and see what happened. After all, we couldn't be sure whether Miss O'Finn would actually do anything. It's one thing to talk about tearing down a statue that's been in the square for two hundred years, but it's another thing to actually do it. I thought that if Monty and the others kept their heads down, it was possible that it would all die down.'

'Did the Defence League appear to accept that?'

'They said that their only goal was to protect the statue, sir. As long as Miss O'Finn didn't try to cause harm to John Bonhomme, she had nothing to fear from them. I also made an appointment to see Miss O'Finn in her office at St Cecilia's School, to talk to her about it.'

'When was that?'

PC Barnett finds the place in his notes. 'This was on 12 March, sir, three days before the incident.'

'Yes. Who was present at your meeting?'

'Just Miss O'Finn and myself.'

'And, refreshing your memory from your notes, officer, please tell his Honour and the jury, as precisely as you can, what was said.'

PC Barnett picks the notebook up, finds the place, and reads with obvious care.

'I explained to Miss O'Finn that, as a police officer, I had concerns about the possibility of a breach of the peace if she attempted to take the statue down, and I cautioned her against using any kind of force to damage or remove it.'

'How did she respond to that?'

'She said that if the Council wouldn't do it, she was entitled to do it herself as a private citizen acting in the public interest.'

'Were those her exact words, officer?'

'Yes, sir, they were.'

'What did you say?'

'I explained to Miss O'Finn that under the law, as I understood it, she was not entitled to take matters into her own hands, and I pointed out to her the offences of affray and criminal damage. She replied that she was allowed to do it because of the European Convention on Human Rights and the law of modern slavery.'

'Again, were those her exact words?'

'Yes, sir.'

'Did you understand what she meant by that?'

'Not really, sir. I said I wasn't personally familiar with any legal rule that would allow her to take the statue down, and I told her that I would have to consult my superiors or the Crown Prosecution Service to seek their advice. I strongly advised Miss O'Finn not to take any action regarding the statue until I had received that advice.'

'How did she react to that suggestion?'

'She was what you might call non-committal, sir.'

'Well, did she give you any assurance that she would not take action?'

'No, sir.'

'Did you, in fact, receive the legal advice you requested?'

'Not in time to prevent what happened, unfortunately. I did put in a request to the Chief Constable's office, but I hadn't heard back when the incident occurred three days later. I've heard from them since. I don't know whether you want me to...'

'No, thank you, officer,' Roderick says. 'That may be a matter of law for the court to decide.'

Indeed it may. For the first time, I'm beginning to catch a glimmer of where Kenneth is going with his defence. With the exception of the plausible issue of self-defence on the assault, it seemed to me originally that Deirdre O'Finn was bang to rights on this indictment. But it seems Kenneth has found – or thinks he's found – some esoteric rule that might get her off the hook. It would have to be esoteric, of course – it is Kenneth, after all. I'm not sure he takes cases that don't have some potential to end up in Strasbourg.

'Well, let's move on to the evening of the incident,' Roderick says. 'When did you first become aware that there might be trouble in the square on that evening?'

'At about six-fifteen, sir,' PC Barnett replies after a quick glance at his notes. 'I was on routine patrol in uniform, and I noticed an unusual build-up of people in the square, including a number of people I didn't recognise as inhabitants of Little Brewing. I think there were eight or ten of them when I first observed them. I also saw that Councillor Beveridge was on duty, protecting the statue, together with three or four other members of the Defence League. So, I diverted away from the square, returning about ten minutes later.'

'What did you observe on your return?'

'When I returned, sir, I saw that the number of people had grown to twenty or more, and a number of inhabitants were watching from the edges of the square. At that time, I also saw Miss O'Finn, together with a number of young women, who appeared to be about sixteen to eighteen years of age, wearing the St Cecilia's school uniform.'

'What was Miss O'Finn doing when you first saw her?'

'She was going from group to group, talking to the people who were assembling. She and the young women in uniform also appeared to be distributing a number of items I now know to be lacrosse sticks to those people.'

'What conclusion did you draw from what you saw?'

'I concluded that Miss O'Finn was preparing an attack on the statue, and the members of the Defence League.'

'What action, if any, did you take at that point?'

'I did two things, sir. First, I radioed in to request back-up. I knew that was going to take some time, because any additional officers have to come in from some distance away; but it was obvious to me that, if violence did break out, I couldn't do anything about it on my own. I also approached Miss O'Finn. I told her that she, and those with her, were entitled to engage in a peaceful protest; but I also told her I suspected that she was contemplating the use of force, and I again cautioned her that, in my opinion, if she did, she would be acting unlawfully, and that I would be obliged to arrest her.'

'How did Miss O'Finn respond to that?'

'She continued to maintain that what she was doing was lawful, and she suggested that I should arrest the members of the Defence League, or at least, order them to step away from the statue. I then removed myself and took up a position close to the statue, such that everyone present could clearly see that I was a police officer in uniform, and from where I could see everything that happened.'

'Did that have any effect?'

'Some. One or two people left the square, and a few retreated to the edges of the square. But there was still a sizeable crowd with Miss O'Finn. I counted eighteen in all, excluding Miss O'Finn herself, and including five of her pupils in school uniform.'

'What happened next, officer?'

'I heard Miss O'Finn call out to the members of the Defence League, asking them to move away, so that Miss O'Finn and those with her could destroy or remove the statue.'

'What were her exact words, officer?'

PC Barnett makes a show of consulting his notebook. 'She said, "Step aside, slavery lovers, and let the bastard take what's coming to him."'

'How did the Defence League respond to that?'

'They declined to step aside, sir.'

'Once again, officer…'

'Councillor Beveridge replied, "Fuck off back to Ireland, you mad pervert. We're not going anywhere, and neither is John Bonhomme."'

'What happened then?'

'Miss O'Finn raised both her hands in the air and shouted to those with her, "Right, let's get this done, then." At this time, she was holding a lacrosse stick in her right hand, sir. She then ran towards the statue, and those with her followed, also brandishing lacrosse sticks and hammers. I shouted, "Stop!" as loudly as I could, but they ignored me.'

'What did you do then?'

'Well, there was nothing I could do to stop them, and I couldn't keep observation on all of them, so I decided to concentrate on Miss O'Finn and Councillor Beveridge, who I judged to be the main protagonists, sir.'

'What did you see occur between the two of them?'

'I saw Miss O'Finn head straight for Councillor Beveridge, waving her lacrosse stick in the air, and shouting. Unfortunately, due to the amount of noise, I was unable to hear what they were saying, but it was clear that they were angry and shouting at each other. I then saw Miss O'Finn strike Councillor Beveridge on the head with the lacrosse stick, and I saw that Councillor Beveridge was bleeding heavily from a wound to the head, where she had struck him. Councillor Beveridge then sat down close to the plinth, and I saw that he was using his phone. I later learned that he had called 999 for an ambulance. A member of the public also appeared to offer him first aid, and he moved away from the plinth at that point.'

'Officer, was Councillor Beveridge holding anything before Miss O'Finn struck him?'

'Yes, sir. He was holding a cricket bat.' The officer turns to look at me, and then the jury. 'He is a member of the village team, sir. He made fifty not out against Bury St Edmunds last season.' The jury have a good snigger, as does Kenneth.

'Did he really?' Roderick comments, without sniggering at all.

'Some mute inglorious Cowdrey, perhaps?' Kenneth suggests.

'I do wish my learned friend would not interrupt,' Roderick complains grumpily. I give Kenneth a look, which he acknowledges with a slight wave of the hand, though I have to admit, I did think it was quite funny.

'Did Councillor Beveridge do anything with the cricket bat before Miss O'Finn struck him?' Roderick asks.

PC Barnett thinks for some time. 'Not that I saw, sir. He was holding it and waving it around while they were arguing, but I didn't see him threaten to hit her with it, or anything like that.'

'What did Miss O'Finn do when Councillor Beveridge started to bleed? Did she offer him any assistance?'

'No, sir, she did not. I saw Miss O'Finn approach the statue of John Bonhomme. She took a hammer from inside her coat, and I saw her strike the statue a number of blows with the hammer. I noticed that one of the blows dislodged a piece of the statue's left arm, sir. At that stage, others were attacking the statue in a similar way. The Defence League were doing their best to stop them, and they had two or three men who arrived as reinforcements from the Cat and Fiddle; but they were outnumbered, and it did seem inevitable that the statue would be completely destroyed.'

'Did something happen to prevent that?'

'After some time, sir, and I couldn't tell you exactly how long, but after some time, I heard the sound of sirens, which indicated that my backup was on the way. This caused quite a few of Miss O'Finn's supporters to drift away, as did many of those watching from the edges of the square. By the time the six additional officers arrived, we were down to eight to ten hard-core supporters, not counting Miss O'Finn and her pupils. At about the same time, an ambulance arrived. The crew examined Councillor Beveridge and eventually took him to hospital.'

'What did you do once your backup was in place?'

'I pointed out to the officers those individuals I had seen attacking the statue, and further pointed out that some of them were in school uniform, and probably minors, and asked the officers to take all their particulars with a view to interviewing them at a later stage. I also pointed out the members of the Defence League, and asked that the same should be done in their cases. It was a complicated situation, sir, and I felt the need to take advice from my superiors about what action to take, so I was reluctant to arrest anyone at that time – with one exception.'

'Who was that exception, officer?'

'Miss O'Finn, sir. I had personally seen her commit the offences of assault occasioning actual bodily harm – perhaps even causing grievous bodily harm – and criminal damage. I informed Miss O'Finn that I was arresting her on suspicion of those offences, and cautioned her.'

'Please tell the jury the words of the caution.'

'The words of the caution are, "You do not have to say anything, but it may harm your defence if you fail to mention, when questioned, something which you later rely on in court. Anything you do say may be given in evidence."'

'Did Miss O'Finn make any reply to the caution?'

PC Barnett reads from his notebook. 'Yes, sir. She said, "You're on the wrong side of history. You can't stop this. We've got most of it done tonight. We'll be back to finish the job. Next time, Bonhomme is gone." I then seized Miss O'Finn's lacrosse stick and hammer, sir, and advised her that I was confiscating them, and that they would be used in evidence. I instructed her not to go anywhere, and in due course, after officers had taken the particulars of everyone present, she was taken to the police station. Miss O'Finn was kept in custody overnight because I was not satisfied that she had ceased to pose a threat to the peace. She was interviewed the following morning in the presence of her solicitor, and later charged with the offences.'

'Yes, thank you, officer. His Honour and the jury have heard that the others present in the square that evening were dealt with by way of cautions and warnings. Could you briefly explain why that was done?'

'Yes, sir. This was based on the advice I received from my superiors, and from the Crown Prosecution Service. It was felt that, as I had focused on what was going on between Miss O'Finn and Councillor Beveridge, my evidence about the conduct of others present would very likely be insufficient for there to be a reasonable prospect of conviction. In the case of the pupils from St Cecilia's, of course, we had to notify their parents, and in due course, warnings were given to them by a senior officer. Those who had assisted Miss O'Finn in attacking the statue agreed to accept cautions. In the case of the Defence League, it was felt that they would not have been charged with any offences in any case, as they were doing no more than standing guard over the statue, and so no further action was taken in their case.'

'Thank you, officer,' Roderick says. 'Now, if we could turn to Miss O'Finn's police interview, please. Would you assist me by reading the questions you asked, and I will read Miss O'Finn's answers, and any remarks made by her solicitor.'

'I can read my own answers, thank you very much,' Deirdre O'Finn ventures from the dock. 'Why does he have to read them for me?'

'That's the way it's done, Miss O'Finn,' I reply. 'Mr Lofthouse is entitled to present the prosecution case without input from the defendant.'

'Well, he better not get all sarky when he reads my answers,' Deirdre adds. 'I gave serious answers, and I want everybody to take them seriously.'

'I'm sure Mr Lofthouse wouldn't dream of being sarky, Miss O'Finn,' I observe.

'Perish the thought, your Honour,' Roderick replies.

And away we go. It's never the most interesting part of a trial. With the best will in the world, an hour or two reading our way through a lengthy interview, one question and answer at a time, poses a challenge to any jury's ability to stay awake. Roderick and Kenneth have agreed that they should have a transcript to follow, and we take a short break halfway through, which helps to some extent, but it's still an uphill battle. Despite its length – one suspects that Miss O'Finn's personal history includes a kissing of the Blarney Stone – the interview doesn't add much to what we already know. There is to be no hint of denial, no trace of regret. John Bonhomme was a slave trader, and it is only right that his memory should be erased. Not only that: we also learn, as presaged in Roderick's opening, that the man had the effrontery, in one of his writings, to suggest that women and girls should not be educated. To do so, Miss O'Finn's inquiring sixth-formers discovered, could bring no benefit to the world and could serve only to distract them from their rightful duties towards their families, in particular their husbands.

The most illuminating passage is her description of hitting Monty Beverage with the lacrosse stick. She hit him, she insists, because he was about to use his cricket bat on her, while calling her names and abusing her for being trans, and she had no other way of defending herself. Well, that at least is coherent, and would entitle the jury to acquit her on the assault charge if they think it may be true. But the rest is the European Convention and the law of modern slavery, which in her mind entitle her to represent the enlightened members of society in tearing down the statue of John Bonhomme. But she doesn't draw our attention to any specific rule of law to that effect, and neither does her solicitor. We are still just as much in the dark about her defence as we were before the interview.

That concludes PC Barnett's evidence in chief. I'm not going to ask Kenneth to begin his cross-examination so late in the afternoon. It feels like a very long day – and besides, Stella has an emergency bail application for me to hear once I've released the jury for the day. So the saga of John Bonhomme is adjourned until tomorrow.

When I return to chambers later, after refusing bail to a hopelessly recidivistic residential burglar, I find an email from Sir Jeremy Bagnall inquiring into the progress of my report on Hubert. I'm rather taken aback. It's not Jeremy's way to email me. Like me, he grew up in an age long before there were such things as emails, and although we have both learned to use them, they will never be our weapon of choice. It would be far more like Jeremy to call, or even to arrive unannounced and make himself comfortable in my armchair while he waits for me to finish in court. The email, it seems to me, confirms previous signs that he's not happy with what's going on, and would like to find a way out if he could; and at least it does provide me with a way to be evasive. I send him an email in reply, to the effect that my report on Hubert is underway, but has been delayed by events in my courtroom in a very difficult case – news of the Suffolk statue wars will undoubtedly have reached the Grey Smoothies by now, so my excuse is quite credible – and I would be grateful if I could submit it early next week. I leave chambers without waiting for a response. On the way out, I call into Hubert's chambers on the off-chance, but it seems that he has long since left for the Garrick Club.

* * *

Tuesday morning

I take myself in to court early this morning, because I have a premonition that difficult points of law are about to raise their ugly heads. I'm not convinced so far, by the vague references to the European Convention and the law of modern slavery, that Deirdre O'Finn has any legal justification for her attack on the statue of John Bonhomme. But as a judge, you develop a sense of foreboding about such things, with vivid images of the Court of Appeal in action – images which in my case, since last week, have become rather more vivid than they used to be. And knowing Kenneth as I do, I'm fully expecting the vague references to be superseded by more specific ones before too long. I need to be prepared.

I am under no illusions. Only an incurable optimist would hope to find anything useful on the law of modern slavery in what passes for a library at Bermondsey Crown Court, and sure enough, beyond confirming that slavery is illegal – which I already suspected – I come away little the wiser about that subject. But I do find an annotated copy of the European Convention on Human Rights, which I check out by scribbling my barely legible initials where indicated in the register. The register was installed by Stella three or four years ago, in an effort to try to keep track of our books, which had a tendency to disappear, often being found months later in some forgotten corner of the building. The system isn't working very well, it seems: the last entry is dated more than a year ago, indicating that we are either ignoring the register, or not making very much use of the library. Feeling virtuous for having dutifully signed it out, I take the European Convention back to chambers, and start ploughing my way through anything that might be relevant to taking down statues of slave traders.

But RJs rarely have much peace and quiet for such luxuries as legal research, and today is no exception. As I am immersing myself in the basics of freedom of expression, my phone rings. It's Stella, and she sounds frantic.

'Judge,' she says, breathlessly, 'I need you to come down to the car park. Now.'

'The car park?' I ask. 'Why do you need me in the car park? Stella, I'm in the middle of something. Whatever it is, can't Bob deal with it?'

'No, Judge. It's about to get out of hand.'

'Out of hand? What... you mean, a disturbance or something?'

'You could put it that way, Judge, yes.'

'Well, call security, or find a police officer.'

'They're already here, Judge. I'm afraid that's part of the problem. Please: come now.'

I have no idea what she's on about, but Stella isn't given to joking around, and obviously, there's something amiss. Reluctant as I am to drag myself away from the European Convention, I have no choice but to go and see for myself. As I don't drive to court, I rarely have occasion to visit the car park. It's at the back of the building, and my only connection with it so far is the happy one that the car park was the site of the discovery of the famous Bermondsey cannon. Today, it's the site of something quite different.

When I get there, everything seems quiet enough. Stella is standing just outside the door with Dan, our head security officer, his colleague Eric, and two uniformed police constables, who, I assume, are here in connection with cases in our list. When they see me, they all make an effort to stand up straight.

'So, what's going on?' I ask, as lightly as I can.

'Eric picked this character up on our CCTV in the office, sir,' Dan replies. 'He had the correct code for the car park, and he was driving in, as if to park. But he isn't one of our regulars, and he isn't listed in the book as a visitor, so Eric was keeping an eye on him.'

On cue, Eric takes over. 'I wasn't unduly worried, sir,' he says, 'until he got out of his car, and I noticed that he was carrying this.' He reaches behind him to retrieve an item that must have been propped up against the wall, and holds it up gingerly for me to inspect. My eyes open wide. No wonder there's been a bit of a panic. This would have got any security officer's attention. It's a full-size sword – the real thing, clearly an item that could cause some serious damage in the right – or wrong – hands. Security are used to confiscating knives, hammers and various other potential weapons at the front entrance, and they show up clearly enough on the security apparatus there. But a sword is something else again, and whoever drove into the car park with this one was about to gain access to the building without going through security.

'So, I asked these officers to join us,' Eric adds.

'My colleague and I arrested him for possession of an offensive weapon, sir,' one of the officers says. 'I cautioned him, to which he replied, "You blithering idiot, don't you know who I am?" I will say this for him, sir: he gave us no trouble. He made no effort to threaten us, or use the weapon against us. He surrendered it immediately without any resistance. I was about to take him off to the nick. But this lady insisted that we send for you before doing anything else, sir. I'm afraid I don't know who he is.'

I do. It dawns on me in a flash. I know before I confirm it by taking a couple of steps past the officers to look at the possessor of the offensive weapon, who is sitting forlornly in a chair someone must have brought for him – Stella, probably – some distance away from the door. I immediately take in the old-fashioned blue-black velvet jacket and waistcoat, the frilly lace ruffle adorning the front of the shirt, the knee-length breeches, the black tights, the patent leather court shoes, and the cocked hat held in the left hand. Yes, I know all too well who he is, and it's quickly dawning on me that Bermondsey Crown Court has just suffered what the media call a public relations disaster.

'Officer,' I reply, 'did you happen to notice the way in which this gentleman is dressed?'

'I did, sir. I did wonder whether it might have some terroristic significance. We all went on a course last year, where they said that terrorists often adopt some particular form of dress.'

'Oh, for God's sake,' the suspected terrorist mutters.

'Officer,' I say, 'did they also explain to you during your training that it's a defence to a charge of possessing an offensive weapon if you have a reasonable excuse for having it with you?'

'Yes, sir.'

'Did they explain that it may be a reasonable excuse if you have a weapon with you as part of your formal ceremonial dress?'

Finally, there's a flicker of light in the eyes. 'Oh. Yes, sir. You mean, like soldiers, or the Sikhs, with their daggers?'

'Exactly so.'

The officer glances across at the man he's charged with possessing an offensive weapon, and almost accused of being a terrorist, and the first signs of doubt are visible in his face. True, the intruder doesn't bear much resemblance to a soldier or a Sikh, but he's obviously dressed up for some reason or other.

'Oh, dear,' he says.

'Officer, allow me to introduce Sir Roger Pennycook, the High Sheriff of Suffolk. Sir Roger, I think I'm right in saying that you are wearing your ceremonial dress this morning, and that the sword is part of the dress; is that correct?'

The High Sheriff pushes himself up out of his chair. 'That's correct. The sword represents the High Sheriff's duty to offer protection to those working for the Crown, such as Her Majesty's Judges.'

There is an awkward silence for some time.

'I'm sorry, sir,' the arresting officer says. 'I had no idea.'

'Neither did we,' Dan adds.

'Well, somebody must have had an idea,' I protest. I must admit, I'm getting a bit hot under the collar now. When news of this gets back to Suffolk, and even worse, to Stephen Gulivant and the Grey Smoothies, it's yours truly who's going to look like the idiot. 'We've known about the High Sheriff's visit for some time, and apparently we gave him the code for the car park. Why weren't we prepared?'

'If I may, Judge,' Stella replies, in her most diplomatic tone of voice, 'we were expecting the High Sheriff, but we didn't know he would arrive at court wearing his ceremonial dress. I suppose I assumed that he would dress for court in chambers, once he'd arrived, like the judges. I can only apologise. But as far as Security are concerned, what they saw was a man carrying a sword in the car park, and…'

'They thought there might be a problem,' I say, completing the thought for her. 'I'm sorry, Sir Roger, but we do have a lot of trouble with people trying to bring weapons into court, and the staff are trained to be vigilant.'

The High Sheriff nods. 'Of course,' he replies graciously. 'This ceremonial dress stuff is murder to put on, especially the tights, and I like to get dressed before I leave the house, so that my wife can help me with it. It's never a problem at home in Suffolk, because they're used to me at court. It never occurred to me that it might be different here at Bermondsey. I should probably be the one apologising.'

After which, mercifully, the crisis is quickly resolved with handshakes all round. But by this time, I'm already late for court, so I whisk the High Sheriff away to chambers, replete with sword, and get into my own ceremonial dress. It fleetingly occurs to me to wonder whether the Grey Smoothies would consider allowing judges to wear a sword with our courtroom gear. There are days, I reflect – such as yesterday – when it might come in useful. The High Sheriff may have been reading my mind. By now, we're both a bit more relaxed than we were in the car park, and we've agreed on 'Roger' and 'Charles'.

'I hear you had some trouble with some of the good people of my county yesterday, Charles,' he says. 'I must say, I'm very disappointed to hear that.'

'Well, feelings are running high, Roger,' I reply. 'There were some outbursts in the public gallery. I had to ask some of them to leave, and eventually, I felt I had to close the public gallery completely.'

'Disgraceful,' Roger says, and I sense that he means it. 'People like that are letting the side down. We do pride ourselves on being fairly civilised in Suffolk.'

'I'm sure you are,' I reply. 'But there are always a few who have to cause trouble, aren't there? And when you get a situation like the John Bonhomme statue – well, there are bound to be a few who want to blow off steam.'

'Are you opening the public gallery this morning?' he asks.

'Yes. It's a public trial, so we'll give them a second chance. But if it's the same story today, we'll have to close it down again pretty quickly. I can't have the jury being exposed to this nonsense for the whole trial.'

We pause at the entrance to the courtroom. Dawn is about to bang on the door with her ceremonial gavel to announce our arrival.

'Don't worry, Charles,' Roger says. 'They're going to behave themselves today, I promise you.'

Having admonished everyone to be upstanding, Dawn leads us into court. Roger and I stand together before taking our seats. I'm just about to introduce him, so that everyone knows who he is, and, hopefully, no one else tries to arrest him for possessing an offensive weapon, when he preempts me.

'Good morning,' he begins, without reference to me. 'My name is Roger Pennycook. I'm the High Sheriff of Suffolk. Part of a High Sheriff's duty is to sit with the judges and protect them in the name of the Crown. Judge Walden is trying a case from my home county, and so I'm sitting with him here in Bermondsey to offer the court my protection.' He then focuses his gaze on the public gallery, draws the offensive weapon from its scabbard, and lays it in front of us on the bench. 'This sword,' he continues, in a rather chilling tone, 'represents my protection of the Court. I trust that everyone, including my fellow visitors from Suffolk, will take note, so that the trial can take place in a peaceful and orderly fashion.'

With that, Roger turns, bows to me, and takes his seat. I take my seat beside him, the sword glinting in the lights of the courtroom before us.

Roger has certainly made an impression on Bermondsey Crown Court. It's not every day someone draws a sword, having declared their intention of protecting the court, and it's not just our visitors from Suffolk who are duly impressed. Even Kenneth seems in awe as he stands to begin his cross-examination of PC Barnett.

'Officer,' he begins, with one eye on the sword, 'where do you stand on the question of John Bonhomme? Should he stay or go?'

Nice opening gambit. PC Barnett has to think about that one.

'As a police officer, I don't think it's for me to express a view on that matter, sir,' he replies eventually.

'Really?' Kenneth continues blandly. 'Because I rather thought you had expressed a view when you answered questions put to you by my learned friend Mr Lofthouse.'

'Did I, sir?'

'Well, let me read you my note of a reply you gave to Mr Lofthouse when he was asking you about the dispute over the statue. Let me know if I've got it wrong, but my note is that you said this: "Most people in the village are very attached to Mr Bonhomme's statue. Well, it's been there for a very long time, and it's what the village is known for. We are all very proud of it." Do you recall saying that?'

'I may well have said that, sir, yes.'

'Yes. Well, what interests me, officer, is your use of "we". You say, "*We* are all very proud of it." When you said "we", who were you referring to?'

'I was referring to people who live in Little Brewing.'

'Yourself included?'

'Yes.'

'So, in fact, officer, you have taken sides, haven't you? You're on the side of John Bonhomme staying where he is: isn't that right?'

Roderick stands. 'Your Honour, PC Barnett is a police officer. It's not proper for my learned friend to push him into taking sides, as he puts it.'

'I'm not the one pushing him,' Kenneth points out. 'It was my learned friend who asked the question. And he's not just here as a police officer: he's here as a witness – a prosecution witness. If he has a bias for or against one side or the other in this case, it's only right that he should declare it.'

He's right of course, and Roderick doesn't seem inclined to continue the debate. I nod.

'I agree, Mr Warnock. Answer the question, please, officer.'

The witness shuffles uncomfortably in the witness box.

'Well, yes, sir. I do believe that the statue should stay in pride of place, where it's always been.'

'Did you make Miss O'Finn aware of that opinion when you went to the school to warn her against taking matters into her own hands?'

'No, sir. I didn't think it would be appropriate to do so while carrying out my duties as a police officer.'

Kenneth stares at him for some time – not a comfortable experience for anyone. With his slightly dishevelled look, the wig never quite straight on his head, and the decidedly manic smile, he can have a formidable air about him. Having been the object of the same stare a number of times, I know exactly how PC Barnett is feeling.

'Did you not indeed, officer?' He pauses again, briefly. 'Are you a member of the John Bonhomme Defence League?'

'No, sir. Again, given my position as a police officer…'

He allows the words to drift away into the ether. Kenneth smiles.

'But you'd like to be, wouldn't you?'

'Oh, really…' Roderick protests, rather half-heartedly.

'When you saw Miss O'Finn and her supporters rush towards the statue, was there a part of you that wanted to take off the uniform and join Councillor Beveridge and the others in defending John Bonhomme?'

If Roderick was making an objection, he hasn't bothered to pursue it, so I'm not going to intervene.

'I was on duty as a police officer, sir. That's all that mattered to me – to do my job and try to keep the peace. Whatever personal opinions I may have played no part in it.'

'When you saw the confrontation between Miss O'Finn and Councillor Beveridge, you couldn't hear what they were saying because there was so much noise all around: is that right?'

'Yes, sir.'

'You saw Miss O'Finn hit Councillor Beveridge on the head with her lacrosse stick?'

'Yes, sir. I did.'

'But you couldn't hear what might have led up to it?'

'What led up to it was that she wanted Councillor Beveridge out of her way so that she could destroy the statue – which is exactly what happened.'

'And because she was on the wrong side of the argument – trying to take the statue down – did you assume that she was the aggressor in the altercation between the two of them?'

'No, sir. I judged her to be the aggressor because she and the mob she had with her rushed towards the plinth and attacked the Defence League.'

Kenneth stares again. 'Not because you saw what was going on between the two of them?'

'Well, yes, I saw what happened between them.'

'Councillor Beveridge had his cricket bat, didn't he, officer, ready to make another fifty not out?'

Roderick briefly considers making an objection, but the jury are chuckling, and he wisely thinks better of it.

'He did have his bat with him, sir, yes, as I said before.'

'Did he threaten to hit Miss O'Finn with it?'

'Not that I saw, sir.'

'Officer, are you sure you didn't assume that Miss O'Finn was the aggressor because, as you saw it, she was on the wrong side of the argument?'

'Certainly not.'

Kenneth nods. 'Well, let's move on. You told the court that everyone involved in trying to take down the statue was dealt with by way of caution, with the notable exception of Miss O'Finn: is that right?'

'That was decided by my superiors and the Crown Prosecution Service.'

'Well, yes. But your superiors and the CPS weren't there, were they? All they knew about it was what you reported to them. So, they would have relied on your recommendation, wouldn't they?'

'They did ask me for my opinion, sir, yes.'

'And, so that the jury will understand, a caution is an alternative to prosecution: a formal police warning, which can only be given when the person being cautioned has admitted to a police officer that they have committed an offence: yes?'

'Yes, sir.'

'But Miss O'Finn wasn't given that option, was she?'

'No, sir. She was not.'

'In fact, she also had the distinction of being the only person to be arrested on that evening, didn't she?'

''I saw her commit at least three serious offences, sir.'

'Did you also see others present commit offences?'

'Yes, sir.'

'Was Miss O'Finn the only person to be arrested?'

'Yes, sir.'

'In the case of the members of the Defence League, no one was either prosecuted or cautioned, were they?'

'That is what the CPS decided, sir.'

'Again, on your recommendation?'

'I can't speak to what the CPS lawyer may have thought, sir, but that was my recommendation, yes. They were the ones being attacked.'

'So, in summary, officer, does it come to this: that while everyone else was cautioned, or in Miss O'Finn's case, prosecuted, your fellow supporters of John Bonhomme were given a free pass?'

Roderick leaps to his feet, and mutters something about that being an improper question. But by the time he's finished the objection, Kenneth has already resumed his seat without waiting for an answer.

I'd been expecting Roderick to re-examine PC Barnett and try a little rehabilitation, but he seems in a rather subdued mood today – or perhaps he thinks, as do I, that Kenneth has landed a few decent blows on his witness, and the damage might only get worse if he gives the officer another chance to explain himself. Instead, he calls April Collins.

'How old are you, April?' Roderick begins.

'I'm seventeen, sir.'

'And are you a sixth form pupil, and indeed, are you also head girl at St Cecilia's Academy for the Daughters of Gentlefolk, just outside Little Brewing?'

'Yes, sir.'

'Do you remember Miss O'Finn coming to take over as headmistress at the school?'

'Yes, sir. I was in the lower sixth then.'

'And, once she had arrived, did you have any classes with Miss O'Finn herself?'

'Yes. Miss O'Finn teaches English and social studies. English is my subject, so I had her for that. But she also included the entire sixth and lower sixth forms in one large social studies class, which met once a week, on Friday mornings.'

'Was that unusual?'

'Yes, sir. Classes are generally kept quite small at St Cecilia's, and they would meet two or three times a week. Also, it was compulsory. You're supposed to make your own choice of courses once you get to the lower sixth, but everyone was required to take her social studies class.'

'Did Miss O'Finn explain why the course was compulsory?'

'She said that it was important that we all learned to think independently, and question authority. She explained that these days, universities expect to see that you can think for yourself – well, the best universities, anyway. So she wanted to have a class where we could all do some research, and then talk about some controversial social issues.'

'Did she create one particular project for you?'

'Yes, sir. I think this was the second or third time the class met. Miss O'Finn asked us whether we knew about the statue of the poet John Bonhomme, in the square in Little Brewing. We all knew the statue, of course. You can't miss it. You see it every time you walk through the village, and the villagers tell you all about it.'

'What did the project consist of?'

'Well, first, we talked about how things like the statue could set the whole tone, even for a town or city, if the person was famous, you know, like Florence Nightingale or Lord Nelson.'

'And what was the problem with that?'

'I suppose the question was, whether he was really a good role model. Miss O'Finn asked us what we knew about John Bonhomme himself. I think most of the girls knew nothing at all, except his name and the fact that he'd written some poetry. I knew a bit more, because of English being my subject. I had actually borrowed a book of his poetry from the library, and I'd read some of it. But I don't remember it giving much personal information about him – except that he was French, but he'd come to England and married a local woman, and he'd settled in Little Brewing.'

'What did Miss O'Finn ask you to do?'

'We were to split up into small groups and do our own research, and see what we could find out about John Bonhomme – especially anything that might be different from his image in the village.'

Roderick smiles. 'Something scandalous, you mean?'

April returns the smile. 'She didn't put it like that, sir. She was talking about questioning authority. But I had the impression that she would be pleased if we came up with something scandalous, yes.'

'How did your group carry out its research?'

'Well, we started with the internet, but there was very little there, really, and what there was just repeated the basic history – he was French, but married a local woman, and so on. So, we started on the local libraries, to find out what they had. And that's when we started to find some stuff that blew us away.'

'What did you find?'

'We found some articles, by locals, mainly, and unpublished, so they weren't generally known. But these articles talked about a period of years in his life when he'd lived in the West Indies, Bermuda and St Kitts.'

'What did you find of interest about his time in the West Indies?'

'Well, sir, there were copies of some documents – obviously very old – that the authors had found in the National Archives, or the British Museum, or somewhere, I forget. They suggested that Bonhomme had worked for a man called Benjamin Simple, who was a well-known merchant based in Bermuda. Simple had a regular business in the export trade, but the documents made it clear that he was also mixed up in the slave trade, and Bonhomme was named on the ships' manifests as having made several voyages to America when there were slaves on board.'

'I see,' Roderick says. 'Did these articles say anything else about Bonhomme's participation in the slave trade?'

'Only one thing, sir. They said that, by the time he arrived in England, Bonhomme was a very wealthy man. He owned quite a large parcel of land on St Kitts – I saw the title deeds for that – and they said that he had a considerable sum in gold, far more than he would have earned as a clerk, which was his official job title in Simple's company. Several witnesses apparently saw the gold being unloaded when he arrived in England, and he had some – I suppose now, you would call them security personnel– waiting at the dock to escort him, with his gold, to wherever he was going.'

'Yes, I see. Was there also something about Bonhomme not approving of women and girls being educated?'

April laughs out loud. 'Yes, sir. That wasn't our group. Cynthia Pole's group found that, in a literary commentary on one of his collections of poems. Apparently, he thought that it would only distract them from their duties towards their husbands and families.'

'April, were you present at the vote in the village council on 3 March?'

'Yes, sir.'

'Were you present in the square on the evening of 15 March?'

'No, sir.'

'Why not?'

April pauses briefly. 'I agreed with Miss O'Finn asking for the vote in the village council, sir. It was a decision for the village to take, especially as the statue had been in place for so long. But I felt that she should have accepted the result of the vote. St Cecilia's isn't far from the village, but we're not really part of it. I thought it was wrong to try to take the statue down by force.' She pauses, and smiles. 'Besides, my parents would have killed me.'

Roderick laughs. 'Well, we certainly couldn't have that, could we? April, before my learned friend asks you some questions, I would like to ask you about one more thing the jury might like to know, something you mentioned to me when we were chatting earlier. When you leave St Cecilia's at the end of this school year, what are your plans?'

April positively beams. 'I've been offered a place to read English at St John's College, Cambridge,' she replies.

'Well done,' Kenneth says, getting to his feet as Roderick sits down. 'My own college, as it happens, although they didn't accept women in my day.'

'John Bonhomme would have approved, then,' April replies, to general laughter, in which Kenneth joins wholeheartedly.

'Well said, April,' he says. 'And for the record, whatever John Bonhomme may have thought, I'm very glad they take women now, and I wish you every success.'

'Thank you, sir.'

'I only have one thing to ask you. Did Miss O'Finn put any

pressure on you, or the other girls, to join her in the square on 15 March?'

'No, sir.'

'Because there were only four or five girls there from the school, weren't there? The vast majority of the sixth and lower sixth stayed away?'

'Yes sir. I think most of us were afraid of getting into trouble, in addition to not being sure it was the right thing to do. Miss O'Finn told us that we were all welcome to come with her, but it was to be our decision – we had to learn to think for ourselves. She didn't put any pressure on me, or on any of the other girls, as far as I know.'

'Thank you, April,' Kenneth says.

Roderick tells us that the next witness is to be the leader of the John Bonhomme Defence League, Councillor Monty Beveridge. But not until later.

Lunch beckons, an oasis of calm in a desert of chaos.

When we return to chambers, I'm pleased to note that Roger has remembered to pick up the sword and return it to its scabbard, and that thought leads me to another. It suddenly occurs to me that he has no alternative but to lunch in his ceremonial dress, and I decide to leave my own robes on, so that he won't feel out of place. We are ready for some lunch, and today I've asked Stella to order in some food from Basta Pasta, a nearby Italian café we call on for special occasions. We can't have the High Sheriff exposed to the perils of the dish of the day, especially today – the combination of the dish of the day and being arrested in our car park might just be too much for him. Roger stops me at the door.

'Just before we go in to lunch, Charles, I've been thinking, and if you have no objection, I think I might stay until the end of the trial. I can stay overnight at my club, so it's not a problem.'

I'm not quite sure how to react. Before Roger arrived, I would have probably tried to keep the Suffolk invasion as brief as possible. But I'm getting to like Roger, and once he – and the sword – leave court, there's every chance of hostilities breaking out again, so if he's willing to stay and see it through, I'm thinking it may not be a bad idea.

'That's very good of you, Roger,' I reply. 'But I'd be imposing on you, keeping you away from Suffolk for so long. The way things are going, this trial will probably last most of the week. It might even stray into next week if the jury are out for a while.'

'I'm very glad to do it,' he says. 'It's my county that's on trial, and as High Sheriff, I feel I have to do what I can to make sure we give a good account of ourselves. As you said yourself, Charles, you can't have the jury being exposed to that kind of nonsense from a few self-appointed vigilantes.'

'Well, we'd be very pleased to have you, Roger, of course,' I say.

When we arrive in the judicial mess, I see that Basta Pasta is already being dispensed by a lady they've kindly sent along to help out. I also notice that in addition to Marjorie and Legless, Hubert has not only come in to lunch today, but also seems in a cheerful enough mood. I'm glad to see him, but I'm really not sure how to approach him and I'm feeling rather nervous about it. As a result, I'm a bit slow getting started on the introductions. But it turns out that, in Hubert's case, at least, I needn't have worried about it.

'Roger,' he says, 'I'd heard you were going to be with us today. How are things?'

Roger smiles. 'I was hoping I might see you, Hubert. Very well, thanks. How are you keeping?'

'Can't complain,' Hubert replies.

'You two know each other, then,' I ask, stating the obvious in my surprise.

'Yes, of course,' Hubert replies. 'Roger's a fellow member of the Garrick. We don't see as much of him as we would like, since he insists on living in darkest Suffolk, but he does favour us with his presence from time to time.'

'My time isn't my own this year,' Roger explains. 'Being High Sheriff is a full-time job. They keep you busy, believe you me – no time for frivolities such as an evening at my club. I should be back to normal again next year, once I've handed the job over to someone else. But I'm going to stay at the club while I'm here this week, so there's no reason why we shouldn't have dinner, if you're free.'

'Free as a bird,' Hubert replies. 'How about this evening?'

'With pleasure.'

I introduce Marjorie and Legless, and we settle down to enjoy a splendid lunch.

'I'm sorry you had all that trouble this morning, Roger,' Hubert says. 'I must say it's coming to something when we invite a guest and then do our best to have him arrested and hauled off to the nick before he can even get into the building.'

Of course, the story will have made the rounds very quickly, to the general amusement.

Roger laughs. 'It was my own fault, Hubert,' he replies graciously. 'It should have occurred to me that I was trying to get into a strange court carrying an offensive weapon.'

'Security should have been aware,' Hubert says, 'shouldn't they, Charlie?'

'It was a simple mistake, one anyone could have made,' I reply.

'You see, Roger, sometimes resident judges take their eye off the ball,' Hubert continues, 'spending more time worrying about how their judges are doing in court instead of concentrating on the task at hand, which is making sure the court is being properly run.'

There is an awkward silence for some moments.

'We have a guest with us, Hubert,' Legless points out quietly.

'One we've treated rather badly,' Hubert insists.

'Even so...' Legless replies.

'Please don't be concerned, Hubert,' Roger says. 'No harm done. In fact, looking back on it now, it's actually rather funny. It's a story I can dine out on for years. And I'm thoroughly enjoying my visit to Bermondsey.'

'It shouldn't have happened,' Hubert insists, but the wind has gone from his sails now, and he sounds rather sheepish.

'Hubert, if it's bothering you, feel free to treat me to a dry martini before dinner,' Roger says, 'and we'll say honour has been satisfied.'

We all laugh. It occurs to me that, if Roger has never served in the diplomatic corps, the country has lost a natural talent. As if by magic, the atmosphere returns to normal, and the delicious lunch soon has everyone chatting away about other things. But Hubert is a problem that isn't going away.

* * *

Tuesday afternoon

Councillor Monty Beveridge is a large man, carrying rather too much weight, which has left the light grey suit he's wearing some distance behind. He takes the oath in an almost petulant tone, and gives the impression that he is a man with something on his mind, and that we are likely to hear all about it before too long. Once again, I find myself grateful for Roger's presence with me on the bench, and the sword gleaming in the light in front of us.

'How long have you served as a councillor in Little Brewing?' Roderick is asking.

'For almost twenty years now. We are elected for three years, and I'm serving my seventh term.'

'You're obviously a popular figure in the village, Mr Beveridge,' Roderick observes.

'I've always tried to apply traditional values and common sense,' Beveridge replies, apparently by way of explanation of his remarkable political longevity. 'People still value those things in villages like Little Brewing.'

'Yes, I'm sure,' Roderick says. 'When did you first become aware that a demand was being made to remove the statue of John Bonhomme?'

'Rumours were floating around the village from some time in February, and I was hearing all about it in the Cat and Fiddle.'

'The Cat and Fiddle being the village pub, as the jury have heard?'

'The Cat is the centre of life in the village. Everyone is in and out the whole time. I'm there almost every evening. That's where I get the information I need to do my job as a councillor. If you relied on the council staff, you'd never have a clue what's going on. But after a couple of hours in the Cat, you've heard it all.'

'What exactly did you hear by way of rumour?'

'Well, we already knew that…' He suddenly stops and turns towards me. 'I'm sorry, Judge, but I'm not going to call him "Miss". I'll call him "O'Finn" if you don't mind.'

Muttering breaks out in the public gallery on both sides, and I see Deirdre wearing a dark expression in the dock. But Roger's presence, and a slight move of his right hand towards the sword, are having their effect, and it doesn't quite rise to the level where I need to intervene.

'You are free to refer to the defendant by her surname, if you wish,' I reply. 'But if you use the male form, you'll be spending some time in the cells, as I've had occasion to warn a previous witness – of which I'm sure you are fully aware. You're not in the Cat and Fiddle now, Mr Beveridge. The court's patience is wearing thin, and you would be well advised not to try it. Now, please answer Mr Lofthouse's question.'

Beveridge stares menacingly at me, but after some seconds it gradually dawns on him that I'm not about to change my mind.

'We knew O'Finn had become head… head teacher at St Cecilia's,' he says, 'and obviously, there was a lot of talk just about that, about the danger those poor girls were in, and what did the board of governors think they were doing…'

'Your Honour…' Kenneth says, half-standing.

'Last chance, Mr Beveridge,' I say. 'Once more and I'll hold you in contempt and have you taken down to the cells.'

'Somebody,' he continues, 'I think it was somebody who knew one of the teachers there, found out that O'Finn had asked the more senior girls to try to dig up some dirt to smear John Bonhomme. Then, we heard that they were saying he'd been involved in the slave trade, or some such. And before you can say Jack Robinson, I hear there's going to be a vote in the Council about taking Bonhomme's statue down.'

'How did that vote come about, do you know?'

'Yes, I do. Any councillor can call for a vote on any subject affecting the village, and O'Finn had leaned on my colleague, Councillor Brenda Meggs, to demand a vote on whether we should take the statue down.' He shakes his head. 'If you want something like that done, Brenda's your girl – she's the village tree-hugger.'

'How did you react to that?'

'I talked to the other councillors and straightened them out, and we won the vote eight to one.'

'But that wasn't the end of it, was it, Mr Beveridge?'

'No, it wasn't. Almost straightaway, we were hearing that O'Finn was going to take matters into… its… own hands, and then the article in the *Star* appeared, and we knew we had a real problem.'

'You were afraid that some action would be taken against the statue?'

'Yes. Obviously, it's vulnerable all the time, out there in the open. It wouldn't take someone with a hammer long to destroy it, even if they couldn't make it disappear completely, and she'd already said she was going to do it. She was going to get the girls involved too – get them into trouble, introduce them to crime to end their school careers, very nice.'

'Did you decide to take any action to safeguard the statue?'

'Yes. A group of us in the Cat had a meeting and we decided that we weren't going to stand for it. We weren't going to allow Bonhomme's statue to be removed or defaced, especially by a nosy interloper like O'Finn.'

'When you say "a group of us…?"'

'There were ten to twelve of us, men who know each other well, men who've lived in or around the village all their lives, including the vicar, I may say – right-thinking men who weren't going to tolerate this kind of nonsense. We decided to set up the John Bonhomme Defence League, whose purpose would be to do whatever was necessary to protect the statue.'

'What steps did you consider to be necessary to protect it?'

'There was only one thing we could do, really – we had to keep a watch over it, especially at night. We didn't think O'Finn would have the nerve to do it in broad daylight or the early evening, when there were people around, and PC Barnett would be out on patrol; and besides, you can see the square from where we sit in the Cat, so we could keep an eye on it at long distance until later at night. That's when we thought she would do it – late at night. So, we drew up a rota and took it in turns standing guard over the statue at night.'

'Did you stay out there all night?'

Beveridge actually smiles. 'That's the story we put out on the street, so O'Finn would think there was never a time when we weren't watching. But the truth is, we usually knocked off and went home between one or two if everything was quiet. We were losing too much sleep as it was.'

'Mr Beveridge, were you on guard duty – if I can put it that way – on the evening of 15 March?'

'Yes, I was.'

'Who was with you?'

'There were five of us, all members of the League: Gerry Sullivan, Bernard Fink, Ed Carter, Bob Atherton, and myself. The vicar had said he would volunteer that evening, too, if he could.'

'At what time did you begin your vigil?'

'About six-thirty.'

'Wasn't that rather early for you to start?'

'Yes, it was. Usually, we wouldn't have begun until ten at the earliest. But we'd received reports in the Cat that O'Finn and some of the St Cecilia girls had been spotted in the village, and PC Barnett had reported that there were an unusual number of people in the square. It just felt like something was going on, so we decided to take no chances.'

'And when you'd been on duty for an hour or more, did something happen?'

'Yes. As PC Barnett had said, there was a good crowd gathering in the square – I don't know who they were – not people from the village, I can tell you that. O'Finn was there, with several of her girls– all dressed in their school uniforms, if you please. She was handing out hammers and some things that looked like hockey sticks, but with, like a bag, at one end.'

'Lacrosse sticks,' Roderick says.

'Lacrosse, right. So, O'Finn's organising these people, and arming them with these sticks, and hammers and such like, and then he – she, sorry – starts marching them towards us like the Grand Old Duke of York. It was obvious that she was going to attack us, and the statue.'

'Yes. Let me ask you this, Mr Beveridge: did you and the other members of the League have any things with you that could be used as weapons?'

'Yes. Well, we knew that O'Finn's mob would be carrying weapons they could use to destroy the statue, and they could quite easily decide to use them on us first if we didn't get out of their way, couldn't they? So, when we went on duty, yes, we would carry something with us, in case we had to defend ourselves. Usually, it would just be brooms or whatever we could borrow from the Cat. But some of the lads brought their own items.'

'What was your item, Mr Beveridge?'

'I would have my cricket bat with me.'

'And again, for what purpose?'

'Just in case I had to defend myself.'

'Tell his Honour and the jury what took place next.'

'Well, O'Finn ordered us to leave, so that the mob could get to John Bonhomme. We told her that wasn't about to happen, and…'

'Do you remember the exact language that was used?'

'No, not really. It was a madhouse. Everybody was shouting at the same time. It wasn't parliamentary language, on either side, I can tell you that.'

'Then what happened?'

'Then O'Finn screamed at the mob, "Come on, let's get these slavery-loving so-and-sos out of the way," or something to that effect, and they charged us – twenty or more of them, all waving those sticks and hammers. And this with PC Barnett standing right there, in uniform, ordering them to stop it. They didn't pay any attention to him at all – which gives you some idea of what the girls at St Cecilia's are being taught in their social studies class these days. We did our best to defend ourselves, and protect John Bonhomme, but we were outnumbered. We did land a few blows on them, but they did a lot of damage to John – well, you've seen the photographs, I'm sure. If the police reinforcements hadn't arrived when they did, they would have done for him – he would have been gone.'

'Mr Beveridge, let me focus on Miss O'Finn for a moment. What did she do when the charge began?'

'Charged right up to me, and ordered me out of the way, or else... I said I wasn't moving – and I'm sure I wasn't very polite about it, any more than O'Finn was. And the next thing I know, he – she, whatever – whacks me over the head as hard as she can with her lacrosse stick. She just raised it in the air and brought it down on my head without any warning.'

'Mr Beveridge, before she hit you, did you make any move to hit her with your cricket bat?'

'No, I did not.'

'Did you threaten to use violence against her, or did you say or do anything that might have made Miss O'Finn fear that you were about to use violence against her?'

'No, I did not.'

'What effect did the blow to the head have on you?'

'It knocked the stuffing out of me. I was stunned. I didn't know what day it was. I remember sitting down, up against the plinth, and I could feel a trickle of blood on my head. I think I dropped my bat. After that, it's all a bit of a blur, except I do remember seeing O'Finn taking her hammer to poor old John Bonhomme. She had a free run at him – there was nothing I could do to stop her. I remember PC Barnett and the vicar coming to see if I was all right, and there were some other people too, I don't know who they were.'

'The jury will hear the medical evidence, Mr Beveridge, so I needn't ask you about it all in detail now. But did someone call an ambulance, and were you taken to hospital?'

'Yes. They took me to West Suffolk Hospital in Bury St Edmunds. They stitched me up, and they kept me in overnight for observation because they thought I was probably concussed. I was discharged with painkillers and what have you the following morning. I had headaches for weeks afterwards.'

Roderick nods. 'Thank you, Mr Beveridge. Wait there, please. There will be some further questions for you.'

'Mr Beveridge,' Kenneth begins, 'you remember my learned friend Mr Lofthouse asking you about the vote in the village council, don't you?'

'Yes, I do.'

'I want to ask you about something you said about that, and I made a note of it at the time. Correct me if I've got it wrong, but when my learned friend asked you when you found out there was to be a vote, did you say this: "I talked to the other councillors and *straightened them out,* and we won the vote eight to one?" Is that what you told his Honour and the jury?'

Councillor Beveridge has appeared reasonably confident about giving evidence thus far, but he's suddenly looking rather ill-at-ease. He shifts his weight from foot to foot, and takes some time to reply.

'I believe I did say something like that, yes. It was just a figure of speech.'

'A figure of speech?' Kenneth asks. 'Really? Would you care to explain to his Honour and the jury what that figure of speech means?'

More hesitation. 'We had an informal meeting in the Cat, and talked about the situation.'

'Who had an informal meeting, Mr Beveridge? Who was present?'

'The eight of us who voted the same way.'

'In other words, the entire Council, except for the tree-hugger, Councillor Meggs?'

'It's true that Brenda wasn't present, yes.'

'Why wasn't Councillor Meggs present?'

Hesitation again. 'I'm not sure. I mean, it wasn't planned – it was just a spontaneous thing. We all found ourselves in the Cat having a drink, and we started discussing the vote. As I said before, everybody's in and out of the Cat all the time. That's all there was to it.'

'So, it just happened that all the councillors spontaneously found themselves in the Cat and Fiddle, except for Councillor Meggs?'

'Yes.'

'What did you say to your other colleagues, in Councillor Meggs's absence, to "straighten them out?"'

There's a long pause, after which Councillor Beveridge takes a deep breath, and looks as if he's deciding to take the plunge in some way.

'I reminded all my colleagues that O'Finn had only just arrived in the area,' he replies. 'She was fresh off the boat from Ireland. She didn't know Little Brewing from Chelsea. She lived up at the school. She didn't understand what the village is about, and she didn't make any effort to find out. She didn't try to talk to any of us, to find out who we are, or what we had to say. She just presumed she was entitled to waltz in and order us around, order us to destroy our statue, that we've had in the square for more than two hundred years. I mean, who does she think she is? It's not on.' He pauses again. 'So, that's what I told my colleagues,' he adds authoritatively, 'and they agreed with me.'

'When you say that she made no effort to talk to you,' Kenneth asks, 'are you suggesting that she should have become a regular at the Cat and Fiddle?'

'No,' Beveridge replies. 'She could have talked to us at the Council chamber, made an appointment to introduce herself, or invited us up to the school. There were lots of ways of doing it. She would have been welcome at the Cat, had she chosen to come. The previous headmistress, Miss Blair-Smyth, paid us a visit from time to time, not regularly, but once in a while, and she would have a port and lemon with us – that was her drink, Miss Blair-Smyth, port and lemon – and we used to chat with her. O'Finn could have done the same.'

Kenneth allows some time to pass. 'Is that a serious answer, Mr Beveridge,' he asks, 'that Miss O'Finn would have been welcome at the Cat and Fiddle?'

'Certainly,' Beveridge replies, but with less confidence than his last answer.

'She would have been welcome to come and be called "Mr O'Finn" or "Desmond", would she, welcome to come and be called a "pervert", be told that she posed a danger to her pupils, told to go home to Ireland?'

Beveridge shakes his head. 'We wouldn't have said that…'

'All those things have been said in this courtroom, during this trial, Mr Beveridge,' Kenneth points out. 'At the Cat and Fiddle, there's no judge to threaten you with a night in the cells, is there? Do you really suggest to the jury that she would have been welcome there?'

There is no reply. Kenneth doesn't insist on one.

'The truth of the matter is this, isn't it, Mr Beveridge? You dislike Miss O'Finn because you're prejudiced against her as a trans woman, and you dislike her for daring to encourage her pupils to ask questions about your local hero, John Bonhomme, for exposing him as a slave trader after the village had covered that fact up for two hundred years...'

'That's not true,' Beveridge shouts in reply.

'And when Miss O'Finn confronted you at the plinth, you did what you would probably have done at the Cat and Fiddle, if she'd ever made the mistake of showing her face there: you threatened to practice your off drive on her. You made it clear that you were about to use your cricket bat on her, to teach her what happens to people who have the cheek to question what goes on in your village? And that's why she hit you first with the lacrosse stick, wasn't it? She had no choice. It was the only way she could defend herself against you and your cricket bat.'

'That is not true,' Beveridge positively bellows. 'I never got the chance to use my bat. She walloped me over the head with her stick before I had any chance to defend myself.'

He suddenly turns towards the jury.

'In any case, Desmond is a bloody pervert, isn't he? And God only knows what he gets up to with those poor girls at St Cecilia's. Miss Blair-Smyth must be turning in her grave, poor love. And he's here for five minutes, and he thinks he can throw his weight around, and mess around with our John Bonhomme after two hundred years? Well, not on my watch, that's all I have to say about that: not on my watch.'

Next, he turns towards the dock.

'You know what, Desmond, why don't you just fuck off? Fuck off back to fucking Ireland, and good riddance.'

And finally, towards the bench.

'Are you going to send me down to the cells now?'

'Yes, I am, Mr Beveridge,' I reply. 'I hold you to be in contempt in the face of the court. You will remain in custody overnight until the court sits tomorrow morning, and thereafter, until you offer the court a full and sincere apology for your conduct. I will ensure that you are offered legal advice at no cost to yourself. Take him down, please.'

There is a spontaneous outburst of cheering on one side of the public gallery, and boos and obscenities from the other. To her great credit, Deirdre O'Finn remains calm, and doesn't react. I am about to read the public gallery the riot act again, and perhaps even announce that I'm shutting it down for the duration, but before I can get a word out, Roger stands, draws himself up to his full height, and seizes his sword. He says not a word, but fixes both sides of the gallery in turn with a stern stare. The noise dies away almost at once.

Carol stands, and whispers to me. 'Judge, I think Emily Phipson is still on her feet in Judge Dunblane's court. Shall I ask her if she will have a word with Mr Beveridge once she's finished there?'

'Yes, thank you, Carol,' I reply, 'good idea.'

No one has the energy to take the case any further today, and I gratefully agree with Roderick's rather subdued suggestion that we should adjourn until tomorrow morning.

'Well, that was great fun,' Roger says, once we're back in chambers, 'though it's dreadful to think of the inhabitants of Little Brewing actually electing that man a village councillor.'

'For the seventh time, if I recall rightly,' I say. 'There's no accounting for taste, I suppose.'

We both start to change into our street clothes. Roger's wisely taking no chances – he's not going outside dressed as High Sheriff again. He's brought his civvy gear up from his car, and I've told him he's welcome to leave his regalia in chambers with mine while he's with us. I've had one or two qualms at the thought of the Grey Smoothies finding out that I'm keeping a sword in my wardrobe, but there's no reason why they would, and I've decided not to worry about it.

'No, I suppose not,' Roger agrees. 'Look, I'm sure you have things to do, Charles, and I need to touch base with my office; so with your leave, I'm going to take myself off to the Garrick and flirt with a dry martini. I'll see you tomorrow.'

'Well, thank you again for your protection today, Roger,' I say. 'It certainly did the trick, didn't it? Just as a point of interest, have you ever had to wield your sword in anger before while protecting a court?'

'Never,' he replies. 'It's my first time.'

'Well, you wielded it admirably,' I say. 'Oh, and Roger, before I forget, I spoke to my wife last night, and told her you'd be staying on. She insists that you must come and have dinner with us tomorrow evening.'

'That's very kind of you both, Charles,' he replies. 'But I don't want to be a bother.'

'You won't be any bother. It will be our pleasure, and Clara loves a chance to make her signature vegetarian lasagne.'

'Well, that sounds delightful,' Roger replies. 'I will look forward to it.'

'She also says, as you're staying over unexpectedly, that the washing machine is at your disposal if you have need of it.'

Just after Roger has left, and I am settling down to read an application to change conditions of bail, Stella knocks and comes in. She's wearing her trademark look of impending doom, which is familiar to all of us at court. You have to wonder sometimes, just from looking at her face, whether London is burning, or a biblical flood is imminent. It's usually something a bit less serious, but the look never fails to get my attention. Today is no exception. She is in full angel-of-death mode. She closes the door confidentially.

'Can I have a word, Judge? It's about Judge Drake.'

I close my eyes briefly. 'Yes, of course, Stella. Come and sit down.'

She seems hesitant. 'There's something very odd going on, Judge,' she begins, 'and I'm not quite sure what to do, if anything. Earlier this afternoon, I was contacted by Barbara, my opposite number at Winchester. She told me Judge Drake had been in touch with her personally, by phone.'

'He called the list officer at Winchester? What for? What possible reason could he have for doing that?'

'That's a good question, Judge. Barbara got the impression that he wanted to set up some arrangement with her, whereby he could go and sit at her court now and then when she needs an extra judge.'

I am conscious that I'm staring at her. 'But that doesn't make any sense,' I point out.

'I know. That's why I'm having trouble working out what's going on. Barbara herself didn't seem sure exactly what he wanted.'

'Winchester's not even on our circuit – it's on the Western Circuit.'

'Yes, Judge. And in any case, if I understand it correctly, if Judge Drake wanted to sit at any court away from Bermondsey, he would have to apply through our presiding judge.'

'Yes, that's right,' I reply. 'And off circuit, of course, he'd have two presiding judges to contend with.'

'Barbara said, at one point, Judge Drake seemed to be asking if he could sit at Winchester as a deputy circuit judge. Apparently, he thought that might mean he wouldn't need permission from the presiders.'

'But he'd still need permission from the Grey Smoothies,' I point out. 'They're in charge of deputy judges.'

'Yes, Judge.'

'And sitting as a deputy implies that he would have retired,' I add.

'Yes, Judge.'

'Let's assume he sees the writing on the wall at Bermondsey,' I suggest after some time. 'So, he announces his retirement here, and then what…? Does he think he can arrange to sit as a deputy under the radar, far away, in Winchester, without the presiders or the Grey Smoothies noticing? Is that what's going through his mind?'

'That's the conclusion I eventually came to,' Stella replies, 'but I can't work out how he could possibly get away with it. All right, there are times when all list officers need an extra judge urgently – as you know yourself, Judge. But when that happens, they either bring in a recorder, or if it's a case they can't give to a recorder, they ask their presiders to find them a judge. No list officer's going to approach a judge personally and ask him to sit.'

'No,' I agree. 'And does he think they don't read judgments of the Court of Appeal in faraway reaches of the realm like Winchester? I just don't get it.'

'And that's what worries me more than anything else,' Stella says. 'It's his state of mind. It's not rational – and he's sitting in court, trying cases. I'm worried that things could get even worse for him. I mean, if Mr Justice Gulivant and the Grey Smoothies find out about this…'

'You mean, *when* they find out. They'll have a collective heart attack.'

She closes her eyes. 'I'm sorry, Judge. If I'm out of line, I… but I just don't know what to do.'

'No, you're quite right, Stella. Things were coming to a head anyway, but we can't ignore it any more. We can't let the grass grow on this.'

'Barbara hasn't told anyone else,' Stella says. 'I asked her not to, until I'd had the chance to talk to you. But I have to get back to her. What do you want me to say?'

'Ask her not to say anything for now,' I reply after some

thought. 'I'll contact her resident judge myself, and discuss it with him. He will probably want to tell the presiders, and I don't see how I can really argue with that. What I have to do is think of a way to approach Judge Drake and find a solution we can all live with, before the wheels fall off the bus completely.'

Stella looks at me. 'How will you do that?' she asks.

'God only knows,' I reply.

* * *

Wednesday morning

'She has some nerve, if you ask me, sir,' Elsie says, 'coming over here from abroad and laying down the law to those poor people about what they can have and can't have in their village square. The cheek of it!'

'It's always your foreigners though, innit, sir?' Jeanie joins in. 'I thought all that was supposed to have stopped when we voted to leave the European whatsit.'

'That's what they told us,' Elsie confirms. 'But it's always the same, innit? You can't trust a word they say.'

I'm buying two ham and cheese baps this morning. This isn't greed on my part. If Roger is to be with us all week, I want to make sure he has options outside the canteen. I'm also conscious that he may not want to be on his best behaviour in the judicial mess every day, and may prefer to have lunch in chambers. That would also free up Legless, Marjorie and Hubert to have their usual lunchtime banter, ask each other's advice, and talk about what's going on in their courts, without seeming to be ignoring a High Sheriff. The occasional lunchtime guest is inevitable, and not unwelcome; but as a judge, lunchtime can be the most important time of your day, if you have a real problem and not much time to solve it. Often, a word or two from a colleague is all it takes. I can't deprive them of that for the whole week.

'Miss O'Finn has every right to be here, Jeanie,' I point out, 'and she's the headmistress of a very good girls' school in Suffolk.'

'But in that case, sir,' Jeanie says, 'she should know better than most how to behave, shouldn't she? What kind of example is that to set to young girls? And how did she get to be a headmistress, anyway, being, what do they call it, trans, or whatever?'

'It probably went in her favour, didn't it?' Elsie replies. 'That's the way it goes now, innit? They're all scared to death of being accused of, what do you call it – something or other-phobia – aren't they? They probably thought they'd get in trouble if they didn't make her headmistress.'

'They had a teacher at the school near me,' Jeanie says, 'and it turned out he was on the run. He was wanted in Scotland for robbing a bank.'

'That wasn't a case of discrimination, then, was it?' I point out.

'No, sir,' Jeanie agrees, taking my money and handing me my baps. 'That was just your usual case of them not knowing what they're doing.'

'I think my auntie Maude was trans,' Elsie says suddenly, as I'm leaving.

Jeanie looks at her, eyebrows raised. 'I doubt it, Elsie,' she replies. 'I mean, that was years ago, wasn't it? They hadn't invented things like trans then. What makes you think that, anyway?'

Jeanie shrugs. 'I don't know. She just looked more like a man, didn't she? She smoked those small cigars. And she supported Leyton Orient.'

George's newspaper stand is my next port of call, to pick up my copy of *The Times*. George is very well informed about all kinds of news, not just the kind that dominates the front pages. I sometimes think he must have read every page of every paper and magazine he has for sale, although that would obviously be impossible. But I've lost count of the number of times he's directed me to references to the court or myself in publications other than *The Times,* and I suspect he offers the same service to all his customers. How he does it, I have no idea. He directs my attention to several articles about the Suffolk statue, and I invest in one or two of the tabloids, mainly to show my appreciation.

'What I can't understand, guv,' he says, handing over my change, 'is how they bring themselves to do it. I mean, when you think about the surgery involved. I'll be honest with you, guv: I go weak at the knees just thinking about it. And, at the end of the day, it can't really make them into a woman, can it?'

'That's a complicated question, George,' I reply, walking away with a cheery wave before he can continue the discussion. I'm not going anywhere near that one.

The first order of business, after the daily laying down of the sword on the bench, is to have Monty Beveridge brought up from the cells. I have to ask him whether he's considered his position, and is prepared to apologise for his conduct in court yesterday. He won't be naturally inclined to say he's sorry – I have no doubt of that – but a night in custody does sometimes concentrate the mind. Also, I see Emily Phipson in court, and if Emily has had the chance to counsel him, it may have had its effect. Emily is a no-nonsense member of our Bar, and she will have advised Monty in no uncertain terms that one night in custody is unlikely to be the end of the story – further nights are looming large, as is the prospect of a substantial fine.

As soon as he is brought up, Emily stands.

'Your Honour,' she says, 'I've had the opportunity to speak with Mr Beveridge, and he's had the opportunity to reflect on his outburst yesterday. He instructs me that he very much regrets it. I would ask your Honour to understand that the damage to the statue of John Bonhomme has been a highly emotional matter for Mr Beveridge, and he became angry, particularly in the course of being cross-examined by my learned friend Mr Warnock. I wasn't in court for the cross-examination of course, but Mr Beveridge tells me he considered it to be extremely hostile, and because of that, he lost his temper. He is prepared to apologise, and, your Honour, he assures me that it will be a genuine apology. He asks me to make clear that his reaction yesterday was out of character, and that there will be no repetition.'

She resumes her seat.

'Thank you, Miss Phipson,' I say. 'Mr Beveridge, stand up please. I've heard what Miss Phipson has said. Is that correct?'

'Yes, your Honour,' Beveridge replies quietly. 'I apologise unreservedly to the court and to Miss O'Finn for my behaviour. It was out of character, and it won't happen again.'

I had been thinking of adding a fine to his misery, but Emily has persuaded me that the episode is now closed, and I quickly conclude that the best course is to let it go.

'Very well, Mr Beveridge,' I say. 'The court accepts your apology. You are free to go. However, I am ordering you not to attend court again during this trial, unless you are recalled to give further evidence. And I will add this: you have good reason to be grateful to Miss Phipson for persuading me that I do not need to take the matter further. Do you understand?'

'Yes, sir.'

Today is not going to be particularly interesting in terms of evidence, but it should be less emotive, and less likely to attract comment from the public gallery. Roderick begins with the distinctly unemotive medical evidence arising from Monty Beveridge's stay in hospital. There's no dispute about it, so the medical report is read to the jury. There's nothing new in it. They stitched him up and kept him in for observation overnight, just in case. The only real point of the evidence is to prove that Councillor Beveridge did in fact sustain actual bodily harm, but there's never been any doubt about that – in law, actual bodily harm covers any physical injury, however slight, and Beveridge's injury certainly wasn't slight. The only issue there is whether the blow might have been struck in lawful self-defence.

Next, we hear a number of witness statements read to the jury. The evidence of these witnesses is also undisputed, so there's no need to require them to attend court. Roderick concludes by reading some agreed facts, which mainly concern the monetary value of the statue, the extent of the damage sustained, and what will be required to repair it. The evidence of monetary value is relevant to the jurisdiction of the Crown Court to hear this case – smaller cases are heard in the magistrates' courts – but it is of limited interest to the jury. Roderick may also be planning to ask me to make a compensation order to cover the cost of repairs, if Deirdre is convicted. He may be disappointed. Compensation orders are only made where the amount in question is firmly established or undisputed, and I would be very surprised if that proves to be the case here. At present, they don't have a firm number. John Bonhomme may have to seek redress in his local county court.

As his final witness, Roderick calls the officer in the case, DS Farmer, a pleasant, youngish woman representing the Suffolk constabulary. She gives evidence in a restrained, orderly way. She comes across as a natural diplomat, a trait which has probably been tested to its limits in this case. She took over what must have been a very difficult investigation.

By the time PC Barnett's backup arrived, many of those she would have wanted to interview had disappeared. PC Barnett had focused his attention almost exclusively on Deirdre O'Finn and Monty Beveridge. Most of those still at the scene were either suspects, and thus not obliged to say anything, or witnesses with an axe to grind, either pro- or con-John Bonhomme. There was a serious lack of independent witnesses, who might have given her some kind of objective picture of what had happened. So DS Farmer had to start from scratch, interviewing some of them as witnesses, others as suspects under caution, and putting fragments of evidence together. Somehow, she managed to identify many of those who had been present, and did a remarkable job in recommending who was, or was not, to be cautioned.

Next comes the inevitable. DS Farmer turns to the arrest of Deirdre O'Finn, and her interview under caution at the police station, with her solicitor in attendance. As I've mentioned before, the reading of a defendant's interview, though essential, is never one of the most engrossing parts of a trial. The officer reads the questions put to the suspect, and counsel reads the replies, and any interventions by the defendant's solicitor. Some are better at doing this than others – Roderick and DS Farmer are by no means bad. But with the best will in the world, and even with a transcript to follow, there is always a danger of the jury beginning to drift off. You have to take breaks now and then, to keep everybody sane, particularly with an interview as long as this one.

It goes on and on. Deirdre took full advantage of her opportunity to berate John Bonhomme and Monty Beveridge and his ilk, with numerous references to the European Convention on Human Rights, and the law of modern slavery, though interestingly, without any attempt to go into detail. Occasionally, here and there, such as on the issue of self-defence, she manages to give a few answers relevant to the case. But her answers generally are rambling and repetitive. From her attempts to intervene and keep Deirdre on track, for the most part unsuccessful, you can sense DS Farmer's frustration. Mercifully, when we are about halfway through, it's lunchtime, and we have an extended break. Eventually, mid-afternoon, it finally comes to an end. Kenneth cross-examines DS Farmer briefly, after which Roderick declares the prosecution case to be closed.

Kenneth gets to his feet.

'Your Honour, a point of law arises, which, I anticipate, may take some time. Of course, the jury are not concerned with points of law. Rather than keep them waiting unnecessarily, may I suggest that your Honour release the jury now for the day, and hopefully we will be ready to proceed with them first thing tomorrow morning?'

I've been expecting this, of course, and Kenneth's suggestion is a sensible one: we're going to need some time to resolve the issues he's about to raise. The jury, having sat through a rather tedious day of evidence, are only too glad to escape for the remainder of the afternoon. They fairly bound out of court behind Dawn.

'Your Honour,' Kenneth begins, 'I have a submission of no case to answer with respect to count one, the charge of affray, and count 3, the charge of criminal damage. I do not make any submission on the assault occasioning actual bodily harm, count 2. I accept that the issue of self-defence must be left to the jury.'

I nod. 'Yes, Mr Warnock. If I'm not mistaken, then, you're about to direct my attention to the European Convention on Human Rights and the law of modern slavery.'

Kenneth laughs.

'Your Honour may be forgiven for expecting that,' he replies. 'I'm afraid that, as your Honour may have gleaned from listening to the interview, Miss O'Finn is rather obsessed with the European Convention on Human Rights and the law of modern slavery, although sadly, without the advantage of much actual knowledge or understanding of them. I've tried to talk to her about it, without much success, I'm afraid. But I'm not going to direct your Honour's attention either to human rights or slavery.'

There aren't many barristers who would talk about their clients like that, but I've heard Kenneth do it before, and I've always thought of it as one of his most refreshing traits. I'm sure they've discussed it, and when I glance towards the dock, Deirdre doesn't seem in the least distressed about it. In fact, I think I detect a thin smile.

'In that case, Mr Warnock,' I reply, 'what *are* you going to direct my attention to?'

Kenneth grins, in the enigmatic way he does when he's about to launch one of his more esoteric legal theories.

'Something far more basic,' he replies. 'I propose to direct your Honour's attention to the law of nuisance.'

'Nuisance?'

'Yes, your Honour. As your Honour knows, nuisance is one of the Common Law's oldest causes of action. Nuisance simply means an interference with another's right to use and enjoy his land without such interference. If my neighbour diverts his stream so that it floods my field, or allows his trees to grow so that they encroach on my land, and drop leaves, and prevent me from accessing my fence, he commits a nuisance.'

He pauses, apparently to make sure I'm following – another trait of his, less refreshing. I nod to reassure him.

'It's also well established, your Honour, that the person affected by a nuisance has the remedy of abating the nuisance.

In other words, if he is unable to resolve the matter by discussion, he is entitled to protect his property, and ensure his ability to enjoy his land, by taking direct action.'

'I'm not following, Mr Warnock,' I say. 'No one has been diverting streams or allowing trees to overhang property in this case.'

'No, your Honour. But a nuisance occurs whenever the right to use and enjoy land is affected. In this case, of course, the land is public land, used and enjoyed by the public as a whole rather than one owner, but that doesn't matter. That just means that we have a public nuisance, rather than a private nuisance. The public have the same rights as a private owner, namely, to abate the nuisance if the party causing the nuisance refuses to remove it.'

I stare at Kenneth for some time.

'But what nuisance is there in this case?'

'Your Honour, the inhabitants of Little Brewing, and indeed, the wider public, have the right to use and enjoy the village square. By refusing to remove the statue of John Bonhomme, when he has been unmasked as a slave trader, the village council has interfered with those rights. People today don't want to be identified, or have their village identified, with the slave trade, but they are inevitably reminded of it every time they walk into the square. It's an affront to people of colour in the area, and as such, a source of embarrassment, perhaps even of shame. It is a gross interference with the people's right to use and enjoy the square. It was within the power of the village council to remove the nuisance: they were asked to do so, they were given every opportunity to do so, but they refused. In my submission, Deirdre O'Finn merely did what any member of the public would have been entitled to do – she attempted to abate the nuisance by removing the statue herself. This wasn't an affray, your Honour, it was the exercise of the legal right to abate a nuisance. Miss O'Finn was legally entitled to act as she did.'

Apparently regarding what he has just said as self-evident, Kenneth stops and shows no sign of elaborating further. He may have been expecting me to ask one or two questions, but Roderick takes the silence as his cue to jump in.

'Your Honour,' he begins, 'my learned friend was good enough to apprise me of his argument in general terms this morning before court sat.'

It would have helped if I'd also been on Kenneth's list of those to be apprised – at least to the extent of knowing whether I would be dealing with the European Convention or the law of nuisance – but I've been a judge long enough to know better than to expect notice of such things. Counsel are given to springing arguments on judges without warning, mainly because they are still thinking about them and refining them up to the last moment, and aren't always sure what the final version will look like. I have no right to complain – I was the same when I was at the Bar – and besides, judges shouldn't need notice, should they? As we all know, judges carry the whole canon of law around in their heads.

'The difficulty with my learned friend's argument,' Roderick is telling me, 'is this: a nuisance is something that affects the use and enjoyment of the land in a physical way – as my learned friend's examples of the diverted stream and overhanging branches illustrate very well. A nuisance physically affects the rights of all those entitled to use the land. That's not the case here. Members of the public have full access to the Little Brewing village square today, just as they always have. No one has built a fence around the square, or diverted a stream across it. It's still open to all in exactly the same way it has been for the past two hundred years. My learned friend's submission fails for the simple reason that there is no nuisance, and, therefore, nothing to abate.'

'But if I understand Mr Warnock's submission correctly,' I venture, 'he takes the view that the presence of the statue is a cause of embarrassment or shame for the inhabitants of Little Brewing, and that adversely affects their right to use and enjoy the square. Why isn't that a nuisance?'

'As the evidence in this case shows, your Honour,' Roderick replies, 'that simply isn't the case. Some members of the public, such as Miss O'Finn, may take that view, but if you go down to the Cat and Fiddle and talk to Councillor Beveridge and the other members of the Defence League, they feel no embarrassment or shame at all. For them, their use and enjoyment of the square is the same today as it has always been – with the possible exception of feeling obliged to spend more time there, to defend the statue. In other words, my learned friend's nuisance is all in the mind. By the same token, if the village council had voted to take the statue down, would he then argue that the Defence League's enjoyment of the square had been affected? It doesn't work: the presence of the statue doesn't affect the use and enjoyment of the square as such; it's no different from Trafalgar Square.'

I stare at him. 'Trafalgar Square?'

'Yes, your Honour. When they were trying to work out what to put on the fourth plinth in Trafalgar Square, various things claimed to be works of art appeared for a time, and were then replaced. It caused endless controversy, of course, but people still used and enjoyed Trafalgar Square as usual. And, your Honour, this case illustrates perfectly why my learned friend's argument not only doesn't work, but is downright dangerous. If the public has a right to abate a nuisance, that right must be exercised by the public as a whole. You can't have individuals or groups claiming to act in the name of the public. If you allow that, you're going to have exactly what happened in this case – an affray caused by the so-called abatement being resisted by members of the public who disagree. It's a recipe for breaches of the peace and civil disorder.'

I look over to Kenneth to see whether he wants to reply, but he seems confident of having made his point. I've learned over the years, that, even if you feel fairly sure of your decision, there's a lot to be said for allowing it to percolate around the brain overnight, or at least over lunch, if time permits. It tends to make your delivery of the ruling somewhat more coherent. Besides, in some cases, you need to take a second look, or even a third look at it, because legal submissions can sometimes appear deceptively simple, when in fact, they're hiding a wealth of complexities counsel may not have fully explored. This one seems very straightforward – sufficiently so to be suspicious. I have time in this case, and it makes sense to take full advantage of it.

'I'm not going to rule on your submission this afternoon, Mr Warnock,' I say. 'I want to make sure I do it justice. I want to think about it overnight.'

Kenneth positively beams. 'As your Honour pleases. I'm much obliged.'

The law of nuisance isn't the only subject I have to worry about this afternoon. There is another demon at my door, and the time has come to confront it. At just after four, I steel myself and make my way to Hubert's chambers. It seems I'm just in time – he's gathering his things together with the air of a man in haste.

'Oh hello, Charlie,' he says on seeing me at his door. 'I was just on my way out.'

'Yes, so I see,' I reply. 'I don't want to keep you, Hubert, but I do need a quick word.'

With obvious reluctance, he sits down on his sofa, and waves me into a chair.

'I can't stay long,' he says. 'I promised Roger a quick martini before he sets out for dinner with you and your good lady wife.' He pauses before adding, 'And if it's about your judgment, I don't want to talk about it. I said all I intend to say at lunch.'

'In the first place, Hubert,' I reply, 'it wasn't *my* judgment. True, I delivered it, but it was the judgment of the Court, which consists of three judges, all of whom agreed that we had no choice but to allow the appeal.'

'In that case,' he retorts, 'why didn't you get one of the others to deliver it? For God's sake, Charlie, you're my RJ.'

I nod. 'I tried, Hubert. I raised that point with Stephen Gulivant, but he insisted. He seems to think it's an experience everyone should have, to allow an appeal from a judge they know – some kind of rite of passage for new judges sitting in the Court of Appeal.'

'Rite of passage? Bollocks. Oh, come on, Charlie. He was just having a laugh behind your back.'

'He was presiding, Hubert. I was in no position to refuse.' I pause for some time. 'And you might think about this: I did do my best to keep my criticism of you as moderate as I could. That might not have been the case if one of the others had taken charge of it.'

There is a long silence.

'Well, it's ancient history now,' Hubert ventures eventually. 'I'm sure I'll get over it. Onwards and upwards.'

'It's not quite that simple, Hubert,' I say. 'The Grey Smoothies are taking an interest in the case. I've had a visitation from Jeremy Bagnall.'

'Jeremy Bagnall? What the hell has it got to do with Jeremy bloody Bagnall?'

'They think you're past your sell-by date,' I reply. 'They're wondering whether you've been experiencing confusion in other cases. They've asked me to report to them, following which they're going to ask Stephen Gulivant to have a word with you.'

'Have a word with me?'

'In all probability, to talk you into retiring in the near future.'

Hubert stands, abruptly, walks towards the window and peers outside. He is silent for some time.

'Well, that's not going to happen,' he says defiantly.

'It may be better than the alternative,' I point out.

Hubert returns slowly to the sofa.

'All right. Look, Charlie, perhaps I did lose the plot a bit in that one case. But I wasn't the only one. Those bloody Bradley people were deliberately muddying the waters. After they were arrested, they did their best to confuse the police, and they succeeded. The identification procedures were a mess. The whole investigation was a mess. Even the prosecution weren't sure what had happened.'

'Perhaps so, Hubert, but…'

'Apart from that, I've been perfectly fine in court. You can ask anybody.'

'I have,' I reply as gently as I can. 'I asked Piers Drayford and Emily Phipson. What do you think they had to say?'

He doesn't reply.

'And yesterday, I was hearing about your sudden interest in Winchester. What on earth is all that about?'

'Who told you about that?' he asks, in an outraged tone of voice. 'That's confidential. I'll…'

'Their list officer called Stella,' I say. 'She didn't know what to do. Hubert, you know as well as I do that you can't just go and sit at some court on another circuit and expect nobody to notice. What on earth were you thinking?'

'I'm not going to retire until it's my time,' he insists, 'which is still some time away.'

'It's just under two years away,' I reply. 'The Grey Smoothies have finally worked it out.'

There is a long silence.

'There must be something we can do about this nonsense,' he says, eventually. But he sounds deflated.

'I don't know,' I say. 'I'm thinking about it. I'll need to offer the Grey Smoothies some assurance that, if they do leave you *en poste*, you're not going to go completely off the rails. I'm not sure yet how I'm going to do that. But Hubert, if I do find a way and I stick my neck out, you have to work with me. I can't have nonsense like making overtures to other courts behind my back.'

He nods. 'Understood.'

He stands and returns to his spot at the window.

'I'm a good judge, Charlie,' he says.

'Yes, you are,' I reply. And then, for no reason I can account for, I suddenly add: 'Tell me: what was the best piece of judging you ever saw during your career?' As soon as the words have left my mouth I'm thinking, that's a bloody silly question to ask. How would I answer it? I'd have to think for hours. But to my amazement, he doesn't hesitate for a moment.

'I remember it clearly, Charlie,' he replies, 'as if it were yesterday. It was what made me want to become a judge one day, if I could. I wasn't long out of pupillage. I'd only just been taken on in chambers. And one morning, I'm sitting at my desk working on some opinion or other, when my clerk, Albert, rushes in. He's in a total panic. My former pupil-master, Jack Hornby, has had a case come into the list for two o'clock in the Court of Protection. But Jack's doing a case down in Brighton, and he's not going to be back by two o'clock. Albert's got nobody else available, so he's talked the solicitors into letting me do it.'

I can't resist a smile. 'The Court of Protection? That's a bit rarefied, isn't it? I'm not even sure what goes on there.'

'Jack had a number of cases in protection while I was his pupil,' Hubert replies, 'so I wasn't entirely in the dark. But, as you can imagine, it was a bit daunting.'

'It would probably have made me leave the Bar there and then.'

'So, after lunch, I make my way to court. My brief's not very helpful. All it tells me is that my client, "the patient", is about seventy years old, his family think he's lost touch with reality, and they've brought proceedings to take charge of his money and other assets, which are apparently quite substantial. So, I try to interview my client. I'm asking him questions, but he's not answering. Instead, he's standing there, in the middle of the conference room, eyes closed, and waving his arms around – as though he's conducting a symphony orchestra. When the case is called on, I still haven't got a word out of him.'

'It sounds like a nightmare,' I say.

'Anyway, we've been listed in front of Mr Justice Warby, a chancery judge I don't know at all. He calls on my opponent, representing the family, who tells him he's applying for a guardianship order, and roughly what the case is about. During which time, my client is standing in the middle of the courtroom, still conducting his imaginary orchestra. Then, I assume, it's my turn.'

He suddenly turns to face me directly.

'But instead of calling on me, Warby ignores me completely, steps down from the bench, walks across the courtroom and stands right in front of my client. "I'm terribly sorry," he says, "but I've been trying to place that piece you've been conducting. It sounds very familiar, but I can't quite place it. Would you mind refreshing my memory?" And bugger me,

Charlie, the client actually opens his eyes, and speaks. He says: "It's the Jupiter, of course – Wolfgang Amadeus Mozart, Symphony number 41 in C major." "Of course," Warby replies, "how silly of me. I should have recognised it. Look, I hope you won't mind my saying this, but I thought you took the second movement a bit on the quick side."'

I can't help laughing out loud.

'So, the client says: "Did you really? That's strange. I'm usually criticised for taking it too slowly. But, you know, it is *andante cantabile,* so you have to be careful not to let them rush it – the strings, in particular, tend to want to go too fast." "No," Warby says, "What you did was interesting. I thought it brought out the rhythm of the movement very nicely."'

'Amazing,' I say.

'And you know what, Charlie? Warby and my client then have a perfectly lucid conversation for about twenty minutes, during which time he explains to the judge that his family have been trying for years to get control of his assets, and asks him not to let them get away with it. Warby then denies the application for guardianship pending a full evidential hearing. What happened after that, I don't remember – the case went on for ages, and Jack dealt with it. But I've never forgotten what Warby did. And, as I say, it was what made me want to become a judge. I never had the brains for the High Court bench, of course, but still…'

I leave quietly, surreptitiously depositing the Reverent Mrs Walden's flyer for her aging course on Hubert's desk.

* * *

Wednesday evening
Roger arrives for dinner exactly on time, bearing a dozen mixed red and white roses, and a couple of bottles of a very

decent looking Margaux, which instantly endears him to the Reverend Mrs Walden and enhances my already high opinion of him. Over the Reverend Mrs Walden's classic vegetarian lasagne, a spinach salad, and a home-made chocolate mousse invented specially for the occasion, we all three chat like old friends. Given that High Sheriffs hold office for a year only, it had never occurred to me that they would have any real cache of war stories – though if Roger's experience on his first morning at Bermondsey is in any way typical, they should certainly have one or two worthwhile tales to tell. Roger certainly does. Some are drawn from the distinguished naval career he enjoyed before his retirement – if that's the right word, in his case – but many are the fruit of his time as High Sheriff, which is now almost two thirds over. He tells them modestly, with a quiet, self-deprecating humour, and all in all he proves to be an utterly charming guest.

While the Reverend Mrs Walden is in the kitchen, making coffee at the end of the meal, he suddenly leans across the table.

'Actually, Charles,' he says, 'I hope I'm not out of line, but I did want to ask you something, if I may.'

'Of course,' I reply.

'I don't quite know how to put it. Tell me if it's none of my business, but… is Hubert in trouble?'

'Well, I…'

'It's just that… well, I had dinner with him at the Garrick yesterday evening, and he…'

I smile. 'I'm sure he explained to you what a terrible resident judge I am, and how I gave a monstrously unfair judgment against him in the Court of Appeal.'

Roger returns the smile. 'At great length – through two and a half courses, if I recall rightly.' We both laugh. 'But as I say, I probably shouldn't be asking you.'

'No,' I reply. 'Actually, Roger, any insight you may have would be very much appreciated, as a matter of fact. Hubert became very confused during the case in question. It was a difficult case, three defendants and serious issues of identification. It would have been a challenge for any judge. But unfortunately, having got himself confused, he wouldn't let counsel enlighten him, and he ended up giving the jury faulty directions – and probably getting them just as confused as he was. The problem is that the powers that be are now thinking that perhaps it's time for him to retire. You know Hubert, so you probably know that any talk of retirement is like a red rag to a bull.'

He nods. 'That's what he's afraid of, Charles. He sees the sword of Damocles hanging over his head, and he's worried that it's about to fall…'

The Reverend Mrs Walden returns with coffee, and he stops abruptly.

'There's no need to hold back on Clara's account,' I assure him. 'She knows all about Hubert's situation.'

Clara sees the direction of travel of the conversation instantly.

'In my pastoral capacity,' she explains, 'he came to me after the death of his wife.'

Roger nods. 'Of course. I know losing her was very difficult for him.'

'It devastated him,' she replies. 'He's still not really over it.'

She pours the coffee for us all, and I produce my prized bottle of Martell VSOP cognac to go with it.

'Is there anything you can do for him?' Roger asks.

'I'm not sure. If it wasn't for this, Hubert would be expected to retire in about two years' time. But the civil servants are worried that he could mess up a lot of other cases in that time. I'm trying to think of a compromise solution everyone could live with, but so far, it's eluding me. If you have any thoughts, I'd be grateful.'

Roger takes a deep draft of his cognac. 'Well, what occurs to me,' he replies, 'is that it would help if you could buy him some time.'

'I'm not sure I follow...'

'Hubert's greatest fear is that he will have to retire immediately. You have to understand that, since his wife died, the court and the Garrick have been the two mainstays of his life. He needs time to adjust – to think about what his life will be like with one of the mainstays gone. For all his bluster, Charles, Hubert is a realist. He knows he's going to have to retire at some point, if only because of age. But it's too soon – especially if it will always be associated in people's mind with this case.'

'But if we could fend it off for some time...?'

'My impression is that, if you can buy him some time, time to restructure his life in his mind, there would be less resistance than you might expect when the inevitable day comes.'

'That makes sense to me, Charlie,' the Reverend Mrs Walden says.

I nod. 'It would help if he came to see you again, wouldn't it?'

'It might. If he asks for help, it might make it easier. But actually, Hubert is a lot more resilient than we give him credit for. With enough time, he'll get there anyway.'

'I agree,' Roger says.

* * *

Thursday morning

The morning does not begin auspiciously. Before I can even take the lid off my latte, Stella presents herself in my chambers, wearing her best Titanic look, to inform me that Sir Jeremy Bagnall's secretary has been on the phone to her. It seems that Sir Jeremy wants a conference at my earliest convenience, with Sir Jeremy himself, and Stephen Gulivant, to discuss an important administrative matter. He was also inquiring into the progress of my report. So, no prizes for guessing what that's about. I may not be able to kick the ball as far down the road as I'd hoped. But I can't worry about that immediately. I have legal issues to grapple with. I ask Stella to call his office back, explain to them that I'm in the middle of a very difficult case – I know Jeremy is aware of the Suffolk saga – and promise we will arrange a conference as soon as we can.

And then, as I'm settling down to enjoy my morning latte while I ponder the mysteries of the law of nuisance, with the aid of an out-of-date treatise on tort law I unearthed in the library, my phone rings. It's Philip Barth, my opposite number at Winchester Crown Court. His list officer will have told him what's going on, and he seems to find it all rather humorous.

'I've known Hubert for years, Charlie,' he begins. 'He's always marched to the beat of a different drummer, shall we say, but what on earth is going on at Bermondsey?'

'Between the two of us?'

'Yes, of course.'

'They're saying Hubert is losing the plot.'

Philip laughs. 'Oh, come on, Charlie, Hubert has his own plot, always has. He's never bothered trying to follow ours. He's one of the last great eccentrics of our profession, perhaps *the* last, and I've always said that we will all be the poorer when he finally hangs his hat up.'

'It's not that simple, Philip,' I reply. 'I'm afraid there is some evidence to back it up, and it's all moving rather quickly.'

He doesn't respond immediately. 'I read your judgment in the Court of Appeal, of course,' he says. 'But are you saying that wasn't just a one-off? I mean, let's be honest, we all have our bad days at the office, don't we? For God's sake, I got reversed a couple of months ago for making a complete pig's ear of my direction on evidence of bad character. It happens to us all once in a while.'

'It's not a one-off, Philip,' I reply, 'and what's worse is that I think Hubert himself is aware that there may be a problem. He may be feeling desperate about it. Why else would he try to set up an arrangement to sit with you on the QT?'

'Yes, well, we're all a bit mystified,' Philip admits. 'Obviously, he could never get away with a caper like that.'

'Exactly, Philip. It's not rational. That's what I'm trying to deal with.'

'What can I do to help?' Philip asks, after a silence.

'Well, the last thing I want is to add to his problems – or mine. I'm sure your first instinct is to tell your presider all about it, and put him in touch with mine. But if you could at least hold off on that for a short time, it might make all the difference. I have a feeling that, if I can just have a little time, we may be able to sort it out.'

'I can do that, Charlie,' Philip replies. 'The presiders have enough to do as it is, and there's no urgency. I've told Barbara not to reply to Hubert, and I will ask her not to talk about it to anyone else. I'm sure we can hold the fort here while you work it out at your end.'

'Thank you, Philip,' I say.

'So, do you really think Hubert will have to retire at long last? I mean, his retirement, or not, has been an ongoing saga for years, not to mention a source of great entertainment for us all.'

'I'm afraid so.'

'Well, that will be the end of an era,' he says. 'We shall not see his like again.'

*

'The defendant applies to me to withdraw counts one and three from the jury, on the ground that there is no case to answer,' I begin, once court has been assembled, without the jury. 'It is conceded that, in relation to count two, the question of self-defence must be left to the jury to decide.

'Mr Warnock submits that, even if Miss O'Finn committed acts which might otherwise amount to causing an affray and criminal damage, she cannot be convicted of those offences in this case because she was acting lawfully to abate a public nuisance. This case concerns the presence, in the village square in the Suffolk village of Little Brewing, of a statue of the local poet, John Bonhomme. The statue has been in exactly the same place ever since it was commissioned, more than two hundred years ago. But recently, the subject of the statue, Mr Bonhomme, has come under renewed scrutiny as a result of some research carried out by the sixth form at a nearby girls' school, St Cecilia's. The research was undertaken on the instructions of the school's headmistress, the defendant, Deirdre O'Finn.

'According to the school's head girl, April Collins, who conducted some of the research and who gave evidence before the jury, their inquiries revealed that before settling in Little Brewing, Mr Bonhomme had resided in Bermuda and St Kitts, and while there, had been active in and had made a considerable amount of money from the slave trade. There was also a suggestion that he had written disparagingly about the idea of providing education to women, apparently on the ground that it would serve only to distract them from their matrimonial and familial duties, though I'm not sure how much that adds to the issue now before me. It is not necessary for me to make any finding, and I expressly do not make any finding, about whether or not Mr Bonhomme was in fact involved in the slave trade, or, if he was, to what extent. Suffice it to say, that Miss Collins's evidence provides a clear basis for someone to believe that he had some such involvement, and that is sufficient for present purposes.

'Mr Warnock's submission is based on the proposition that the continued presence of Mr Bonhomme's statue in the square, now that there is good reason to believe he may have been a slave trader, constitutes a public nuisance. The public's right to use and enjoy the space of the square, the argument goes, has been adversely affected because the public will be embarrassed or ashamed to have to walk past the statue of a slave trader. The statue is a particular affront, Mr Warnock suggests, to people of colour, and perhaps also to women generally. It is an interesting question whether or not the case would be different if the statue had been commissioned now, with that information being generally available. In that case, the installation of the statue would be in question, rather than simply the decision to leave it where it has been for two hundred years. It was not suggested in argument that the position would be different in that case, but it seems to me that it might have some bearing on the argument.

'Mr Warnock goes on to argue that, if he is right about the existence of a public nuisance, any member of the public would be entitled to abate the nuisance by removing the statue if the relevant authority refuses to do so. That latter condition is certainly satisfied. There is no dispute that Miss O'Finn requested the village council, which is responsible for such matters, to remove the statue, but after a debate and a vote, the Council declined to do so. The remaining question is whether or not Miss O'Finn was entitled to abate the nuisance as a member of the public affected by it.

'Mr Warnock submits that any member of the public may exercise the right to abate a nuisance affecting public land.

Mr Lofthouse, on the other hand, submits that Mr Warnock cannot be right about that. He points out firstly, that nuisance must involve some physical interference with the use and enjoyment of the land, and that there is no such interference here. He further points out that many members of the public, far from feeling any embarrassment or shame when using and enjoying the square, are firmly of the view that the statue of John Bonhomme should remain in place. So much is clear from the evidence in this case. The evidence of Councillor Beveridge and the Reverend Mr Pratt, dealing with the formation of the John Bonhomme Defence League, amply illustrates the point. Indeed, the evidence shows that the affray charged in count one occurred specifically as a result of the very obvious differences of opinion within the Little Brewing community. Mr Lofthouse adds that, if Mr Warnock's submission does in fact represent the law, it would be very dangerous, because it would virtually guarantee breaches of the peace, and perhaps serious disorder in cases such as this.

'It seems to me that Mr Lofthouse must be right. Allowing that abatement may be a remedy for nuisance, the first point is that nuisance must be a physical interference with the use and enjoyment of the land. As I have already said, if it were proposed to install a statue of Mr Bonhomme for the first time now, it is possible that the result might be different. But no physical change has been made to the square at all – indeed, Miss O'Finn's whole complaint is not one of physical interference, but of the absence of physical interference. Any discomfort felt by someone using the square is, it seems to me, in that person's mind, and not in the physical appearance of the square, which has remained essentially the same for more than two hundred years.

'Mr Lofthouse is also correct, in my view, in submitting that even if there were a nuisance, and even if abatement were an appropriate remedy in the absence of action by the relevant authority, Miss O'Finn cannot be heard to claim that she was acting on behalf of the public when it is abundantly clear that a very significant section of the local population – indeed, for all we know, it may be the majority – are firmly in favour of the statue remaining in place, indicating that their enjoyment of the square is not in any way diminished.

'For these reasons, it is my view that there is a case to answer in respect of counts one and three, and I shall leave those counts to the jury accordingly.'

Kenneth stands immediately.

'In the light of your Honour's ruling, may the jury be brought down to court, and may count three be put to Miss O'Finn again?'

Of course, Kenneth is experienced enough to advise his client that, in the absence of the claim of abating a nuisance, there is no possible defence to the charge of criminal damage. He could continue in the hope of getting some kind of sympathy verdict. But Kenneth isn't the kind of advocate to pin his client's hopes on that, and he has wisely suggested that she avail herself of whatever credit I and the jury may give her for saving the court's time, once I ruled against her legal defence. The interesting thing is that he isn't asking for count one to be put again. Apparently, he still has some ingenious answer up his sleeve to the charge of affray.

When the jury are in place, I explain to them what has happened, and what is about to happen.

'Please stand, Miss O'Finn.' Carol says. 'Miss O'Finn, in count three of the indictment, you are charged with criminal damage. The particulars of the offence are that you, on or about the 15th day of March, without lawful excuse, damaged a statue valued in excess of £20,000, belonging to the Little Brewing Village Council, intending to damage the said statue, or being reckless as to whether the said statue would be damaged. How say you: are you guilty or not guilty?'

'Guilty,' Deirdre replies quietly.

This provokes the first serious reactions from the public gallery since the advent of the shrieval sword. By now, there are only four determined spectators on each side, but they have, it seems, lost none of their partisan attachments, and for some reason they see the defendant's change of plea on count three as a pivotal moment in the trial.

'Send her down now, Judge,' a member of one faction shouts. 'What are you waiting for? She belongs inside. Fucking with our statue? Pervert bitch.'

'Try that trans stuff with the lads in prison and see what happens to you,' another adds.

Obviously, the other side is not going to allow this to pass without challenge.

'She's been framed. It's Beveridge and his crew who should be going inside.'

'No platform for slavery in Suffolk! Free the Little Brewing martyr!'

This latter demand becomes the theme of a brief chant. But there aren't enough of them for a credible chant, and it soon dies away. In fact, neither protest looks like lasting long. I'm pleased to see, out of the corner of my eye, that the jury is no longer disturbed, if they ever were, by such outbursts. They are sitting calmly in the jury box, one or two of them smiling, enjoying the show. Roger, on the other hand, is far from calm. He is on his feet, his trusty Excalibur in hand, and he is pointing it in a distinctly threatening manner in the direction of the public gallery.

'It's all right, Roger,' I say quietly, putting a hand on his arm to invite him to sit back down, which, with obvious reluctance, he eventually does. 'I think the court staff have this one covered.'

I order the public gallery to be cleared, which Dawn accomplishes single-handedly by the simple expedient of approaching the public gallery and pointing to the door of the court while wearing her best frown.

'Members of the jury,' I say once calm has been restored. 'You have heard Miss O'Finn plead guilty to count three in open court, having had the benefit of legal advice from her counsel and solicitor, and in the light of that change of plea, you may think that the only possible verdict you can return on count three is one of guilty. So, rather than take up any more of your time, and the court's time, on that count, I'm going to ask you to return that verdict now. If the gentleman closest to me in the front row would kindly act as your foreman, just for this purpose?'

It's a strange procedure for the judge, in effect, to invite the jury to return a verdict of guilty. Juries always look surprised. But, of course, if I'd gone with Kenneth on his submission, I would now be directing them to return a verdict of not guilty. It would be an awkward situation if a jury ever declined to follow the direction, but mercifully, they seem to understand, in both cases, why it is the right thing to do. Their *ad hoc* foreman duly declares, in response to Carol's questions, that they do find the defendant guilty on count three, and that guilty is the verdict of them all.

'My name is Deirdre O'Finn.'

For her appearance in the witness box this morning, the defendant has chosen a black top, emblazoned across the chest in white with the words 'Trans Pride' and underneath, 'Deirdre: She/Her/Hers.'

'Miss O'Finn,' Kenneth begins, 'I think you originally hail from Ireland, is that right?'

'From Cork, yes, but I've lived and worked in this country for the past ten years.'

'What is your profession?'

'I am a school teacher.'

'What post do you hold currently?'

'I am the headmistress of St Cecilia's Academy for the Daughters of Gentlefolk, just outside Little Brewing.' She pauses. 'But I'm suspended pending the outcome of the trial.'

I doubt I'm alone in court in thinking that the suspension probably became permanent about five minutes ago.

'The jury haven't heard very much about St Cecilia's,' Kenneth continues. 'Tell the jury what kind of school it is.'

'It's one of the leading residential schools for girls in the country,' Deirdre replies. 'We take all levels, from prep school, to an upper sixth form. The school was founded in 1875 by a wealthy philanthropist. It's always had an outstanding academic record. Our girls regularly gain places at Oxford and Cambridge, and a number of prestigious universities abroad. Of course, the fees are on the high side, but the parents don't seem to mind, as long as we keep up our standards.'

Kenneth pauses. 'Miss O'Finn, the court has heard that you are a trans woman – in other words, you were born a man – and, I think, given the name of Desmond – but you have transitioned to become a woman: is that right?'

'That is correct,' she replies. Suddenly, she turns to me. 'And, if I may, your Honour, I would like to say how much I appreciate the way I've been treated by the court staff, who have gone out of their way to be helpful and accommodate me while I'm at court.'

'I'm very pleased to hear that, Miss O'Finn,' I reply. 'I will pass your comment on to the court manager.'

Something about her vote of thanks makes me look at her closely, and what I see is remarkable. Since she started to give evidence there has been a real change in Deirdre's demeanour. The defensiveness and nervousness are gone. She seems confident, even authoritative, as if she feels she's now back in her own element, rather than the court's. The slogan-shouting activist has disappeared and has been replaced by a teacher, and a scholar.

'Miss O'Finn,' Kenneth resumes, 'what was the reaction among the parents to your appointment as headmistress at Cecilia's as a trans woman?'

'There were a few who complained about it,' Deirdre replies. 'Well, there always are, aren't there? You could appoint Dorothy Hodgkin headmistress and some parents still wouldn't be satisfied. But most of them were fine with me. Only two or three actually pulled their daughters out of the school. The governors have been wonderful. They promised to support me, come what may. They believe it's about time the school came to terms with the twenty-first century.'

'Was there anything specific the governors encouraged when they appointed you?'

'Yes. During my interview, I had expressed the view, quite strongly, that the one thing St Cecilia's was failing to do was to develop the pupils' sense of independence and capacity for critical thought. They needed more guidance in forming their own opinions and having confidence in expressing them. The governors agreed with me, and they have encouraged me to develop those strengths in the girls.'

'How do you go about doing that?'

'I held a staff meeting shortly after I arrived, and explained to the staff what I wanted to achieve. You can encourage independence of thought regardless of what you're teaching, so I asked them all to take that on board.' She smiles. 'Some of the older members of staff, who've been at the school for eons, turned their noses up, and pretended not to understand what

I was talking about. But most of them responded positively, especially the younger ones.'

'What did you do in relation to your own classes?' Kenneth asks. 'Incidentally, what are your subjects?'

'English and social studies. One thing I did was to create a new social studies class, for the sixth forms, which I made compulsory. It took the form of supervised research, because research is another skill we don't focus on enough, but when they get to university it's a skill they really need.'

'Before I ask you more about that, Miss O'Finn,' Kenneth says, 'tell the jury this: you were accepted at the school, but how were you received in the village of Little Brewing?'

'I think the answer to that is clear from what we've seen during this trial,' she replies. 'Let's just say I failed the Cat and Fiddle test.'

The jury laugh out loud, and several are nodding.

'Would it be fair to say that you encountered hostility because of your being a trans woman?'

'Yes, that would be fair to say.'

'What was the first research project you assigned to the new social studies class?'

'Well, I was trying to find something close to home, something they would be familiar with, and I wanted to see whether they could challenge what they'd been told about it. And one day, I was walking through the village square, and I found myself staring up at the statue of John Bonhomme, and suddenly, it came to me. John Bonhomme was a local hero – all the girls knew who he was, and the chances were they'd all bought the conventional Little Brewing back story.'

'Did you know, when you assigned the sixth form the research on Bonhomme, that he had a history in the slave trade?'

She laughs. 'No. I had no idea. That was gold dust, a gift from the gods. You know, I thought there must be some skeleton in his closet. English is my subject, so I was interested in him as a poet, and I'd already read enough to know about his views on women, specifically his views on the education of women. I fully expected the girls to find that material, and I thought that in itself would be enough to wind them up. But when they found the trail to the slave trade, I couldn't believe it.'

'How did that progress to the idea of having the statue removed?'

'Well, when we realised that this local hero was a slave trader, all the girls were pretty incensed – some more than others, but it's fair to say that we were all shocked. And actually, it was one of the girls – I can't remember who, now, and it may be that it was more than one – who came up with the idea of asking the village council to remove the statue from the square. I agreed immediately.'

'How did you yourself feel about what the girls had discovered?'

She nods quietly for some time. 'I was very angry. When you're trans, you think differently about a lot of things, because of the discrimination you encounter every day yourself. I know a lot of people would say, "Why should we care about what went on in the eighteenth century? Those were different times." But, if you suffer discrimination yourself, you know that the times today aren't all that different. There are different kinds of abuse now, but they're still abuse, and you take it personally, because you're a victim of abuse too.'

'How did that affect your attitude to the statue?'

'I decided in my own mind that the statue had to go, one way or the other. We would start with the village council, as the girls had suggested, because that was the easiest way, and after all, it was their statue, so it was their responsibility. So, I contacted Councillor Meggs, who I'd been told might be sympathetic, and explained the situation to her, and she arranged the vote. But as we know, it went against us.'

'Miss O'Finn,' Kenneth says, 'when you say that the statue had to go, one way or the other, I think we all understand what you mean. But I want to ask you this: did you put any of your pupils under any pressure to participate in a forcible removal of the statue?'

'No, I certainly did not. After the vote, I explained to them what I intended to do, and why, and I said that if any of them felt strongly and wanted to join me, they would be welcome. But I explained the dangers, including Beveridge's so-called Defence League, and I told them I expected them to ask their parents' permission before doing anything of that kind. In the end, three or four of the more senior girls said they wanted to come with me, but most of them didn't. I told them it didn't matter to me, as long as they thought it through for themselves.'

Kenneth pauses to consult his notes.

'Well, let me turn to the events of 15 March. Was that the date you chose to try to take down the statue?'

'Yes. I didn't want to let the grass grow after the vote in the village council. I wanted it to be fresh in everyone's minds that the council had passed on the opportunity to do the right thing. And they were already trying to put the frighteners on me. I'd already had the village bobby calling round to warn me off, lecturing me about all the possible offences I would be committing if I as much as laid a finger on John Bonhomme. He wasn't interested in anything I had to say about having a right to take action myself – that wasn't on his radar at all. So, I could see the way the wind was blowing – there was no point in delaying it.'

'Miss O'Finn, the jury has heard evidence that in the early evening of 15 March, there was a gathering of people in the village square, perhaps twenty or more, in addition to you and the pupils you had with you. Do you know who those people were?'

'I didn't know all of them. But I'd had quite a few messages of support after the vote, mainly from people outside the village who'd heard what was going on. I let those people know what I was planning. I said I could use some help and they would be welcome to come along and join in if they had a mind to.'

'The jury also heard evidence that you provided those with you with hammers and lacrosse sticks. Is that right?'

'Yes. The hammers were only for use in destroying the statue. The lacrosse sticks were in case they were needed for self-defence. Beveridge and his mob were always tooled up to the teeth when they were protecting the statue, and that's what we were expecting. We had no intention of being the first to use force, but we had to have some way of defending ourselves.'

'Miss O'Finn, I think you agree that you and those supporting you made the first move – you advanced towards the statue: is that right?'

'Yes, that's correct. But I would like to point out that before advancing, we did call on Beveridge and his mob to get out of the way and let us take the statue down.'

'Do you recall the language you used to say that?'

'Not exactly. It was something to the effect of, "stand aside and let John Bonhomme get what's coming to him." But I don't recall my exact words.'

'Did Councillor Beveridge respond to that?'

'Yes, he did. Again, I don't recall his exact words, but it was a combination of insults – I was a pervert, and I should fuck off back to Ireland – and defiance – if I wanted the statue I should come and fucking get it, and see what fucking happens. And as he said whatever he said, he was waving his cricket bat at me.'

'What happened then?

'I called out to those of us who wanted the statue gone that it was time to act. We advanced on the statue with the intention of achieving our objective.'

'Were you successful?'

'Not entirely. We did succeed in doing considerable damage to the statue, but we were unable to remove it. I would like to say that, if Beveridge and his mob had allowed us to remove it, there would have been no need to damage it. We were quite happy for it to be put on display somewhere else, with an explanation about Bonhomme. We just wanted it off the square.'

'Why were you unable to remove the statue?'

'As I said, Beveridge and his crew were doing their best to stop us. Fighting broke out, and although we outnumbered them, they were able to stop us removing the statue long enough for the police reinforcements to arrive.'

'Miss O'Finn, the jury has heard that, during the fracas, you struck Councillor Beveridge over the head with your lacrosse stick. Is that right?'

'Yes.'

'Tell his Honour and the jury why you did that.'

'I had no choice. Beveridge was abusing me verbally in the way I've already indicated. He also kept threatening me with violence. At one point, he even said he would kill me – well, actually, to quote his exact words, he would "fucking do for me", because I was "useless fucking Paddy bog scum". Shortly after that, he raised the cricket bat above his head and shouted, "you're fucking history". It was obvious that he intended to hit me with the bat. I believed I had no choice but to hit him before he could hit me.'

'What, specifically, did you believe might happen if Councillor Beveridge hit you with his cricket bat?'

'I believed that I could have suffered a very serious injury, perhaps even a fatal injury.'

'Miss O'Finn, the jury has heard that Councillor Beveridge called an ambulance and that he was taken to hospital, and that while he was sitting on the ground, you attacked the statue, rather than rendering him any assistance. What do you say about that?'

She nods. 'With the benefit of hindsight, I wish I had done some things differently. At the time I didn't realise that he was seriously injured. It's true, he was sitting on the ground, but he was conscious and he was speaking on his phone, so I admit I did take advantage of his being out of action, which gave me a clear run at John Bonhomme.'

'The jury has also heard that you believed that you were legally entitled to remove the statue by force, by virtue of the European Convention on Human Rights, or the law of modern slavery...'

She smiles. 'You put me right on the law, Mr Warnock, so...'

They share a laugh.

'I did. But leaving aside the precise legal reasons, did you believe then that you had a legal right to remove the statue?'

'Yes, I did.'

'You've mentioned that you feel you might have done certain things differently with the benefit of hindsight. Has hindsight changed your belief about your right to remove the statue of John Bonhomme?'

'No. I accept what you told me about the law.' She pauses. 'But even if the law doesn't help me, I still believe I have a moral right, or even a moral obligation to do whatever I can to prevent women and people of colour being offended and insulted every time they walk across the square in Little Brewing.'

'Do you regret what you did?' Kenneth asks.

'No, I do not.'

Kenneth quietly resumes his seat.

'Miss O'Finn,' Roderick begins, 'you told the jury that PC Barnett had tried to "put the frighteners" on you.'

'That's exactly what he did.'

'Well, is another possible interpretation that he was simply trying to warn you that you were in danger of breaking the law?'

'That's not the way it came across. You had to be there.'

'But you'd made it clear publicly, hadn't you, that you intended to remove the statue of John Bonhomme by any means you could – including by force if necessary?'

'Yes. That's true.'

'Would you not agree, Miss O'Finn, that if a police officer has information that activities are being planned that are likely to lead to violence, he has a duty to do what he can to discourage those activities?'

'In general, yes, I would agree.'

'And would you also agree that the most obvious way for the officer to do that is to talk to those involved, point out that they may be breaking the law if they go ahead with their plans, and do his best to encourage them to rethink their plans?'

'I suppose so, yes.'

'PC Barnett warned you about two offences in particular, didn't he, causing an affray, and criminal damage?'

'He did mention those offences, yes.'

'You ignored his advice, and now you're charged with those very offences in this indictment, aren't you?'

'Yes.'

'On the evening of 15 March, Miss O'Finn, did you give the

signal for your supporters to join you in advancing towards the statue of John Bonhomme?'

'Yes, I did.'

'Those supporters including some girls from St Cecilia's school, wearing their school uniforms?'

'The girls who were there with me came of their own volition.'

'These were girls of fifteen, sixteen years of age entrusted to your care as headmistress by their parents: yes?'

Deirdre does not reply. There is only one possible answer to that question, and Roderick doesn't insist on hearing it spoken aloud.

'Were your supporters carrying hammers and lacrosse sticks?'

'Some had hammers, some had sticks, some had both.'

'Provided by you?'

'I provided the lacrosse sticks, obviously. That's not the kind of item most people have at home. But some people brought their own hammers.'

'When you ordered the advance on the statue, were you aware that Councillor Beveridge and other members of the Defence League were present, defending the statue?'

'Of course.'

'Were you also aware that they were also armed with items such as Councillor Beveridge's cricket bat, that were capable of being used as weapons?'

'Obviously.'

'Obviously. And, Miss O'Finn, when you ordered the advance on the statue, was it therefore also obvious to you that what you were doing was going to lead to violence?'

'Not necessarily. I asked them to withdraw and allow us to take the statue down peacefully, and I gave them every opportunity to leave. If they'd done that, there would have been no violence.'

'Did you honestly expect them to withdraw, Miss O'Finn?'

Deirdre actually smiles, rather sheepishly. 'No.'

'And, of course, by the same token, if you and your supporters had withdrawn, there would have been no violence, would there?'

She doesn't reply. Again, Roderick doesn't press her.

'Miss O'Finn, you told the jury that you hit Councillor Beveridge with your lacrosse stick because you were afraid that he was about to hit you with his cricket bat, you feared that you might sustain a serious injury, and you had no alternative but to strike first: is that right?'

'Yes, that is exactly right.'

'You could have walked away, couldn't you?'

'No, I couldn't. Beveridge was out to get me, and he had his bat in the air. There was no time to walk away.'

'What about running away?'

'I didn't think that was an option. It was all happening too quickly.'

'Was it a frightening experience, having to hit somebody with a lacrosse stick to avoid serious injury yourself?'

'Yes, of course it was.'

'But if you were frightened, after you had hit Councillor Beveridge, you had a clear opportunity to walk away, didn't you? He was injured, wasn't he? He wasn't coming after you then.'

'Why should I walk away?'

Roderick seems taken aback for a moment, but with his long experience, he recovers almost immediately.

'Miss O'Finn, Councillor Beveridge was injured – he was bleeding from his head, wasn't he? He was calling for an ambulance. Did it not occur to you to make sure that he was all right?'

She hesitates, just for a moment, but noticeably.

'He didn't seem to be seriously hurt. He was sitting down, talking to someone on his phone.'

'Calling for an ambulance.'

'I didn't know that. I thought he was probably calling his mates in the Cat and Fiddle to come and help him.'

'You also had fights going on elsewhere around the statue, in which people were using weapons. It was only a matter of time before someone else was injured. Are you seriously telling this jury that you did not stop and think that perhaps this was getting out of hand?'

'No. I did not.'

'No. In fact, Miss O'Finn, frightened as you say you were, far from walking away or seeing if Councillor Beveridge needed help, you ran up to the statue and attacked it using your hammer, didn't you?'

'I did try to remove or destroy the statue, yes. That's why we were there.'

Roderick glances up at me. 'With your Honour's leave, if the usher would be kind enough to show the witness exhibits 1 and 2…'

Dawn has them in Deirdre's hands in a flash.

'Miss O'Finn, do these photographs, our exhibits 1 and 2, show the damage you and your supporters did to the statue of John Bonhomme on the evening of 15 March?'

Deirdre peruses them with what seems like a self-satisfied smile.

'Yes, they do.'

'What part of that damage did you inflict personally?'

She holds up exhibit 2 for all to see.

'I was in position by the left-hand side of the statue, so I would have struck the left-hand side, the body and legs.'

'And what was your intention when you struck the statue in that way?'

'To prise it loose and remove it, or, failing that, to destroy it.'

Roderick pauses for some time.

'Miss O'Finn, I'm curious about one thing. Your head girl, April, told the jury that, in addition to the suggestion that John Bonhomme was a slave trader – which seems to be debatable, to say the least – he was also opposed to the education of women and girls, which can be proved easily through his writings. You're a teacher. Yet your campaign to take the statue down was based on the question of the slave trade, and you've hardly mentioned the question of education.'

Deirdre smiles. 'You're a perceptive man, Mr Lofthouse,' she observes.

'Thank you,' Roderick replies, unable to resist returning the smile. 'I don't get that a lot.' Kenneth chuckles to himself, as do one or two jurors.

'You're quite right,' she agrees. 'To tell you the truth, as a trans woman and a teacher, it's education for women and girls I'm really passionate about. There are so many places in the world where education isn't available to them. John Bonhomme died more than two hundred years ago, but he's still alive and well in spirit. I feel I have to try to do something about that – even if it's only killing off his statue rather than his opinions.'

'But the slave trade was more likely to resonate with people generally, better publicity: was that the thinking?'

'Yes. I suppose it was.'

Roderick nods and resumes his seat. 'Yes, thank you, Miss O'Finn. That's all I have, your Honour.'

Kenneth stands. 'No re-examination. Unless your Honour has any questions…?'

'No, thank you,' I reply at once.

'Please return to the dock, Miss O'Finn,' Kenneth says.

'Your Honour, there is a matter of law that arises. May the jury retire for a few minutes?'

Roderick stands. 'Your Honour, I see the time. Perhaps it may be best to release the jury until after lunch. By the time we have dealt with my learned friend's application, we're bound to be very close to the break.'

I glance at my watch. Roderick is quite right. I hadn't noticed – I must have been more absorbed than I realised in Deirdre O'Finn's evidence.

'Yes, very well,' I say. 'Two o'clock please, members of the jury.'

They troop out of court under Dawn's ever watchful eye.

'Your Honour,' Kenneth says, once they have left court, 'I only have one witness to call on Miss O'Finn's behalf. But my learned friend tells me that he objects to my calling this witness to give evidence. We have discussed the matter in an effort to resolve it, but without success, and it seems that we need your Honour to rule.'

'All right,' I reply. 'What is the dispute?'

'Your Honour, the witness I propose to call is Niamh Gibson, who is a professor of social history at Trinity College, Dublin. Professor Gibson has made a particular study of the situation regarding the education of women and girls throughout the world, and the effect that it has on women. She has also studied campaigns to promote education for women, and has a book on that subject coming out shortly.'

'So, she's being called as an expert witness?' I ask.

'Yes, your Honour.'

Well, it wouldn't be like Kenneth not to come up with some novel ideas, and he is certainly not disappointing. His foray into the law of nuisance was interesting, but an expert witness to help the defendant to explain her feelings to the jury sounds unlikely. Perhaps Kenneth sees himself as snatching at straws anyway, in which case he might well try his luck at providing the jury with something eye-catching.

'Well, I'm sure Professor Gibson's work is very important,' I venture tentatively, 'but I'm not sure what it has to do with the case this jury has to decide.'

'Your Honour, this is an unusual case by any standards. It's not your average case of affray, such as juries deal with day in, day out. The jury may find Miss O'Finn's motivation of considerable interest. Professor Gibson will explain to the jury how seriously Miss O'Finn takes the whole question of women's education, and why it would be likely to inspire her to do something like taking down the Bonhomme statue, which might otherwise be difficult for the jury to understand.'

You can see that Roderick is itching to respond, and he is on his feet in a flash.

'Your Honour, how deeply Miss O'Finn may or may not feel is irrelevant to the questions the jury has to decide. The prosecution are not require to prove motive. If we prove the acts Miss O'Finn committed, and the necessary intent, then the case is proved. If the jury are not sure of those things, then they will acquit. The jury don't need an expert to assess Miss O'Finn's state of mind. In my submission, her state of mind is perfectly obvious from the evidence they have already heard, including the evidence Miss O'Finn has just given. Professor Gibson's evidence is irrelevant and inadmissible.'

'I'm afraid I have to agree with Mr Lofthouse, Mr Warnock,' I say. 'I can't see how the evidence could possibly help the jury.'

Kenneth knows better than to flog a dead horse.

'As your Honour pleases.' He offers his rather creepy smile, the wig perched perilously to one side of the forehead. 'Well, that does at least save some time – Professor Gibson is in Dublin, and I couldn't have got her to court until Monday. Your Honour, I have no other live witnesses, but I do have a number of written character references, some fifteen in all. My learned friend has seen them, and he tells me that he has no objection to my reading them to the jury.'

'No objection whatsoever,' Roderick confirms.

'I'm much obliged to my learned friend. In that case, your Honour, I can read the references after lunch, after which I will close my case, and we'll be ready for closing speeches.'

And so to lunch, an oasis of calm in a desert of chaos.

'Charles, how long do you think the case has left to run?' Roger asks when we're back in chambers. 'I'm only asking because I have a rather full schedule in Suffolk next week, but having come this far, I would like to see the ending if I can.' He grins. 'And if you're going to reopen the public gallery for the verdict, you might need some protection.'

Roger's right about that. It's something I've been turning over in my mind. The verdict is the finale and climax of any trial, and no judge wants to close the public gallery when the jury return to court for the last time. On the other hand, trouble when the verdict is announced can be particularly challenging in any case with a hint of controversy, a category which certainly includes the saga of John Bonhomme and Deirdre O'Finn. There's no denying that Roger's presence has helped considerably in keeping things under control during this week, but if serious disorder breaks out when the verdict becomes known, I can't let Roger loose with the sword. He's already brandished it with apparent intent once, and I wasn't entirely sure he was bluffing. What I am going to need is Dawn, and a number of police officers, in addition to our own security.

I calculate aloud. 'Well, let's see. Speeches this afternoon, probably start my summing-up towards the end of the afternoon, and finish it tomorrow morning. So, let's say, jury out some time around eleven or eleven-thirty, if all goes according to plan.'

'So, no guarantee of a verdict tomorrow?'

'No. Fridays are always tricky for verdicts. There's always a feeling that it would be nice to get it done and get started on the weekend, so you can get a quick verdict on a Friday. But in other cases, they know they can't do it in an afternoon, and then they sometimes shut up shop, and say, "We're coming back next week anyway; let's leave it until Monday". You can never tell.'

'I would have thought this would be a shut-up-shop case,' Roger suggests. 'It's not going to be easy for them, is it?'

'You know, that's what I've been assuming for most of the week,' I reply, thinking out loud, as much for my own information as Roger's, 'but now, I'm not so sure. When you think about it, she's admitted everything the prosecution have to prove, hasn't she? She has a shot on the self-defence, but on the affray, she gave Roderick everything he asked for in cross-examination. If you take the emotion out of the case, it's fairly cut and dried.'

Roger smiles. 'Yes, but I'm not sure you can take the emotion out of this, Charles. John Bonhomme is a divisive figure.'

I return the smile. 'In Suffolk, undoubtedly, but not necessarily in London. That's why Ipswich lumbered us with it. A Bermondsey jury is more likely to focus on the facts. I'm not saying it's all over, but I think Deirdre is up against it. In any case, Roger, you have more than done your duty here as High Sheriff. Nice as it would be to have your company again, I know how busy you are, and I wouldn't dream of asking you to come back next week.'

There is a knock at the door. Stella opens it and enters quietly.

'Sorry to disturb, Judge. I'm glad I've caught you. I thought you might have gone into lunch already…'

'No, still here. What have you got?'

'I just thought I should let you know that Sir Jeremy and Mr Justice Gulivant want to come for their conference, as they're calling it, tomorrow, at lunchtime. Sir Jeremy's office called earlier. They didn't say so in so many words, but I got the impression that the time isn't negotiable. I imagine Meredith will be with them too. Shall I order sandwiches and drinks as usual?'

I nod. 'Yes. Thank you, Stella.'

She leaves as quickly and quietly as she came.

'It's none of my business, of course,' Roger says, 'but do I take it that would be about Hubert?'

'Yes, I'm afraid it would,' I reply.

'Charles,' he says suddenly, 'why don't you come to dinner at the Garrick this evening, if Clara doesn't mind? It would give you a chance to talk to Hubert again and get a feel for how the land lies. It may be easier for Hubert having me there as well, and this may be our last chance.'

I nod, and reflect for some time. 'That might not be a bad idea,' I reply.

The door opens once more. This time it's Marjorie, who doesn't enter at all quietly, but with a noticeable spring in her step.

'Hello, Roger,' she says. 'I hope I'm not interrupting, Charlie, but I called into the mess, and saw that you hadn't come in for lunch yet, so I thought I might find you here.'

'As you have,' I reply. 'How can I help?'

She smiles. 'Oh, I think I'm the one who may be able to help,' she replies. 'Stella says you're having an attack of the Grey Smoothies tomorrow, to discuss Hubert's *confusion*.'

She places a distinct, and rather strange, emphasis on the word 'confusion', as if to make sure that we will keep it firmly in mind. I'm suddenly intrigued.

'Bad news does travel fast,' I say.

'It does, but in this case, Charlie, it's just as well that it does. You see, when I heard about the forthcoming conference, I was suddenly reminded of a case I read the other day. It's a commercial case in the Civil Division of the Court of Appeal, from about a year ago.'

'A commercial case?'

'I'm sitting as a deputy in the Commercial Court in a couple of weeks' time,' she explains, 'and I was preparing for the case they've given me. Anyway, I thought it might interest you, so I've brought you a copy of the report. I'm glad I found you here. I didn't want to give it to you with the others looking on.'

'*Mellor and others v Vaughan Beatty Enterprises PLC and others*,' I read aloud from the first page of the report. 'And I would be interested in a commercial case because…? Oh, no. Don't tell me you're going to ask me to fill in for you in another civil case.' I turn to Roger. 'The last time Marjorie asked me to take one of her civil cases, I found myself seeking refuge in a pub in darkest Cambridgeshire, while the bomb squad defused some World War Two magnetic bombs buried in the very plot of land the parties were fighting over.'

Marjorie laughs aloud. 'Notwithstanding which,' she tells Roger, 'Charlie organised a mediation right there in the pub, and settled the damn case while the parties were three sheets to the wind – a feat that will live for ever in the annals of civil litigation. Absolutely brilliant.'

'That wasn't what you said at the time,' I point out. 'At the time, you said I must have lost my mind to hold a drunken mediation in the pub, and God only knows what would happen if it ever went to the Court of Appeal.'

She nods. 'Yes. Well, there was that, too. But you did get the result, Charlie. Anyway, you needn't worry. I'm not asking you to do another civil case. I just think you might find this report worth reading.'

She stands and moves towards the door. 'See you at lunch.' As she is leaving, she turns back towards us and, again with a strange intonation, murmurs the word, 'confusion'.

I put the law report on my desk to await my attention, and in we go to lunch.

* * *

Thursday Afternoon

Both closing speeches are commendably brief. I suppose, as I tried to say to Roger, that once you keep the emotion out of it, this case isn't particularly complicated. Deirdre has in effect coughed up to causing an affray, and the question of self-defence on the assault charge is one which presents the jury with a clear choice. Roger is right up to a point, of course – you can't take the emotion out of this case entirely, and there's always the possibility of a sympathy verdict – but we are in Bermondsey now, not Little Brewing, and with two experienced advocates like Roderick and Kenneth at the helm, the jury will be left in no doubt about what they have to decide.

Roderick, of course, can't resist returning to his poetic theme.

'As I said when I opened the case to you on Monday, members of the jury, John Bonhomme isn't the only poet who comes to mind. Thomas Gray identified the characters to us in his celebrated *Elegy*, didn't he? I'm sure you remember.

> *Some village-Hampden, that with dauntless breast*
> *The little tyrant of his fields withstood;*
> *Some mute inglorious Milton here may rest,*
> *Some Cromwell guiltless of his country's blood.*

'Well, you have the little tyrant of the fields, who has done her best to render the village Milton, John Bonhomme, mute inglorious; and you have the village-Hampden who withstood her with dauntless breast. Now, members of the jury, let me make it clear again that Deirdre O'Finn was perfectly entitled to express her view that the statue of John Bonhomme had become an affront to women and people of colour, and should be removed from the village square. As long as she pursued that goal by peaceful, lawful means, she did nothing wrong, and at first, she did exactly that. She wrote articles in the *Star*, the local newspaper, and she lobbied the village council to hold a vote on the question, which was duly done. All of that was perfectly right and proper. It was after the vote had been lost that the problems started.

'Miss O'Finn would have you believe that, after she had gone public with her determination to take the statue down by any means, including force, when PC Barnett came to see her, he was trying to "put the frighteners" on her. But it is more likely, isn't it, that the officer was simply trying to calm things down and prevent trouble? Be that as it may, there can be no doubt, can there, members of the jury, that from that moment onwards, Miss O'Finn knew what she was planning would be unlawful and would lead to her being prosecuted? With that in mind, let's look at the evidence...'

Which he does clearly and concisely, and without any further poetic allusions.

Kenneth can't resist laying into the inhabitants of Little Brewing generally, and the *habitués* of the Cat and Fiddle in particular, as a bunch of narrow-minded, prejudiced Neanderthals, who were determined not to listen to Deirdre's legitimate concerns about John Bonhomme, not because they didn't see their merits, but because they couldn't cope with the idea of having a trans woman in their midst – particularly when that trans woman had been appointed headmistress of their revered St Cecilia's school. That much is obvious, Kenneth adds, from the demeanour and behaviour in court of Councillor Monty Beveridge and the Reverend Mr Phineas Pratt, on whom the prosecution rely as witnesses against the defendant they so much dislike and despise. They are not so much village Hampdens, he suggests, as a pair of village Falstaffs – they might be funny in a less serious context.

So far, so good. After this, however, Kenneth would clearly prefer to say as little as possible. He does an excellent job with the self-defence, inviting the jury to picture Monty Beveridge, passionately defending the iconic statue, cricket bat in hand, ready to make another fifty not out. He has the jury chuckling, and I wouldn't be surprised if he's done enough to turn them in his favour on the assault count. But when it comes to the affray, it's pretty obvious that there is not much he can say. It's a dilemma that all barristers face once in a while, and sometimes there's nothing you can do but tacitly acknowledge that the evidence is against you. Most do it by emphasising the burden and standard of proof, reminding the jury that they may not convict unless the prosecution has proved the case so that they are sure of the defendant's guilt. Say that and sit down is the usual approach. But Kenneth goes a step or two further.

'You must bear in mind, members of the jury,' he adds, after dealing at length with the burden and standard of proof, 'that it is your sole prerogative to return verdicts. You are the sole judges of the facts. But in our courts, juries are also the judges of much more. You are the guardians of our rights, including the right to express our views, and perform necessary acts when the public interest demands it. It is your duty to ensure that those important rights are not taken away by our government, or by our prosecutors...'

Which, of course, is when Roderick leaps to his feet with a most uncharacteristic display of vigour that takes everyone by surprise, to tell me that there is a point of law, and to ask that the jury retire to allow us to discuss it. Dawn quickly ushers them out of court.

'I will see counsel in chambers,' I say, on impulse.

'Do you want me to stay here?' Roger asks.

'It might be best. We'll only be a couple of minutes.'

'Kenneth, what are you thinking?' I ask once we are seated in chambers.

He seems taken aback. 'Judge?'

Unbidden, Roderick takes it upon himself to explain. We're in my domain in chambers, and he really shouldn't, but in this instance I don't mind at all.

'You're inviting the jury to acquit without regard to the evidence and the law,' he says, 'asking them to ignore the judge's directions and return a sympathy verdict. I think it's called jury nullification, technically. It's not allowed.'

'We all know that there are such things as sympathy verdicts,' I add. 'But you can't suggest it to the jury. You could get into serious trouble, Kenneth.'

Kenneth has turned rather pale.

'I am so sorry, Judge. I had no idea I was going too far.'

Roderick casts a sceptical look up towards the ceiling, but actually, I'm inclined to believe Kenneth. We've all done it. You start out making a respectable enough argument, and it suddenly drifts out of bounds – and although he came close, he didn't actually invite the jury to rebel against the law in so many words. He may have Roderick to thank for his prompt intervention, which closed him down before he could transgress. He stayed on the right side of the line, and the jury may not have taken in the full significance of what he was on the verge of suggesting. All the same, I can't let it stand.

'You will have to tell the jury that their power to return a verdict must be exercised in accordance with the evidence and the law,' I say, 'or I will – and if I do it, I will have to be pretty blunt about it. I'd also have to report you to the Bar Council.'

'Of course, Judge,' Kenneth replies.

We bring the jury back and Kenneth makes a show of emphasising that any verdict the jury returns must be in accordance with the evidence and the law, and in accordance with my directions.

I begin that process, but I'm not going to try to finish the summing-up this afternoon. Fortunately, there are a number of set pieces in every summing-up, which any judge can deliver by rote after a modest amount of experience – the roles of judge and jury, the burden and standard of proof, and the importance of following the law and ensuring that the verdict is based on the evidence. Since I have some time left after that, I also give them the definition of the two offences they are still concerned with – affray, and assault occasioning actual bodily harm – and take them through the basic legal principles they need to understand, including intent and self-defence. I decide to stop there. I will review the evidence with them tomorrow morning.

Having released everyone for the day, we return to chambers. Roger is anxious to get back to the Garrick and arrange a suitable table for us for this evening. I invite him to go on ahead. I have some work to do in chambers, including reading the mysterious judgment of the Court of Appeal in the case of *Mellor and others v Vaughan Beatty Enterprises PLC and others*. The headnote – the brief summary of the court's findings helpfully provided by law reports – tells me that this was about a contractual dispute of some kind, which involved an eye-watering amount of money, and that the judgment of the High Court was reversed. It also tells me that the judge who decided the case in the High Court was Mr Justice Gulivant. Suddenly, I find myself quite drawn to the novel experience of reading the report of a commercial case.

* * *

Thursday Evening

I have something of an ambivalent attitude to gentlemen's clubs. I joined the Oxford and Cambridge years ago, after a good deal of moral pressure from my old college, and a special offer on my first year's membership. But I'm not a regular there. I've never been what they call clubbable. I could never bring myself to haunt a club night after night, as Hubert haunts the Garrick. It's understandable in Hubert's case. He's suffered from loneliness ever since his wife died, and his many friends at the Garrick are an important part of his life. But many of the members you see in the bar there have no such excuse, and how they keep up conversation over drinks and dinner, evening after evening, is a mystery to me. Not to mention how expensive it must be. I do take myself off to tea or dinner at the Oxford and Cambridge occasionally, usually when the Reverend Mrs Walden has invited engaged couples or the women's circle to the vicarage for the evening, and it seems advisable to make myself scarce. We go there for dinner together once in a while to celebrate a birthday or anniversary. But most of the time we hang out at one of our local haunts, the Delights of the Raj or La Bella Napoli, where it's a bit less formal, and you don't have to dress up.

Inevitably, I'm invited to other clubs for dinner from time to time, and I generally enjoy the experience. On one notable occasion I had the privilege of being entertained at Boodle's by none other than Sir Jeremy Bagnall. But most often the invitation comes from Hubert, and it's to dine at the Garrick. I've always had an excellent dinner there, the ambiance is interesting, and so are some of the people you meet, the membership being drawn mainly from the legal and the theatrical professions. But I always feel a bit furtive when I cross the club's threshold, as if I'm venturing into forbidden territory – which I would be if the Reverend Mrs Walden had her way. The Reverend Mrs Walden disapproves of the Garrick because of their famous – or, in her view, infamous – refusal to admit women as members, and she's not shy about reminding me of this antediluvian attitude, any more than she is about reminding Hubert when she gets the chance. The Reverend isn't alone in that view, of course, but it's her face I see as the porter directs me to the bar, where Hubert will be waiting.

This evening he's waiting with Roger, both of them already well into a dry martini.

'Charlie,' he says by way of welcome, 'how good of you to visit me in this den of iniquity. I do hope your good lady wife hasn't given you too much of a hard time. I know she doesn't approve of our goings-on here at the Garrick.'

I smile. 'She doesn't approve of the fact that she couldn't be elected a member.'

Hubert nods. 'But she's always welcome for dinner, Charlie,' he replies. 'You must bring her one evening, so that she can see for herself. People don't understand that. We have nothing against women. They've always been welcome as guests. What will you have?'

I decide to join them with a dry martini. The conversation is light until we go into dinner. Roger has secured a quiet enough table in a corner, well away from the long members' table. We enjoy the soup of the day to start, and then settle down to a braised steak, accompanied by a very acceptable club red.

'So,' Hubert begins, wiping his lips with his remarkably large Garrick club napkin, 'I hear the Grey Smoothies are descending on us tomorrow?'

'Yes,' I reply. 'Well, Sir Jeremy, presumably with Meredith in tow – and Stephen Gulivant.'

He looks up. 'Why would Stephen Gulivant be there?'

'At one point,' I reply, 'Jeremy thought it might make it easier for you if they brought in a judge from outside, rather than have me talk to you.'

'I don't need to talk to Stephen Gulivant,' Hubert growls, 'any more than I need to talk to Jeremy Bagnall.'

'You're not going to talk to anyone tomorrow,' I reply. 'Tomorrow is for me to talk to them, to report on what I've found out about you. You know what I'm going to say. Then I'll listen to what they have to say, and we will see how the land lies after that.'

'What's your feeling about that, Charles?' Roger asks.

'I honestly don't know, Roger.'

'Nothing good,' Hubert mutters, 'that's for sure – not with those two characters trying to stitch me up.'

I shake my head. 'We can't just dismiss this, Hubert; we can't just wish it would go away. They wouldn't be with us tomorrow unless they had concerns about you, and we can't pretend they're not real concerns. What we need to do is find a way to put their minds at rest.'

'They've already made their minds up,' Hubert replies. 'There's nothing to put at rest.'

'I don't think so,' I reply. 'If that were the case, I don't think they would have delayed matters by asking me for a report. They would have acted straightaway. As it is, they're giving me the chance to make a case for you.'

Hubert puts down his knife and fork, and looks at me. For the first time, I detect just a hint of resignation.

'What kind of case could you possibly make, Charlie,' he asks, 'after your judgment – yours and Stephen's – in the Court of Appeal, and that other case Piers and Emily told you about? It's all pretty damning, isn't it?'

I see Roger turn towards me also.

'What case would you make,' I ask after some time, 'if you had to put their minds at rest tomorrow?'

'What case would I make?'

'Yes. Hubert, you're talking about carrying on for another two years. I'm assuming you wouldn't be thinking in those terms unless you had confidence that you could do the job well. I know you too well to think you'd want to continue if you thought you were losing the plot. So, convince me that you're not a danger to the cases you will be trying for the next two years. Make that case for me.'

He is silent for some time, during which the waiter arrives to remove our dinner plates and tempt us with some suggestions for dessert.

'Do you remember those two benefit fraud cases I had a year or so ago?' he asks eventually.

'Yes, of course.'

'I had two benefit fraud cases called Bourne and Karsten,' Hubert says, more to Roger than to me. 'They were very similar – in terms of the method used in the fraud, they took place at about the same time, and so on – so much so that the police and the CPS thought Bourne and Karsten were in cahoots, and they wanted to try them together for conspiracy. But the evidence wasn't there, and I ordered that they be tried separately.'

'Quite rightly,' I say. 'I read through the files, and I agreed with you.'

'So, we tried them back-to-back,' Hubert continues, 'and in the second trial – I can't remember which way round it was, and it doesn't matter – I called the defendant by the wrong name when I was asking him some questions during his evidence. I called him Bourne when it should have been Karsten, or *vice versa*.'

'Why was that, Hubert?' Roger asks. 'Do you know?'

'Yes,' Hubert replies without hesitation. 'I remember it clearly. There was a young woman in the public gallery – I have no idea who she was – but she reminded me of Joan, her hair, what she was wearing, and I was distracted. It only lasted for a moment, but that was enough to distract me. Nothing came of it. Counsel corrected me, I made a joke of it with the jury – how terrible it is to get old, and so on – and we carried on. But the Grey Smoothies had to interfere, as usual, putting two and two together and making five.'

'Jeremy came to see me about it,' I say. 'I persuaded him it was nothing to worry about.'

Hubert looks at me. 'You never told me, Charlie, but presumably, you did that by telling him I'd had a vision of my late wife?'

'No,' I reply. 'As a matter of fact, I didn't. I thought that was a personal matter, and I didn't see any need to share it with Jeremy.'

Hubert seems genuinely taken aback. 'I assumed that was why they are taking a renewed interest now. What did you say to him, for heaven's sake?'

'I told him that you had explained the situation to me, that I accepted your explanation, which was a highly personal one, that I didn't think there was any cause for concern, and I asked him to accept that from me – which, somewhat to my surprise, he did.'

We sit silently for some time, during which the waiter takes our orders for dessert.

'Have you seen Joan again since then?' Roger asks.

'Not while I've been in court,' Hubert replies. 'But elsewhere – it happens once in a while. There will be some woman in the street or on the tube who reminds me of her, or dresses like her. I don't really think it's Joan, Roger. I'm not crazy. I know it's an illusion. It only lasts for a few seconds. But it is disturbing when it happens.'

'Of course,' Roger says. 'It's bound to be.'

'I've been seeing your good lady wife, Charlie,' Hubert says, turning to me. 'I'm sure she's told you all about it.'

'I know you've seen Clara,' I reply, truthfully, 'but not what you may have said to her. She would never divulge anything you've talked about.'

'She was a great source of comfort after Joan died. I will be seeing her again.'

'I'm glad to hear that,' I say. 'You couldn't be in better hands in my opinion. Well, I'm biased, of course, but…'

We share a smile.

'Hubert,' Roger says, 'even if you haven't seen Joan in court, have there been times when you're thinking about her during a trial? The mind does tend to wander, doesn't it? I must admit, mine certainly has this week. Interesting as it all is, you can't stop other thoughts coming in, can you?'

I look at Roger. It's an insightful question.

'That's true,' I agree. 'It happens to me all the time, and not all trials are as absorbing as Miss O'Finn. Sometimes I have to make myself concentrate.'

Hubert nods. 'Yes, I do think about her sometimes when I'm in court,' he replies. 'My mind can drift. I give myself a good talking to, and I'm back. But I can't deny that I may be somewhere else in my mind for some time, and there are moments when I'm not quite sure what's been going on.'

Roger glances in my direction.

'Hubert,' I say, 'would you mind if I do tell Jeremy about Joan this time?'

He thinks for some time.

'Not if you think it might help. As long as you don't give him the impression that I'm seeing things... no, if you think it might help...'

* * *

Friday Morning

Having fended off a determined cross-examination by Elsie and Jeanie about the likely verdict in the case of Deirdre O'Finn – and a suggestion that if they don't want John Bonhomme's statue in Little Brewing, there's a pub in Walthamstow that might be interested, as long as there's a discount for the damage – I progress to George for my copy of *The Times*. Today, George has something else for me as well, a copy of the *Star,* no less, all the way from Suffolk. It's hot off the press, and the editor appears to have decided to devote almost the whole issue to a blow-by-blow account of the trial. The seats reserved for the press have been fully occupied since it started, and evidently one of the *Star*'s reporters has been assigned to cover this away fixture. I have a sudden vision of the inhabitants of Little Brewing rushing from their homes to the newsagents, coins in hand, to secure their copies as soon as the print is dry. I'm sure Roger will be interested to flick through it, as will I. You'd be amazed at how little resemblance the evidence, as reported in the columns of many publications, can bear to the evidence actually given in court; and I shudder to think what spin the editor has put on my closing of the public gallery and my committal of Councillor Beveridge to the cells. I suspect it may be the main topic of conversation in the Cat and Fiddle for some time.

'You are a marvel, George,' I say. 'How do you find all the stuff you do?'

He shrugs modestly, but I know the compliment pleases him. It's fully deserved. George has an uncanny knack for tracking down even the most obscure reports of trials and other goings on at Bermondsey Crown Court, and I know he does similar research for all his regulars. How he keeps track of it all is a mystery.

'Nothing to it, guv,' he replies. 'These local papers can be difficult to find in London, but everything's available to those who know where to look.'

He shakes his head when I try to pay him for the *Star*.

'It didn't cost me anything, guv. One of my mates found it for me and donated it – well, he owed me a favour, didn't he? So, where is this Little Brewing place, anyway? You'd think they'd have better things to do than argue over whether to tear down some old statue, wouldn't you? Still, that's the way it goes now, innit? If your maiden aunt wouldn't approve of something, we can't have it, can we? Have to tear it down. I'll tell you what, guv: with all these vandals on the loose, it's a wonder we have any bloody statues left in this country. And as usual, the Labour Party isn't lifting a finger…'

I excuse myself with renewed thanks.

While Roger immerses himself in the *Star*, I have my usual Friday morning chat with Stella about the forthcoming week.

'I've got another weird one for you, Judge,' she says with a smile.

'I'm not sure I can survive much more weirdness,' I reply. 'What's it about this time? Please tell me it's got nothing to do with statues.'

'No, Judge, no statues. Two elderly ladies, sisters, in Kennington, supplying cannabis from their house. They were growing the plants themselves in the attic. Barbara and

Marcia Hyde-Booth. Both over eighty. You'd think they'd know better at that age, wouldn't you?'

'I don't know what to think any more,' I reply.

'Too true, Judge. Security need to know whether you're going to open the public gallery back up today, since there's a possibility of a verdict. They've already got people gathering outside. They're asking whether they should let them in, and if so, whether we should have a couple of police officers on standby, just in case.'

'Yes, on both counts,' I reply. I only finished agonising over this late last night, but I'm not disposed to close the gallery on a possible verdict day, if I can help it. We were able to control the kind of demonstrations we had during the week, and my instinct is telling me that we can do the same again.

'Right you are.' She consults her notes. 'Oh, and Judge, we've had a request from Councillor Beveridge to be allowed back into court. You remember, you ordered him not to come back to court again. But he says he's learned his lesson, and he will he very well behaved if you give him another chance.'

My immediate reaction to this is 'no'. But something makes me hesitate.

'What do you think?' I ask Stella.

'Well, actually, Judge,' she replies cautiously, 'I was thinking it might not be a bad idea. He probably wouldn't take the chance of being held in contempt again, and he might be able to calm things down if they do start to kick off.'

'I agree, Charles,' Roger says, looking up briefly from the *Star*. 'He does have some influence with the Bonhomme crowd, which is the most likely source of any real trouble. It might help.'

I nod. 'All right. Let's bring him into court before we have the jury in, and I'll make it clear to him what we expect of him, and what's likely to happen if he lets us down.'

All of this goes according to plan, and I duly conclude my summing-up – in the presence of a visibly chastened Councillor Beveridge – and send the jury out to begin their deliberations just after eleven. Roger and I return to chambers, escorted by Dawn, pending whatever pleas of guilty or applications Stella is going to send our way to keep us occupied while they're deliberating. Roger hasn't brought it up again, but I'm aware that the question of when the jury might return is still looming large in his mind, and I decide to ask Dawn what she thinks. Ushers spend a lot of time with juries, and although they would never discuss the case with the jurors, they often develop a feel for whether the jury will agree on a verdict, whether the verdict will be unanimous or by a majority – and how long they may need before they're ready to return it. Juries are the most unpredictable of creatures, and regularly take everyone in a case by surprise. Even experienced ushers like Dawn can misread the tea leaves. But her record is impressive.

'Sir Roger is worried about whether he's going to miss the verdict if he has to return to Suffolk tomorrow,' I say. 'It's not a straightforward case. I could see them being out for a while. Any thoughts?'

Dawn doesn't even hesitate.

'Oh, no, Judge. This isn't going into next week. We'll get a verdict this afternoon.'

Roger and I stare at her.

'What?'

'Oh, yes, Judge. This lot made their minds up some time ago.'

Before lunch, I sentence a defendant who has pleaded guilty to several counts of residential burglary, which takes some time – not because there's any doubt that he's going inside for a decent stretch, but because the story of Chummy's lengthy campaign takes Piers Drayford some time to narrate

on behalf of the prosecution, and because Emily Phipson
has to do her best with a long, rambling pre-sentence report,
containing a number of totally unrealistic recommendations,
and then make her own, as always, scrupulously realistic
and competent plea on Chummy's behalf. Finally, lunchtime
arrives. I'm not going to pretend that there's any question of
an oasis today. Roger quietly departs for the mess, while I
prepare for my visitors.

As predicted, Sir Jeremy and Stephen Gulivant are
accompanied by our cluster manager, Meredith, who will take
notes. Taking notes is something of a fetish in the world of
the Grey Smoothies. Once something is recorded in a formal
Grey Smoothie note, it acquires an almost religious status. It
is thereafter deemed to be true, not to be questioned, and the
record is carefully preserved for posterity. I would be fully
within my rights to make my own record of the proceedings.
I've done that on various occasions in the past, usually by
means of having Stella sit in with her trusty hand-held tape
recorder. But I don't want a record of this. Before getting down
to business, we make a token assault on the unappetising
sandwiches supplied by the kitchen.

'Well, Charles,' Jeremy begins, wiping his hands with his
paper napkin with a look of some distaste on his face, 'as you
know, I've asked for this conference because we need to talk
about where we stand with Judge Drake – Hubert – in the light
of your recent decision in the Court of Appeal. You kindly
agreed to make some inquiries about whether this appears
to have been an isolated incident of confusion, or whether or
not there have been other indications that might give rise to
concern. The floor is yours.'

Meredith is poised, pen in hand.

'Yes,' I begin. 'First of all, Jeremy, I'm grateful for the time you gave me. I've had my work cut out with this Suffolk case, as you know.'

Jeremy exchanges a furtive smile with his note-taker.

'Yes indeed. Meredith tells me there are all kinds of interesting stories making the rounds about the High Sheriff of Suffolk and his sword. Anything I should know about – officially, that is?'

'No, Jeremy. The High Sheriff has been extremely helpful,' I reply without elaborating, 'as well as being a pleasure to have at court.'

'I'm delighted to hear it – good diplomatic move on our part, having him here, of course. But I shouldn't have interrupted you. You were saying…?'

'After we spoke, I made inquiries, as discreetly as I could, of people who would know if there was anything wrong – the list officer, and counsel who have appeared in front of Hubert recently.' I pause. 'There was one other case that was concerning.'

Jeremy and Stephen exchange looks.

'Go on.'

'There was a case in which Hubert appeared to confuse the offence charged in the indictment with a previous conviction which had not been admitted in evidence. It became necessary for him to discharge the jury. This came from counsel in the case, both very experienced.'

Stephen shakes his head.

'He was confused?'

'So it would seem.'

Stephen turns to Jeremy. 'Well, that rather settles it, doesn't it?'

'Settles what, Stephen, if I may ask?' I intervene before Jeremy can reply.

'Well, it's obvious, Charles, isn't it? He must retire or be retired. We can't let him loose for another two years when he can't keep the facts of a case straight in his mind. He can go with full honours, of course, but he has to go, and go before too long.'

'Is that your view, Jeremy?' I ask.

Jeremy doesn't respond immediately. 'Well, two cases in which he has exhibited confusion must be cause for concern, mustn't they, Charles? Don't you agree?'

'I agree that there is cause for concern,' I reply. 'But I'm not sure it's necessary to take drastic action at this stage. Whenever Hubert retires, it's going to come as a huge blow to him. The court is his life – well, the court and the Garrick Club – not to mention the fact that he is widely respected because he is a good and highly experienced judge. If we make him retire now, while the Brady case is still being talked about, it would be an unnecessary humiliation. At the very least we should allow some time to elapse, so that his retirement isn't linked in people's minds to the Court of Appeal.'

Stephen is looking very doubtful, but Jeremy is nodding. I decide to press on.

'I have an alternative proposal,' I say.

Jeremy raises his eyebrows. 'By all means, let's hear it.'

'I would like you to consider leaving Hubert in place for now – partly, as I said, to avoid the association in people's minds – but also because as RJ, I don't think there is any immediate threat to the court.'

'Really, Charles?' Stephen says. 'How many times must a judge become confused before it does constitute a threat to the court? Surely, it could happen in any given case, with God only knows how much risk of injustice, and waste of resources in terms of discharging juries, or even further appeals.'

'Stephen has a point, Charles,' Jeremy says. 'Something could go seriously wrong. My Minister may even be questioned in the House about why he left a judge in place knowing he had a history of confusion.'

'I do understand that, Jeremy,' I reply, 'and I wasn't suggesting that we take no action at all. But... I'd like to ask you something, if I may. Do you remember, somewhere between a year and two years ago, you and I had a conversation about Hubert becoming confused in another case? It was one of two cases of closely related benefit fraud, and he became confused...'

'Another example?' Stephen interjects. I ignore him.

'He became confused, for one very brief moment, between the two defendants. I reassured you that I didn't think there was a problem. I asked you to accept that from me without my telling you what had happened, and you kindly agreed.'

'I remember.'

'Well, with Hubert's permission, I want to tell you now. What happened in that case was that he saw a young woman in the public gallery who reminded him of his late wife, Joan. Joan's death hit him very hard. He's still not over it. But on this occasion, it caused him to lose concentration, just for a moment or two. No harm was done. Counsel corrected him, and they carried on with no further problem.'

'He saw his dead wife in the public gallery, Charles, is that what you're saying?' Stephen asks.

'No, Stephen, that's not what I said. I said that the young woman reminded him of Joan and caused him to lose concentration for a very brief time.' I turn to Jeremy. 'At the time, I thought that the death of his wife was a personal matter. I would have told you if you'd pressed me, Jeremy, but I'm grateful that you didn't.'

Jeremy nods. 'Has there been any recurrence of that episode? Has he been reminded of her in court since then? Is that what's going on here?'

'He says not. But from talking to him, I have no doubt that Joan's death is the major factor in whatever confusion he has experienced.'

'Yes, I see,' Jeremy replies.

'Even if that's the case, it's still a problem, isn't it?' Stephen insists. 'Look, Charles, I'm not unsympathetic to the man. It's a terrible thing for anyone to go through. But the question is: can we be sure that it's safe to leave him on the bench?'

'That is the question,' Jeremy agrees.

'I believe my proposal will put your minds at rest,' I say. 'It's based on the fact that Hubert is now working with a counsellor to help him to come to terms with Joan's death. Both Hubert and the counsellor believe that it is going well. So, what I propose is that we allow the therapy to take its course. But at the same time, I, or one of the other judges, will make ourselves available to Hubert, so that he can come to us at any time if he starts to experience confusion again. The difference now is that Hubert understands what's going on, so if it does happen again, he won't panic. If he feels any confusion, he will ask for help, either from one of us, or preferably from counsel in whatever case he's trying.'

'That sounds like a lot of responsibility for you and the other judges to take on,' Jeremy muses.

'I don't think so, Jeremy,' I reply. 'The confusion has never been something that happens every day, and as he gets better, it will die away. That's not just my speculation, by the way – I happen to know that his counsellor agrees.' I pause. 'The other thing is this. As he comes to terms with losing Joan, the compulsion never to retire will fade away. I don't think he will stay for two years. My guess is that he will go of his own volition before then.'

There is a prolonged silence.

'Well,' Jeremy says eventually, 'I must say, Stephen, I'm

inclined to give Charles's proposal a chance to work. Obviously, we can't let it drift on indefinitely, whatever happens. If there is a significant incident that causes problems, we would have to step in and act. But if the counsellor is right and a solution is within reach, I'm inclined to give it a chance.'

Stephen shakes his head. 'Confusion is confusion, Jeremy,' he insists. 'It's too much of a risk.'

I think for a moment. If I'm going to deploy my secret weapon, the moment has arrived. Should I, shouldn't I? There's a lot at stake for Hubert. I have to try.

'It's interesting you should say that, Stephen,' I say. 'The other day, my colleague Marjorie Jenkins suggested I read a decision of the Court of Appeal. It was in the Civil Division, commercial case – not my kind of thing at all – but Marjorie sits as a deputy High Court judge, as you know, and she thought I might find it interesting. What *was* the name? Miller...? No... Mellor, that was it, Mellor and others and somebody else and others – something like that, doesn't matter. Anyway, the court reversed the decision of the High Court judge at first instance, because he'd got the law wrong. But that's not how they put it. They said that the judge was obviously *confused* as between two quite different principles of law, and although counsel did their best to steer him in the right direction, he remained *confused*, with the result that his judgment on the facts of the case was fundamentally flawed. As a result, the Court of Appeal had no alternative but to order a new trial in front of a different judge – they couldn't just substitute their own view of the case. It made me think: what do we mean by *confusion*? It seems to me that there can be all kinds of confusion, and they afflict everyone from time to time, but not all the time. No one would suggest that this judge should retire because he made an error of law, would they? Happens every day.'

I stop to assess the effect of Marjorie's contribution to the campaign. The look on Stephen's face tells me it's hit home. He throws up his hands.

'Well, all right. I suppose we can give him some time. But we need to keep a close eye on the situation, Charles.'

'Of course,' I reply.

* * *

Friday Afternoon

As foretold by the prophet Dawn, the jury return to court just after three. Most juries, when about to return a verdict, look a bit tense, and sometimes even traumatised. But not this jury. They look relaxed, smiling and quietly chatting as they take their seats in the jury box. Dawn was right. This jury made up their minds some time ago.

The public gallery is full, and I notice that Councillor Monty Beveridge is sitting prominently in front of the John Bonhomme contingent. I remember what Stella and Roger had to say about letting him back in and try my best to see it as a good sign. But in any case, we have a good contingent of security and police officers in place, not to mention Dawn, and the High Sheriff, sword in place, on the bench.

'Before we take the verdicts,' I say, 'I want to make something clear. In the earlier stages of this trial, there were some disturbances in the public gallery, as a result of which I had to close the gallery for some time, as well as forbidding certain individuals from further attendance. This resulted in a disruption of the work of the court. Let me make it abundantly clear today that the court will not tolerate any outbursts or other improper behaviour while the verdicts are being returned, or afterwards. I expect all those in the public gallery to treat the court with proper respect. If there is any trouble, those responsible will be prosecuted for contempt of court, and for any other offences they may commit. I hope I have made myself clear.'

I nod to Carol, who asks Deirdre O'Finn and the foreman of the jury, a middle-aged woman, to stand.

'Members of the jury,' she says, 'you have already returned a verdict on count three of the indictment. Madam foreman, please answer my first question either "yes" or "no". Members of the jury, have you reached a verdict in respect of counts one and two of the indictment on which you are all agreed?'

'Yes, we have,' the foreman replies.

'On the first count of this indictment, charging Deirdre O'Finn with affray, do you find the defendant guilty or not guilty?'

'Guilty.'

'You find the defendant guilty, and is that the verdict of you all?'

'Yes, it is.'

'On the second count of the indictment, charging Deirdre O'Finn with assaulting Monty Beveridge thereby causing him actual bodily harm, do you find the defendant guilty or not guilty?'

'Not guilty.'

'You find the defendant not guilty, and is that the verdict of you all?'

'Yes, it is.'

To my surprise, and relief, the verdicts are received in silence and without any obvious reaction from the public gallery, except for the look of outrage on the face of Councillor Monty Beveridge at the verdict on count two, the clear implication of which is that Deirdre O'Finn had felt obliged to defend herself against a threat from his fifty-not-out cricket bat. In the dock, Deirdre O'Finn remains impassive.

Kenneth stands slowly.

'Your Honour, it seems to me that a pre-sentence report would be of limited assistance in this case. I don't know whether…'

'I do intend to ask for a report, Mr Warnock,' I reply. 'I will extend Miss O'Finn's bail until the time of sentence.'

Kenneth nods. 'Much obliged, your Honour.'

I'm sure Kenneth fully expected me to agree with him. As a matter of fact, I do agree with him – I don't think a report will be of any use at all. Deirdre O'Finn isn't your common or garden offender, beset by problems caused by some combination of drink, drugs, unemployment and bad judgment. Sentencing Deirdre O'Finn involves considerations of a different order altogether. I'm asking for the report because I want an iron-clad excuse for not agreeing to any suggestion that I should sentence her today. For one thing, I need time to reflect on the sentence I'm going to pass, and the report will buy me three weeks. For another, I wouldn't dream of passing sentence in the febrile atmosphere in court in the wake of the verdicts. The public gallery has been admirably restrained thus far, but I'm not about to push my luck. Time needs to pass to allow the heat to dissipate. Three weeks sounds about right.

I instruct Deirdre not to leave court until she's spoken to the probation officer to make arrangements for the report to be prepared, after which I gratefully adjourn for the day.

'Well, Charles, I've thoroughly enjoyed my time with you here in Bermondsey,' Roger says, sheathing his sword for the last time in my chambers. 'Thank you so much for having me.'

'It's been a pleasure as well as a boon to have your protection, Roger,' I reply. 'You've been a tower of strength. And I'm grateful for your input about Hubert too. That's been invaluable.'

'I've hesitated to ask, but…'

'It didn't go too badly,' I say. 'I think we can salvage something for him, as long as he perseveres with Clara, and works with us on his trials.'

'I'm very glad to hear that,' Roger relies. 'It would be terrible to lose Hubert prematurely. He is such a character.'

'He certainly is that,' I agree.

'You and Clara must come and spend a weekend with us,' Roger says, smiling. 'Goodness only knows what impression you must have formed about Suffolk, sitting through this trial. Martha and I would love to show you that it's really not that bad. Some parts of it are positively delightful.'

I can't help laughing. 'I'm quite sure the people we've had to deal with this week aren't in any way representative of Suffolk, Roger,' I reply. 'We'd love to come and see for ourselves. The only problem is that the weekend is Clara's busy time. She doesn't have a curate currently, so it's hard for her to get away.'

'I could always have a word with our vicar,' Roger suggests. 'I assume Clara's bishop could talk someone into covering for her if she received an invitation to be our guest preacher in Aldeburgh, couldn't he? And if you came during the arts or poetry festival, there are all kinds of thing going on – it can get very lively.'

'Let me ask her,' I reply.

It suddenly seems very quiet without Roger's cheerful conversation. I need to go and talk to Hubert, who will be waiting for me anxiously in his chambers; but I need a few moments to take some deep breaths and let the stress of the day begin to subside. I sit down behind my desk, close my eyes, and go through a rhythmic breathing routine I learned many years ago from the Reverend Mrs Walden. When I open my eyes, I notice that Stella has left the draft list for next week on my desk for my perusal. I peruse it, casually at first, but then, as my eyes fasten on one of the cases she has listed for trial, with more intensity. An idea is coming to me. Almost at once, I'm tempted to reject it – I realise at once that it would be a gamble, surely far too great a risk. But, try as I may, I can't bring myself to dismiss it out of hand. Feeling suddenly energised again, I make my way to Stella's office, where I find her immersed in a file.

'Stella,' I say, 'the list you left for me, is that the final edition, or the late draft?'

'The late draft, Judge. I should have the final version out in an hour or so.'

'Could you hold the front page for a while?'

'Judge?'

'*Colson and others*: isn't that the fraud they sent us from Southwark?'

'Yes, Judge. It has to start on Monday, and they didn't have anyone free to take it. It's a four-hander, four to six weeks. I gave it to Judge Jenkins as soon as it arrived, so that she would have time to prepare.' She smiles. 'Judge Jenkins *is* our resident fraud expert, isn't she?'

'She is. But I may want to try something different with this one.'

She smiles again. 'Do you want to try it, Judge? Fraud isn't usually your cup of tea. You're usually only too glad to leave them to Judge Jenkins. I suppose I could give her the Hyde-Booth sisters.'

'No,' I reply. 'I'll take the sisters. But if he's agreeable, I'm thinking of giving *Colson* to Judge Drake.'

I see Stella choke back something she was about to say. She stares at me in bewildered silence. I'm sure she's wondering whether Hubert isn't the only one losing the plot.

'If Judge Drake can deal with a four-handed fraud lasting four to six weeks,' I explain, 'it would shut the Grey Smoothies up, wouldn't it? They could hardly claim that he was past his sell-by date then, could they?'

'No disrespect, Judge,' Stella says eventually, 'but in the present circumstances, that's a big "if".'

'I know. That's why I can't do it without his agreement – and without Judge Jenkins's agreement to help him with it.'

'Help him with it?'

'You know Judge Jenkins as well as I do, Stella. She will have been devouring the files over breakfast. She will know the case inside out by now. All I want her to do is have a daily session with Judge Drake, to make sure he's on track. To be honest, I'm not sure it will be a problem. Judge Drake has done frauds before.'

'Not for some time, Judge.'

Stella is looking doubtful, and she may well be right. The same thought occurred to me as soon as the idea suggested itself to me. If it works, all well and good, but there's every chance that it could turn into a total disaster. But she's thinking about it, and to my surprise, not only does she not suggest that I must be losing my marbles – she actually comes up with a point that hadn't occurred to me.

'On the other hand, Judge, it's harder to blame someone for being confused in a six-week fraud than in a three-day robbery, isn't it?'

We share a smile. 'It is, Stella. It is indeed. Can you hold the front page while I have a chat with him?'

'The list can wait, Judge. Take all the time you need.'

'You said, if it was really bad, you'd come and see me at lunchtime,' Hubert says as I enter his chambers. 'So, I assume the worst didn't happen. Is there some hope?'

'Candidly, it went a lot better than I'd expected,' I reply. 'Without giving you a blow-by-blow account, I'm not sure about the whole two-year stint, but I think we have a good shot at getting you a year, or thereabouts. But... well... the thing is, Hubert, I'm going to need your full cooperation.'

He stares at me. 'Don't say it like that, Charlie,' he protests. 'When have I ever not cooperated? Anyway, cooperate with what, for God's sake?'

'I want you to talk about the cases you try, with me or Marjorie, for a minute or two each day.'

'What?'

'Just so that you can tip us off if there's been any feeling of confusion, you know, if you were to see someone who reminds you of Joan, or... well, in case there's any confusion. All we would do is remind you that you can always ask counsel for help, or ask us for help. That's all. I would expect, almost every day, it will be a matter of a minute or so, "Everything all right?" "Yes, everything's fine", and so on. But there may be the odd day, when it would help to chat about the case for a few minutes. That's all it is, Hubert.'

He does not reply immediately.

'And if I agree, and keep out of trouble, the Grey Smoothies will leave me in peace?'

'Yes.'

He nods, and picks up his copy of Stella's draft list.

'Well, in that case, Charlie, we can begin with that one-handed, day-and-a half, GBH you've given me to tax my brain on Monday, can't we?'

I find myself coughing awkwardly.

'Ah, yes... well, as a matter of fact, Hubert, I'm hoping we might agree on something of a change of plan for Monday.'

PART FOUR

THE TWILIGHT OF THE GODS AND GODDESSES

THE TWILIGHT OF THE GODS AND GODDESSES

Monday morning

It's time to begin a new case, but the echoes of last week stubbornly refuse to fade. For one thing, it's my first morning for almost a week without a sword in front of me on my bench, and it's wielder, the High Sheriff in his distinctive ceremonial dress, seated next to me. And for another, I'm reduced to asking myself a question I never thought would cross my mind: where is Kenneth Warnock when we need him? It has actually occurred to me to have someone call his clerk and find out whether, by any chance, he may be free. I can't do that, of course, but I have a feeling that it would be a huge boon this week to have the king of bizarre legal arguments involved in the case I'm about to try, or at least available for consultation.

Stella, I have discovered, has kept from me two rather important facts about the case of the two eighty-plus-year-old Hyde-Booth sisters. Firstly, they are representing themselves; and secondly, this isn't a case of their being denied legal aid, or not being able to afford it: they are going to present a 'defence' that isn't a defence at all, and I would be amazed if there is a barrister or solicitor, other than Kenneth, who would want to get mixed up in it. I am, of course, being totally unfair in suggesting that Stella has kept these two facts from me. True, she didn't mention them in conversation, but I could have discovered both facts at any time, quite easily, simply by opening and reading the file – a step I took belatedly this morning while sipping my latte. I could just as well have done it on Thursday or Friday. I do have the excuse that I was rather preoccupied last week, and I suppose one way of looking at it is that, even if I had read the file then, there would have been nothing I could do about it: so why spoil my weekend worrying about it? Of course, I'm searching for straws of consolation.

Cases where a defendant is representing himself, or herself, are always something of a nightmare. They take longer, and they are very tricky to manage. The defendant usually has no idea how to question a witness, or address the jury, and may not even fully understand the charge, or what defences she may have. So as the judge, I have to explain to her how each phase of the trial works, what she is allowed, and isn't allowed to do, and, inevitably, to advise her to some extent, about how to conduct her case. I may sometimes even ask a few questions on her behalf, and raise points of law that require some answer from the prosecution. In short, I have to bend over backwards to help her, and somehow do so without seeming to take sides – for which I rarely get any thanks. Defendants are inherently distrustful of the judge's intentions, and suspicious of anything I suggest. American judges and lawyers, perhaps in an effort to mitigate the horrors of such trials in their own minds, refer to them in Latin, as cases in which the defendant is acting *pro se*. Personally, I can't see how it can make any difference to put it in Latin. Whether the defendant is representing herself, or acting *pro se*, these are never easy cases to deal with. And I've got two defendants acting *pro se*, both over eighty, with a defence I can't allow the jury to consider. It's a case that cries out for Kenneth Warnock.

Well, if I don't have Kenneth, at least I have Susan Worthington. Susan is prosecuting. She's excellent: always well prepared, good on the law, generally very measured in tone, but more than capable of putting the fear of God into a witness – or even a jury – when she deems it necessary. I've asked her whether she has any objection to the two sisters leaving the dock and coming to sit alongside her in counsel's row. She agrees without hesitation. It's the only way to make sure they can hear what's being said in court, and that we can hear what they have to say. Once they are in place, Carol asks them to stand. I consider telling them they don't have to stand if it's difficult, but they both spring to their feet with considerable agility, and no sign of distress at all. There is a close resemblance between them and they are dressed in a curiously similar way, dark blouses with medium length skirts, and low heels. Each is sporting a mourning brooch, one brown, the other a dark green, and an impressive string of pearls – whether genuine or not, my untutored eye can't say – but impressive, nonetheless.

'Are you Barbara Hyde-Booth?'

'Yes, your Honour,' the sister to my left replies.

'And are you Marcia Hyde-Booth?'

'Yes, your Honour.'

'Good morning, ladies' I begin. 'I hope you don't mind my asking, but you are rather similar in appearance: are you twins?'

'No, your Honour,' Barbara replies. 'I'm a year older than Marcia – I'm 83 and she's only 82 – but we do look alike and people do sometimes confuse us. That's why we wear different coloured brooches – mine's brown, and Marcia's is green.'

An absurd thought flashes through my mind: if all defendants were as considerate as these two, perhaps it would make Hubert's life easier.

'You can call us "Miss Barbara" and "Miss Marcia" if you like,' Barbara adds. 'It's easier than saying "Miss Barbara Hyde-Booth" and "Miss Marcia Hyde-Booth all the time".'

'Thank you,' I reply. 'Now, let me address you both for a moment. I see that you're not legally represented today. You're perfectly entitled to represent yourselves, of course, but I have a duty to advise you that it does put you at something of a disadvantage. I will give you all the assistance I can during the trial, but it's not like having your own lawyer. You're not used to the court's procedure, and you probably don't know much about the rules of evidence. An experienced barrister or solicitor would be able to present your case more effectively than you can on your own. I don't know whether there is any financial reason for your not having a lawyer, or whether there is some other reason, but I would be prepared to grant you both a short adjournment if you wish to seek representation, even at this late stage.'

This, of course, is why everything takes longer with defendants acting *pro se*. I already know the answer to the question I've posed, but I have to hear it from them.

'Thank you, your Honour,' Barbara replies, 'but we will represent ourselves. It's not a matter of money, and we have taken advice from a solicitor, although he did say that it would not be helpful for him to represent us in this case.'

'You don't have to answer this question,' I say. 'Anything said between you and your solicitor…'

'…is privileged,' Barbara interrupts, to my surprise. 'Yes, we know, your Honour. Our late father was a barrister, you see – many years ago now, of course – but he used to appear in some big cases at the Old Bailey, and we learned a lot from him.'

'I see,' I say, trying to ignore Susan's grin. 'Well, all I wanted to ask you is this: it's very unusual for a solicitor to advise a client not to be represented at a trial in the Crown Court. If you don't mind telling me, did he explain why?'

'He said it was because he didn't think we have a legal defence,' Marcia chimes in.

'He didn't think it would be professionally proper for him to represent us under those circumstances,' Barbara adds.

Susan's grin has subsided now, and she stands.

'Your Honour, I hesitate to intervene...'

I nod. I'm having the same reaction.

'It would only be professionally improper if he tried to present a defence he knew to be without foundation,' Susan says. 'Even then, if it was even questionably arguable, he would be perfectly entitled to ask for your Honour's ruling before abandoning it. In addition, he could advise the defendants during the trial, make objections to the prosecution evidence, and take any legal points that might arise on their behalf.'

It is one of the wonderful features of our legal system that the prosecution has an overriding duty of fairness, especially where the defendant is unrepresented, and like all our prosecutors at Bermondsey, Susan is always scrupulous about it.

'I agree, Miss Worthington,' I say. I turn to the two sisters. 'I hope you understood what Miss Worthington said. The point is that a solicitor or barrister can represent you in various ways, even if he can't advance a particular line of defence. You would be well advised to change your minds about this, and as I say, I would be glad to adjourn for a short time to allow you to be represented.'

'Both you and Miss Worthington have been very kind,' Barbara says. She glances at Marcia, who nods. 'But we would still like to represent ourselves.'

I stare at her.

'May I ask why?'

'Because we believe our defence *should* be a legal defence,' she replies. 'It would be a defence in natural law, and we believe that denying us the right to present it to a jury would be a violation of our human rights.'

'We might even have to go to Strasbourg and complain to the court there,' Marcia joins in.

Susan is grinning again.

'Would you like to outline for me what the defence is?' I ask.

'It's exactly what we told that nice police officer when she interviewed us,' Barbara replies. 'The government has no right to make the use of cannabis illegal. It's a violation of natural law and human rights. And if the government is not allowed to make it illegal, we shouldn't be convicted.'

'"*Nulla poena sine lege*,"' Marcia adds, leaning forward confidentially, as if to remind me that the full weight of Strasbourg may one day descend on me if I dare to violate natural law. Just in case it's needed, she offers a translation. '"No penalty without law." Our father taught us that.'

Susan stands again, slowly.

'There may be an alternative course open to the court,' she suggests. 'Your Honour could appoint counsel as *amicus curiae*, even if the defendants represent themselves.'

Amicus curiae, a friend of the court. It's not a bad idea. The barrister appointed is there, technically, solely to assist the court with difficult questions of law. But in practice, they will feel free to raise any points that may need to be examined. It's a stretch. This case is not notable for its difficult questions of law. But it's in a good cause, and if Susan is happy about it, my sense is that I can get away with it. I whisper to Carol.

'Who do we have at court who may be free at some point today?'

She quickly consults the computer. 'Aubrey Brooks is in two sentences in Judge Jenkins's court. I could ask Judge Jenkins's clerk to take him on one side and see if he would be willing, and if so, we could move him up the list. But he will still need time to prepare. It would mean not starting the trial until after lunch, perhaps even tomorrow morning.'

I nod.

'Miss Barbara, Miss Marcia, what's being suggested is that I should appoint a barrister as what's called a friend of the court…'

'An *amicus curiae*,' Marcia says. 'We understand.'

'It won't affect your representing yourselves, but it will provide the court with some legal assistance in case it's needed. I think it may be advisable, and I'm going to adjourn for a short time to inquire into whether it is feasible. I hope we won't keep you waiting for too long. I will extend your bail throughout the trial. You're free to leave court for now, but don't leave the building unless I've released you for lunch, and listen for the tannoy.'

I retire to chambers and Dawn brings me some coffee. About an hour later, she ushers in Susan – and Aubrey Brooks, looking dapper as always in his double-breasted jacket. I am glad to see him. Aubrey sits as a recorder, and is generally regarded as a safe pair of hands – and I wouldn't want to have less experienced counsel for this. Getting him is a stroke of luck – he had a trial in the list at Inner London for this afternoon, but the officer in the case is indisposed, and they've had to adjourn it.

'I understand the court regards me as a friend, Judge,' he says, smiling. 'I'm flattered. It's not an experience I've always had elsewhere.'

We laugh. 'I know I'm imposing, Aubrey,' I reply, 'but I think they will pay you a fee, since I've asked for you as *amicus*.'

Aubrey waves the subject of a fee away.

'Susan tells me we have a couple of old biddies who've been running a cannabis business, and are threatening to go to Strasbourg unless we say they're entitled to do it under natural law?'

'Something like that,' I agree, 'but "a couple of old biddies" doesn't do them justice. They are both very sharp, believe you me.'

Aubrey nods. 'I don't know whether Susan agrees with me, but it seems to me that what we have here is two defendants who admit they are guilty, but won't *plead* guilty. All you can do, Judge, is give them their day in court. I'm not sure there will be any real issues of evidence. I can work with Susan on that, and come up with the answers as we go along. But at the end of the day, Judge, I would probably be bound to advise the court that they have no defence in law, so barring a sympathy verdict of some kind – which seems unlikely in a case of commercial drug supply – they will be duly convicted.'

'The problem, Aubrey,' I say, 'is that I'm obliged to give them such assistance as I can in presenting their defence. But if they don't have a defence…'

'Then, I think you will have to say so, Judge,' Aubrey says. 'I will look at it again, but I wouldn't lose any sleep worrying about the Court of Appeal, much less Strasbourg. I can't see any legal basis for what they're suggesting.'

'There isn't any legal basis,' Susan agrees. 'They're trying it on, Judge, that's all it is. They're hoping for a lenient sentence. You can't blame them at their age, I suppose, but that's all it is. They're hoping for some sympathy from you.'

'Well, thank you both,' I say. 'Can we be ready to start at two o'clock?'

'We're all ready to go,' Susan confirms.

'I'm as ready as I'll ever be,' Aubrey says.

* * *

Monday afternoon

Often, if you don't get your trial started first thing on Monday morning, when you are finally ready, you find that you're a few jurors short of a panel – and you have to wait until late stragglers arrive, or jurors have been selected from the panels in the other courts. I have been worrying about not starting until after lunch, particularly given the time it might take to find jurors available for a lengthy fraud case such as the one Hubert is starting today. But mercifully, the jury manager has succeeded in sending us fifteen jurors in waiting, which ought to be enough in this case. None of the potential jurors knows the defendants, or anyone else involved in the case, or has heard of the allegations against the Hyde-Booth sisters, so we have the luxury of taking the first twelve whose cards Carol picks out of her jar at random.

I take some time, not only to give the jury the usual pretrial directions – about not discussing the case with others, not doing their own research, including on the internet, and ignoring any press reports of the case – but also to explain to the jurors why the elderly defendants are sitting in counsel's row, and that, at their invitation, we are going to be calling them 'Miss Barbara' and 'Miss Marcia'. They're a youngish jury, six men and six women, with the usual variety of cultural backgrounds you get with Bermondsey juries. I explain, too, that despite Aubrey's presence, the sisters are not represented, and that I will be giving them such assistance as I can to present their case. This makes no difference to the jury's task, which is to listen to the evidence and return a true verdict according to the evidence. I do my best to explain Aubrey's role, though I'm not sure how much sense it makes to them – or to me, for that matter – that the court has its own counsel but the defendants don't.

'Members of the jury,' Susan begins, 'as his Honour has explained, I appear to prosecute in this case, while my learned friend Mr Brooks is here to assist the court with legal matters. Miss Barbara and Miss Marcia are not legally represented. This is not a complicated case, and I will be quite brief. I've asked the usher to give out copies of the indictment, one between two, and I see that you now have those. If you will look at the indictment with me, you will see that Miss Barbara and Miss Marcia are charged with one count of conspiracy to supply cannabis, a controlled drug of class B, over a significant period of time. The prosecution cannot say with certainty for how long the defendants have been operating their drug business, and so have opted to allege a time frame of one year, though the evidence will suggest that it was in fact significantly longer. His Honour will explain to you later in the trial that a conspiracy is simply an agreement to do something unlawful. In this case, the Crown say that together, Miss Barbara and Miss Marcia operated a discreet, but sophisticated business, cultivating cannabis plants, and supplying cannabis to customers in return for money, in a quiet and outwardly respectable residential area of south London.

'Members of the jury, their business came to light as a result of information picked up, quite by chance, by a police officer, DC Jill Mason, whose case this is. DC Mason will tell you that one evening in March of this year, she was off duty and was in a public house with her partner, for purely social reasons, when she overheard discussion between two men sitting at the next table. These men were talking openly about "weed" being available at an address in Barkworth Road, a street in South Bermondsey, from two ladies they referred to as the "Goddesses of Weed."'

'Loose lips sink ships,' Miss Marcia comments disapprovingly, with a glance in the direction of the jury.

'Still,' Miss Barbara adds, 'the "Goddesses of Weed" – that's not bad, is it?'

The jury are smiling, and several are raising hands to mouths, to avoid being seen to be laughing too obviously.

'Please don't interrupt, ladies,' I say. I briefly contemplate sending the jury out and lecturing the Hyde-Booth sisters about the folly of making silly, self-incriminating comments. But it won't do any good. The jury have already got the picture, and for Miss Barbara and Miss Marcia, avoiding self-incrimination is no longer what this case is about – if it ever was.

'Sorry, your Honour,' Miss Barbara replies, apparently on behalf of them both.

'The following morning,' Susan continues, 'DC Mason reported what she had heard to DCI Isherwood, who supervises drug investigations in that area of South London, and asked his permission to visit the address in question undercover, in order to investigate. DCI Isherwood agreed, and a few days later, DC Mason visited the house in Barkworth Road at about seven in the evening. She knocked on the door. It was answered by Miss Marcia, who asked what she wanted. DC Mason intimated that she wished to purchase cannabis, and after explaining that she had found out about the house through gossip in the pub, was admitted. DC Mason will describe the scene for you. She will tell you that it was as far from the popular image of a drug den as could be imagined. Every effort had been made to create a pleasant and affluent environment. The living room at the front of the house was expensively and tastefully decorated in the style of a Victorian drawing room...'

'Edwardian,' Miss Marcia insists with a suggestion of irritation. 'Victorian, my foot. It's Edwardian. Anyone can see that.'

I am poised to intervene, but this isn't Susan's first trial. She's had defendants try to disrupt her openings before, and she isn't about to let the Hyde-Booth sisters slow her down. She is quite content to plough ahead, ignoring the chuckles in the jury box.

'Edwardian – I do apologise; I stand corrected. In the style of an Edwardian drawing room, with comfortable armchairs, and subdued lighting provided by ornate lamps, with classical music – I'm told a Mozart string quartet – playing in the background. There were several men and women present, some smoking cannabis, the smell of which was very noticeable. Others were drinking tea, and cakes were available on the dining table. DC Mason asked if she would be obliged to smoke the cannabis at the house, or whether she could take it away, and was told that she was free to stay and smoke at the house, or take it away, as she preferred. Miss Barbara invited her to have a cup of tea, which DC Mason did. DC Mason then purchased cannabis at a cost of £25 and left the house.

'During the following seven days, DC Mason visited the house on two further occasions, again purchasing cannabis to the tune of £25, as on the first occasion. DCI Isherwood also assigned a second officer, DC Jason Bridge, to visit the house undercover on two different days. DC Bridge also purchased quantities of cannabis, which he removed from the premises. Both officers noted that on each occasion they visited the house, there were customers smoking cannabis on the premises, most enjoying tea and cakes at the same time.

'At the start of the following week, members of the jury, DCI Isherwood obtained a search warrant for the premises. With DC Mason and a number of uniformed officers, he visited the house at seven o'clock in the evening to execute the warrant. The scene that awaited the officers was much the same as it had been on the occasions of the undercover visits. The officers seized a substantial quantity of cannabis, and took the particulars of six people present who were smoking cannabis. These six people were then released, on condition that they agreed to attend the police station at a later date for interview. Having established that the two sisters owned the house, DCI Isherwood then arrested Miss Barbara and Miss Marcia on suspicion of supplying cannabis. They were both taken to the police station, and later interviewed in the presence of the duty solicitor.

'Members of the jury, you will hear the interviews read to you in due course. But I should tell you now that the most interesting fact to be revealed during the interviews was that, not only were the defendants supplying cannabis, they were also producing it. During their interviews, both sisters told DC Mason that they owned a second house in Stockholm Road, not far from the house in Barkworth Road, where the cannabis was being sold. DC Mason adjourned the interviews and obtained a search warrant for the house in Stockholm Road, which she visited, with a number of uniformed officers, later that same evening. In that house, members of the jury, the officers found that the second floor was dedicated to the cultivation of cannabis plants. There was enhanced lighting and heating apparatus, and altogether, the house had all the hallmarks of a professionally run cannabis cultivation factory. The officers recovered twenty-six mature cannabis plants, a number, the Crown say, which, taken together with the equipment, clearly indicates a commercial operation, rather than growing one or two plants for personal consumption. Not on a huge scale, but certainly a commercial operation.'

'What does she expect?' Miss Barbara asks. 'Does she expect us to work for nothing?'

'Does she know what a decent female cannabis plant costs these days?' Miss Marcia wonders aloud.

'Enough,' I say. 'Please don't interrupt. You will get your chance to speak in due course.'

'Yes, your Honour,' Miss Barbara replies, quietly.

'Members of the jury,' Susan says by way of conclusion, 'at the end of the trial, his Honour will direct you about the law, and I anticipate that he will direct you that the Crown bring the charge and the Crown must prove it so that you are sure of guilt, if you are to convict. Nothing less than that is enough for a conviction. Miss Barbara and Miss Marcia do not have to prove their innocence. In fact, they don't have to prove anything at all.' Susan glances up at me. 'Your Honour, I will call DC Mason.'

'I swear by almighty God that the evidence I shall give shall be the truth, the whole truth, and nothing but the truth.' DC Mason turns briefly to face me. She is tall and slim, and has an air of quiet confidence about her. 'Jill Mason, detective constable, attached to Kennington police station, your Honour.'

'Officer,' Susan begins, 'on the evening of 7 March this year were you off duty, and did you have occasion to go somewhere?'

'Yes. My partner, Jeff, and I decided to go out for a couple of drinks. We went to the Marquis of Wellington in Druid Street.'

'What time was this?'

'Seven, seven-thirty.'

'Was the pub busy at that time?'

'There were a good number of people, but it wasn't crowded. We were able to find a table for two without any problem.'

'Did anyone come to your attention during the evening?'

'Yes. I noticed two gentlemen sitting at the table next to us.'

'Can you describe these gentlemen for us?'

'They were both in their fifties, I would say, well dressed – jackets and dark trousers, and one of the gentlemen was wearing a tie. They were drinking pints of beer, but they were not in any way drunk.'

'Officer, let me ask you this: were you trying to spy or eavesdrop on these gentlemen?'

'No, not at all. I was off duty. I was there with my partner for an enjoyable evening out. I wasn't thinking about work.'

'But did you nonetheless overhear some conversation that attracted your attention as a police officer?'

'Yes, I did.'

'What did you hear?'

Miss Marcia is on her feet with surprising agility.

'Your Honour, I apologise for interrupting. I may be wrong. But from my recollection of things our father used to tell us, I believe that question may call for hearsay.'

Aubrey somehow manages to keep a perfectly straight face, which, I confess, is more than I can.

'As your Honour's *amicus*,' he says, 'I believe Miss Marcia – and my late learned friend Mr Hyde-Booth – are correct. Any answer the witness might give would clearly be hearsay.'

Susan has at least one respectable response to this, and she would be entitled to point out that no one objected during her opening speech, when she told the jury exactly what had been said. But her sense of fairness prevails, as it always does, and she concedes graciously, without my intervention. Besides, she hasn't been able to suppress her smile any more than I could.

'I'll deal with it in another way,' she says. 'Officer, as a result of what you heard did you do anything?'

'Not immediately. But on returning home, I made a note of what I'd heard – not word for word, but the substance of it – and the following morning, I reported it to DCI Isherwood, the officer in charge of drug investigations for South London.'

'Did you make any particular request or recommendation to DCI Isherwood at that time?'

'Yes. I asked for his permission to visit an address in Barkworth Road SE16, working undercover.'

'For what purpose?'

'To investigate whether or not drugs were being supplied at the premises.'

'Do you need the permission of a senior officer to work undercover?'

'Oh, yes, always. There are protocols that have to be established – protocols for the officer's safety, such as the identity you will use, codes for signalling that you need help if things go south, procedures for meeting your supervising officer to be debriefed, and so on. And then there are administrative protocols, such as authorisation to spend a given amount of money on things such as drugs, establishing a chain of custody of the drugs, and preserving them as evidence. It's not a simple matter to go undercover.'

'I take it from what you say that there is always an element of danger in going undercover?'

'Yes. Initially, you're walking into a situation you may know very little about. Drug dealers can often be highly paranoid. They tend to suspect anyone new of being a police officer, and they may try to test you by putting you in a difficult position, such as inviting you to take drugs yourself on the premises. You have to be prepared for anything.'

'It's not paranoia if they're really after you,' Miss Barbara comments.

'In fairness,' DC Mason adds, 'I do want to make it clear that, because of what I'd heard in the Marquis of Wellington, I wasn't concerned about safety in this case, and at no time did I ever feel threatened. I had a good idea what I was dealing with before I went in...'

'The "Goddesses of Weed,"' Miss Barbara says, to loud laughter across the court.

'Yes,' DC Mason agrees, after laughing as loudly as everyone else.

'Did DCI Isherwood give you permission to visit the premises in Barkworth Road undercover?'

'Yes, he did. I was given the identity of Jill Perry – you generally try to keep your own first name, since you're so used to being called by that name. According to my legend, I was a teacher, getting burned out by all the paperwork I had to do, and needing a little something to brighten my evenings after a hard slog at school.'

'And she played the part brilliantly,' Miss Marcia comments. 'We would never have suspected her for a moment, would we, Barbs?'

'Never in a million years,' Miss Barbara agrees. 'Oscar material, I'd say.'

'When did you first visit the house in Barkworth Road?' Susan asks.

'On 9 March, at about seven in the evening.'

'Describe for the jury what happened.'

'I approached the house and rang the doorbell. The door was opened by a lady I didn't know at that time, but now know to be the defendant Miss Marcia. I introduced myself using my undercover identity, and stated that I was interested in buying some cannabis. As soon as the door was opened, I noticed a very pungent odour of cannabis.'

'Which you were familiar with, no doubt, because of your experience as a police officer?' Susan asks.

DC Mason smiles. 'And because of my previous experience as a university student who was sometimes invited to parties,' she adds.

'Of course. Did Miss Marcia invite you in?'

'Yes, she did.'

'What did you see on entering the house?'

The officer shakes her head. 'I was absolutely astonished,' she replies. 'I found myself, not in your typical drug den, but in a living room, beautifully decorated and furnished – and the Victorian style thing was my mistake; I understand now that it was in the Edwardian style. Sorry for the confusion. There were leather armchairs, three comfortable-looking sofas, one or two *chaises longues*, and three very elegant coffee tables. Classical music was playing quietly in the background.' She smiles again. 'And it was a Mozart string quartet – I'm right about that.' She turns to me. 'I studied music at Uni, your Honour.'

'Number fourteen, in G major,' Miss Marcia adds, by way of confirmation.

'What happened once you were inside the house?'

'Miss Marcia invited me to sit down at one of the coffee tables, which I did. I observed that there were six other people, four men and two women, present in the living room, all except two of whom were smoking joints. I noticed that all these individuals were smartly dressed and had an affluent appearance, and for the most part, seemed to know each other. I deduced that from the fact that they were conversing in a familiar way. So, this too, made the drawing room very different from what you'd expect to find in a drug den.'

'It's not a drug den,' Miss Barbara insists, 'and we're very particular about our clientele – we don't cater to the riff-raff.'

'Miss Barbara then approached me, and introduced herself and Miss Marcia to me, and we chatted about inconsequential things for a minute or two. Miss Barbara brought me some tea and a cake, which I accepted.'

'That was on the house, I take it?'

'It was, yes.'

'Did there come a time when the conversation turned to what I might call business matters?'

'Yes. I explained my situation, as per my legend, and stated to Miss Barbara that I wanted to buy some cannabis. I told her that I had never bought cannabis before, and asked for her guidance. She talked to me knowledgeably for some time, and recommended a particular cut as being good quality, but not too strong. I asked whether I had to smoke it at the house, or whether I could take it away, and she replied that it was my choice. I was welcome to stay and smoke at the house, have tea, and get to know some of the other customers – actually, she called them "guests" – or I could take it home.'

'And did you enter into a transaction with Miss Barbara?'

'Yes, I agree to purchase cannabis from her at a cost of £25, which was within the allocated funds approved by DCI Isherwood. Miss Marcia wrapped it up for me in a strong black garbage bag, for the purpose of minimising the odour of the cannabis.'

'And, just to make sure we're clear, was what you purchased herbal cannabis – there wasn't any cannabis resin, sometimes referred to as "hash?"'

'No. From my observation, the defendants dealt only in herbal cannabis, and not in resin.'

'I should think not,' Miss Barbara comments. 'Awful, messy stuff. Never could abide it.'

'I take it, officer, that you took the cannabis you purchased away with you?'

'I did, sir. I went directly from Barkworth Road to the nick – the police station, sorry – where I placed the cannabis in the custody of DCI Isherwood, with a view to its being preserved for evidential purposes.'

'And is it available, should anyone wish to see it?'

'Yes, it is.'

Susan turns to me. 'Your Honour, if the court wishes, I will ask DCI Isherwood to produce all the cannabis purchased for inspection before closing my case.'

'That's up to you, Miss Worthington,' I reply. 'It might interest the jury to see it.' I see a few enthusiastic nods in the jury box. 'But I'm afraid they won't be able to take it into their jury room,' I add, just to quash any thoughts of malfeasance. The nods turn to chuckles.

'Officer,' Susan continues, 'did you visit the house in Barkworth Road on any other occasions?'

'Yes. I visited the house on two further occasions, 12 and 16 March, and on both occasions, I made an identical purchase of cannabis for the price of £25, and again, the cannabis purchased was taken straight to the station and placed in evidence.'

'Who did you deal with on those occasions?'

'I dealt with both defendants. Miss Barbara would take the money, and Miss Marcia would wrap up the cannabis for me.'

'Are you aware that DCI Isherwood also assigned another officer, DC Jason Bridge, to make visits to the premises at different times, and that DC Bridge also made purchases of cannabis there?'

'Yes, I am aware of that.'

'As a result of the investigations made by you and DC Bridge, was further action taken?'

'Yes. On 22 March DCI Isherwood applied for a search warrant for the premises in Barkworth Road, and at about seven o'clock on that evening, DCI Isherwood and I executed the warrant together with a number of uniformed officers.'

'The object being…?'

'The object being to seize and preserve any drugs and other evidence on the premises, and to arrest the defendants for supplying a controlled substance, if there was evidence of that at that time.'

'Officer, let me ask you this. You had visited the premises undercover. Would it be usual for you to be part of the team executing the search warrant?'

'No, usually, an undercover's identity is protected as far as possible, so they wouldn't be involved in the arrests. But I don't do undercover work – this was a one-off for me – I wasn't going to use that identity again, and DCI Isherwood thought, given the defendants' age, that it might be advisable to have a police officer they knew involved. It can get quite fraught when you're executing a warrant. I had struck up a friendly relationship with the defendants, which helped to keep things calm.'

'How nice of Mr Isherwood,' Miss Barbara comments.

'When you entered the premises, what did you find?'

'Much the same as on the other occasions I'd been there. On this occasion, there were two men and two women smoking joints when we entered. Miss Barbara and Miss Marcia were chatting with them. Tea, coffee, and cake were provided. DCI Isherwood explained that we were police officers and that we had a search warrant, and ordered all those present to stop what they were doing and stay where they were. Uniformed officers took particulars of the persons present who were smoking, and they were then released on condition that they reported to the police station at a later date, to be interviewed. The uniformed officers then made a thorough search of the premises, resulting in the seizure of several kilos of a herbal substance, later tested and found to be herbal cannabis. The officers also found and seized the sum of £245.50 in cash.'

'That was from our pensions,' Miss Marcia complains. 'When are we going to get it back?'

'What happened with respect to the defendants?'

'DCI Isherwood advised both defendants that they were

under arrest on suspicion of supplying a controlled substance, and cautioned them.'

'Officer, please remind us of the words of the caution.'

'The words of the caution are, "you do not have to say anything. But it may harm your defence if you fail to mention, when questioned, something which you later rely on in court. Anything you do say may be used in evidence."'

'Did either defendant make any reply to the caution?'

DC Mason turns to the relevant page in her notebook and reads carefully.

'Yes. Miss Barbara said, "Cannabis grows naturally in English soil. How can it be illegal to use it? What are you going to ban next, radishes, rhubarb?" Miss Marcia replied, "Our father always said it would come to this in the end, a police state. What did we fight the war for? That's what I want to know." The defendants were taken to the police station and interviewed under caution, in turn, by DCI Isherwood and myself in the presence of the duty solicitor.'

'Yes. Officer, I am going to ask you in due course to help me to read the interviews in full. But for now, I want to ask you about one particular matter that came up during the interviews, one which caused you to undertake further investigation. Tell the jury about that please.'

'Yes. Miss Barbara was interviewed first, and of course, we asked her about the source of the cannabis found at the house in Barkworth Road. We were expecting to hear that they got it from a dealer. But to our surprise, she told us that they produced the product themselves by growing and preparing cannabis plants, with some casual help in the form of manual labour from two young men who lived locally, whom she declined to name. She added that this activity was being carried out in another house she and Miss Marcia owned, in Stockholm Road SE16, which is a short distance from Barkworth Road.'

'On hearing that, what action did you take?'

'We immediately adjourned the interview, and with the duty solicitor, we began the interview with Miss Marcia. We confronted her with what Miss Barbara had told us and invited her to comment on it. She immediately agreed that what Miss Barbara had said was true. At that point, it was clear to DCI Isherwood and myself that we needed to take immediate action to seize and preserve any evidence there might be at the address in Stockholm Road. By this time, it was after midnight, and we advised both sisters that we would have to keep them in custody overnight, and conclude their interviews the following day. DCI Isherwood rang round the list of night duty magistrates, to obtain a search warrant for the premises in Stockholm Road.'

'Officer, explain to the jury why that was such an urgent matter.'

'Well, at that point we had to assume that, once news of the sisters' arrest reached their customers, and perhaps the local lads and others who might have been working with them, someone might try to destroy or remove evidence from the premises. It was important to prevent that, and to secure the evidence ourselves without delay.'

'Was DCI Isherwood successful in obtaining a search warrant?'

'Yes, he was.'

'What did you do next?'

'DCI Isherwood rounded up four uniformed officers from the canteen and pressganged them in the middle of their bacon sandwiches, and we immediately went to the address in Stockholm Road. We didn't know whether we would find anyone on the premises, so we had brought equipment with us to effect a forcible entry if we had to. But in fact, when we knocked on the door and announced ourselves, the door was opened by a man who appeared to be in his early twenties, casually dressed, who stated that he was "just looking after the place for the old ladies."'

'That would be George, I suppose,' Miss Barbara asks her sister, apparently oblivious to the fact that she is interrupting the evidence.

'That's what I would have thought,' Miss Marcia replies, 'but the papers they sent us said it was Bernie.'

'They must have swapped shifts without telling us,' Miss Barbara observes accusingly.

'Please don't make comments while the witness is giving evidence,' I say.

'Continue, officer,' Susan says.

'DCI Isherwood informed the man that we had a warrant to search the premises for evidence of the cultivation of cannabis plants, and advised him that it would be in his best interests to cooperate with us.'

'And did he cooperate with you?'

'He did. He immediately led us to the second floor, where we found clear evidence of the systematic cultivation of cannabis plants. There were twenty-six plants at different stages of development. There was a sprinkler system in operation. There was also LED lighting. LED refers to high density discharge lamps. These lamps produce an intense artificial light, which, when used correctly, benefits the growth and development of the plants.'

'What happened then?'

'DCI Isherwood told the man we had found in the house that he was under arrest on suspicion of cultivating plants of the genus cannabis, and cautioned him, to which he made no reply. DCI Isherwood then determined that it would be better to postpone a full search of the premises until daylight, especially as we would need the assistance of forensic experts to seize the plants and the paraphernalia we had found and preserve them as evidence. The assistance we needed would not be available until the following morning. So, we took the decision to secure the premises overnight, leaving an officer on guard. Officers resumed the search the following morning with a forensic team. I wasn't involved in that, but it is within my knowledge that the plants and equipment we had found were seized at that time.'

Susan pauses for a few moments, to consult her notes.

'Yes. Thank you, officer. Finally, based on your experience as a police officer, are you able to assist the jury about the significance of the quantity of plants and the use of LED lighting in relation to the cultivation of cannabis plants?'

Aubrey stands. 'Your Honour, I'm not sure what answer my learned friend is looking for with that question. If she is asking whether it indicates a commercial operation rather than production for personal use, it may be that, technically, it would be better coming from DCI Isherwood than from this officer. I'm not sure it matters, but since I am your Honour's *amicus…*'

Susan nods. 'I will leave it for DCI Isherwood,' she replies. 'Your Honour, that's all I have for this witness.'

We have some time before the usual end of the afternoon session, but the sisters Hyde-Booth have already had a long day, and are beginning to look slightly weary. I'm not going to explain to them about cross-examination and make them put questions to DC Mason this afternoon.

'We will leave it there for the day,' I announce. 'Ten o'clock tomorrow, members of the jury. Please don't forget what I've told you about not discussing the case with anyone else.'

* * *

Monday Evening

When I arrive back at the vicarage this evening, the Reverend Mrs Walden announces that she has booked us a table at La Bella Napoli, one of our favourite venues for a relaxed dinner in the evenings. Tony, the owner and head chef, and proud native of the eponymous city, does a wonderful sea bass, and for a few favoured customers, will prepare an Insalata Caesar at your tableside, adding a touch of theatre to a tasty dish. The Reverend and I can claim some credit for the tableside preparation. Tony had always done it in Italy, but had gradually abandoned the practice in London because of what he saw as our frantic lifestyle, which gets in the way of a leisurely meal. But in a case I tried some time ago, there was evidence of two Italian chefs yelling at each other while brandishing meat cleavers, ostensibly while arguing about the correct way to make Insalata Caesar, in particular whether it was essential to use eggs rather than mayonnaise. The real argument turned out to be about the fact that they had been targeted by an organised crime syndicate as a result of gambling debts accrued by one of them. But by the time that became clear, Tony, who had heard about the case through the grapevine, was involved, and insisted that eggs were the preferred ingredient, and that the salad was traditionally done at tableside. After that, it became a standing joke between us, and he now does it for us every time, and always with eggs, not mayonnaise.

But I am only too aware that the Reverend Mrs Walden has things on her mind other than sea bass and Insalata Caesar. When she wants to talk about something serious, we almost always end up at La Bella Napoli or the Delights of the Raj, and tonight I know exactly what the topic of conversation will be. The Reverend is not your average vicar. She supports a number of causes not usually associated with the Church of England, or, for that matter, with Christianity in general. For example, her views on sex and marriage are not exactly orthodox, and have sometimes raised eyebrows in her congregation. But her manner somehow enables her to embrace a certain degree of freedom of thought without causing offence, and her bishop has always been remarkably supportive. The legalisation of cannabis for all purposes has long been one of her causes, and she has attended numerous rallies over the years, in addition to lobbying our MP on the subject.

'I can't believe you're prosecuting those two old ladies, Charlie,' she begins, once the tableside theatre has concluded. 'How old are they?'

'I'm not prosecuting them,' I point out. 'Susan Worthington is prosecuting them, on behalf of the Crown Prosecution Service. They're early eighties, I forget exactly.'

She stares at me. 'You're the judge. There must be something you can do.'

'Such as what?'

'Such as throwing the case out.'

'Clara, I can't throw a case out because of a defendant's age – well, not unless they're unfit to stand trial, mentally or physically – and believe me, none of that applies to the Hyde-Booth sisters. They're both as fit as a fiddle, and neither of them has lost a single marble.'

She takes a deep breath. 'All right. I'm sorry. I know it's not your fault. But it's just so unfair to prosecute people for using a plant that occurs naturally, especially when it's a couple of elderly dears who like to take a puff in the evenings.'

I pause before finishing my Insalata Caesar, which, as ever, has been wonderful.

'Clara,' I say, 'I don't know where you're getting your information about the case – I assume from your friends in the pro-cannabis group – but please allow me to point something out. The Hyde-Booth sisters are not two elderly dears taking a puff in the evenings. They are two extremely shrewd businesswomen, who've been running a highly successful – and highly profitable – commercial operation to supply cannabis to a well-heeled clientele for any number of years now. Their cannabis plants don't just occur naturally, I assure you. They're cultivated in a well-equipped greenhouse, with LED lighting, carefully regulated temperatures, and all mod cons.'

'So what?' she replies. 'We grow fruit and vegetables in greenhouses all the time. It's convenient and efficient. But they still grow naturally if we let them. Charlie, I could grow cannabis plants in our garden at the vicarage, alongside the carrots and sprouts.'

I go hot and cold for a moment. 'You're not, are you?' I ask. I'm sure I must sound rather alarmed.

She laughs out loud. 'No, of course not. But my point is: I could.'

I recover somewhat. 'They even contribute to the local economy,' I continue, 'by employing two lads to look after the plants for them while they're developing. The police aren't sure how long they've been at it, but it's been a long time, and they would still be at it, if it hadn't been for a bright young DC keeping her ears open, and hearing a conversation between two of their customers that she wasn't meant to hear.'

We drink some wine for a while, a lovely house Chenin Blanc Tony recommends to go with the sea bass.

'What's their defence?' she asks.

'Well, that's the strange thing about this case,' I reply. 'As far as I can see, they don't have one, and they don't want one. They admitted everything to the police when they were arrested, and they're in the process of admitting everything in court. They've both refused to be represented. I've appointed Aubrey

Brooks as *amicus curiae* – a friend of the court – to point out to me any legal points I'm missing, but I think Aubrey agrees with me.'

'But they must be saying something by way of defence,' Clara insists. 'Otherwise, why didn't they just plead guilty and have done with it? They'd get a discount on sentence for that, wouldn't they?'

The sea bass arrives, and we take some moments to savour the first delicious bites.

'Yes, they would – if they pleaded. But it's almost as though they're saying, "We're guilty, but we're not going to plead guilty, and you can't make us."'

'Why would they do that?'

It's a good question. I pause to take a sip of wine.

'I think it's a matter of principle. They feel the same way you do. Cannabis occurs naturally, and it's wrong to prosecute people for using a plant that grows naturally. I understand the argument, but it's not a defence. It's an offence to cultivate and deal in cannabis, they're going to be convicted of that offence, and I will have to sentence them. That's what's really bothering me, if you want to know.'

She stares at me. 'Well, surely, you'll give them a slap on the wrist, won't you? What else can you do with two elderly women like that?'

'It's not that simple, Clara. We have sentencing guidelines, and these women have been running a well-oiled commercial operation. They should be looking at a custodial sentence.'

'You don't want to do that,' she insists.

'No, of course I don't. But if I do anything else, I have to come up with a reason the Court of Appeal will buy when Susan complains to them that I've passed an unduly lenient sentence. It's not easy when the defendants not only show no remorse, but keep telling whoever will listen to them that they're entitled to do what they were doing under some kind of natural law.'

We finish the sea bass and enjoy the wine in silence for some time. Tony returns with the dessert menu and the obligatory complimentary glass of Lemoncello.

'How did the day go for Hubert?' she asks from behind the dessert menu. 'Wasn't today the first day of that big case you've given him?'

'Yes,' I reply. 'They didn't get any further than swearing a jury and the start of the prosecution's opening, which I'm told is going to take a couple of days. So there was nothing very much for Hubert to do today, except to take good notes. Marjorie says he's in good form. She's going to check on him every day. She says the first real challenge will be a week or so in.'

'What's happening a week or so in?' she asks.

'Hubert will have to decide whether to let in the evidence of two financial experts the prosecution wants to call,' I explain. 'The defence says their evidence is inadmissible. It's the kind of decision he's made countless times before. He just has to keep everything straight in his mind, and he should be fine.'

'He will be fine,' she replies.

Tony comes to inquire how our dinner has been, which of course, is wonderful. We follow his recommendation, ordering the chocolate-hazelnut tiramisu, and chat for a few moments as we sip the Lemoncello.

'There's going to be a demonstration outside court tomorrow,' she says suddenly, once Tony has retreated to the kitchen. "Save the Bermondsey Goddesses.""

I stare at her.

'Clara…Why didn't you tell me before. I should alert security,' I say.

'Oh, not that kind of demonstration,' she replies. 'It will be six or seven members of the group with home-made placards. And they're not going to enter the building.' She pauses. 'Actually, I should say, *we* are not going to enter the building. I'm going to be with them.' She sees my transient look of alarm. 'Don't worry, Charlie. I'll be discreet. I won't do anything to embarrass you, I promise.'

I believe her. We've been here more than once before in aid of various causes, and she never has.

* * *

Tuesday morning

'I think they should be left alone to make a few bob if they can,' Elsie says as she puts the finishing touches to my ham and cheese bap. 'I know I shouldn't say that, sir, but it's hard to live on just your pension if you're a woman, and that's the truth, especially at their age.'

'What is it they call them in the paper?' Jeanie asks, '"the Goddesses of Weed?" And both of them not a day under eighty. Well, I mean, you have to laugh, don't you, sir?'

'It's not a laughing matter for me,' I point out.

'Well, no, of course, sir, you being a judge...'

'I have to take it seriously. Supplying drugs is a serious offence, Jeanie, especially when you do it for money.'

'They gave my grandchildren a good talking to about it at school, just last week, didn't they?' Elsie replies. 'Quite right, too. You have to keep it from the youngsters if you can, don't you? But my old man says a whiff or two can't do you any harm when you get to our age.'

'I'm not sure I'd want to do it myself,' Jeanie says, 'but if people want to try it, I don't see why they shouldn't. I don't think they should ban it altogether.'

'And what about those people from Jamaica, you know, the what's-its...?' Elsie asks.

'Rastafarians?' I suggest.

'Yes, those are the ones. I mean, they use it for their religion, sir, don't they? It doesn't seem right to penalise them for that, does it?'

Mercifully, I succeed in gathering up my bap and change, and making my escape before being drawn into that discussion.

George has several newspapers to show me today, because they feature a photograph of the Hyde-Booth sisters leaving court yesterday afternoon, smiling for the camera and generally looking rather pleased with themselves. Two also claim to have interviews with the sisters, who make good use of the platform to extol the virtues of plants that grow naturally in English soil.

'You'll have to warn the jury, won't you, guv,' he observes presciently, 'you know, just in case they've read them?'

George doesn't miss a trick when it comes to selling newspapers. He's quite right, of course, and he has been selling me newspapers for long enough now to know how these things work. I buy one of each, plus *The Times*, as usual, which, I'm gratified to note, appears not to regard the Hyde-Booth sisters as front page material.

Arriving at court, I see one or two members of the pro-cannabis league starting to position themselves outside the main entrance, banners in hand. There's no sign of the Reverend Mrs Walden as yet, but I'm quite sure she's right – they're not going to cause Security any concern. Even so, I divert to the judges' entrance at the rear of the building as smartly as I can, so as not to attract attention.

The jury having been duly warned, and DC Mason having returned to the witness box, it's time for me to explain to the defendants about cross-examination, even though they will no doubt insist that they picked up the essentials long ago from their father.

'This is your chance to ask DC Mason any questions,' I explain. 'If there's anything she has said that you believe to be incorrect, or if there's any additional information you believe she can provide, something she hasn't mentioned yet in her evidence, this is your time to ask her about it.'

They confer quietly for a few seconds. Miss Marcia stands.

'Your Honour, everything she said is quite correct – except for the Edwardian thing, of course – so we don't need to ask her anything like that. But there is just one thing we would like to clarify.'

'Yes, of course,' I reply.

'Officer,' Miss Marcia says, 'is it true that, even left to its own devices, a healthy cannabis plant is capable of growing to full maturity if planted in England?'

DC Mason looks at me, smiling. She is aware that she's being asked to serve as an expert witness, and quite rightly, she wants to give me the chance to say that, technically, she's probably not an expert, before answering. Aubrey stands.

'Your Honour,' he ventures tentatively, 'it may be that that evidence would be better coming from DCI Isherwood than from this witness.'

Before I can gather my thoughts, Susan rides to the rescue.

'That won't be necessary, your Honour,' she says. 'The Crown does not dispute that cannabis plants can grow successfully to maturity out of doors in the United Kingdom.'

'Thank you, Miss Worthington,' Miss Marcia says politely. 'I'm very grateful.'

'Though I should make it clear,' Susan adds, 'that we also say that that fact has no relevance whatsoever to the question the jury have to decide in this case.'

Miss Marcia looks a bit less grateful now. But after this, things speed up considerably. Since no one has any more questions for DC Mason, Susan calls DC Bridge, to deal with the visits he paid to the house in Barkworth Road. His evidence is essentially a replay of DC Mason's, and Susan takes him through it at quite a pace; the sisters have no questions, and we have soon finished with our second witness. Then there follows the inevitable reading of the police interviews, Susan reading the part of the officers, and DCI Isherwood reading the part of the defendants. As ever it's a tedious process, and by the time we have completed it, with a merciful coffee break in between the two interviews, we are all grateful to be within sight of lunchtime. At this point, Carol whispers that Stella needs me to take a plea of guilty to an ABH, a traditional Saturday night punch-up at the George and Dragon, said to have been provoked by differences of opinion about the relative merits of Millwall and Charlton Athletic football clubs.

The defendant is a merchant seaman of previous good character, and everyone wants him to be sentenced today, in the hope that he will be allowed to rejoin his ship, which is due to put to sea at Harwich tomorrow, *en route* to various exotic ports of call. Hubert was due to do it, but he doesn't want to interrupt the prosecution's opening in his fraud case, so Stella would like me to take it. I'm very glad to – both for Hubert's benefit, and also to give the sisters a breather before Susan closes her case and the ball drops into their court. I impose a stiff fine on the errant mariner, to be paid before he leaves court, and make my way to lunch.

An oasis of calm in a desert of chaos. And, today, so it is. Hubert seems very cheerful, and while tucking in as heartily as ever to the dish of the day, billed as a mushroom and leek risotto, gives us a vivid, humorous verbal portrait of one particularly arrogant member of the Bar we all know, who is representing one of his defendants. The mood quickly spreads among us, and we all enjoy lunch.

* * *

Tuesday afternoon

If the morning came to a speedy close, the afternoon seems determined to outdo it. After presenting the jury with a written confirmation of the Crown's capitulation on the question of cannabis plants flourishing in the countryside of England, Susan declares her case to be closed. It's time for me to explain to the sisters what their options are at this stage of the trial, and it's important stuff. Usually, the jury would be in court while I do this, so that they can see that fair play is maintained. But I'm not sure how the sisters will react to what I'm about to tell them. It may well be that they will have a few comments, some of which the jury shouldn't hear. Not only that, but I will almost certainly need to have a discussion with Aubrey about whether they have any kind of defence to the charge in the indictment, and if not, how I should direct the jury about that unusual circumstance. So, I decide not to bring the jury into court just yet. I will explain to them what's been going on later.

'The time has now come,' I begin, 'when, if you wish, you may present your case to the jury, by giving evidence yourselves, calling witnesses, producing any relevant documents you may have, or all of those things. But the first thing I must make clear is that you are not obliged to give evidence, or to present a case. No defendant ever is. The prosecution has the burden of proof, and unless they prove your guilt so that the jury are sure, the jury may not convict you. Whether or not you give evidence, or present a case, doesn't change that in any way. You don't have to prove your innocence. In fact, you have no burden of proof at all. The jury are not allowed to take into account whether or not you give evidence, or present a case, and they certainly may not convict you because you choose not to. I will make all that clear to the jury when I sum the case up to them.'

'We don't have a case to present,' Miss Marcia replies, 'except that cannabis plants grow naturally in British soil. We're not selling some artificial drug that has to be manufactured from chemicals in a laboratory. We've never done that, and we never would. We don't believe in drugs like that. Our product is totally, one hundred per cent natural. It's not right that we should be prosecuted for using plants that grow naturally in our own soil. It's against natural law. Not to mention that cannabis is far less dangerous than tobacco, which is deemed to be legal.'

I suddenly have a vision of the Reverend Mrs Walden standing outside court with her colleagues in the pro-cannabis lobby, waving her banner.

'I'm afraid that doesn't provide you with any defence in law,' I reply. 'I know that cannabis has been legalised in various places abroad, and I'm aware that there is considerable support for this country to follow suit. But Parliament hasn't yet taken that step, and until they do, it's illegal to cultivate cannabis plants and to supply cannabis.'

'I suppose we will just have to go to that court in Strasbourg, then,' she replies.

'I won't stop you telling the jury about your views on cannabis if you give evidence,' I say, 'if there are other matters you want to bring to their attention – as long as you understand what I've said about it being no defence in law.'

I'm ready to move on to the next point, but the sisters are ahead of me.

'If we were to give evidence, your Honour,' Miss Marcia asks, 'would Miss Worthington be able to cross-examine us?'

'I was just coming to that,' I reply. 'Yes, if you give evidence under oath, she would be free to cross-examine.'

'She would be free to ask us about our business, how long we've been in business, our income and expenditure, all of that?'

I can't help smiling grimly. Apparently, the Hyde-Booth sisters have been reading up not only on trial procedure, but also on confiscation proceedings – proceedings the prosecution can bring after a conviction to try to recover the proceeds of crime, which are probably already a gleam in Susan's eye. I'm sure that's a major concern – the sisters are more than sharp enough to realise that cross-examination would be an excellent way for Susan to collect some data to start building her case, and the proceedings could well cover their two houses, as well as their financial assets.

'She would,' I confirm. 'But, of course...'

Miss Marcia raises her hand as I am about to reassure her that I would make sure that Susan's questions were proper. She confers quietly with her sister for some time.

'There's no point then, is there?' Miss Barbara concludes, in due course. 'Not if she can ask us all about it. We won't present a case, your Honour.'

'You will have to reply individually,' I say.

'I won't be presenting a case,' she replies.

'Neither will I,' Miss Marcia echoes.

Susan stands. 'Your Honour, in that case, given that the defendants are not represented, and are not presenting a case, I will not be making a closing speech.'

That's the usual course for the prosecution to take in this situation, avoiding overkill and taking advantage of the opportunity to appear scrupulously fair to the defence. So now, in a matter of a few minutes, we suddenly find ourselves approaching the end of the trial. There's nothing left except for me to sum the case up to the jury. But first, I feel the need for some reassurance from my *amicus curiae*.

'Well,' I say, 'Mr Brooks, just before we bring the jury back, let me ask you this. As I've said to the defendants, it seems to me that they haven't raised any matters that would afford them a defence in law.'

Aubrey stands. 'I think that must be right, your Honour.'

'At the same time…'

'At the same time, your Honour would wish to avoid giving any appearance of directing the jury to convict. I would respectfully suggest that your Honour can properly direct the jury in this way: your Honour can make clear to them that the defendants have offered no defence as such; but that they are not obliged to offer a defence. The prosecution have the burden of proof, and the jury can only convict if the prosecution have proved the case against the defendants so that they are sure of their guilt.'

'So, I'm giving the standard direction on the burden of proof, but in this case, unlike others, I have to be very careful not to give the impression that the jury have no real choice but to convict. They will draw that conclusion for themselves, but I must avoid the temptation to suggest it to them.'

Aubrey nods. 'I would submit that if your Honour avoids that one temptation, he will be quite safe, both from the Court of Appeal and from Strasbourg.'

'Not from Strasbourg,' I hear Miss Barbara mutter darkly.

My summing-up doesn't take long. It's been a short case, and there are no real legal issues. I explain about the burden and standard of proof, take the jury through the indictment to give them the legal definitions surrounding the offence, and remind them very briefly of the evidence. With

Aubrey's advice at the forefront of my mind, I stop there. I didn't time it, but if I took half an hour I would be surprised. I retire to chambers for a cup of tea. Stella hasn't given me anything to do while the jury is out, so I pick up *The Times* and start browsing. This lasts for about ten minutes: at which point Carol puts her head around the door looking rather shocked.

'We have a verdict, Judge,' she announces.

I stare at her in astonishment. 'What? They can't... They've only been out for...'

'Yes, I know, Judge. Dawn's bringing them down now.'

It takes a few minutes to assemble court. No one has been expecting a verdict so quickly, and Carol has to tannoy to bring Susan and Aubrey hurrying from the robing room or the canteen.

'Your Honour,' Carol says with a meaningful look, once we are all present and accounted for, 'twenty minutes have elapsed since the jury retired to consider their verdicts. Would the defendants please stand. Would the foreman please stand.'

The foreman is a smartly dressed young woman, who I noticed was taking copious notes during the trial. She doesn't appear in the least concerned about the short retirement time. Nor, for that matter, do the remaining jurors.

'Members of the jury,' Carol continues, 'please answer my first question either yes or no. Has the jury reached a verdict in relation to both defendants on which you are all agreed?'

'Yes, we have,' the foreman replies at once in a confident voice.

'On the sole count of this indictment, charging the defendants with conspiracy to supply a controlled drug of class B, do you find the defendant Barbara Hyde-Booth guilty or not guilty?'

'We find the defendant guilty,' the foreman replies.

'You find the defendant guilty, and is that the verdict of you all?'

'Yes, it is.'

'On the same count, do you find the defendant Marcia Hyde-Booth guilty or not guilty?'

'We find the defendant guilty.'

'You find the defendant guilty, and is that the verdict of you all?'

'Yes, it is.'

'Thank you, members of the jury,' Carol replies, no doubt expecting the foreman to resume her seat. But the foreman hasn't quite finished yet. She turns towards me.

'Your Honour, we have convicted the defendants because the evidence left us with no choice. But we wish to add that in our opinion, the defendants should be treated leniently, and in particular, should not be sent to prison. The jury believe that as cannabis is now so widely accepted, and is less dangerous than some legal products such as tobacco and alcohol, it would be wrong to impose a sentence of imprisonment. We also draw attention to the defendants' age, and the effect prison would have on them. We would like to ask the court to make this statement part of the court's record, and to bear it in mind when Barbara and Marcia are sentenced.'

'Well, thank you, members of the jury,' Miss Barbara says.

'That is so kind of you,' Miss Marcia adds.

The vision of the Reverend Mrs Walden and her banner returns. I see that every eye in court is on me. Carol is still on her feet, clutching her copy of the indictment, apparently not quite sure what to do.

'Madam foreman,' I ask, 'is the statement you have just made supported by all the members of the jury?'

She looks around the jury box. Every head is nodding.

'Yes, it is, your Honour.'

'Well, thank you,' I reply carefully. 'I will certainly take what you've said into account when I pass sentence – which will not be today. Please understand that I can't say what the sentence will be at this stage. I'm going to order pre-sentence reports, and we will see what they have to say. But when the time comes, I will take what you've said into consideration.' I glance down at Carol, who has now recovered and resumed her seat. 'And I will ask the clerk to ensure that each member of the jury is informed of the date of sentencing so that you can attend court if you wish.'

The foreman nods. 'Thank you, your Honour.'

I release the Hyde-Booth sisters on bail pending sentence, and admonish them not to leave court until they've made arrangements with the probation officer for the pre-sentence reports. I've been half-expecting Susan to alert the court to the possibility of confiscation proceedings, but she has remained studiously silent – probably in deference to the jurors.

That evening, throughout dinner – her signature vegetable lasagne, washed down by a nice Aldi Reserve white Burgundy – I can't help noticing that the Reverend Mrs Walden is wearing a broad grin. At first I find it rather irritating, but before too long, after a glass or two of the white Burgundy have started to take effect, I have to admit that she's entitled, and eventually I can't resist sharing it.

* * *

Four Weeks Later, Monday morning
For some bizarre reason, I keep asking myself what it would have been like for Marie Remert if her jury had returned the expected verdict of guilty: to have spent years of your

life writing pre-sentence reports for offenders, and now find yourself reading a report prepared by someone else for your own sentencing hearing.

I think it's because I seem to have been besieged recently with difficult sentences. Sentences you would prefer not to pass keep you awake at night – at least in my case, it's the only aspect of a circuit judge's work that has that effect. But it's odd to be kept awake by such a case when the jury have rescued you from having to confront it. I've agonised unnecessarily about giving a former probation officer, a woman of exemplary character, what appeared to be the inevitable custodial sentence for pouring a kettleful of boiling water over her husband's head. I've wondered what kind of pre-sentence report I would have had before me. I'm sure it would have reminded me of the psychological abuse she had put up with for years before the fateful day. But I still can't come up with an answer. I suspect I would have tried to get away with two or three years, knowing full well that the Court of Appeal would probably condemn it as unduly lenient in due course. But at least, I reason questionably, that wouldn't be my fault. And this in a case I don't even have to deal with.

But if Marie Remert, presumptive accomplice of Ginger the leaping cat, is one case I don't have to worry about this week, there are two others on the immediate horizon that I can't avoid. I now have pre-sentence reports for Deirdre O'Finn, scourge of Suffolk slave trader statues, and for Barbara and Marcia Hyde-Booth, purveyors of cannabis to the gentlefolk of Bermondsey. And if that isn't enough to guarantee a fraught week, Hubert is about to begin his summing-up in the fraud case of *Colson and others*. By Friday, I'm thinking, I may be in the market for a holiday.

But it's not Friday yet, it's only Monday, and today I have to sentence Deirdre O'Finn for causing an affray, and criminal damage, during her leading role in the onslaught against the statue of John Bonhomme in Little Brewing, Suffolk. To my relief, the public gallery is only sparsely occupied. It's a strange thing. During the trial, unless I kept the public gallery closed, we had a constant gathering of supporters and opponents of John Bonhomme – and therefore, also of Deirdre O'Finn – and Dawn, aided by security had the task of keeping them apart. They still managed to hurl abuse at each other, and at Deirdre O'Finn, and even with the presence of the High Sheriff it was often tense. You would have thought that the same suspects would be in evidence again for the climax, either to show their support for the defendant at the time of sentence, or to encourage the court to pass the most severe sentence possible. But there are only one or two on each side, and they seem perfectly well-behaved.

Roderick Lofthouse has the first word. His role today is fairly formal. He reminds everyone of the history of the case, including the defendant's previous exemplary character, and takes me quickly through the sentencing guidelines. Then, he adds this detail.

'Your Honour, there is one more matter. I have been in contact with the Little Brewing Village Council to see if they could assist with the likely cost of restoring the statue. Once I explained the court's interest in the matter, they were quite helpful, and disclosed that they have been working with one or two experts to evaluate the damage. I'm told that they are now confident that the cost of a full restoration will be about £5,000, and they would accept that amount as a proper settlement, if it were to be offered, let us say, in a future civil action. Unless your Honour has any further questions...'

'No, thank you, Mr Lofthouse,' I reply. 'That is very helpful.'

Kenneth is on his feet in a flash.

'Your Honour, may I get the question of money out of the way as quickly as I can? I'm grateful to my learned friend. He had provided me with that information, and as a result, Miss O'Finn instructs me that she is able to pay that sum, relying on family sources to assist her, and that she is willing to do so – there will be no need for the Council to sue her. I mention that in case it should prove to be relevant. But I do so with some diffidence, as I hope your Honour understands. May I now move on to other matters?'

'By all means, Mr Warnock.'

'I have three points to make on Miss O'Finn's behalf, and three only.'

Kenneth looks more focused than usual. His habitual smile is missing, and he has been meticulous in straightening his wig. He appears altogether more serious, and it was a good call to deal with the money up front. He can't ignore it, but he doesn't want to give me the impression that Deirdre is trying to buy her way out of trouble with an offer of money. He mentions it in passing, and moves on quickly – exactly the right way to do it.

'My first point is that her conduct in this case is entirely out of character. I have submitted a total of eight references from character witnesses. I hope your Honour has had a chance to read them.'

'I have,' I confirm.

'I'm much obliged. My second point is that what she did was the result of serious errors of judgment in allowing herself to be carried away by a cause she believed in, that she has learned her lesson, and that the court can be assured that nothing of this kind will happen again.

'The third and final point is this: both Miss O'Finn and I accept that a custodial sentence is inevitable. But I will seek to persuade your Honour that there is a strong case for suspending that sentence, and I will be calling a witness, who I hope will assist the court in reaching that conclusion.

'Let me begin with my first point: how did this happen? Your Honour, Deirdre O'Finn's background has nothing in it to suggest criminality. She was brought up in Cork, in a conservative catholic house; she received an excellent schooling; she went on to take a first-class degree at Trinity College, Dublin, since when she has devoted her life to teaching. Your Honour has read the statements from members of her family in Cork, from friends, and from her childhood parish priest. Everyone agrees that there is nothing to suggest that she would behave as she has in this case. It is entirely out of character.'

'I notice,' I say, 'that the family character witnesses include her father, but not her mother. The pre-sentence report suggests that there has been some ill-feeling over her transitioning.'

'That is something of an understatement, your Honour,' Kenneth replies at once. 'My instructing solicitors did approach the mother for a statement, but she flatly declined to give one – and that may be a fact of some significance in this story. The sad fact is, your Honour, that Deirdre's mother disowned her the moment she came out as trans. Mrs O'Finn still insists on referring to her as her son, Desmond, and has vowed never to speak to her again. Her father, and other family members, have struggled with Deirdre's change too, but they have come to terms with it sufficiently for them to remain in contact. But I'm afraid Mrs O'Finn is a lost cause in that respect and I'm sure your Honour will understand that this has caused Deirdre a good deal of pain and anxiety, which, in my submission, may well have contributed to the situation she finds herself in today. The author of the report suggests that connection, and I would submit that it is very likely correct.'

I nod. 'Yes, I see, Mr Warnock.'

'Your Honour, my second point follows on from my first. We have a woman from a conservative background, who has transitioned from male to female both psychologically and physically, adopting a woman's name, and living in all respects as a woman. She also turns out to be a gifted teacher, teaching with great success in Ireland before coming to this country – your Honour will have seen the two glowing references from head teachers for whom she worked...'

'Yes...'

'But then, she is offered what must have seemed like her dream job – headmistress at St Cecilia's Academy for the Daughters of Gentlefolk – not only a very prestigious position, bur also one that allows her to start to develop her own ideas about education, especially those about encouraging independent thinking in girls. She starts to put her ideas into practice, and lo and behold, the perfect opportunity presents itself, when her pupils start to discover some uncomfortable truths about the local hero, John Bonhomme.'

'Who is conveniently represented by a statue in the middle of the village square,' I observe.

'Your Honour, yes. And at first, she did everything right – writing articles in the *Star*, bringing her pupils' research to the attention of the public, and finally inducing the village council to take a vote on whether the statue should be removed. You really can't fault her at all for any of that. Her pupils are learning about thinking for themselves, standing up for their principles, about the importance of the press, and about the workings of democracy.

'I would ask your Honour to remember that after the vote, if not before, she finds herself on a collision course with the Cat and Fiddle brigade, which not only wants to protect John Bonhomme at all costs, but also despises her, because the idea of a trans woman as headmistress of a leading girls' school doesn't fit into the Cat and Fiddle *Weltanschauung*, and they are never going to let her forget it. In her eyes, they have joined forces with her mother against her. Your Honour knows how she was treated only too well – it even played out in your Honour's courtroom through Councillor Beveridge, and almost led to violence – not in the Cat and Fiddle – but in this courtroom, in front of your Honour and the jury.'

'I understand that, Mr Warnock,' I say. 'But even so, it's some distance from there to leading a crowd of twenty or more fellow-travellers in an affray, armed with lacrosse sticks and hammers.'

'It is, your Honour. I've spoken with Miss O'Finn about it at some length, we have worked our way through the pre-sentence report, and at the end of the day, it seems clear that she allowed herself to become obsessed with the statue because it symbolised everything Little Brewing and the Cat and Fiddle stood for. She should have stopped herself, she should have listened to PC Barnett's good advice, of course she should. But by then she was a very angry woman.

'I should add, too, your Honour, that Miss O'Finn wasn't responsible for recruiting everyone who turned up in the square on that evening. There were many local people who agreed with her, and were only too anxious to help. They didn't need to be persuaded.'

'But she did provide the weapons,' I point out, 'and she did get some of her pupils mixed up in it.'

'Yes, she did,' Kenneth replies. 'Your Honour, all I can say is this: since her arrest, Miss O'Finn has had a lot of time to think about what happened, and she assures me that she never wants to be in this position again. If I may put it in this way, she has learned her lesson. She will continue to believe strongly in the causes she espouses, but she assures me that she knows now where to draw the line. Given her background and her previous good character, I would respectfully submit that your Honour can feel safe in accepting that assurance.'

He pauses. 'May I move on to my third and final point?'

'Please do,' I reply.

'Your Honour, my final point is that there are strong grounds for suspending the sentence that Miss O'Finn and I both recognise is inevitable, and in support of my submissions, I would like to call a witness, Lady Gwendolyn Marchant.'

'By all means,' I say.

Lady Marchant is an imposing figure, tall and thin, wearing an elegant, but understated suit in muted colours. She takes the oath in a clear, confident voice.

'Please give the court your full name, Lady Marchant.'

'Gwendolyn Maud Marchant.'

'And, among various other activities, are you the chairwoman of the Board of Governors of St Cecilia's Academy for the Daughters of Gentlefolk, which, as the court has heard, is a prestigious school for girls, situated near the village of Little Brewing in Suffolk?'

'Yes, I am.'

'For how long have you been in that position?'

'For almost ten years. I served as a Governor for seven years before that, and in fact, I'm an old girl of the school.'

'So, you've had a long association with St Cecilia's?'

'A very long association.'

'Yes. Lady Marchant, when did you first meet Deirdre O'Finn?'

'When she interviewed for the position of headmistress. She came to us with excellent recommendations from Ireland, and it was our view that she was by far the strongest candidate. She had some very original ideas about education, which the Board felt would benefit the school. Schools like St Cecilia's, which tend to do the same things year in, year out for generations, can get stuck in the mud if they're not careful. Sometimes you need someone to come in with a fresh vision for the school, shake things up a bit.'

'Was one of Miss O'Finn's ideas that it was important for girls to be encouraged to think independently?'

'Yes. That was one of the things we found to be of particular interest.' She turns towards me and smiles. 'It wasn't like that at St Cecilia's in my day, your Honour, I assure you.'

I return the smile. 'No, I'm sure.'

'And were you aware of the research she had some of her more senior pupils do into John Bonhomme?'

'Only in very general terms, when it began. But I read the correspondence in the *Star*, and of course, I was aware of the vote in the village council.'

'What did you think about that?'

'I thought it was splendid.'

'But then, of course, there was the affray in the village square.'

'Yes.'

'Please tell his Honour what view the Board of Governors took of that.'

Lady Marchant sighs and shakes her head.

'Well, obviously it came as something of a shock, particularly when we learned that some of our pupils had been involved. The Board held an emergency meeting on the following day. We agreed that, in view of her arrest, Deirdre would have to be suspended with immediate effect, and we asked her deputy to take over on an interim basis until the situation is resolved.'

'What were your other concerns?'

'We also agreed that we would have to contact the parents as a matter of urgency, especially sixth-form parents, and even more especially, those whose daughters had been involved in the incident in the square.'

Kenneth pauses for just a moment or two.

'When you contacted the parents, did their reaction surprise you in any way?'

'Yes, it did. There were some parents who were horrified, of course, and seven took their children out of school immediately. But, to be honest, we'd been expecting much worse.'

'What was the more general reaction?'

'Well, the first reaction we were aware of came from the pupils, rather than the parents. We received numerous requests, and eventually a petition, from the fifth- and sixth-formers, defending Deirdre and asking that she be reinstated.'

'Really? What reasons did they give for that?'

'A very large number said that Deirdre was the best teacher they'd ever had. Several described her as a "breath of fresh air", and four or five said their lessons with her were the "highlight of their time" at St Cecilia's. And then, we started to get similar messages from parents. Quite a few parents said that Deirdre was right to out John Bonhomme as a slave trader, and to demand that his statue be taken down, and they were proud of their daughters for joining in the campaign.'

'That's remarkable,' I observe. 'Did they say those things in so many words?'

'They did, your Honour. I think they'd also heard from their daughters about how Deirdre was being treated by Councillor Beveridge and the others in the Cat and Fiddle because of… well, you know, because of her personal history… and they felt they should support her. All in all, the school actually came out of it in quite a positive light. We actually gained a few pupils as a result, from some progressive parents.'

'Lady Marchant,' Kenneth continues, 'has the Board of Governors reached any decision about Miss O'Finn's future, if any, with St Cecilia's school?'

'Yes. We held a meeting after the verdicts were returned, and the unanimous opinion was that if she should remain at liberty, we would reinstate her as headmistress, but the reinstatement would be conditional for the first twelve months.' She turns to me again. 'Your Honour, please understand that we are not trying to suggest to the court what sentence should be imposed – of course, that is a matter for the court, not for us. But if the sentence leaves Deirdre at liberty, that would be the course we would take. I have discussed the matter with Deirdre at some length, and I have made it clear to her that the only way, if she wants to remain at St Cecilia's, is to accept our terms. She understands the situation, your Honour.'

'When you say "conditional",' I ask, 'what does that mean, exactly?'

'It means that we would monitor her, to make sure that she is serious about avoiding the kind of provocation that led her astray in this case. She would have regular meetings with me, or with my deputy, every week, so that we can spot any worrying signs and deal with them before they go too far. We don't want to interfere with her teaching, but we have to be as sure as we can be that we're not going to find ourselves here again a year from now.'

'Yes, I see,' I reply.

'Not only that,' Lady Marchant continues, 'but it seems to me that what happened was the result of her becoming isolated.'

'Isolated?' I ask.

'She came over here from Ireland, where her friends and family are. Little Brewing is a small, self-contained community. She was an outsider, she didn't make many connections, and she had no one she could really talk to. Hopefully, the condition we would impose would rectify that situation to some extent.'

'Didn't she have colleagues on the staff she could talk to?'

'Oh, most of them would chat to her over coffee, I'm sure,' Lady Marchant agrees, 'the younger ones particularly. But when you're headmistress, there's always some distance they feel they have to keep – they don't want to get too close. And, to be perfectly honest, some of our more senior staff never took to Deirdre, and I'm afraid some of that had to do with her transition. The Cat and Fiddle isn't the only hotbed of narrow-mindedness, your Honour. There were those who couldn't, or wouldn't, see past their rather outdated image of St Cecilia's, and sadly, Deirdre suffered because of it. But the Board feel that with our encouragement, she has the potential to be an outstanding headmistress, and we are hoping that we can give her the chance to prove it.'

'Unless I can assist further…?' Kenneth asks, after Lady Marchant has retired to the public gallery, mercifully choosing to sit with the pro-Deirdre faction.

I'm not one of those judges who likes to retire, just for the sake of retiring, before passing sentence. It's hardly ever necessary. Once you've read the pre-sentence report, reminded yourself of the sentencing guidelines, and listened to what counsel has to say, you almost always know what the sentence is going to be. Besides, why prolong the suspense? Sentencing hearings are tense enough as it is. But there are times when you do need to get out of court for a few minutes, just to make sure that you've got it right, and that you're not going to regret what you're about to say. On the rare occasions I retire, it's because counsel has made an exceptionally compelling speech in mitigation, which is what Kenneth Warnock has just done in this case. To be honest, I can't remember when I last heard one as good: concise, persuasive, realistic, and not a single word irrelevant. He's given me a number of things to think about very carefully. I need to take a deep breath and go over it all in my mind. So, for some twenty minutes I sit in chambers, gazing out of the window and wondering whether I'm about to do the right thing.

'Stand up, please, Miss O'Finn. As Mr Warnock has said, the question I have to decide is not whether to impose a custodial sentence, but whether or not I can properly suspend that sentence.

'On 15 March you led what can only be described as a mob – a mob which included some of your pupils, young school-girls – in a determined effort to destroy or remove the statue of John Bonhomme. You did so, having armed the mob with lacrosse sticks and hammers, knowing full well that Councillor Beveridge and others were defending the statue, and you did so against the explicit orders of the one police officer on duty. You must have realised that there would be violence. You created a situation in which it was possible that one or more of those present would suffer serious injury. The pre-sentence report describes that as an "error of judgement". All I say about that is this: if your "error of judgement" had ended as badly as it might have, there would be no question of a suspended sentence. You would be facing an immediate term of imprisonment of some length. The same would have been true if the jury had convicted you of assault occasioning actual bodily harm against Councillor Beveridge. Fortunately for you, in the event, neither of those things happened.

'You owe a debt of deep gratitude both to Mr Warnock and to Lady Marchant. They have presented the other side of the case very forcefully. I have read the character references, from which it is clear that you are a person of previous exemplary character. It goes without saying that you are highly intelligent; everyone who knows you agrees that you are a gifted teacher, and someone who is very creative in developing her work. I accept also that you have had significant difficulties to cope with in your life, not only within your family, but also in the community of Little Brewing. I take all those matters into account. I am told that you have learned your lesson, and that there will be no recurrence of your "error of judgement". Frankly, Miss O'Finn, I am not sure that I would have been persuaded by those considerations alone in such a serious case. It is the evidence of Lady Marchant that, at the end of the day, has persuaded me that the right course is to suspend the sentence. The fact that she and the other governors believe that they can trust you in the role of headmistress after everything that has happened, and are prepared to give you a chance to prove that you can avoid trouble in future, speaks volumes for you, and that is what has made the difference.

'Please listen carefully to what I am about to say. On count one, the charge of affray, the sentence will be one of imprisonment for twelve months. On count three, the charge of criminal damage, the sentence will be one of imprisonment for six months, to run consecutively to the sentence on count one, making a total of eighteen months. That total sentence will be suspended for a period of two years. What that means is that, if you commit no further offence within the next two years, it will be over – you will hear no more about it. On the other hand, if you do commit a further offence within two years, you will be prosecuted for that offence, and the sentence I pass today may be activated and added to whatever sentence is passed for the new offence. Do you understand?'

'Yes.' Almost inaudible.

'In addition, it will be a condition of the suspension that you report to me here at court every two months, so that I can be satisfied that you are attending your meetings with

Lady Marchant or her deputy, and that you are staying out of trouble. You will agree dates with the clerk before you leave court. Understood?'

'Yes.'

'I will make a compensation order in favour of the Little Brewing Village Council in the amount of £5,000, which is to be paid within three months. And finally, there will be an order restraining you from approaching within one hundred yards of the village square in Little Brewing, and that order will remain in effect for two years. Any violation of that order is punishable by imprisonment. Do you understand those orders?'

'Yes.'

'Very well, Miss O'Finn. Finally, let me make it clear to you that you have come very close to going to prison today. I can say with some confidence that, if you offend again, the result will be very different. Very well. That's all.'

'Thank you, your Honour,' she replies. It's still not easy to hear her.

I send Kenneth a note, congratulating him on his excellent representation of Deirdre O'Finn, and the result he's achieved for her. He sends me a witty reply, attributing his success to his ritual prayers in front of the Bermondsey cannon in the foyer of the court.

Much later, just before going home for the day, I infiltrate myself into Marjorie's chambers, something I've been doing regularly since the beginning of the *Colson* case. She always receives me with a good grace, though I know there are times when it irritates her, especially, as is the case today, when she's trying to work and I'm interrupting. This afternoon she's half-way through reading a judgment of the Court of Appeal.

'Any word...?' I ask.

'No. Charlie, I haven't had time to drop into Hubert's court. I have a trial to conduct in my own court, you know.'

'Yes, I know. All I'm asking is…'

'I haven't heard anything untoward, which has to be good news. But this is a two-day summing-up, and today was day one. Look, Charlie, I've been over it with him. It's the kind of summing-up where you can't remind the jury of every piece of evidence – you'd be there for a couple of weeks. You have to take a broad-brush approach– has there been a fraud, if so, how was it done, what do the defendants have to say about it? You've done cases like that. You know the kind of thing.'

'And did he seem…?'

'If you ask me, he's right on top of it. I could be wrong, but I've been talking to him about this case every afternoon for four weeks now, and I don't think I am.' She pauses. 'Charlie, Hubert may be experiencing the odd moment of confusion here and there, but he's still a very bright man, and a good judge. That hasn't changed.'

* * *

Tuesday Morning

You would never think that two pre-sentence reports could be so different. Yesterday, I was inundated by a vast amount of detail about Deirdre O'Finn, a careful analysis of her professional and social life since her arrival in Little Brewing, and a variety of suggestions about sentencing options. It was almost an *embarras de richesse*, a bit too much information that leaves you struggling to keep sight of the wood in the midst of so many trees. The report on Barbara and Marcia Hyde-Booth could be from a different genre.

It offers five rather obvious observations: that the sisters come from a well-to do background and are comfortably off; that they have always remained single; that it is hard to explain how they came to be involved in supplying cannabis; that they were supplying cannabis on a moderate commercial scale; and that because of their age and close relationship, a prison sentence could have a seriously deleterious effect on their physical and mental health. The report concludes, or more accurately, fades away without offering any semblance of an answer to any of the questions I have to deal with. I understand, to some extent. You have to sympathise with any probation officer charged with the task of interviewing the Hyde-Booth sisters. I'm sure getting information out of them must have been like getting blood out of a stone. But that reflection offers little comfort. I have to pass sentence on these two ladies, and I could do with some help.

To my amazement, when I take my seat on the bench, help arrives, and from an unexpected source. I see Aubrey Brooks in counsel's row. His assignment as *amicus curiae* should have ended with the trial, and I assume he is there out of courtesy, just in case he can be of further assistance. But I'm in for a surprise, and it is a welcome one.

'Your Honour,' he says, 'the defendants have asked me to represent them in connection with the proceedings today, and any further proceedings. Neither my learned friend nor I see any conflict in my doing so, and we hope your Honour agrees.'

'I see no objection at all, Mr Brooks,' I reply, my relief no doubt all too obvious in my voice, 'and I think that's a very wise decision on the part of the defendants.'

The relief wanes a little as I look around the courtroom. I'm going to have a lot of critical eyes on me today. The press are well represented, of course – this case is a reporter's dream, and the Hyde-Booth sisters have become national news. Seven members of the jury have taken up my invitation to attend, and Dawn has accommodated them in the jury box. The public gallery is full, with some of its occupants displaying home-made badges bearing the legend, "Save the Goddesses". And the Reverend Mrs Walden has quietly taken a seat in the back row. So, no pressure, then.

I force myself to focus. Susan reminds everyone briefly of the facts, and starts to walk me through the sentencing guideline. It doesn't bode well for the defendants. The guideline clearly indicates a substantial custodial sentence for any defendant cultivating cannabis plants and supplying cannabis on a commercial scale. The only leeway lies in the uncertainty about the scale of the sisters' operation and the length of time for which they were in business. None of this is clear from the available evidence, a point Susan very fairly goes out of her way to concede. But even making the most generous of assumptions in their favour, the guideline offers the sisters little comfort. Susan concludes by telling me that she is not inviting me to make any financial orders today, because the Crown Prosecution Service is still considering the question of confiscation proceedings.

'Your Honour,' Aubrey begins, 'my clients have instructed me to make two things clear at the outset. The first is that they stand by their view that they should not have been prosecuted for using a plant capable of growing naturally in British soil, and that they have no regrets about making cannabis available to their customers, many of whom smoke only to alleviate terrible pain, which might otherwise become unbearable. But the second point is this: both sisters assure the court through me that, regardless of the sentence passed on them today, they have now retired, and will not engage in that activity again under any circumstances.

'Your Honour, I have, of course, already made them aware of the sentencing guideline, and they are under no illusions about the likely sentence in any case of this kind. But that, I submit, is what should cause your Honour to think long and hard about the proper sentence in this case. In my submission, the expression "case of this kind" is meaningless in the context of this case. There are a number of highly unusual – indeed, I would go as far as to say unique – features of this case which mark it out from any other cultivation or supply case. It is certainly unique in my experience, and I must now take a few minutes of the court's time to trace the history of the defendants' connection with cannabis, in order to direct your Honour's attention to those features.'

'Take as many minutes as you wish, Mr Brooks,' I say.

'Thank you, your Honour. A number of years ago now, the sisters had an elderly great-uncle who lived in York. Sadly, the time came when they learned that this gentleman was dying of a terminal cancer, and so they went to York to visit him for the last time. He was at home during his final illness, and while they were there with him, the sisters could not help but notice that he was smoking cannabis on a daily basis. Their initial reaction to what they saw, your Honour, was one of shock, and indeed, horror. They come from an eminently respectable family, as your Honour heard during the trial, and they regarded anything to do with drugs as beyond the pale, as their father and other family members had drummed into them from an early age. They were even more horrified when, one evening, they met the dealer who was supplying the uncle with his cannabis, a frightening young man who obviously worked for very undesirable people, who was very aggressive when it came to payment, and who tried to suggest that the uncle might want to consider trying some cocaine in addition to the cannabis.

'But they also saw something else, something the uncle's doctor and nurses quietly admitted: that the cannabis had a remarkable effect in alleviating what might otherwise have been intolerable pain, and did so without the side-effects of more conventional medicines. Barbara and Marcia were profoundly affected by what they saw, and after their uncle's death, they started to do their own research into cannabis, and had a number of long conversations about what they found. Central to this was the realisation, which has now been alluded to many times in this case, that cannabis is a plant, and one quite capable of growing unaided in British soil. In their minds, this separated cannabis from drugs that are essentially chemicals, and have to be manufactured in laboratories; and when they compared the negative aspects of cannabis to those of tobacco, a plant whose use is perfectly legal, they concluded that the prohibition on the use of cannabis – especially by people in a condition like their uncle's – was unconscionable.

'Your Honour, while not exactly rich, the sisters were certainly well off. In his will, their father had left them the two houses the court has heard about in Barkworth Road and Stockholm Road, together with enough money to allow them to live comfortably enough without working, as long as they were not too extravagant. They became aware of men and women in their area who would benefit from cannabis in the same way as their uncle had, and a plan began to form in their minds. They decided to do their best to create a safe setting for those who needed cannabis to have it. This meant having nothing to do with street drug dealers, and nothing to do with those involved in organised crime.'

I shake my head. 'But how did they hope to do that?' I ask. 'They had no experience of that world, and whatever they set up, surely there was nothing to stop established dealers from infiltrating it, and taking it over without a second thought.'

'That is exactly right, your Honour,' Aubrey replies, 'but they reasoned that the kind of operation they had in mind would pose no threat to the street dealers, because they would be supplying only people known to them, who would be the kind of people who would never take drugs in other circumstances. They would create a small operation, and one that had no dealings with drugs other than cannabis. In addition, if they operated exclusively from their two houses, including cultivating their own plants in that private setting, there would be no need for them to interface with the street dealers at all. Indeed, they calculated that they had a good chance of flying under the radar. And that was exactly the kind of operation they established. By now, they had conducted very detailed research, and they were well informed about the mechanics of cultivating cannabis.'

'But they couldn't do it all themselves,' I point out. 'They would need some help, people to watch over the plants at night and so on. There was bound to be some risk.'

'There was, your Honour. But they were very careful to choose young men and women with no criminal records, whom they paid very well indeed, not only for their work but for their discretion.'

'How did they acquire their customers?'

'Your Honour, they started by keeping their eyes and ears open in the pub, and gleaning what information they could about people with conditions similar to their uncle's. But, of course, that wasn't enough to defray the expense, much less make a profit. So, they began to recruit another class of customer. These were respectable people of mature age, rather like the sisters themselves, who would never normally dream of taking drugs of any kind, but might be bold enough to try cannabis in a safe setting. They came up with the idea of tea and cakes in the elegant sitting room in their own house, which could hardly be further removed from the street drug scene. They also did their best to build a personal loyalty in the customers, to protect the operation. It was important that the customers should not gossip about them – although sadly, it was exactly that, a careless conversation in the pub – that was to be their undoing in the end. Ironically, Miss Barbara tells me that they were reluctant to accept DC Mason at first, because she was too young, although her manner and the cover story she used convinced them in the end that she would be safe.'

'So, it wasn't just about supplying pain relief for the terminally ill, was it?' I ask. 'They were also supplying those who smoked for the pleasure of it.'

'That is true, your Honour,' Aubrey replies, 'and they saw nothing wrong with that. But it is also true that the tea and cakes approach was essential – it was that service that brought in the money, so that they could supply the medical patients without charge. Your Honour, they did make a modest profit, as any business has to, to survive, but this was never about making money. The Hyde-Booth sisters have never needed to supply drugs for money. They have always seen themselves as providing a valuable service to a section of the public.'

'A service they knew to be illegal.'

'Yes, your Honour. They tell me that they kept a close eye on developments in different parts of the world, and saw that the clear trend was towards decriminalisation, either specifically for medical purposes or more generally. They thought it was likely that the same would be true of this country before long. But it hasn't come in time for them.'

Aubrey pauses. I'm sure he knows what I'm thinking – that all of this would have been far more effective if one or both of the sisters had given evidence under oath about it. But they still have the same concern they had during the trial – if they do go into the witness box, there is nothing to stop Susan from cross-examining, and starting to build a case for confiscation proceedings. It's an impossible dilemma. Aubrey has, however, given it some thought and has found what might be at least a partial solution.

'Your Honour, I'm going to call DCI Isherwood to give evidence about one or two matters.'

This obviously isn't coming as a surprise to DCI Isherwood or to Susan. The officer is already striding towards the witness box. He takes the oath and formally introduces himself to me.

'Detective Chief Inspector,' Aubrey begins, 'you have been in court while I have been addressing his Honour this morning, have you not, and you have heard what I have said?'

'I have, sir, yes.'

'In the course of your investigation, did you interview any of the sisters' customers who visited the house in Barkworth Road?'

'Yes, altogether I interviewed twelve customers.'

'And just as a point of interest, were proceedings brought against any of the customers?'

'No, sir.'

'In the course of your interviews with the customers, did you glean any information which would either confirm or contradict anything I said to his Honour?'

I see Susan twitching. Her instinctive reaction is to object. Any answer to Aubrey's question would be blatant hearsay, and in a trial, I wouldn't dream of allowing the witness to answer it. But she remains in her seat. She has calculated, quite rightly, that I'm going to treat whatever DCI Isherwood says with caution; but I'm not going to ignore it, and it never looks good for the prosecution to stand in the way of possible mitigation evidence.

'I did sir,' DCI Isherwood replies. 'It was my impression that the defendants made every effort to keep their operation free of interference by the local street dealers, and certainly never dealt in any drugs apart from cannabis. I spoke to one customer who was very seriously ill with a painful condition, who told me that they refused to accept money from him for his supply of cannabis. I also accept, having also interviewed the defendants, that they do sincerely believe that cannabis should be legal.'

'Thank you, Chief Inspector,' Aubrey says. He's far too experienced to push his luck by asking for too much detail. 'Does your Honour have any questions?'

'No, thank you,' I reply. 'You may step down, Chief Inspector.'

'Thank you, your Honour.' But DCI Isherwood does not immediately step down. Instead, he shifts uneasily from foot to foot for several seconds, before turning to look at me directly. 'If I may, your Honour, there is something else I would like to say.'

I glance at Susan and Aubrey, both of whom are poised to respond, but neither of whom knows quite what their response should be. Susan again errs on the side of caution. Aubrey is probably thinking, "In for a penny, in for a pound". What DCI Isherwood has to say might be very good for him, or it might be very bad. But he started this ball rolling, and he can't credibly stop it now. As no one objects, I indicate to DCI Isherwood that he is free to speak.

'I just wanted to say this, your Honour. I am aware, of course, of the recommendation made by the jury, and I wish to add that every officer involved in this investigation, myself included, agrees with that recommendation. That's all I wanted to say.'

There are approving mutters in the jury box and the public gallery. Aubrey, of course, could hardly be more delighted, and he can't conceal his smile. Susan, on the other hand, looks distinctly miffed. She grinds her teeth. She can't really say anything in court, of course, but one suspects that there may be a few words exchanged backstage later in the morning.

'Thank you, Chief Inspector,' I say. For the second time, I invite him to step down, and this time he does, with some alacrity.

'May I put one question to the defendants directly?' I ask Aubrey. He looks rather surprised, but quickly agrees. Both sisters stand immediately, without being asked.

'Mr Brooks has assured me,' I say, 'that you have now both retired from the cannabis business, and that there will be no further dealing of that kind. Are you both willing to give me the same assurance personally?'

'I give that assurance freely,' Miss Barbara replies at once.

'As do I,' Miss Marcia adds. 'Today your Honour is witnessing the Twilight of the Goddesses.'

They resume their seats in unison. For the second time in two days, I retire to consider sentence – a new, and not entirely welcome record.

When I return to court some twenty minutes later, the same eyes confront me – the jurors, the friends of the Goddesses, Aubrey and Susan, the Reverend Mrs Walden, and, of course, the Hyde-Booth sisters themselves. I invite everyone, including the sisters, to take their seats. Defendants or not, I'm not about to make them stand up during the whole of my sentencing remarks. For one thing, I have no idea how long it is going to take. Even with twenty minutes to scribble some notes, this is not going to be straightforward. It takes me almost a minute to arrange my notes and begin, and the eyes remain glued to me throughout,

'The sentencing guidelines,' I begin, 'are one of the better innovations introduced into our court practice in recent times. They provide a range of sentences for a given offence, which not only helps judges to identify the lines along which they should be thinking, but also promotes consistency in sentencing as between different judges, and different court centres, so that defendants can reasonably expect that the sentence to be imposed has nothing to do with the accident of which court centre or which judge their case is assigned to.

'But a guideline is just that – a guideline, not a rule or an inevitable result. What judges have to do is to follow the guideline, unless it appears that there is good reason to depart – upwards or downwards – from the sentence, or range of sentence suggested by the guideline, in which case the judge must identify the reasons for the departure. In my experience, and I suspect in the experience of judges generally, any departure is usually likely to be modest and not hard to justify, although there are cases in which it can be more difficult. But I have never before encountered a case in which it has been suggested that the kind of sentence, or range of sentence, suggested by the guideline for an offence is not only too severe, but may actually be entirely inappropriate, to the point of resulting in an injustice. But in this case, it seems, that proposition has been put before me, not in so many words, but by way of necessary implication – not only in counsel's speech in mitigation, but also in a recommendation by the jury endorsed, I'm told, by every police officer involved with the case, including the Detective Chief Inspector in charge of the investigation.

'The clear suggestion is that this is not a case in which an immediate custodial sentence would be appropriate. The difficulty with that suggestion is that on any reading of the guideline dealing with the cultivation of cannabis plants, it would seem that such a sentence is effectively inevitable. There is room for debate about the length of the sentence, as there always is, but as to the principle to be applied in a case of cultivation on a commercial scale, there seems to be little, if any, room for debate.

'The features of this case which are described as highly unusual, if not unique, and which are said to take this case outside the usual scope of the guideline, were drawn to my attention by Mr Brooks in his able and cogent address in mitigation. In essence, these defendants, sisters, are ladies of more than eighty years of age, and, apart from this case, women of impeccable character. It is said that they dealt in cannabis primarily for the benefit of customers suffering terribly as the result of serious illness, to whom they supplied the cannabis free of charge; that they took infinite pains to ensure that there should be no interference by street dealers, and that they cultivated plants in one of their own houses for that reason; that they never supplied any drug other than cannabis; and that making money was never their motivation. They invited customers to their other house, where they could smoke in safe, comfortable surroundings, or purchase cannabis to take away, the emphasis being, again, on a safe environment.

'Underlying their operation is a sincerely held belief that it is wrong to forbid the use of cannabis because the cannabis plant is capable of growing naturally, unaided, in British soil. That, of course, provides no defence under our law – they knew from the outset that they were breaking the law – but it does explain their attitude to cannabis, and to the business they established.

'Based on everything I have heard, I accept that the matters I have just outlined represent the circumstances of this case, and the description of the case as highly unusual, if not unique, seems to me to be fully justified. What I have to decide is whether I should depart from the guideline in a very significant way – effectively ignoring it – as I have been invited to do; or in deference to the sympathetic features of the case, follow it with a relatively minor adjustment of the length of the sentence. I need hardly add that it is a question I have found to be far from easy, but at the end of the day, I find myself compelled to find that the guideline, while not inappropriate to almost any imaginable offence involving cultivation, is so far removed from doing justice in this particular case, that a radical departure from it is required.'

I glance up at Barbara and Marcia.

'Stand up please, ladies. After much anxious reflection, I have concluded that to send you to prison today would be, not only deleterious to you, given your age and personal circumstances, but also wrong in principle, given that what you did was a statement of principle rather than a deliberate commitment to crime. It was, of course, a very serious error of judgement, and one that must not be repeated. I accept your assurance that you have retired, and that today does represent the Twilight of the Goddesses. I sincerely hope that is the case, because, should you come before the court again for any similar offence, I assure you that the outcome will be very different.

'The sentence of the court today is that, on the sole count of this indictment, in each of your cases, there will be a sentence of two years imprisonment, suspended for two years. That means that provided you commit no further offence in the next two years – and that means any offence – that will be the end of it. If you do commit a further offence, you will be prosecuted for that offence, and the sentence I pass today may be activated in addition to the sentence for the new offence. Do you understand what I have said?'

'Yes, your Honour,' in unison.

'Very well. I am not asked to make any further orders today. Are there any other matters I need to deal with?'

Susan and Aubrey both stand, and assure me that there are not. I leave the bench for the sanctuary of chambers with as much haste as I can decently muster. As I am leaving, I am aware of a round of applause emanating from the jury box and the public gallery. I must admit that I rather enjoy it.

A few minutes later, Dawn brings me a note from the Reverend Mrs Walden. It reads: *'Bravo, Charlie. Well done. Dinner on me this evening, your choice of venue.'*

I tell Dawn to let Aubrey and Susan know they are welcome to a cup of tea after they've finished up in court, and half an hour later, they duly appear.

'I wanted to thank you both,' I say. 'It was a very difficult case, and your guidance was invaluable.'

Aubrey smiles. 'Well, I think you got it exactly right, Judge. I'm not sure Susan agrees, but it was a courageous decision, any way you look at it.' He suddenly puts on a mischievous air. 'You can't ask her, of course, Judge, but I can. Come on, Susan, are you going to take this to the Court of Appeal as an unduly lenient sentence?'

Susan returns the smile, a touch ruefully. 'What, with a jury recommendation endorsed by God only knows how many police officers? It's up to the CPS, of course, but if they ask me, I will probably suggest they don't want to be asking the Court of Appeal to send two ladies over eighty straight inside in the face of all that.'

'What about confiscation proceedings?' I ask.

'The CPS have asked me to talk to Aubrey and see what we can work out,' she replies.

I'm surprised. 'Really? I would have thought it was fairly straightforward. You've got two houses where crime was committed, and you've got the legal presumptions about recent income being the proceeds of crime.'

'Yes,' Susan replies, 'but it doesn't have any of the usual hallmarks of large-scale crime. There's been no sudden unexplained wealth, no acquisition of property here or abroad, no attempt we can find to hide money, no foreign bank accounts – none of the usual things we hang our hats on in confiscation proceedings. It may come down to asking a judge to confiscate their two houses and leave them destitute. I'm not sure we have the appetite for it in this case. So, if Aubrey and I can reach an accommodation which costs them something, but also leaves them something, that's the way we would probably go.'

'We'll get there, Judge,' Aubrey adds.

* * *

Friday Afternoon

After the excitement of the first two days, the remainder of the week has been something of a let-down. Stella has a two-week trial for me starting on Monday, so she didn't want to risk my starting even a short trial this week. Consequently, I have been dealing with the list – plea and case management hearings, sentences, and assorted applications not reserved to a particular judge. The list is an essential institution, and someone has to take it, and when one of us becomes free, it means that the other judges can continue with their trials without taking time out for their share. We all try to be good-natured about it when our turn comes around, and this week it's been mine. But needless to say, the list is not exactly enthralling compared to the drama of Monday and Tuesday, and the only good thing to say about the list today is that it has been fairly short. Since lunch I've been reduced to sitting at my desk, scanning the latest supplement to *Archbold*, just to make sure I haven't missed any vital new developments.

But just after three-thirty, Marjorie puts her head around my door, apparently in a state of some excitement.

'Come on, Charlie,' she says, sounding almost out of breath.

'Come on where?' I ask.

'Hubert's jury is back,' she explains. 'They're returning their verdicts.'

I need no second bidding. I'm with her at the door in a flash.

'When did they go out?' I ask, as we walk briskly along the corridor towards Hubert's court. 'Wednesday morning, wasn't it?'

'First thing Wednesday morning. He finished summing up on Tuesday afternoon, but it was too late to send them out then.'

'How many counts?'

'Four defendants, two counts each, so eight in all.'

I reflect anxiously. 'So, they've been out for two days after a four-week trial with eight counts. Two days is a bit quick, isn't it?'

She smiles. 'Oh, come on, Charlie, you know how it is with juries. You can never tell. It might be a shade on the quick side, but that doesn't mean there's anything untoward. I'd be more concerned if they'd been out for two weeks.'

By the time we enter Hubert's courtroom using the public entrance and quietly take seats in the public gallery like the spectators we are, the jury have finished returning their verdicts, and Hubert is discussing arrangements for pre-sentence and other reports with counsel. Marjorie has quietly summoned Julie, Hubert's usher, to ask what happened.

'Guilty all round,' Julie whispers proudly, 'all four defendants, all four counts, all unanimous verdicts.'

Once the sentencing arrangements have been agreed, and the defendants have been taken down to the cells, I can't help noticing that everyone except counsel – solicitors, police officers and the one or two members of the public present – are leaving court, almost as if their departure is being orchestrated. It turns out that it is. The apparent culprit is Jeffrey Percival QC, who has been prosecuting. He is someone we don't see much of at Bermondsey. It is a bit beneath him, certainly not his regular hunting ground. He generally frequents the Old Bailey and Southwark Crown Court, where he has built a highly successful practice prosecuting fraud and other serious crime. Defence counsel are in the same league, two Silks, and two very senior members of the Bar. We have attracted a star-studded cast for the case of *Colson and others*, no mistaking that, and they have been in front of Hubert for four weeks. After looking around court confidentially, but with some care, Percival stands to address Hubert.

'Your Honour, I've asked that the courtroom be cleared for a moment or two, so that only counsel and court personnel are present. I see that we have Judge Walden and Judge Jenkins with us, and I am glad that they will hear what I'm about to say.'

'Yes, Mr Percival,' Hubert replies. He is smiling, although if he knows what's coming, he is giving nothing away.

'Your Honour, this has been a challenging case on all sides,' Percival continues, 'and I've been asked to speak on behalf of all counsel to say, if I may do so respectfully, how much we have appreciated your Honour's conduct of it. It has lasted for some four weeks, which was exactly what was anticipated, and we have had verdicts in two days. The case has been tried fairly and with consideration for all the parties. We all feel that the smooth running of the case has been due entirely to your Honour's patience with the witnesses, your mastery of the facts and the law, and of course, your Honour's summing up – which we all agree was not only concise, but as clear and helpful as could have been wished for.'

'That's very kind of you all, Mr Percival,' Hubert replies modestly.

'What we would like to do,' Percival continues, 'and this is why I asked to have a limited audience, is to hold a case dinner. Your Honour would be the guest of honour, and if that meets with your Honour's approval, we will liaise with your Honour's clerk to ensure that we choose an acceptable date and venue.'

'In reply, Mr Percival,' Hubert says graciously, 'I would like to say that whatever I may have done in this case owes a great deal to the assistance I received from counsel. Your submissions, and the way in which the case was conducted throughout, were admirable on all sides of the case – a model of how it should be done. I really am very grateful to you all. And, of course, a case dinner would be very pleasant. Thank you all.'

I become conscious of staring at Hubert, and hurriedly turn to whisper to Marjorie.

'Well, congratulations, Marjorie. I don't know what you did, but whatever it was seems to have worked wonders. Thank you for the time you took over this.'

But she shakes her head. 'In all honesty, Charlie, I didn't really do that much. Yes, we chatted about the case in the evenings, and once or twice I pointed him in what I thought was the right direction. But I didn't try this case: Hubert did. He did this, not me.'

'Before we adjourn, Mr Percival,' Hubert is saying, 'since I have my resident judge, Judge Walden, here, I would like to suggest that the dinner might have something of a double purpose.'

'Your Honour?'

'I am going to take this opportunity to announce that in due course, probably towards the end of the year, I shall be retiring from the Bench. Of course, I fully hope and expect that there will be more than one dinner in my future, but this will be a very welcome start.'

Jeffrey Percival is, of course, just as taken aback as the rest of us, but he recovers admirably.

'I'm quite sure that you will have many dinners, your Honour,' he says, 'but I am glad that we will be the first, and I'm sure I speak for everyone in saying how much your Honour will be missed, and offering our very best wishes for your retirement.'

There is a silence in court that seems to go on forever. Eventually, Hubert smiles.

'Thank you, Mr Percival. I don't know whether Judge Walden wishes to say anything about what I've said?'

I stand.

'Judge Drake,' I say, 'I do believe that the day on which you retire will go down in history as the Twilight of the Gods.'

Percival turns round towards me. He nods and smiles.

'Hear, hear,' he says quietly.

Just as we are leaving court, Legless appears as if from nowhere.

'I hear I'm missing all the excitement,' he says with a grin. 'What's going on?'

'You are,' I confirm. 'Convictions all round, and counsel on all sides inviting Hubert to a case dinner.'

'The real excitement,' Hubert says, 'is my announcement of my retirement, which I made just after accepting their kind invitation to dinner.'

'Your what…?' Legless stares at us all for several seconds. 'You're not serious, Hubert… When?'

'Oh, sometime towards the end of the year, after Stella's had time to make her plans. There's no definite date. I just felt it was time.'

Legless continues to stare, until we all have to laugh.

'Well,' he says, recovering admirably, 'this calls for a suitable celebration. This way, please.'

We follow Legless along the judicial corridor, as he leads the way to his chambers, and make ourselves at home. Legless rummages around in the bottom drawer of his desk and produces a bottle with a flourish, like a magician plucking a rabbit from a hat.

'Charlie, if you don't mind, the proper glasses are in the bookcase. You know where, don't you?"

'Delighted,' I reply. I know where because I've done this before – albeit not often. I know what's in the bottle, too. Legless is something of an authority on Scotch single malts, and he has very occasionally treated me to a glass on some special occasion. But it's not a regular occurrence. He's not parsimonious in the typecasting sense often attributed so unfairly to Scotsman. He is careful with his single malts, but I'm sure their price alone is a sufficient justification for that. I make my way to the bookcase, and find his set of six beautiful heavy whisky glasses, tucked away in the left-hand corner, exactly where they were the last time I benefitted from his largesse. I carry four of them carefully over to his desk.

'This is very good of you, Legless.'

'Glendronach, twenty years old,' he replies while pouring for us. 'A particularly fine drop. I don't open this beauty without good reason, I don't mind telling you.'

'Well, I think we have every right to a small celebration,' I say. 'Hubert has had a triumphant fraud, with dinner to follow, and let's not forget Marjorie's imminent departure for the dizzying heights of the High Court.'

'Hubert and Marjorie,' Legless toasts, raising his glass.

I echo him, and all four of us take a draft. It commands silence for some time. A particularly fine drop it undoubtedly is.

'And while we're on that general subject,' Legless says, after savouring his draft to the full, 'I would like to take this opportunity to mention an appointment of my own, which has just been announced.'

We all stare at him. I can't even begin to work out what he could be referring to. I haven't heard anything about any appointment in the offing for Legless, and as his RJ I'm pretty sure that I would have heard about it. I know Stella would have heard about it, and she would have told me. So, what can be going on? Is he going to be an RJ somewhere, perhaps?

'You are in the presence,' he continues, 'of the most recently appointed Independent Judicial Officer of the Rugby Football Union.'

Marjorie smiles. 'You mean, adjudicating on red cards, and whether players get suspended or not?'

Legless nods. 'Exactly so, Marjorie, and I will have jurisdiction at the highest levels – internationals, the Premiership, the European competitions, everything. If I may so, a jurisdiction every bit as vital as the High Court.'

'No question about it,' Marjorie agrees. 'Congratulations, Legless. Well done. You are perfect for it.'

I almost sigh with relief. 'So, Stella isn't going to have to worry about replacing you too?'

'No, no. Don't worry, Charlie. I will still be haunting you here at Bermondsey. It's a part-time thing, weekends and evenings mainly. But they tell me you get invited to some good functions, in addition to how interesting it will be.'

'Well done,' Hubert and I say, almost in unison.

We raise a toast to the RFU's new star.

Hubert drains his glass and replaces it on Legless's desk.

'Well, thank you for the tipple, Legless. Very well done. I'm sorry to leave you all, but a busy evening awaits. I have to go and see my vicar, and then it will be time to take my accustomed place in the bar at the Garrick for my pre-dinner snifter. I wish everyone a fine evening.'

Legless turns to me. 'Aren't you worried about Hubert, Charlie?' he asks.

'After today – and indeed, after the last four weeks?' I reply. 'No. I don't think I am. Should I be?'

'I could have sworn I heard him say he was going to see his vicar.'

'Yes. I believe he did say that.'

'And you're not concerned he might be getting confused again?'

'Not in the least, Legless,' I reply. 'Not in the least. Actually, I'm rather encouraged.'